The Argentinians

By J W Finch

To Bron
Hope you Enjoy it!

[signature]

Finch, JW.

The Argentinians / JW Finch.

ISBN-13: 978-1507586181

ISBN-10: 1507586183

First Edition.

For Dessy.

A man is always the same person underneath even if he does not use his real name.

That man can still be a hero whichever name he uses.

.

Contents

Prólogo

In the military the recruits learn many skills in great detail, most of which are not much use when they finally leave. Unless they get lucky and find their way into a niche market. Only a few find such opportunities. Opportunities which tend to pay very well. Two such men are Robert Dixon and Andrew Cooper. They served in many conflicts across the world together building up a long lasting, trusting friendship. In their line of business they needed to be able to trust each other totally, both in ability and morally.

They met in basic training in the late 1980s, serving in the same units throughout their ten year military career, serving on active duty more times and in more places than is committed to public records.

When each man had been wounded, the person they relied on to get them to safety was the other. Every time one of them was injured, his recovery was aided by the constant companionship of the other. Friendship as close as this rarely develops in civilian situations, where the threat to life is far more distant. A friendship that grew stronger with each covert mission they undertook. Each mission honing their skills in the field.

Both men left the military at the same time, where they found their opportunities were limited due to their very specialised skillsets, until Rob had a chance meeting with an ex-officer who was looking for their skills. Both parties had something each other needed. Rob had the skills, the officer represented an organisation with the financial security. The job was not something Rob could do alone so he asked the only person he could trust, his long term friend, Andy, resulting in a successful partnership in the only niche market they could thrive.

Many lessons were learnt in that first job, it was completed perfectly thanks to the honed skills of the pair. The methodology to completing the job had proved troublesome. They had learnt a valuable lesson that anonymity and deception were essential tools necessary to get close to their target safely. Their skills in these areas needed improvement.

One valuable lesson was that being British can sometimes close more doors than it opens. There is a lot of mistrust of the British in many parts of the world. Mistrust that exists because of the close relationship between the UK and the USA. A relationship that has been used to influence foreign governments.

The anti-British feeling and the desire to retain some anonymity was addressed by taking another nationality. They tried several options, before settling on a couple of nationalities they would pass themselves off as depending on the situation. Both nationalities had a historical anonymity between Britain on the battle field as well as the sports field, providing the perfect identity cover. Argentina and Germany.

Developing the skill of deception was not so easy. This is a skill they had to learn from scratch and fine tune for their own needs. Deception utilised techniques such as misdirection, concealment and sleight of hand, techniques that they could only learn from experts with a lot of experience and skill. Experts that they sought out and studied from intensely. An incredibly detailed back story was created which would aid them, whilst also providing some protection for their personal lives in the future.

The final area they became experts in was Psychology, learning to read and predict people they had just met with precision. They combined all of their new skills with their current combat skills and the ability to plan everything in detail so precise that they made themselves very attractive in their particular line of work. The training took time. It was nearly a year after their first job before they were ready for the next. The time gap didn't affect their new careers, as they had earned enough acclaim in that first job to warrant further work.

Their reputations were eventually sealed as one of the prime options in this line of work. Governments and other agencies needed them when there was a situation that needed resolving that could not be completed officially. Situations that required sufficient degrees of separation to prevent major diplomatic issues and allow plausible deniability.

It would have been difficult to advertise their skills publicly. A sufficient network of trusted contacts had been built up to be able to secure regular work. Each job increased the risk to their real identities. After ten years of such work they were nearly financially secure enough to live comfortably for the rest of their lives, but still needed to work for a couple more years.

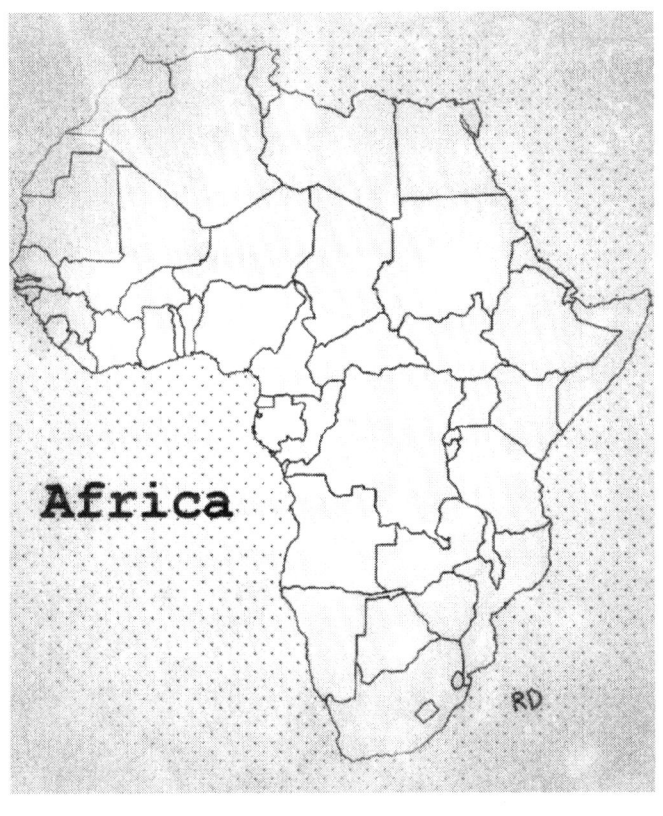

Africa

RD

Capítulo Uno

One drawback in this line of work is that you tend to spend a lot of time travelling.

As the plane taxies slowly along the runway towards the terminal, most of the passengers get ready to take their hand luggage and depart as fast as possible. Two of them just sit motionless, they are in no hurry. There is a small jolt as the plane comes to a halt, the seatbelt lights go out and the cabin bustles into action.

The two motionless passengers are casually dressed in jeans with plain jackets covering Argentinian football shirts, disguising their true nationality, giving them the anonymity they prefer. Their hair is long, their faces covered in stubble, finishing off the appearance they want to portray as two scruffy backpackers. The wait for the queue to exit the plane takes ten minutes, the two men are in no hurry, preferring to be almost the last off the plane, as they know that customs would pull them over to go through their bags with a fine toothed comb. Getting selected for a search by customs was a routine affair for them. Customs officers seem to think a long haired backpacker always has something hidden in their bags. With these two backpackers, the customs officers are always disappointed.

This time they pass through without a hitch. South African customs officers generally aren't interested in people that arrive on flights from the more affluent European countries. Rarely is there opportunity to find contraband being brought into the country on a small scale. Backpackers tend to come into the country looking for their kicks rather than bringing them in with them.

Outside the terminal the backpackers make a phone call from a public phone booth before they survey the range of taxis available to them. They have 50 kilometres to go, so need a taxi that will make the distance. The available taxis are very good by African standards, most of them are less than five years old and have few dents in the bodywork. Poor bodywork is not a problem, the mechanical aspects of a taxi are more essential when travelling in Africa. The two men talk to a couple of the drivers to try and determine the state of their transport. Never an easy task when the drivers will say exactly what they think will guarantee the fare. One simple question sorts out the issue.

One driver is delighted, while the other walks off to find other potential patrons. The winning driver is even more delighted when they inform him he has to take them 50 kilometres, a good payday for him, one which will earn him more than the taxi payment he has to make this month. He is grateful he had a mechanic look at his engine more recently than the other driver.

As the journey starts, the driver asks for an advance of the fare to finance the extra fuel needed for the journey. One of the backpackers, Rob, is happy to oblige, he has had his fair share of African taxi journeys where the taxi has run out of fuel. The advance ensures that this is one less thing to be concerned about, making the journey more relaxing.

Outwardly, Rob is the calmer of the two men, slighter in stature than his companion, although still standing just over six feet tall. His muscular frame sitting below a chiselled, lean face with mouse coloured brown hair. His companion, Andy is around the same height, but much broader with a friendly round face underneath jet black hair.

The journey passes uneventfully, featuring the type of questions airport taxi drivers ask. Where are you from, why are you visiting South Africa, where are your wives. Questions they had been asked countless times before, in countless taxis which wouldn't be fit to drive on British roads. Questions for which they had a pre-prepared set of answers for. They do not intend to give anything away about their true identities.

After over an hour they pull up at a ranch in the middle of the bush land. A typical South African ranch, muddy brown, single storey with a veranda all the way around. The building itself had very few windows, bug control indoors being more important than heat control.

A large man is waiting by the ranch door. When he sees the taxi arrive he displays the largest smile the two men have seen in a long time, his white teeth glinting in the dwindling sun. His weather beaten face a result of too many sunny days tending the ranch, a face that is very round and complimented by two very welcoming blue eyes. It is the sort of face that has made instant friends with many people as it implies he is very friendly and a lot of fun. This has served him well in many dangerous situations.

The taxi driver is paid, with a large tip soliciting much more gratitude than the passengers would like. They gather their bags and walk up to the man greeting him as a very old friend.

"How are you doing, Petre you old Devil?"

"Fine thanks, Dixie, although life is getting a lot more heated here now."

"Still getting good food I see." Andy states, as he pokes the man in the stomach.

"Always the joker, Coops, some things never change!"

Petre was one of the few remaining people to call them Dixie and Coops, a throwback to when they served together in units where first names were rarely used. Petre leads them into his house. "Come inside, you must need to rest and we have a lot of catching up to do. I already have dinner prepared for us, afterwards we can get down to business."

The three walk inside the ranch, where the guests are shown their rooms. Each one has a separate but plain room. It is sufficient for their needs. After freshening up, the guests gather in the dining area for the type of extravagant affair Petre is renowned for. The table is far too large for the three men, it is too large for a dozen men, but Petre has entertained a lot in the past, it is better to have too much space than too little. A necessity when owning such a large ranch in South Africa, when you have many contacts and old friends to keep pleased.

The table is covered in a variety of different food dishes from the region, interspersed with enough salad bowls for two each. The centre piece is a baked sweet-curried mince, topped with a savoury egg custard, known as Bobotie. The colours of the dish are striking, with the yellow of the egg custard complimenting the deep brown of the mince. Bobotie is one of Petre's specialities. Both guests have enjoyed it with Petre many times when they worked together.

The smell of the vibrant spices from the dish, combined with rich beef aroma reminds Rob of a time when they were much younger, much more reckless and fearless. A time when they were on the cusp of making their names within the military as the efficient machines which had led to their current way of life.

The meal is served by a young girl who attends to their every need. She ensures their water glasses are never less than half full and that they will never want for side salad for many months to come. There is no alcohol at the meal, a tradition that Petre is very fond of. He believes that it distracts from the enjoyment of the food. In his view, fine wine, beer or spirits should be enjoyed separately. The three enjoy the food in relative silence for ten minutes, just exchanging the odd compliment about the food.

During a lull, Petre puts his cutlery down and addresses his guests.

"Things have changed in this country a lot in the last few years, none of the old guard seem to pass through any more. You are the only two to have visited in the last six months."

Andy is the first to respond. "I know a few have taken to office jobs, but as you know, I couldn't be tied to a desk, my wife likes the style of living I have given her." He then pauses embarrassed, remembering that this is the first time they have seen Petre since his wife died.

"Coops, don't be sad, I have mourned for my wife, she wouldn't have wanted me to be morose, it has been nearly two years, besides I am thinking of moving on. A lot of my countrymen have moved to the UK, there is a lot of money to be made there, this place is completely falling apart now."

They carry on the conversation, talking fondly of old times, of some of the freelance missions they were part of when they had left their respective militaries.

Petre had met Rob and Andy when they were in Zaire together. Rob and Andy had left the British Army, found civilian life too dull, so became soldiers of fortune for a while until they found their current line of work. It was an easy way to earn a lot of money doing what they were trained to do. Petre had also gone the same way after National Service in the South African army. Africa was the land of opportunity for ex-soldiers, where many found themselves fighting for various causes, mainly for the money, sometimes for the kicks.

During their careers they had built up a large network of friends, sometimes on opposing sides, but all fighting for the same cause, making themselves rich. Petre was one of their closest friends from that time, he had helped them on many of their trips back to Africa.

Weapons were easy to get on the African continent, just not that easy to get in, unless you were an arms dealer. Rob and Andy were arms dealers when it was convenient to be, it was a way in to many circles that most wouldn't want to get into, they just didn't sell any arms, their work was always done well before they sealed a deal.

Petre stored some of the more hard to come by weapons for them, which they could use in a 'sales pitch', however as most of the tools of their trade had to be discarded after each job they needed new supplies often. Petre had the connections to replenish them, which he eagerly did. It was an easy way to supplement his income without too great a risk.

"I have got the normal items you use, would you need anything else?"

Petre knew the nature of their work, however he never knew the details, he wouldn't want to. Sometimes it is better to be in the dark, especially with the type of people that were involved in some cases.

Andy was the closest of the two to Petre, having visited with his wife on several occasions. He was also the least serious of the two, preferring to crack a joke to ease a tense situation. "Old friend, when have you known us to need anything else! We really only need what we always use."

Rob was much more pragmatic, finding himself most at ease when he had meticulously planned the minor details of each job.

This time Rob had an extra requirement. "We will need a new car this time, we are not worried about attracting attention, we have a long way to go. It's all very well having the most run down car you can find, but we'd also like to get there in comfort for a change."

This was not a problem for a man of Petre's means.

"I can get my hands on a new 4 x 4 quite easily first thing in the morning. What about the name for registration?"

The two Brits looked at each other, then at Petre with large smiles.

Rob explains. "We're going to be using the Argentinian identity this time. We have spent some time on our background story and don't want anything on the registration that will raise suspicion."

"Last time we hired a car under the name Mario Kempes, we were asked for our autographs at several stops, better use something less obvious, like Ricardo Villa." Coops quips. This joke passes Petre by as he has never followed what the English call Football, the only sport he had an interest in was Rugby.

"Nope, I have that covered already." Rob not even acknowledging the joke, too many years of similar comments have taught him to ignore Andy when he uses lines like this. "We'll use a common name, which won't raise any questions when checked out. We will be using a few different identities before we get to our destination, so use a plain, generic name."

"When are you planning on leaving?" Petre enquires.

Andy responds to Petre's question. "We'd like to leave the day after tomorrow, as long as that is fine with you, we are not in too much of a rush. We have a day or two leeway and it's good to spend some time with old friends." Andy was very fond of Petre, he never enjoyed these brief flying visits.

"Excellent, you can try some of my home grown wine then. I've exported some of it to the UK, it went down well, sad thing is, it is not a large money earner, if it was I may stay here for good."

"Well I can, but Dixie doesn't touch alcohol anymore!" Coops reveals with delight.

"I like to keep a clear head, besides my body can't take it anymore. There will be a time for it when we retire." Rob resigns with a sigh. He looks at Andy with disdain. He never enjoyed being called Dixie and knows Andy is mocking him slightly as the only person he tolerates it from is Petre. He hasn't got the heart to tell Petre he doesn't like the name.

Petre gets up and goes into the kitchen, returning with a bottle of unmarked red wine and pours some out for Coops. The wine is a very dark red, it has a faint aroma of the spices that accompanied the Bobotie, but mixed with strong aromas of the local berries and cherry. The aroma is strong enough to tempt Rob to put down his tea and have a sniff of the glass. He had thought of himself as bit of a wine connoisseur in earlier years, but eventually realised that connoisseurs did not consume wine by the gallon.

"Very sweet and spicy, I can see why this would go down well in the UK. The aroma is far superior to much of the plonk we get there." Rob swills the glass around, breathing in the aroma, but not tasting the wine. He leaves that to Andy, who is nodding his approval.

"Why isn't it a good money earner?" enquires Coops. "I could drink this all night."

"If you are an unknown brand hitting the UK, the supermarkets are your main outlet, they only want to sell it at rock bottom prices." Petre says regrettably. "You have to spend a fortune entering contests and winning medals for your wine before you can command a premium price for it. It's something I haven't got the time or inclination to do, so I tend to sell a little locally, export small batches to the UK and save the rest for guests."

They talk for a few more hours, reminiscing about old missions, laughing at some of the close scrapes they have had and how fortunate they are to be here. One stray bullet half an inch in another direction would have been all it would have taken to change that. Rob suddenly announces that he is going to get some sleep around midnight, stating it has been a long trip, he would like to have some rest so he is fresh for the next few days.

"Crikey, you have calmed down mate." Petre exclaims. "Sleep well, I have left a mosquito coil burning for you, we may not get many in here, but it will be enough to stop the odd one that is determined to get some foreign blood."

Andy nods after Rob, he knows his companion well enough not to question his actions, or to persuade him to do anything against his will. Coops also knows that he and Petre will stay up until the early hours drinking his fine wine, probably far too much of it, but he enjoys the company of his South African friend and times like this are getting rarer.

The next day is hot, much hotter than the two guests are used to, but it will help them acclimatise a little. Andy wastes half of the acclimatisation by sleeping in until after midday, whilst Rob makes more use of the time by spending the morning studying maps of the region, drawing some rough outlines in a notebook of his intended route. There is not one piece of detail he wants to miss. He spends some of the time devising alternative plans for every potential scenario on their trip. They cannot afford one small error on this mission as he is far too aware of the increase in competition lately, a by-product in the increase in active service for many western military personnel.

Andy wakes up, pulls open the curtain whilst still in bed, letting go of it immediately when the bright sun dazzles his eyes. He rolls over a few times before forcing himself out of the bed. He pulls on a pair of shorts and a

T-shirt and wanders outside to the sunlit veranda where Rob is sitting at a table reading a newspaper.

Andy tries to seem he is more alert than he is as he shouts his greeting. "Morning!"

"Afternoon more like, late one I take it?" Rob states without looking up. Despite his decision not to drink anymore, Rob understood that Andy needed to overdo it now and again, just as they had together many times when they were serving. He knew when it came to the crunch, there was no-one else that could or would perform as well as his friend. Each person had to have a release, his release at this moment in time was burying himself in his meticulous plans. Many of which are never executed, they are just available if the main plan has to change.

The sunlight causes Andy to rub his eyes as he blinks to adjust to the increased brightness out in the open. "Yes, quite late, we got through a few bottles. Any sign of Petre?"

"He got up about an hour ago, he has gone to town to sort the car out, should be back soon. I was fortunate that I had finished with all our maps before he got up. I wouldn't like him to see something that would potentially put him in danger if our mission went wrong."

Rob knew the way Petre thought, if he knew their route and something went wrong, it would get in the local news quickly. When Petre saw this, he would more than likely drop everything to go looking for them. If Petre didn't know where they were heading, the uncertainty would stop him from taking the risk to find them if a news story broke. Rob had full confidence that he and Andy were the best, that they would be able to handle any incident that affected them. If something did go wrong, the danger would be far too much for Petre to handle on his own. It was an arrogant concern, but he was comforted to know that their actions would not lead to their friend being harmed.

"Route all sorted then?" Andy states nonchalantly, whilst peeling an orange.

"Mostly, some small roads are not marked very well, but we should be in Brazzaville in a few days." Rob knew that if his main plan went without a hitch they would be in Brazzaville in three days.

A car door slamming shut after a crunch of gravel announces Petre's return. He walks around to the back of the house, shouting in Afrikaans at his dogs, two large Rhodesian Ridgebacks. The dogs run off into the field behind the house chasing some unfortunate small animal, as he comes around the corner.

Petre stands in front of the veranda where the two men are sitting. "Everything has been arranged, we'll get the car delivered this afternoon. I take it you want the normal adjustments made to it?"

Rob smiles, Petre knows that they wouldn't dream of having a car without a special compartment to conceal weapons and other material. "Of course, we don't really want our cargo being too obvious at every check point."

"Good, I've already arranged for it to be delivered to my normal body-shop. They are used to me getting compartments added to odd places in my cars."

Coops has been woken up by the strong taste of the orange and seizes the opportunity. "Can we have it painted in a Starsky and Hutch style while you're at it, plus add some large air horns?"

Petre glances at Coops for a second, unsure if he is joking or not, before the realisation strikes that he always is joking when he makes such ridiculous statements. He smirks, before grabbing Coops by the shoulder.

"You old dog, I almost believed you for a second!"

Rob shakes his head, smiling. "You should know him well enough to ignore any of his stupid comments."

Petre lets go of Coops and changes to his business face. "Do you want to check the stock now?"

Andy starts to get in mission mode, realising that he needs to start focusing on what they are here to do. "Nah, we'll wait until sundown, we need to improve our tans. It's better if we are a bit darker this time, we will blend in better."

Petre checks Coops again, but this time he realises he is actually being serious. "Sometimes it's hard to tell whether you are joking or not, Coops."

Coops grins. "Only some of the time, when it comes to actual work, then I know how to be serious, very serious."

Rob grabs Andy this time. "In all honesty Petre, if Coops here didn't know how to be serious when our work was involved, then I don't think we'd be here now. We would have been buried in an unmarked grave years ago."

Petre laughs. "Well thank god for that."

The two Brits spend all afternoon sitting on the veranda, soaking in the sun. They are already tanned, having spent many years working in hot countries, but knew they couldn't go where they were going with slightly pale faces. Barely a word is spoken all afternoon. Rob runs through the route in his head, Andy focuses on what he has been told about this job.

Late in the afternoon the 4x4 is delivered, but it is left in the garage until dark, well after the evening meal. The 4x4 is a white Toyota Land Cruiser, one of the most common vehicles on African roads, the result of being far more comfortable than many of the alternatives. It looks normal from the outside. Andy and Rob go to inspect the vehicle. Andy opens the back, looks inside and takes up the floor base, where a well-hidden compartment has been fitted.

He turns to Rob. "Perfect, this is hard to find if you know it's here."

Petre joins them, very proud that such a good job has been done. "These new ones make it a lot easier to fit a compartment in, almost as if the manufacturers have used it as a design feature. You can get a lot more than you normally take in there. The shop that fitted it have fitted a similar one for me earlier this year, you wouldn't believe how hard it is to detect."

Coops pats Petre on the back. "Damn Handy, as we probably will need a bit more this time, we'll need to take some of the launchers as a show piece, the people we intend to meet will need to be impressed by something more than a few rifles."

Rob measures the compartment and compares it to some notes he has in a small book. "Looks like we can get nearly everything we have stored with you in here, that will impress even the most well-armed of small dictators."

Petre looks at Rob a little concerned. "Dictators?"

"Only a term of phrase my friend, don't worry, we are not starting a coup or anything which will bring unwanted eyes around your place." Rob is slightly annoyed that he could have mentioned even the slightest detail which could have brought trouble for Petre, even if it wasn't true. African states don't take kindly to coups, even the mention of them. There have been too many, too frequently on the continent that even third party states have agreements with others regarding the prosecution of anyone even slightly involved with a coup attempt.

If Rob and Andy had been attempting a coup, the fact that he had mentioned the smallest detail in conjunction with the weapons he needed in front of Petre, could land Petre in a lot of trouble.

In this line of work, the choice of words had to be judged very carefully, even the most innocuous of statements could ruin everything. Rob knew that even Andy wouldn't have made such a faux-pas. Fortunately only the three of them were present and the phrase didn't matter, but Rob wanted to reassure Petre. Petre was a tough man, but he would have had problems he couldn't handle if the authorities believed he was involved in any way in the coup of another African country. "You should know us by now, we don't do anything which would end up on the news, as it would eventually end up with us or some of our friends also in the news. If we did that our careers would be over very quickly."

Petre smiles at this, he knows that his old friends would never get involved in a political situation which would attract any sort of attention. He knows Dixie and Coops well and has faith that their targets are always the type of people that avoid being in the public eye.

All three spend some more time rummaging through the car, before packing some bags into it. A little later another car pulls up outside. Petre goes to speak with the driver, they talk for a while in Afrikaans, which ends with back slapping and laughter.

The car drives off and Petre returns with a holdall.

"Ammunition, plentiful in supply, especially from people who think you are going to use it on the Africans. You should have all you need in here."

He hands the holdall to Andy, who takes a look inside, then turns his head with a wry smile and packs the contents into the compartment.

"That's the thing about the Afrikaners, they are eager to please when they think you may be shooting the Africans, this country has had bad problems since they took control and the Afrikaners think that they can shoot their way back into power."

"As long as he didn't think there was anything untoward happening, I'm happy. For your safety too, Petre, as I wouldn't want your help to lead to word going around you have an arsenal on this farm."

Andy is all too aware how the country has changed in the last decade, the power shift since the end of apartheid has led to a huge increase in violence against white farmers. He would never be able to live with himself if Petre became a victim of the violence due to a little assistance he gave to them. After all, it was only all about money.

Rob finishes loading all of the gear into the compartment. "Fits very well, no one will find it unless they have some inside knowledge, it's the best weapon store we have had, Petre, you're a star."

Petre is aware that their stay is short, so wants to make the most of it by taking in some hunting with them the next day. "What plans do you have for tomorrow and what time are you going to head off the next day?"

Rob looks up. "Well, now we are all fully sorted, I think tomorrow will be the day we head off, it's going to take several days to get where we are going, so an extra day on the road could be very handy. I'd like to get an early start, we have a lot of distance to get covered, so will think of heading off around seven. I've planned most of the route and have pencil marked somewhere to stay each night, but you know what these places can be like so may have to change those plans."

Andy and Petre look surprised, but understand. Petre is saddened slightly, he really wanted to have another day catching up with his old friends, but he knows deep down after the hunting it would be an afternoon of drinking for him and Andy, which would increase the tension between the two Brits. The sensible option is to get the journey started tomorrow, so the work could be finished sooner. The more time spent waiting around would mean more time about thinking what could go wrong. This sort of thinking can lead to mistakes being made at the crucial time.

When they worked together, there was a lot of waiting around. Petre didn't enjoy waiting around for this type of work and he knew the other two would be the same. Get on with it as soon as possible without stopping for reflection was how he liked it. He would be sad to see them go after such a short stay, but their stays generally always were short, so he was used to it. He did hope this stay wouldn't be the last one.

"I'll make sure there is some breakfast waiting for you in the morning, I should be back from checking the cattle by the time you leave, so I will say goodbye then."

Andy and Rob pack the final things into the car, loading plenty of spare water and fuel into the back. They return to the house and retire for what they expected to be the best night's sleep for a few days.

The two awake early next morning, shower and eat a fine breakfast cooked by Petre's housekeeper.

Petre returns while they are finishing up their food. "You have everything you need?"

Andy is in mission mode, the edge of his humour has been taken off. "Sure, you been a great help, Mary cooks such a mean breakfast we won't need to eat for a while."

"She is one in a million, solely responsible for my expanding waist." Petre pats his stomach as he says this and nods in thanks to his housekeeper, Mary.

All three take it in turns to hug each other and say their goodbyes, after they have walked out to the car. Petre and Coops' hug is the longest, accompanied by firm pats on each other's backs throughout. Petre has a strong friendship with Andy, nevertheless there still a very strong bond with Rob, who thanks Petre again while Andy gets into the driver's seat of the Land cruiser.

"Always glad to help you guys out, especially as there aren't many of us around anymore."

Andy leans out of the driver seat window. "Well, we will be around for a lot longer, when you eventually make it to the UK, we will show you some damn good hospitality, we've got many years of it to repay."

Rob shakes Petre's hand, before giving him a final hug, patting him on the back vigorously. Petre reaches into the car to shake Coops' hand. Coops looks his friend in the eyes sincerely. "Take care mate and thanks for everything, we couldn't work without you."

Rob gets in the car, Andy pulls off the handbrake and slowly pulls away, heading off down the dusty road. Petre watches the car until it goes out of view, hoping as he always does that this isn't the last he has ever seen of his friends.

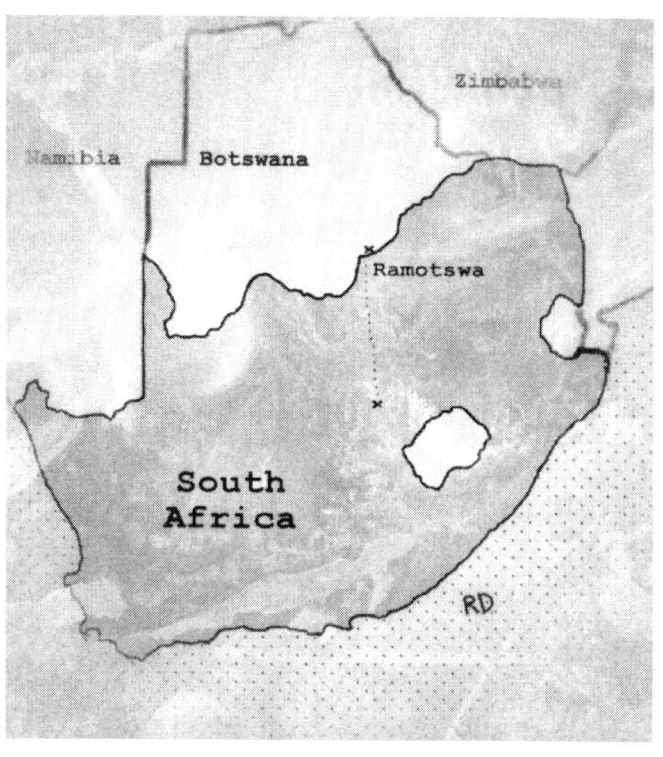

Capítulo Dos

The journey consists of long, hot days as they pass through what many would class as spectacularly colourful landscape, for which any tourist would pay a fortune to experience. The initial part of the journey in South Africa takes them over dusty plains, rich in many shades of brown, from the beiges of the sun drenched sandy undulating grasslands to the dark chocolate colours of the infrequent trees that dot the landscape. It contrasts starkly with the roadside towns along the way, each full of stores lining the road, attracting customers with such a vibrant display of colour and advertising that it would be easy to believe that lights would not be needed on the road at night.

Each store has a different array of colours. Displaying the rival brands of large multinational food and drinks companies on large signs unrelated to the variety of different products on display, all contributing their own distinct colours, from fruit and vegetables to household goods. The one common factor with all of these stores is the adornment of hundreds of second hand plastic bags, a common sight on an African bush store.

After the plains they pass through the verdant green hills of the central highlands, completely covered in lush vegetation, separated by lighter green sun soaked wide valleys with sparkling blue rivers running through the middle. There is also the explosion of colour displayed by the roadside towns, but far less frequently than the amount of towns on the plains. The fertile valleys were too valuable for people to live on as their value lay in feeding the nation and beyond, with far more attractive areas to live than the remote hills, population growth had not taken a large grip in this area.

Finally on this first part of their journey they pass through the bush land close to the border, a mixture of the previous two environments, the browns of the land contrasted by the green covering of small bush vegetation. This area is also filled with the game that attracts visitors on once in a lifetime trips. The type of game that for many people is only ever experienced in documentaries. Lions, Cheetahs, Elephants, Zebras, Hyenas, all living wild, the sight of which would stop most people in their tracks to watch and take photographs. Not Rob and Andy.

Having travelled this land on similar routes before, there were no surprises for them, nothing new they haven't seen many times before up close. This is not a time for sightseeing for them. They had fought conflicts in very similar areas in their post-military careers, so there was a feeling that too much time spent dwelling on the scenery could trigger an old memory of a close friend breathing his final breath, or invoke another similar blood soaked scene. As such it was best not to dwell on the views the land offered. The end of the journey was far more important than enjoying any view.

The journey was broken up with music, a varied selection of songs they had both chosen for driving, mainly middle of the road rock music, interspersed with some British indie guitar bands. This time, like all other times, they would be using a route they have not used before, well not completely. Varying routes is fairly easy due to the variety of northern routes leaving South Africa, there would only be the uncertainty of what obstacles lay ahead on the route, such as which roads would be difficult to pass or which bridges might have been washed away. There was less uncertainty in this case, however as Rob and Andy had spent many years driving in South Africa, so they knew the terrain well, the only uncertain factor was with who they would meet along the way.

Petre had also been invaluable. He would suggest that they might want to try a particular border crossing each time they left him, knowing that they would have to head North out of the country. There was no other way out by land, this would be the only detail of each trip that Petre would know, albeit by assumption, after all if they had work to do in South Africa itself, they wouldn't have put Petre at risk by using his place as the initial base.

This time they headed North-West to the Botswana border, after successfully tackling the border they would head directly north in order to avoid both the Kalahari Desert, which would be a tough crossing and the Okavango Delta, which would be impassable in the rainy season. There are very few routes out of Botswana, but their intention was to head to the sole border crossing into Zambia, which was by ferry at Kazungula, then continue north into the Democratic Republic of the Congo, cross the country in a North-Westerly direction where they would meet the mighty Congo river and cross it into the Republic of the Congo and it's capital situated just the other side.

They had chosen this route instead of the more direct route through Angola as it presented less of a risk,

Angola being considerably more hostile at this time than its neighbours. Their chosen route was longer, with more borders to smuggle weapons through, but the roads would be better and they were less likely to encounter a local war.

Rob had explained the route in great detail to Andy before they left. It was essential that both men knew exactly where they were heading as any indecision or wrong turn could quickly lead to unwanted attention from a variety of sources. The authorities are constantly on the lookout for smugglers, so unfamiliarity with your location can warrant some questioning. At the other end of the spectrum were bandits who were looking for a pay day from a lost traveller who had taken a wrong turning. Rob and Andy wanted to avoid any scenario which may at the least, delay them for a few days or at the worst be life threatening.

They take it in turn to drive, stopping every three hours to switch over, with the time as a passenger spent navigating, meaning it was a tiring way to travel. They had done similar journeys many times before and were conditioned for such travel, spending over 16 hours a day on the road for several days. The alternative of trying to smuggle weapons on a direct flight was less appealing. This was their chosen career, spending long sweltering days in a car, driving through hostile lands was far also more attractive to them than spending 8 hours tied to a desk taking phone calls from irate customers.

After passing though the spectacular South African landscape, they eventually arrive at the border crossing at Ramotswa in the centre of Botswana's southern border. The sun at this time of day was at its highest in the sky. Rob stops the car right next to the border control and both men get out. They walk over to the control which is manned by a couple of border guards, both of whom look disinterested. Both are dressed in the plain but functional olive coloured border crossing uniform supplied by the government.

The two guards are contrasting in size, one of them is much larger than the other. The specks of grey in his hair are a good indication that he is the senior guard. The other indication that he is the senior guard is that the other guard appears much greener and eager to make a good impression on his colleague.

Rob and Andy hand over their papers to the smaller of the two guards, who flicks through the pages of the passport with interest. He is more interested in where they have been than where they are going. His eyes widen on every page turn that reveals another place he has only seen on a map.

The larger of the guards looks them up and down, displaying an obvious dislike of the two travellers that were standing in front of him waiting to pass through his small border post. He aggressively addresses them. "What is your business in Botswana?"

Andy looks him in the eye with a smile on his face. "We are just travelling through, doing the Cape Town to Cairo run."

The senior border guard is unimpressed, he is used to westerners attempting the journey through his country. The amount of people using Botswana as part of the route had increased ever since Zimbabwe started having internal troubles. It used to be the case that one or two people a month would arrive at the border post in Land Rovers, attempting the drive through the country. It was a far tougher and less scenic journey than Zimbabwe, however this now seemed to be contrary, as Botswana was the safer option, which was a more appealing aspect for many travellers who just wanted to get on with the journey. One or two people a month had turned into one or two people a day.

He looks them up and down, they looked similar to many of the Muzungus that pass through, not that he would personally refer to them as Muzungus in the open. Although it was the typical term Africans used to describe westerners, with several regional variations of the commonly used word, after years of mixing with westerners, the guard felt it was a little derogatory. As he looked at the two men in front him, he felt they were a little scruffy, many of his western friends wore suits daily. He also noted that they wore no jewellery, very typical for a Muzungu. He often pondered why the Muzungus did not want to flaunt their wealth to gain respect.

If he had the money they obviously had to be able to buy such expensive cars, he would be covered from head to toe in gold, he would flaunt his wealth, have attractive women hanging off his arms and more importantly would have the respect of all his peers. The Muzungus ambitions did not interest him, he had no interest in seeing the rest of Africa, from what he had heard it looked mostly the same, the same type of landmarks, just in slightly different places. Wealth and respect was far a more tangible benefit that he could understand. "How long will you be saying in Botswana?"

Andy maintains his eye contact and smile despite the obvious hostility. "Less than a week, we are only using transit visas."

This irritates the guard, it was something he heard from every traveller who passed his border post. He always had the same reply to them, which he believed may work one day. "Transit Visas, all westerner only use transit visas. Do you never want to stay in our country? Everyone at this crossing always has only transit visas." He shakes his head, starting to lose interest, thinking of how much gold he could wear for the cost of the Land Cruiser in front of him.

Andy, being tactfully aware that the wrong phrase here could insult the guard's country tries to appease him. "Transit visas are far cheaper than normal visas, although we are only passing through we still get to experience the beauty of your country. We cannot afford weeks in the Okavango like many rich tourists, but if we see what we like, we may upgrade the visa and stay in your beautiful land."

The guard is not impressed, he knows they can afford to stay for weeks in his country. They would like it more than some of the northern countries, but he has heard similar statements from all who have transit visas, none of them tip him well either. He has lost interest and only wants to process the new arrivals, so he can carry on dreaming of riches and trying to teach his younger colleague what life is all about. "Are you carrying any firearms or illegal substances?"

"No." Andy feigns surprise at such a question, but even he knows far better than to make a sarcastic quip to a border guard in answer to such a question.

The smaller guard steps up to the Toyota. "Can you open your vehicle please?"

Andy opens the rear of the car, allowing the junior guard to poke around inside, sniffing some of the bags. He picks up Rob's bag. "Can you open this please?"

Rob opens the bag and the junior guard looks through the contents, satisfying himself that there is nothing untoward that is obvious to the eye, sadly for him nothing that he can impose an on the spot fine for. His colleague would have been impressed with an on the spot fine, it would contribute slightly to his plan to be rich.

This guard is also getting bored now. "Ok you can close this, I have inspected your car, I cannot see anything untoward. You have 7 days to travel through

Botswana." He decides against trying to convince them of the wonderful sights they will miss by using the direct route through as there is another car pulling up behind them which may offer more fruits.

Rob is very gracious, but very eager to leave quickly. "Thank you, very much."

The senior guard tries one futile attempt on behalf of the Botswana tourist board. "Enjoy my country, it has wonderful wildlife."

"We will thanks." Andy knows that they have little chance of stopping to admire any wildlife, even the type that would get top billing on a wildlife TV show.

Rob and Andy get back into the car and drive off, waving to the guards as the smaller one lifts up the red and white striped border post for them. They travel for a few more hours until it gets dark and they reach a bustling town. Rob pulls the car up outside a small guesthouse. Andy goes inside, returning a minute later nodding his head. A compound door is opened to let the car pass in. Once inside the compound they get out, retrieve their day bags and walk across the small courtyard into the guesthouse.

The basic reception is manned by a friendly receptionist who books them in whilst trying to engage in the type small talk that Rob and Andy are too weary to respond to in any detail. They are allocated a fairly basic ground floor room, so basic that it does not even have mosquito nets. However it will serve their needs, they only want a few hours rest and something to eat.

They freshen up after spending all day sitting in the car. A necessity in such a hot country as a rash can quickly turn into something which can compromise a mission. Afterwards they walk along to the hotel restaurant, which in many countries would not meet the description of a restaurant. It was a plain white room, filled with a dozen tables each covered with a cheap PVC table cover featuring a dated floral pattern, surrounded by four chairs. There is no decoration in the room, save a couple of plants in opposite corners. The main thing is that it is clean, which is a comfort as it is an indication that the food is likely to clean also. Rob and Andy both order a stew, which when it appears is as basic as the room, meat, some vegetables with a couple of dumplings in a very thin beef stock, but it fills them well. After the short meal they retire to their beds for whatever sleep they can get.

They only sleep for a few hours, preferring to start early for the long drive ahead. They leave when it is still dark, so the receptionist warns them to be careful as the town can be dangerous at night. They are keen to go, so assure her that they will not be stopping anywhere, just driving right through the town and continuing straight across the country.

The drive through Botswana is not as enjoyable as South Africa as it is a flat country with a landscape very similar to the South African bush land they passed through the previous day. This bush land is less vibrant in colour with the dull yellow- greens of the vegetation being less contrasting to the light sandy browns of the land. The bush land also covers the whole length of their journey through the country, so it will be fairly monotonous.

Fortunately the roads are good and there are less than seven hundred miles to the border. Rob has estimated around twelve hours to travel this section, provided they make good time. This is plenty of time to get to the last ferry at the border crossing with Zambia, which stops for the day at six pm. This gives them a comfortable fifteen hours leeway. Rob is keen to make the border crossing today as it would put them at their destination a day early, giving them more time to investigate their options in Brazzaville.

Again the journey is split into three hour turns to drive, with difference here that the passenger can take a small sleep as the navigation is fairly clear-cut. They stop every other turn to refuel, an easy task due to the high proliferation of filling stations, all provided by the big western household names of Shell, BP or Total. The main difference between these filling stations and their western counterparts is that many were manned by someone who would fill the vehicle for them, often whilst smoking a cigarette, a complete rarity in the west on both accounts.

After nine hours on the road, having spent the last ten minutes studying the map and plotting exactly where they were, Rob turns to Andy to summarise the rest of the trip. "We'll be in Zambia in around four hours' time and in the DRC by tomorrow evening if everything goes OK."

Andy grins, this was his sort of journey, he preferred an easy ride, considering what they generally had waiting at the end of each journey. It was best not to have unpaid action on the way to their missions. "Well it couldn't have been any more straight forward so far, but the DR Congo is not something I am looking forward to, it has always been trouble. Hopefully we won't get too much hassle." He uttered this last line with a hint of sarcasm, they had both had their share of hassle in the DRC, the sort of hassle that has required an armed response to bring it to an end.

Nine years ago, they were working for a large private military company in the area, when they experienced their first taste of the type of hassle common in the Democratic Republic of the Congo when it was known as Zaire. The job was supposed to be a simple extraction of some important mining executives from an area that was being over-run by insurgents starting a civil war against President Mobutu.

The company had underestimated the size and ferocity of the insurgency, only sending one squad to perform the extraction. The squad came under heavy fire as soon as they arrived at the executives' compound, their transport was rendered unserviceable and they had to undertake a week long defence until the company could get assistance to them. If this had been a governmental action, the squad would have been national heroes, however as it was a commercial operation, it didn't merit the same recognition, so went unreported. Rob and Andy conducted themselves with honour, in the former situation would have received the highest possible military honours, however in this commercial situation, they just received a small bonus.

The squad took very heavy losses and Andy and Rob were the mining executives' last effective defence for three days. They defended sensibly, fighting back each attack with tactical efficiency. The attacks were relentless at the start, but grew sporadic but still fierce over the week. The insurgents had many grudges to settle with mining executives, not personal grudges against the men themselves, but against what they stood for and the company that had exploited the population for so long.

Rob and Andy had been working as a team effectively for years before this, but this was their defining moment. They were able to operate efficiently without having to second guess what the other would do, they would know by instinct what each other would do and when they would do it. For many partnerships, the stress involved in that week long battle would be their Coup de grâce, the experience would be something they wouldn't want to repeat, ensuring that they went their own way afterwards.

For Rob and Andy, it made them stronger and convinced each man that the other was the one person that they would trust and rely on implicitly in a conflict. In the last three days, they had killed or wounded over 80% of the insurgents who attacked the compound, suffering not a single scratch themselves.

The attacks petered out dramatically in the last day, with the final few attacks on the compound being shouted threats. The threats were followed by hours of total silence. The stress level was still high in the compound, they had to stay completely alert before assistance arrived. When the transport arrived, the mining executives and what remained of squad were on their way out of the country within ten minutes. The executives were relieved and eternally grateful, the wounded were tended to, whilst Rob and Andy had earned total respect from everyone involved. The two, however were just content with themselves over their conduct and professionalism during a very tough crisis.

In the time that had passed, they had experienced several more armed conflicts in the DRC that had escalated far beyond what was expected. The country had stabilised in the last few years, so this time they knew they were less likely to drive into a full blown military operation, however they did know there may be bandits looking to extract any relative riches from them.

Rob could tell Andy was getting bored and distracted. Rob wanted to ensure they were both sharp for any unplanned active service that they faced. "It's been like driving though a safari park back home so far, when we get to an unpopulated area, it would be a good time to get the guns out, I would like to fire them a few times before we get a crucial point and find they jam."

Andy for once was a little cautious, the less attention they attracted the better. "Thought you'd tried them in SA?"

Rob's preparation has been meticulous, however he does feel that too much preparation and checking is better than too little. "Only fired one shot from each, could do with taking a few rounds through each one, just to make sure we have the feel for them."

Andy shrugs, it's something he is not going to worry about now, it will be another four hours before they arrive in Zambia, so it will probably be the following day before they are somewhere remote enough to test the guns. Anything can happen between now and then, he was going to enjoy the relatively smooth and fast roads as there will not be many like this in the next few days.

Just under four hours later they arrive at the Kazungula Ferry, which would take them the 400 metres across the Zambezi river to Zambia. The ferry port is very busy as it is a hub for the many backpackers and independent travellers crossing into Zambia for its greatest attraction, Victoria Falls. Zambia was the preferred destination for seeing the falls since the troubles started in Zimbabwe, causing tourism in the country to grow exponentially. Zambia was making the most of this, ensuring that this would be the case for many years to come.

The port is full of travellers from all over the world, some on foot, some in a variety of different 4x4s, some in trucks provided by various organised overland adventure travel companies. Many were just relaxing and enjoying the bars and cafes the town had to offer before crossing the river. There was a cosmopolitan bustle of travellers exchanging their own unique experiences of their African journey. It was the largest gathering of western tourists Andy and Rob had seen in a long time in somewhere so remote. It was an ideal opportunity for them to relax a little more and enjoy the atmosphere.

Rob knows what Andy was thinking, he also wanted to have a little time here, but crossing the border was the main priority. "We'll cross first and once the border is out of the way, we can have a night with the backpackers." Andy was delighted, rarely did they have such an opportunity on a mission. Rob had something else on his mind. He had been studying the map. "Livingstone would offer the best night life."

They board the first available ferry, a simple platform packed full of vehicles which took longer to load than it did to cross the river. Once on the other side, the vehicles drive off into a queue with the foot passengers waiting to gain entry to Zambia. They would rarely have such a relaxed passage through a border control. The guard just looked at their passport and waved them through. As far as he was concerned they were just another of the multitude of thrill seekers that Zambia was thriving off, looking to experience a white knuckle raft trip or a bungee jump in one of Africa's newest extreme sports playgrounds.

They immediately head to the M10 to Livingstone, arriving in the town an hour later. Finding accommodation was easy, the amount of places to stay had grown in the last few years as the tourists flooded in, as a result most were of the highest quality. Choosing a place was even easier, they went for the busiest place in town. It was a sprawling one storey stone building with white plastered walls in a Mediterranean style. There were several types of rooms, dorms and a camping area. It had a large outside area with several different patio areas, one with a wooden covering, one with a large pool, another with a fire pit in the centre. There was the obligatory bar in the centre, which served as the hub of the complex.

Booking in is a formality, the receptionist is friendly, notes down the details from their passports, before she gives them the keys to their rooms, after their payment had cleared. They each have a twin room with en-suite facilities. Rob insisted on separate rooms, explaining that sometimes it was relaxing to have some time alone, this didn't fool Andy who knew exactly what sort of relaxation Rob had on his mind.

After showering, they go down to the bar before they head out to eat. The bar is very busy, full of many independent travellers plus a couple of large overland trucks that are using this lodge as their base. Each truck bears the logo of Overland Wonders, a company neither man was familiar with, but as there were so many similar companies offering the escorted adventure experience these days, this didn't surprise them. The sight of the full bar delights both Rob and Andy as it means there would be no shortage of company that night.

Rob orders an orange juice, with Andy opting for a castle beer from South Africa, his favourite local brew. They stand at the bar, surveying their surroundings. There are groups of people scattered all over, some playing board games on the tables, others just exchanging their travel stories. Outside the confines of the bar there is a large group of people around a fire pit. It is hard to tell where everyone was from, but from the sound of the general conversation, it appeared to be a mixture of Europeans, South Africans and Australians, people of all ages. They exchange smiles with a few people, soaking up the atmosphere for a few minutes, without saying a word to each other. Andy smiles as he looks around the room, he is going to enjoy mixing with these people, hearing their stories, whilst relaying edited versions of his own experiences.

Rob is more focused, watching each group of people intently. One person has already caught his eye, near the fire pit. A blond woman, about his age, who is walking around the fire with a note pad, taking details from some of the people gathered around it. She chats to each one, making notes with a friendly vibrancy that sparked something inside him. She reminded him of a past love that hadn't worked out due to his work commitments. His only regret in life was not making more time for her. The regret hadn't stopped him from moving on, he had later married, but he hadn't felt the same passion in his marriage as he had for the earlier woman.

The marriage had broken up after a few years due to his work commitments, but he was still amicable with his ex-wife who had remarried. He sometimes envied Andy for his steady marriage and family life. He wondered how Andy had managed to keep it together for all these years with frequent trips abroad fraught with danger, but for the most part accepted that he had chosen this life and love would be very hard to find, unless there was an exceptional woman involved.

He studied the woman outside the bar intensely for a while. She was very attractive with an athletic body, dressed in cargo trousers and a long sleeved shirt. She

National Insurance Contributions

was obviously more experienced than many of the people she was talking to, who were dressed in shorts and t-shirts. They would learn slowly, that near large bodies of water in Africa, it's wise to cover your limbs, regardless of how hot it is, as insects are more attracted to skin than cloth.

Andy notices Rob staring at the pit, immediately figuring out why. "She's nice, but I can't see her wanting to have much to do with the likes of us, she'll be too occupied with herding the pseudo adventurers she is in charge of." Andy was opinionated when it came to travellers, especially with the type who preferred organised trips as opposed to total independent travel. He felt the organised trips were for people who wanted to feel adventurous without having to be so.

Rob looked at Andy. "I guess, but no harm in trying later on. I'm hungry, it's definitely time to go down the road to grab some food. It should only take an hour after which we can come back for some socialising."

They finish their drinks and head towards the exit, passing the fire. As he passes her, Rob smiles at the woman, who had noticed them, she was instantly intrigued as there was something slightly different about them than other backpackers she had met. Something that only an experienced traveller would notice, they seemed far more worldly wise. She smiles back.

They find a restaurant serving Italian food about five minutes away. It suits them perfectly, as they were unlikely to get sick from it. They are efficiently shown a table and given a menu each. It looked like the restaurant had a high turnover of custom because of its popularity amongst travellers who had been on an African diet for long enough to want some familiar food. They order drinks, which arrive as they are still choosing their meals.

The waiter waits while they select their dishes, which speeds the process up. Andy takes a sip of his beer. "I'm willing to bet this will be a very fast meal." He had looked around, although there were around 30 tables, only a half a dozen were empty, the waiters were bustling around the customers, ensuring that their needs were met quickly. This was unusual for African restaurants, where speed is not normally as important as keeping the customers at their table for as long as possible to maximise the amount of drinks they bought.

Their meals arrive within ten minutes, but they were not about to rush them, engaging in a rare conversation that didn't involve their work. "Have you spoken to your wife or kids since we've been away?"

"No, as much as I would like to, I want to ensure that there isn't a single connection between me and them while we are here, you don't know who listens to calls, paranoid as it may seem, they mean everything to me and I want to keep them out of any danger." Rob was surprised, he thought that Andy would have at least called whilst at Petre's, but understood that if things go wrong, they could be traced back there. "I'm amazed you manage to keep a steady relationship going with what we do."

"It's not easy, but I am fortunate that Wendy is very understanding, she appreciates the life I give her back home. The more trips we do, the more concerns I have though. The more I long for the day when we can stop, but I know it's not necessarily over then as we have affected some people who bear grudges for decades. I guess I will have to find a way to totally disassociate myself from this life when it is over." Rob frowned at this, wondering whether Andy would disassociate himself from everyone.

"Don't frown, I'm not going to drop you as a friend." Andy responded with a big grin on his face, sometimes he was the more sensible of the two. "We just need to work a way to disassociate each other from all of this." This reassured Rob a little, he had paid little thought to their retirement, but knew it would happen sometime, obviously Andy had thought about it more, he had far more to lose.

They are half way through the meal when more customers arrive. Rob was pleasantly surprised that the blond from the lodge was among the party of 6, four male and two female. She smiles at him as they are shown the table next to them. The waiters flock to the table, their orders are taken very quickly, with the food arriving only a couple of minutes later. The waiters seem familiar with everyone at the table as there is lots of chatter between the waiters and the group, some in English, some in Nyanja, the local Zambian language.

Andy and Rob finish their meals before ordering some pancakes for desert, which takes longer than the main course took to arrive. They just sit back with fresh drinks, chatting about football and other topics, any topic apart from why they were really here. The table next to them finish their meals, which had been a noisy affair, then order some more drinks.

One of the men on the table turns to Rob and Andy. "Are you guys here alone? Do you fancy joining us for desert?"

Rob and Andy both get up and drag their chairs to the adjoining table, remaining standing for the greetings. At the table were Chris, John, Mike, Steve, Julie and Kate.

It was Julie that had caught Rob's eye, she seemed to be just as intrigued by him as he was by her. She was around 5'6", long blonde hair with a really attractive face and deep blue eyes. She also seemed to have a lot of spirit.

Chris starts the conversation, explaining that they all worked for Overland Wonders, manning the two trucks. The company insisted on two drivers and a guide in each truck to ensure that the clients were well looked after and had a sense of safety, something that some of the other more dubious adventure companies failed to provide. Formalities over, he focuses on Rob and Andy. "You guys don't look like the normal type of travellers we come across, no offence, but slightly older and much more worldly wise, you must have some interesting stories."

This is Andy's element. "Yes, we worked in the city for many years, built up some successful restaurants, now they are thriving, we have taken time out to see the world. We've been travelling for over a year now, this is our last leg, driving from Cape Town to London." The rest seemed impressed. John more than most. "Wow, it's nice to see a more mature traveller. Have you done it all independently?"

Andy is on a roll. "It's the only way, gives us the freedom to change the trip and we are fortunate not to have any time constraints so can change direction when someone recommends a place worth visiting. I have an understanding wife, who couldn't take the time out from her career and it would have been tough to get the kids out of school. My compatriot doesn't have the same commitments, so when I muted the idea to my wife, she suggested we go together, she knew I would just get restless with the business running itself, fortunately she has managed to meet up with us every couple of months in somewhere exotic."

Julie had taken great interest in the fact that Rob had no commitments, she focuses on him. "So, what was your best part of the journey?"

"Walking 150 miles to Mount Everest last Autumn.it was an amazing trip, I can almost remember every step, with the highlight being the celebration of my birthday in a monastery only 15 miles away from the mountain. We were given some special drinks that the climbing teams had left at the monastery, so I made an exception to my non-drinking rule that night. Next day I remembered why I don't drink anymore!" This wasn't a total lie, he had done the trek three years before, rather than as part of this trip."

Julie is suitably impressed. "You must tell us more of your trip later on, I'm fascinated to hear of places I've not been."

"Have you been to many places?" Rob is starting to get on a roll as the two started to have a separate conversation from the rest of the table, who were being wooed by Andy's experiences. Like Rob's story, none were total fabrications, they just hadn't taken place in the last twelve months. He amazed them with the walk to Shipton's Arch in China, a drinking game with Siberians in the coldest place on earth, sleeping in the jungles of Papua New guinea with local tribes, the stories were too numerous for this one night and the beer was flowing freely.

Julie wasn't listening to Andy, she was focusing on Rob, as he was with her. "Mainly Africa, Australia and South America, I've not really done Asia. I fell into working for Overland Wonders about four years ago after meeting Chris in a Cape Town bar. I have mostly done the same trips ever since, babysitting green students on gap years who want a bit of adventure, but in a bubble. I'm only doing another season before I look at moving back home and settling down. I'm not getting any younger and would like to have a family." This surprises Rob, but he did know that eventually the maternal instinct overrides every other instinct in women. They carry on chatting for the next hour, oblivious to the rest of the table who were growing louder with each round of drinks.

Chris, noticing the concern of the waiters calls things to a halt. "Guys, we don't want to overstay our welcome here, there will be a queue of customers soon, we don't want to get in the way of our welcoming hosts, shall we go back to the lodge for a couple of late night drinks?" The table concurred. The bills are paid and they walk the five minutes back to the lodge as two separate groups, one group of five, the other just two.

John turns to Andy. "Your friend Rob seems to have managed to break through Julie's defences, I've never seen her take such an interest in one person, preferring to remain a little aloof. We were almost at the point of taking bets whether she was a religious missionary, a lesbian or just frigid, as she has never shown an interest in anyone, no matter how hard they have tried in the past." He nodded toward Mike with a smile. Mike was arm in arm with Kate, who had succumbed to his charms.

"I guess it must be lonely on these trips." John grins again. "Not with a group of women travellers who want the full travel experience, if you know what I mean!" He was in his late twenties, as was Steve. It was noticeable that there wasn't much of an age difference between them and the clientele they were escorting, so company was very much in abundance for them. Chris was in his thirties, preferring to maintain some personal distance from clients and colleagues alike.

When they arrive back in the lodge bar it is even louder and busier than before. Two new arrivals have taken centre stage, with a large group of people gathered around them drinking shots with big cheers. Chris approaches the few people still sitting silently around the fire pit. "Guys, we're going to be leaving at 9am tomorrow to see Vic falls. Breakfast is not till 8, so you can join in the fun in the bar, just don't overdo it, the noise from Vic falls can make a bad hangover seem much worse!"

He turns to Andy and whispers. "Sometimes you have to tell them everything they can or can't do." About half the group slowly get up and wander over to the bar, with the rest discussing amongst themselves whether it would be better to go to bed now or sit around the fire for a little longer.

The new arrivals are two South Africans, who had been contracted by the government to create accurate maps of the country. They had been to the remotest of areas in Zambia, areas where no traveller ever goes, taking measurements, so whenever they got to the more populated areas, they made sure they would have a good time. The rest of the guests at the lodge instantly took to them, they were loud, entertaining and very funny, giving very bad tips on how to backpack. Tips such as visiting the book exchange shelf each lodge had, taking a handful of books and swapping them for leaflets they had picked up on their way instead of leaving the customary book in exchange for each one they took.

The loudest of the South Africans was heavy built, whilst his companion was much smaller. Both were scruffy and unshaven, not what anyone would expect to be they typical appearance of a cartographer. No one had managed to catch or if they had asked, remember their names, but it was immaterial, the South Africans were in full flow, initiating drinking games, giving advice to younger travellers and amazing their audience with the many close calls they had in some part of the country, be it with some of the local wildlife or other lodge owners.

The Overland Wonders staff had met them a couple of times in the last year, as they always had spent their recuperation time in Livingstone, so they greet them like old friends. Chris hugs them both before grabbing a drink, still keeping one eye on the rest of the staff, ensuring that they stayed within their limits for the next day.

Andy introduces himself to the South Africans and joins in with the drinking games, while Rob and Julie sit at the periphery spending time getting to know each other. Rob is wary of Andy getting carried away, so excuses himself and goes to speak to Chris. "I take it you are keeping an eye on your guys?"

"I sure am, I want them to have fun, but I also need to ensure we stick to our schedule tomorrow."

This pleases Rob. "Good, can you keep an eye on Andy too, he can overdo things, we have a long journey tomorrow, I don't want to do all the driving."

Chris understands perfectly. "No, problems."

Rob goes over to Andy, but before he can reach him, he is accosted by the large South African, who thrusts a drink into his hand. "Sorry, mate I'm teetotal, but cheers." He clinks their glasses together before giving it to Andy. The South African looks at him oddly. "Teetotal? That word isn't in my dictionary." and gives him a very firm friendly slap on the back, laughing and turned to the rest who were playing his drinking games.

Rob slides up to Andy. "Alright? I'm going to shoot off to bed soon, please don't overdo it, Chris is keeping John, Steve and Mike in check, can you follow his lead?" Andy understands, although his senses were a little dull, he still prides himself in his ability to know when to stop drinking now and again. "Don't worry, I'm not going to be too late, I am too aware that we are entering a potentially hostile country at some time tomorrow."

Rob was reassured when he returns to Julie, to continue from where they left off.

Twenty minutes later, she walks over to Chris, whispers something in his ear, which makes him look at her with raised eyebrows and a smile. He bids her good night, before she returns to Rob, who is standing just outside the bar. They leave together, returning to Rob's room.

Rob was completely surprised by Julie. She had suggested spending the night together before he had a chance to work his magic on her. She told him that she hadn't been with anyone for four years, but as soon as she had seen him, something had stirred inside and after speaking to him, she knew she wanted him, all of him, hoping that this would not be a one off. Rob was delighted and as he didn't drink, he had more than his fair share of one night stands to compensate. He also had surprised himself by developing feelings for Julie so quickly. He was feeling that he would give everything up for her, that is, after they had finished this last mission. He was wary that their backstory hadn't been completely true, although he knew he couldn't tell her now, there may be a time in the near future when he wouldn't have to tell her what he did.

In his room, they caress gently, before simultaneously undressing each other. Both are very pleased with what they see as they stand face to face at arm's length, holding each other's hands. They stand there for a minute, displaying the biggest smiles they had smiled for a long time. They were both incredibly aroused, finally letting go of each other to move the twin beds together as one. They lie on top of each other caressing and kissing, moving from the mouth to various parts of the body, their passion growing stronger with each kiss.

Julie forces Rob on his back and straddles him, gyrating slowly at first, growing faster with every movement. She starts to moan, which turns into a passionate scream. Rob, who normally in the past remained silent during sex, also starts wailing. He had never felt passion this strongly, he was enjoying it more than any sex he had had before. Sweat starts to drip off their bodies, they switch positions a couple of times, first Rob on top, then behind, then side by side, locked in an embrace before Julie returns to the top. Their passion lasts nearly thirty minutes before they both climax and collapse on the bed in each other's arms panting. Rob felt some scorching from the deep scratches Julie had unwittingly gouged into his back, but was slightly pleasured by the way it had been caused by the pleasure he had given Julie.

"That was amazing." They both smile as they said it simultaneously. They lay there for a while, just looking into each other's eyes, with Rob caressing Julie's hair. She spots him slightly grimace.

"What's wrong honey?" Rob rolls over to show her his back, which had started to bleed slightly. Julie was horrified. I'm so, so very sorry, I have never done anything like that before." "It's OK." He was smiling. "I guess I had a profoundly deep effect on you, which makes me feel wonderful. You have the same effect on me." He kisses her lovingly.

In a short period of time, they had become closer to each other than they had with anyone else before. They finally fall asleep in each other's arms, waking at two more intervals during the night to repeat the passion, each time louder, more passionate and lasting longer.

They wake at daylight, tired but content, locked together, gazing in each other's eyes. Rob speaks first. "I don't want this to end." "Neither do I." replies Julie with a tear in her eye. They both know that they would be separated for a while, but not forever. They lay there for another hour, talking about family, hopes for the future and how they could be reunited before getting up and showering together.

It was eight when they emerge from the room, to be greeted by a round of applause by a large group of people in the bar. The large South African shouts at them. "I can see why you don't drink now, but I do think you ought to next time so the rest of us can get some sleep!"

Rob and Julie have breakfast together, with big patches of silence as they contemplated the impending time apart. Rob has been given the Overland Wonders' itinerary, making a promise to Julie that they would meet up soon. Julie had assumed this would be after her trip had finished, she had another four weeks to go, but she knew that it would take longer than for Rob and Andy to finish their trip.

Rob reassures her. "We will meet up sooner than you think, I'm working on a plan." She smiles at this, hoping it would come true. If not, it would only be a couple of months and she had his contact details. They only lived a couple of miles apart back home, they would definitely meet up again in the near future.

They finish breakfast before saying their goodbyes, hugging passionately as everyone else tries to ignore them, but some cannot resist coughing loudly, mainly Chris and Andy.

When she finally lets go and walks to the truck, Julie keeps glancing around, blushing and feeling like a teenager again. Andy walks over to Rob, smiling. "Well, looks like we both had the relaxation we needed last night, time to hit the road, this was a great change in plan!"

Rob looks at Andy seriously. "I think this is more than just a bit of fun, definitely not something I had planned, but sometimes I'm happy to go with the flow."

He gives Andy a friendly little punch as they get their bags from their rooms before getting in the car to resume their journey.

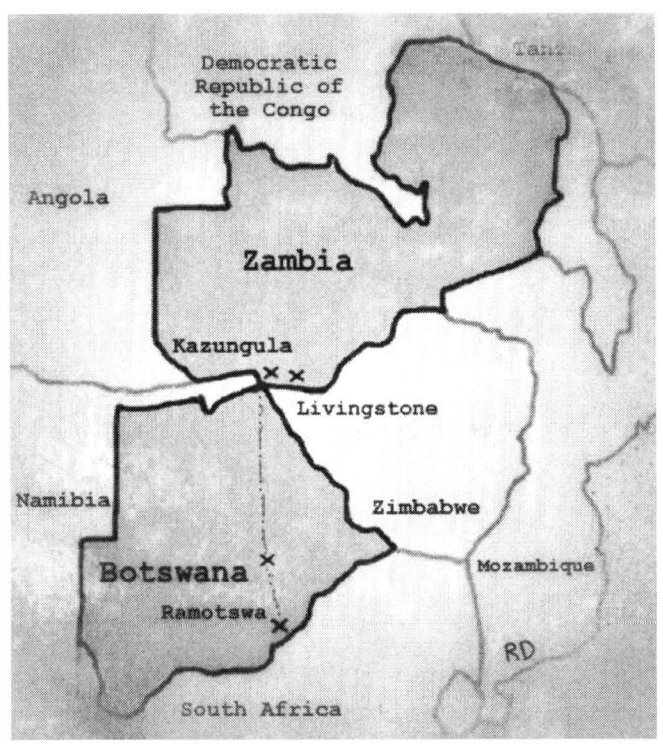

Capítulo Tres

The interior of Zambia is very similar to the region of Botswana they crossed, the terrain is much the same undulating bush land, albeit with less contrasting colours as the yellow-greens and browns, which have converged further due to the increased temperature of the more Northern country. The main surprise to the two travellers was the amount the roads had been improved by since they were last here, which was due to the increase in wealth from tourism. The roads were very good now which would speed the journey up considerably.

Some of the long uncomfortable journeys they have endured in the past are a distant memory as this time they were in a comfortable vehicle, appreciating some of the basic luxuries such as cooling fans. After driving north for twelve hours, they stop off for the night just a couple of hours from the DRC border.

The town they stop off in is very small with only one basic guesthouse, but it has beds and food for them, which are very much appreciated after a long day. They have a quick and basic meal before retiring for the night at around 9pm. They wake at daybreak, shower and take simple a breakfast before heading out to the Land Cruiser. Before they travel the final stretch to the border crossing into the Democratic Republic of the Congo at Kasumbalesa they need to prepare their first disguise to ease their passage.

Andy pulls out some red crosses and logos from his luggage and places them on the bonnet and each side of the car, whilst Rob puts some medical supply kits in full view inside of the car. Once this minor camouflage is complete, they both put on jackets bearing the logo of Médecins Sans Frontières. Border guards rarely turn away aid workers.

The final two hours to the DRC is spent testing each other's medical knowledge as a precaution, but they have used this disguise before and have never been asked anything tricky. They do know that this crossing will be a lot tighter than the southern countries. Tourists are not as common, so the guards will have an instant mistrust of any westerner entering the country.

When they reach the border, they find unsurprisingly that the post is over-manned, with sixteen armed guards, all ready to use force to stop anyone entering their country. Andy had a theory that the more heavily armed a border crossing was, the less the importance of the country. The large presence on the border was a show of force for their neighbours and an attempt to impress the importance of the country on anyone passing through, nothing more.

There was a similar theory on the size of the motorcade of the presidents of such countries, where the size of the motorcade was inversely proportioned to the importance of the country internationally. The dictators of small central African republics often travelled in large motorcades escorted by several hundred troops, accompanied by any available air support, whereas a leader such as Nelson Mandela often travelled in a single car supported by a motorcycle outrider. The show of force was not necessary in countries that were actually important on the world stage.

The Land Cruiser stops next to the border post and the occupants get out with their papers to hand. Four of the guards scrutinise the two men while three stand around the Land Cruiser. The other nine guards stay at their posts with their weapons ready, giving the misguided impression they are prepared for any attempt to illegally break through the border. The guard commander was obvious from his uniform. A uniform that had more gold braid than a western general. All of the guards were waiting for his orders, acting without direct instruction was something that they were too aware must not be done. The post was run like a military unit, a legacy of the recent history of the country.

Volunteers from Médecins Sans Frontières were not an uncommon sight to them. The long civil war ensured that there were plenty of civilian casualties to be treated, leading to a flood of aid workers into the country offering assistance. The border guards viewed aid workers as a strange bunch, none ever looked the same and they couldn't understand why they were so keen to help people they didn't know.

Male, Female, short hair, long hair, all different colours, some smart, some scruffy. One thing they all seemed to have in common was that they were always overly polite and very eager to comply with the border crossing procedures. Aid workers bored the commander, he wanted people to try and cross the border post who were up to no good so he could exert his power on them. He had spent many years in conflicts and yearned for more action than searching through the bags of patronising aid workers.

As the commander starts issuing instructions to the rest of the guards, they instantly leap into action. The guards around the car open the doors and start rummaging around inside. One pulls out the bag of medical supplies that has been placed conspicuously on the top of the other bags and rummages through it. There are plentiful amounts of all types of supplies, most of which are meaningless to him. He is familiar with bandages and some of the more common drugs such as aspirin, but he has never seen some of the supplies of asthma ventilators, catheters, Sphygmomanometers for measuring blood pressure and other assorted equipment before.

One of the other two guards opens the other bags and rummages through, disappointed that there is only clothing and toiletries, whilst the third is checking the inside of the car thoroughly, feeling under the seats, behind the dashboard, opening every compartment he can find. None of them reveals anything of interest.

The commander stares at the car, which is decorated with a distinct red cross logo that is already looking quite old and faded, despite only being stuck on only a couple of hours ago. He looks at the two aid workers and speaks to them in very good English with a taint of a French accent.

"Where are your coats?"

"Sorry?" Andy is a little baffled by the question. He had been asked many things before, even bizarre personal questions at border crossings, but never had he been asked where his coat was.

"Your white coats, everyone from red cross people wear white coats. Where are they?"

The penny drops. "Ah, you mean our white doctor coats. We are not doctors, just volunteers, we do not get given the white coats, we are not important enough. We just have to report to our boss at Kananga, where we will do whatever he says. Only the really important people get the white coats, people like us who get all the bad jobs have to wait to get a white coat."

The commander looks angry for a moment, then bursts into laughter, loud booming laughter. He is bent over with tears almost coming out of his eyes. The rest of the guards stop and stare at their commander. They have never seen him laugh and don't know how to react, looking back and forth at each other and the commander, who gathers himself together after what feels like several minutes, then says something to the other guards in Swahili, but in a dialect that Rob or Andy cannot understand.

The rest of the guards also burst out laughing, which escalates into a fit of hysteria in some, with one actually ending up rolling around on the floor. This continues for a few minutes as Rob and Andy look at each other mystified. Finally the hysteria ends as all the guards instantly gather themselves together when the commander shouts a command. They all stand up straight, with some brushing themselves down. Once they have settled and are totally still, the commander turns his attention to the two westerners.

"My friend, we have many Musungus passing this border, all with the white coats, coming to cure our sick. You are the first we have seen that are not good enough to wear the white coats. We thought ALL Musungus had white coats, now we know, some like you are just like us, not good enough for a white coat. You are nobodies."

Rob still doesn't know if this is good or bad, he just stands there exchanging bewildered glances with Andy. They have passed many borders before, but have never been laughed at for not being important. This potentially could be a very dangerous situation if they are viewed as people who will not be missed in the west.

The commander points at one of the other guards. "My colleague over there said you may be war mongers, but being only two, I told him it wouldn't be a long war and most war mongers fly over the border. Now I find out you are servants to the white coats, you are just like the Africans that they treat with contempt, you have my sympathy."

Rob feels that this is good, if a little insulting, but will take insults and sympathy if it means they will pass this border without incident.

The commander shouts at the guards once more, causing them to all retreat back to their positions on the post. He pats Rob and Andy on the back before getting one of the guards to stamp their Argentinian passports. "You may get in your ambulance and go to help the dying people."

Andy doesn't need to be told twice. He quickly climbs into the driving seat, whilst Rob climbs into the passenger seat and nods his thanks at the guards. As they start drive off through the border the commander shouts at them.

"Enjoy wiping those bottoms for the white coats!"

The enduring image that will remain with them for longer than they would like, is the sight of the whole team of border guards bent over in fits of laughter at their expense. They had never experienced such a bizarre border crossing, but are relieved to have passed through so quickly.

Andy turns to Rob. "Did he just call us ass-wipes?"

"Sure did, I guess they thought that we were going to do the dirty jobs that the doctors get the Africans to do, but I will take being called an ass-wipe at every border crossing if it means an easy passage."

"Could have been worse I suppose."

Rob smiles. "Damn right, we may have had to kill them all. That would have drawn unwanted attention."

The drive through the DRC was very different than the rest of their journey, the infrastructure was not to the same standard as the more developed southern countries. They would remain on the N1 highway all the way across the country from Lubumbashi to Kinshasa, however it was only a highway in name, with a mixture of paved sections and dirt track along the way. Most of the road is cut directly through the tropical rainforest which blankets the whole country. They arrived in the DRC's second largest city, Lubumbashi in an hour of passing the border, driving straight through, keen to spend as little time in the country as was necessary. The more time they lingered, the more likely it was that there would be an incident.

After Lubumbashi, the N1 was nicely paved for a few hours, with their journey only being interrupted by the frequent permanent road blocks they encountered, most of which they were waved through without stopping. A red cross on a white 4x4 is a deterrent to many of the guards manning the roadblocks, it was unlikely that they would be able to solicit a large bribe from aid workers. There had been several well-publicised incidents involving aid workers who have been detained for non-payment of bribes, which was an embarrassment to the country, something the President was keen to avoid, as there was still a large reliance on international aid. He had instructed the forces of the country to only stop aid workers in an emergency. At the only roadblock that they were stopped at, a ten dollar note posted through a narrowly opened window prevented any hindrance of their passage.

Rob had pinpointed a couple of towns they could stay in overnight, the specific one depended on how the road conditions hindered their progress. They wouldn't even consider trying to sleep by the side of the road in such a hostile country.

After a few hours they are in the middle of the sparsely populated rainforest, where Rob decides it would be prudent to get a couple of guns into the front, so they can be accessed quickly if needed. Rob has switched driving duties with Andy and doesn't intend to stop.

"Mate, it may be a good idea to get a couple of the handguns up here, just in case."

Andy doesn't want to stop either, so is happy to climb over the seats into the back. He lies in the foot well on the passenger side, pulls back the carpet and takes a couple of minutes to locate the latch which opens the hidden compartment.

"Petre's man knew how to create an easily accessible hidden compartment, we should buy him a couple of beers we when are there next." He sarcastically moans.

Rob is more pragmatic, he would take a difficult to find compartment any day over an easily accessible one.

"It's better that it takes you a couple of minutes to open it when you know it's there, than have a border guard find it in a few seconds."

Andy closes up and climbs back into the passenger seat. "I know, but I thought that it's now such a necessity for most white South African farmers that he would be able to hide it well and make it accessible very quickly. I'll put that in my feedback form to Petre's man."

Andy examines the guns. All are Glock 22s, 15-round .40 calibre pistols, reliably used throughout the world. One well-placed shot would take a man out easily at short range. That one shot would also have the power to inflict a lot of damage at medium range. Having fifteen shots between reloads is very useful, especially as all of them were suppressor ready, useful for the times when stealth was of the utmost importance. The Glocks were the preferred tools of choice for Rob and Andy's work.

He places two of the guns, each fitted with a suppressor, plus four spare magazines in the glove compartment, then reaches over Rob to place the same arrangement in the driver's door compartment.

The daylight outside is starting to fade, which concerns Rob. He switches on the headlights. "How far is this town?"

Andy gets out a map and switches the internal light on. He spends a few minutes studying it.

"Less than ten miles away, I guess, we should be there in half an hour.

This pleases Rob. "Excellent, I am getting a bit knackered." He suddenly spots something that concerns him in the headlights.

"Fuck, here we go."

Andy looks over the top of the map to see a group of men in the middle of the road, pointing rifles at the car. The road is completely hemmed in either side by thick rain forest, so there is no way to avoid the gunmen.

Rob skids the car to a stop in the middle of the road, leaving the engine running and switching the headlights onto full beam, to make the potential assailants shield their eyes. Andy puts the map away quickly, before switching off the internal light off and grabbing the guns from the glove compartment, placing them between his legs.

They have been in situations like this before. Andy knows that trying to talk your way out of this can quite often end up with you losing your car and its contents at best. It happened to him twice when on active service, in situations when they were not permitted to open fire, even when taking fire. The worst case scenario was ending up in an unmarked roadside grave, a fate which has befallen too many naïve travellers.

Rob initially wants to be cautious, until he understands who the armed men are and what they actually want. "Don't get out until they demand it, then when we do, make sure we both get around to the same side of the car. Don't start shooting yet, I want to see if we can get out of this without unnecessary casualties."

Andy is weighing up the situation, ready to take swift action. "I can only see six of them, only three each, less than two seconds and it is over." He glances over to the thick forest. "At least we have somewhere to hide the bodies so they won't be discovered until we are long gone." He stuffs both guns in his belt under the back of his shirt. Rob sighs as the men approach, but still puts his guns under the back of his shirt.

The hijackers reach the car and knock on the door, beckoning the two occupants to get out. Rob gets out and immediately has a rifle shoved in his face. Andy on the other side is brought around by two of the men and pushed towards Rob. The aid workers both act in deference to the hijackers, to ease them into a false sense of security.

All of the hijackers are talking loudly to each other in a local dialect, seeming to showing a lot of pleasure over the potential riches they have captured. One of them shouts something very assertively, which silences the rest, who remain firm pointing their rifles at their captives.

The leader looks at the two aid workers, using aggressively pigeon English. "Hand over Money."

Rob shrugs his shoulders. "What Money?"

The demand is repeated. "Hand over Money."

Rob responds again. "We have no money, we are aid workers." He beckons to the red crosses on the side of the car.

"We come to help your sick people." trying to install empathy in their attackers.

The leader speaks in his local dialect, which encourages the rest to raise their rifles to a shooting position. This concerns Andy and Rob, the margin for error is going to be very fine. The leader steps up close enough for them to smell his breath. "We have no sick people, only poor people, you help with that."

Rob steps back and turns his pockets inside out, showing he has no money inside. The hijackers start talking loudly amongst themselves, waving their guns around. They get more heated and start to ignore their two captives. Some point to the car as the leader goes back amongst them shouting and pointing to the forest.

This is the moment. Rob looks at Andy and gives a small nod. Simultaneously Rob and Andy reach behind their backs and pull a gun out in each hand, each fitted with a silencer on the end. In a flash they each unload two shots before the hijackers can react, four soft thumps lead to four of them reeling to the ground with terminal headshots. Of the remaining two hijackers, one has dropped his rifle in shock and the leader is fumbling for his. The speed of the two assassins is too great, acting without mercy, a round is placed in each of the remaining hijackers' heads within a second. Both hijackers slump to the ground without a noise. The situation has been resolved in a couple of seconds, in near silence.

The six silenced shots would not have been heard from further than 20 feet away. Rob and Andy stand for a few seconds totally devoid of emotion or remorse, listening for any signs of accomplices. All they hear is silence, eventually interrupted by the breeze over the tops of the trees. They had taken similar actions so many times before, they wouldn't dwell on the loss of the families, the hijackers had died because of their own greed.

Andy breaks the silence. "That's better, a bit of peace and quiet, they became very annoying very quickly. I guess they have never come across ass-wipes before!"

Rob smirks at Coops. Sometimes his quips can have a calming effect, especially after something that would traumatise most people. They wouldn't discuss their actions, there was nothing to discuss, they did what they had to and they knew it, further discussion wouldn't accomplish anything.

The bodies are dragged quickly into the nearby forest, not too far from the roadside. The whole operation takes just a couple of minutes, the important factor was leaving as quickly as possible as they now needed to put some distance between them and this place. The rifles are left with the bodies in the hope that anyone finding them would assume it was some sort of local feud, therefore would be less likely to instigate any sort of official investigation. Decades of civil war and unrest have taught the authorities that investigations can be lengthy, expensive and too much trouble, especially when a local feud is involved.

When Rob and Andy return back to the car, Andy offers to drive, which Rob gladly accepts. They both know that staying only 10 miles away could be asking for more trouble, especially when the dead men are missed. Someone will miss them, possibly sooner rather than later.

Rob pulls the map from the glove compartment and uses a small flashlight rather than the internal light again, mindful of not ruining Andy's night vision. "There is a fair sized town about 60 miles away, should take about an hour and a half."

Andy is happy with 60 miles, enough distance to be comfortable. "Sounds good."

They drive on into the night which thankfully passes without further incident, even after they had stopped and slept in a dirty guesthouse for 5 hours. They leave early in the morning, before sunrise, without waiting for breakfast, they can pick up some roasted maize from a roadside vendor along the route. They continue north west along the N1, passing official checkpoints every 100 miles or so, but they do not attract any interest in most of the checkpoints, paying the obligatory bribe at the couple where they are stopped. The main interest of the checkpoints in this area is stopping insurgents from moving around the country towards the capital.

After the fourth checkpoint of the day, just before noon, Andy checks the map. "We should be in Brazzaville by the end of the day, providing nothing silly happens."

The knowledge that they are near the capital and shortly after that they will be at their destination for this trip is good news for Rob, who has been running the mission parameters around his head. "I think we had all the silliness we are going to get last night. We'd have to be really unlucky to get hijacked twice. It's also about time we speak mainly in Spanish, the tentacles of our target may well stretch this far. Can you also hide anything that could identify us as anything but Argentinian?"

Andy practises his Spanish. "Si" then climbs into the back seat and starts rummaging around, gathering their passports, flight tickets and anything else which could identify them as British or any of the other nationalities they had as a back-up plan. He wraps them in some of the bandages from the medical supplies and tucks away them in the bottom of the gun compartment.

Around 4 hours later they arrive in Kinshasa, an urban sprawl, home to nine million people. Unlike the rest of the country, the city is wealthy, with wide boulevards criss-crossing a central business district which is populated with modern skyscrapers, modest by western standards, but a total contrast to the poorly developed towns found elsewhere in the country. They drive down the wide streets, which have sidewalks bustling with people, walking round the stalls that line the pavements, selling a variety of goods and local food. Many of the stalls are simply sheets placed on the pavement, covered with the goods for sale, a sight that would be unusual in more developed countries.

Kinshasa has nothing to offer the Argentinians on this trip, they had heard many stories about its legendary chaos. This is something they don't have time for now with their main focus being on getting to their final destination, They drive through the whole city without stopping, heading straight for the ferry port on the Congo River. The road reaches the river and follows the riverbank until they arrive at the ferry port, from where they can see their destination. The port is not a busy port, despite their proximity, there is little cross border trade between the two geographically closest capital cities in the world. Passing through customs is a formality, as they approach the border control, the guards spot the red crosses and quickly wave them out of the DRC, not even stopping them to check their passports.

Once in the ferry port, obtaining ferry tickets are a priority. Andy stays with the car, while Rob ventures into one of the nearby buildings. Half an hour passes before he eventually returns with the tickets, looking very frustrated.

"That was absolute chaos, the stories about this place are not exaggerated, I had to bribe about a dozen people to guarantee getting on this ferry." Andy just shrugs his shoulders, bribes were a mainstay of Africa travel, all that mattered was getting the tickets.

This was the second ferry ride of their journey, but when they saw the ferry arriving, they knew it would be a total contrast to the previous one. The ferry that was coming into port seemed to consist of such a large mass of people that they could hardly see the boat. There were people hanging off every piece of the boat they could grab onto. The deck of the boat was totally covered in cargo, not a single vehicle could be seen, which concerned Andy most of all. "I hope you haven't been sold tickets for a car that cannot fit on that thing." Rob doesn't answer, but indicates the few other waiting cars and trucks. Andy is not totally convinced.

The ferry eventually docks, initiating a near riot as people scramble off their various perches and rush to the exit, past the local police who do not bat an eyelid, probably having been paid off not to turn their attention elsewhere. The cargo is unloaded in the most disorganised fashion, the whole process taking nearly an hour, which tries Andy's patience, as he constantly sighs, pointing out the various inefficiencies every few minutes. Once the ferry is clear, one of the officials blows a large whistle, starting another near riot as the hordes of people gathered on the dock rush to the ferry to claim a spot. One of the policemen approaches Rob and Andy and points to the ferry, indicating urgently that they must get on now.

They don't need to be told twice, quickly jump in the car, driving it forward through the crowd which reluctantly allows them through to be guided on board by one of the seamen. They park on board safely and relax, a relaxation that doesn't last long as they start to feel the car rocking. Rob gets out. He is immediately hit by a sack of rice which was just being thrown on board. The cargo is being packed around the car, blocking them in, which causing Rob to get back inside.

"At least in here it'll be a lot more comfortable."

"and peaceful." Andy has wound his window up to block some of the shouting that has filled the air as people fight for the best spots to spend the journey. After half an hour they feel the ferry judder into motion to start the 3 kilometre journey across the Congo river, a journey that takes far less time than it does to load and unload the ferry.

When they dock in Brazzaville, the same chaos that occurred before the crossing started is repeated. The Argentinians are made to wait until most of the cargo is unloaded before they can move the car, finally reaching the border crossing an hour after the ferry has docked. Andy stops the car at the border gate. Two border guards approach the car, Rob leans out of the passenger window, passing them the passports. One guard looks at the passports, whilst the other addresses the two occupants.

"What is your business in the Congo?"

Rob responds. "We are doing a study on the Rainforest for Buenos Aires University." He has a pre-prepared explanation for the red-crosses on the Land Cruiser, but it isn't needed as the guard doesn't even question the livery. He is more intrigued by their nationalities. He has never met someone from Argentina before, but knows all about the sporting achievements of the country.

"Argentina, very good soccer team, Diego Maradona."

Rob smiles, responding in broken English. "You know of Maradona in the Congo?"

The guard is a big fan "Soccer very popular here, bar show it, mainly English league. Argentina unlucky in last world cup."

"Yes, you could say that, the English cheated us again." Andy feels slightly hypocritical as he joins in the conversation. He had once beaten an Argentinian unconscious in a Central American bar in a debate over the 'hand of god goal'. The Argie had made the mistake of saying the word Malvinas in the same sentence as hand of god. Andy was a bit drunk and got carried away. Luckily the Belize authorities were indebted to the British and helped in the cover up.

The other guard finishes looking at the passports and is in the process of approving the visa ."How long you in Congo for?"

Rob looks at him. "About four weeks, as you see we have a visa for one month, arranged with the assistance of your interior ministry."

The guard studies the visa and gives a nod of approval. "All is in order, you may pass after you both fill out this form. Could you both step out so we can just look into your vehicle?"

Both men get out of the car and walk to a small desk by the side of the road, where they are handed a small piece of paper each, accompanied by a very cheap pen. They fill out the forms, while the border guards take a quick look into the car and sniff it loudly. They make grimacing faces and hold their noses.

"You have been on long journey?" One of them asks.

"Yes, we have just been in the DRC studying the rainforest, this was our hotel some nights. No hotels in the forest." Rob pats the car smiling.

"Very dangerous, bandits in DRC rainforest, lucky you not attacked, bang, bang."

Andy smiles to himself. "American Cigarettes can work wonders." then he produces a pack of Camel cigarettes and waves them around. The guards flock over and help themselves. The passport guard takes the whole packet, immediately losing interest in the car. They hand the finished forms to the guard, who waves them across the border.

"Enjoy the Congo, Monsieur."

Rob and Andy climb back into the car, start it up and wave out of the window.

"Thank you señor."

The guards raise their hands and all shout in unison "MARADONA."

Rob grins and drives over the border into bustling Brazzaville, their destination. "That was easy."

Andy gives him a dirty look. "I wasn't happy praising their team, especially after Belize, but its good preparation as I guess we'll be doing that a lot from now on."

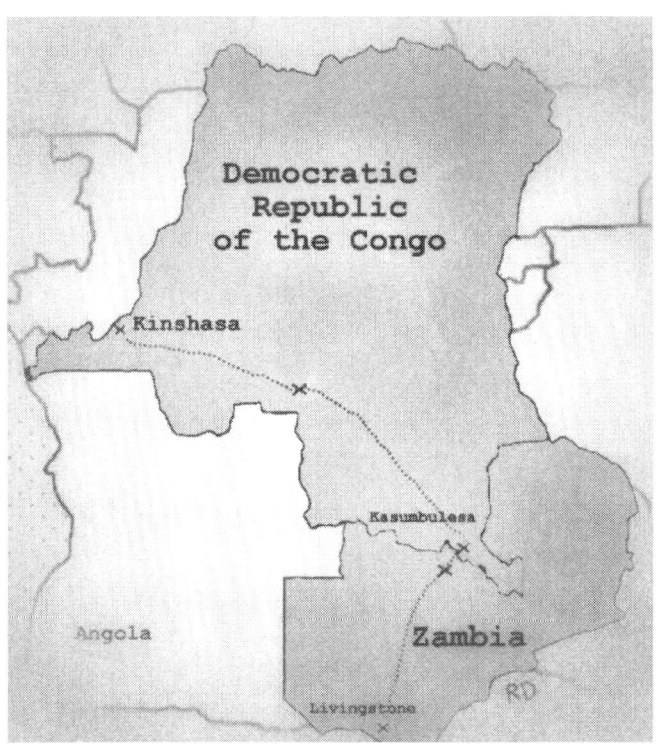

Capítulo Cuatro

Brazzaville is much calmer than Kinshasa. It is also a lot poorer and far less developed, with agricultural land scattered amongst the buildings. Andy navigates as they drive through the streets, which is not an easy task.

"I think we need the second left."

Rob prefers more precision. "Think?"

"This is the worst place I have seen for road names. Hang on, yes, it's this one, the hotel is just down there." Andy has spotted the hotel they have booked into, one of the finest the city has to offer.

Rob is relieved. It has been a long journey to get here. "Damn glad, I need a hot bath and some sleep."

"You're telling me!!" Andy holds his nose, imitating the border guards earlier.

They pull into the courtyard of the Hotel Olympic Palace, a fairly modern design for the area, something that would fit in well with a Mediterranean package holiday resort. A bellhop walks up to greet the car.

"Welcome to the Hotel Olympic Palace. You have a reservation?"

"Yes, Señor Diaz and Señor Cabrera from Buenos Aires University, we have booked a room for 5 nights, we confirmed a week ago."

The bellhop is eager to help, pointing to one side. "Please park here, I will carry your bags in. The car park is to the rear, you can park your car there later."

They get out of the car, get their bags out of the back and hand them to the bellhop. They then walk into the reception.

The reception is clean but bland, typical of the reception in most decent 3rd world hotels, a few plants placed around with a plain wooden desk at reception. Rob approaches the desk and is greeted with a smile by the receptionist.

The receptionist doesn't break her smile. "Can I help you?"

Rob takes care of the formalities. "Yes, we have a reservation for a double room for five nights, under the name of Diaz, from Buenos Aires University. We confirmed via telephone a couple of days ago."

The receptionist studies her reservation list for thirty seconds before finding their names on the list. "Yes, here we are, it is one hundred and fifty dollars a night, can I have a credit card as a deposit please? I also need to see your passports to take down the details."

"We'll pay in advance."

The receptionist is impressed as Rob hands over US$750 in cash and the two fake passports, which she takes and writes out a receipt for before handing back the passports.

When formalities are over, she explains the essentials. "Evening meal is between 7pm and 9pm, with breakfast between 7am and 10am. You are in room 109, the bellboy will show you upstairs. Do you require anything else?"

"No thanks."

The bellhop shuffles up behind them. "This way please."

They are led upstairs to their room, which the Bellboy unlocks and waves them in, placing their bags on the bed. They stand watching the bellhop giving the most obvious guided tour of a hotel room.

The bellhop points around the room, which is fairly basic for the price. A plain wooden floor, bleached white walls, two single beds and a table, plus a sliding door leading to a patio overlooking a medium sized swimming pool. "This is your room, the television channel does not start until 6pm, here is coffee making facilities." He points at a kettle and a couple of cups.

Rob turns to the Bellboy and hands him a dollar bill. "Thank you."

The Bellboy smiles broadly before he leaves, closing the door behind him. Andy looks at the room in depth, checking all of the fittings for anything untoward. He stops when he finds a crude bug in a light fitting, beckoning Rob over.

He writes on a piece of paper. "Knew the government would be checking up on all foreigners, have to be careful what we say, best to do all talking in Spanish. I'm not going to break the bug right away, that may arise some suspicion, I'll wait until tomorrow morning."

Rob starts speaking in Spanish. "Well I'm going to have a bath, got a busy day sorting out the equipment for our research tomorrow."

Rob heads towards the bathroom while Andy carries on searching the room, for any other suspicious items. He looks for a few minutes before writing a short note.

When Rob gets out of the bath, there is a note on the table. "Gone out to have a look around and move the car, the light fitting is only thing which needs replacing."

He is getting dressed when the door opens and Andy walks in.

Rob looks up. "Anything interesting?"

"I phoned our contact from the university, he would like to meet us later. He will be taking us for an evening meal tonight. I'd like to talk to him about the endangered tree we want to find." Tree is the code word they have assigned to their target to fit in with their botanical themed identities.

Rob wants to know more. "Is there enough time to read up on the endangered tree and find out how well protected it is?"

"Our contact indicated that he has got close enough to the tree that he can lead us straight there. A colleague of his, who has seen the tree, will be at the meal tonight. Anyway, we are not meeting him until the same time we had dinner last night, so you have time for some reading."

Rob sits on the bed and starts to read a small dossier he prepared on their target before they started the journey, while Andy lays on his bed and falls asleep.

Andy sleeps for a couple of hours before taking a shower and getting dressed in a designer shirt and trousers. Rob has changed out of his normal attire of jeans and a plain T-shirt, replacing the shirt with an Argentina football shirt, wearing a beige cotton jacket over the top. They go downstairs where they leave their keys with the receptionist.

Andy produces his best smile for the receptionist, trying to get a smile out of her. "We will not need an evening meal tonight, we are meeting a colleague in the town."

The receptionist finally breaks into a smile. "Do you want me to order a taxi? It is not safe to walk the streets at night."

"No we are being picked up on the corner, thanks though."

They walk out of reception and across the hotel entrance to a corner where a plain black Toyota with blacked out windows is waiting to pick them up. They get in the car, which only has one man inside, large heavy set with a well-worn African face. He looks like he has been through many tough situations and can handle himself. They both greet the man with a shake of the hand. They introduce themselves using their aliases, even though he knows they are not Argentinian, whilst he tells them simply he is Michael.

He pulls off into the fairly light traffic Michael speaks whilst he is driving, never letting his gaze divert from the road. "It is safe to talk in here, my government goes to great lengths to ensure that I cannot be detected by anyone. It's not the Congolese they are worried about but the underworld I have infiltrated."

This raises concerns with Rob. "Our hotel room is bugged which we have assumed to be the Congolese government, would it be possible that it is anyone else."

"Yes, it would be the government. They have all hotel rooms bugged, they listen in when a foreigner books in, all the hotels have to notify them of any foreign guests. It's the height of African paranoia. Though they have never acted on any information as far as I am aware, I mean, which foreigner is interested in a country like the Congo for a political war? As for the underworld, they have power in their circles, but not the resources to bug hotel rooms." Michael has reassured Rob a little, although Rob still knows he still cannot relax totally in their room.

Andy joins in the conversation "Well, you don't know who the information is passed on to. People like us don't want to take any chances."

Rob quickly wants to get down to business. "Talking of which, have you managed to set up a meeting with our tree yet?"

Michael is confused. "Tree?"

Rob clarifies. "Our code word for the target, it's best to describe him as the tree, especially as we are supposed to be botanists."

"Ah I see." He is still slightly confused, but carries on regardless, not wanting to appear stupid in front of the westerners. "Yes, I will go into more details tonight, but you will be meeting him in a market tomorrow for a preliminary meeting. If he trusts you, he will easily meet with you somewhere more private. This is the opportune moment for you to fulfil your contract."

Rob doesn't need to be told where to fulfil the contract, he was expecting a private meeting. He prefers to fulfil their contracts with the minimum amount of people around. They can deal with any bodyguards easier in a confined location, but they have to get invited there first. "How well in with him are you? Does he trust you with a lot of knowledge?"

Andy joins in displaying his rare cautious side. "We've seen plans fail at the first hurdle when our contact has been compromised and all hell breaks loose before we get a chance to get close."

Michael wants to reassure them. "I am trusted very much, hence my government using you two instead of me doing it and us losing all I have worked for."

Rob is intrigued by this information. "So this is only one piece of a larger operation?"

"Yes, various agencies have identified this target as a key element in the fight against some regional terrorist groups. He used to be a small time criminal, however his power has grown in the last few years and he has assembled a formidable following. He has managed to gain control of most of the underworld in the Congo, building his powerbase around the control of the diamond industry. He has amassed some considerable wealth and it is believed that he is keen to spread his wings internationally. According to our sources he has formed some important links with some more well-known criminal and terrorist groups around the world. We believe there have been several preliminary meetings discussing alliances between many of the groups. We also believe that the series of meetings is escalating, but intelligence is sketchy. They are likely to meet in places like this, a country that the west does not really care about. You can understand that the government I work for is keen to stop this before it develops into something too big."

Rob and Andy have taken part in similar operations before, taking out a small cog that could start some big wheels turning. Something a government cannot do officially until some major crime has been committed, something many governments are keen to avoid. Rob is concerned for Michael, these types of operations can have serious local repercussions. "Won't your introduction of us compromise your security?"

"No, as I will blame your introduction on a trustee who you will kill. I will just be a driver for you. This trustee will be there tonight. He is keen to impress your tree with new opportunities. He is already taking credit for a possible South American connection that will make him very powerful."

Rob grins. "Everybody wins then."

"Well except the tree and his sapling!" Andy corrects.

All of the car occupants smile as they look out of the windows thinking about the next few days.

Rob wants to ensure they are on the same wavelength from the start. "Can we go through with our cover story that we sent you. Just to make sure there are no small discrepancies?"

Michael runs through the story he has been given. "You are two Argentinian business men with many varied business interests, one of the main interests being the supply of arms to various underground groups. Rodrigo Diaz and Adriano Cabrera. You are looking at the Congo as a good place to invest time due to the diversity of groups all requiring arms. You got into contact with me through my cousin in France, the base you used to contact the Angolan groups you were supplying. You both fought in the Central American civil wars, against the western forces led by the USA, where you developed a grudge against their western imperialism. You were also teenage conscripts in the

Falklands War where you first developed your dislike of Britain and its allies."

"Malvinas war, you'll never hear an Argie talking about the Falklands! The rest is perfect. Have you had to tell them anything else, for example about some of the deals we have brokered?" Andy still flinched whenever he said that word.

Michael shakes his head. "No, just the basics, they were actually looking for a weapons supplier when this came up, so didn't want to know too much to be convinced to meet any weapons dealer, however they have heard about your deals in Africa from other sources. As soon as they knew that you were the guys I was talking about, they were very eager to meet you. I didn't need to tell them anything, your reputations were perfect."

The Argentinians would have been foolish to walk into such a situation based on a word of mouth reference from one man. They both knew well from experience that Africans won't even trust their own brother in normal situations. In situations so deadly, trust has to be earned. They have prepared their backgrounds well, this wasn't the first time they had posed as Argentinians in Africa. Getting into an inner circle of trust can take a lot of work. The Argentinians had spent the last two years building a strong cover story in between completing some other smaller jobs. Rob and Andy knew that with a watertight backstory, they would be able to get very close to some of the international factions that were increasing their power base and causing concern for major governments.

With the help of a foreign government they had actually helped arm rebels in Algeria, making waves ensuring that they would have a reputation that preceded them. Then, the supply of very hard to obtain weapons to a small group in Angola ensured that they would find doors easier to open in sub-Saharan Africa. They weren't sure at the time which doors they would need to open, but had ensured that at least they would be able to knock on them.

Their reputation became legendary when a civil war had broken out in the Sudan. The Argentinians were the middle men for some western governments, supplying a large selection of weapons to the rebels, something that suited all parties involved. The governments got their influence in the war without getting their hands dirty, the rebels got their weapons, and the reputation of the two Argentinians was cemented.

"Excellent, do any of them speak Spanish?" Rob was concerned that although their Spanish was very good, they would one day come up against someone who had grown up in Argentina, someone who would spot their poor dialects. Thankfully, that type of person is rarely to be found in Africa.

Michael has done his background work also. "No, they only speak English and Belgian. They may know some Spanish words, but no-one is fluent. I checked to see if you would have to use English."

Rob has to worry about one less thing, making another of his back-up plans redundant. "I think we are happy using English."

After only fifteen minutes travelling, Michael slows the car down, before he pulls up in a small side street next to a restaurant.

"We are here. I had to take the long way around in case anyone followed us. My contact, Kwanza will be meeting us in a few minutes. He is a trusted person by the tree. He will be taking all of the credit for your introduction. I don't think there is anything else we need to cover."

Rob agrees. "Nope, all bases seem to be covered."

They all get out of the car and walk into the restaurant, which unusually specialises in Ethiopian cuisines. The décor is fairly basic, with beige walls, a few token Ethiopian artefacts sparsely spread over the walls. As they walk in, they are aware that Michael towers above both of them, they didn't realise he was so tall when he was sat in the driver's seat. An African man is there to greet them. He is much smaller than all of them, but is smiling very broadly.

"Hello, hello, my friends, I am your friend Kwanza. I hope you are well. How have you found our fair city?"

"Hello Kwanza, this is Adriano."

Michael points to Andy and Kwanza shakes his hand excitedly.

"Hello, Señor, pleased to meet you."

"And this is Rodrigo."

Kwanza has already taken Rob's hand and also shakes it vigorously.

"Hello, Señor, I am also pleased to meet you."

Kwanza, gestures over the room. "We can sit over here in the corner without being disturbed. The food here is very good, Ethiopian food."

As they survey the restaurant, it is noticeable that there are only four other patrons eating. They all go over to a table in the corner, well away from the other patrons, where they sit on one of the wooden wicker seats around the table. Before they get a chance to say anything, a waiter places a menu in each of their hands. A menu which seems to contain some very basic offerings and a very limited selection of those offerings.

Kwanza is keen to impress the Argentinians right from the start. If all goes well he will gain a lot more respect and power. "Have you eaten this sort of food before?"

Rob and Andy have eaten this food many times before, they know exactly what the food is and more they importantly how to eat it properly. Rodrigo feigns ignorance, knowing that Argentinians who know Ethiopian food may be a bit odd. "No, what do you recommend?"

Michael offers some advice. "The Injera and Doro Wat is very good…,"

Kwanza interrupts quickly. "I try the Doro Wat sometimes, it is from Ethiopia. It has a unique taste."

Both Argentinians look at each other and nod knowingly that they have to be diplomatic in what appears to be a popularity contest, although Michael is happy for it to be this way. Adriano refrains from a sarcastic comment about the food in an Ethiopian restaurant being from Ethiopia. "In that case I will try Injera and Doro Wat." Rodrigo has the same.

Kwanza is pleased they have chosen his selection and calls the waiter over excitedly.

"We will have four Injera and Doro Wat. Bring some Wine too, White should be OK."

Rodrigo catches the waiter's attention. "Waiter, I will just have a bottle of water, unopened please."

"Certainly, Sirs."

The waiter walks off, while Kwanza starts the small talk. "So, you are looking to move into business here?"

Rodrigo takes up the thread. "We are always looking for opportunities. Your country can supply us with many sales, providing your master, Señor Umbekie, has the right contacts and the network to move our merchandise."

They pause while the waiter returns bringing the water and the wine. He pours a glass each for Kwanza,

Michael and Adriano, leaving Rodrigo to open his water and pour it.

Kwanza continues, keen to impress on the Argentinians how important Umbekie is. "I assure you that Mr Umbekie has all the contacts you will need. He is one of the most powerful people in the Congo, he knows many people you have certainly heard of."

Michael joins in to give the importance of his new friends some emphasis. "He also controls enough men to warrant a large initial transaction with you."

Adriano takes his turn to show that the partnership is built on equal terms, keen to impress that there is no stronger partner. "Well that would be beneficial to all of us, as we can obtain merchandise that the west would not like us sharing around, if you understand my meaning."

Kwanza is getting very excited. "I understand very well, my master would be very delighted to test some of this merchandise."

Adriano continues. "We can arrange for some samples to be sent over, but there are a lot of details to be discussed regarding receipt of the delivery. I trust

Señor Umbekie has such facilities in place, it is something we can discuss when we meet him."

Kwanza is also keen to impress that he has a position of power. "I can discuss such matters with you."

Rodrigo decides it's prudent to avoid the possibility of having to go back to the hotel and get some weapon samples at this early stage. "There is no need at this moment to go into such details, all we need to do is meet Señor Umbekie and establish a dialogue to extend to a partnership."

Kwanza is disappointed, but nods understandingly.

Michael proposes a toast. "Let's raise our glasses to what should be a successful venture."

They all raise their glasses.

"Successful venture."

The waiter returns with four plates containing unleavened bread, accompanied by four pots which contain the Injera. Kwanza directs him to place the correct meals, even though all are identical. He then leaves the table. Everyone starts eating, with the two Argentinians rolling the meat into the pancake like a kebab on purpose.

Michael, chuckles, before offering some advice. "No, you don't eat it like that, you are supposed to put some of the Injera from the pot on your plate, then scoop it up in a small torn off section of bread." Whilst Kwanza is too polite to correct them, he glances in disgust at Michael for embarrassing the two people who could make his life very successful.

The Argentinians try eating this way, but feign incompetence. "I think our way was better, easier for the untrained."

The Africans smile and let them eat how they wish. The four continue eating for a while. Kwanza has been watching the Argentinians closely, satisfying himself they are genuine, thinking more and more of what this could mean for him in the eyes of Mr Umbekie, how he will have riches and power and women and lots of gold, all of which would give him the respect of those who he passed on the street.

"There goes Kwanza." They would say. "If you are clever you could grow up to be like him." They would tell their children. He was desperate for this to go well. He didn't want to mess this up. He couldn't believe his luck when Michael had approached him, but was also cautious, was Michael trying to set him up for a fall, to take his place at Mr Umbekie's side. He had made a mental note to keep Michael in his place by ensuring that he would be rewarded with a small but trusted role as Kwanza's aide for his help.

Kwanza had heard a group in Angola had obtained some forbidden weapons, rocket launchers and powerful guns from two international arms dealers that were happy to supply to anyone with the right money. When Michael had overheard Kwanza talking of this, he told him that he had a cousin in Angola who might be able to help. Michael had then arranged for him and Kwanza to make a trip to the border to speak with the Angolan group.

"Two Argentinians, long hair, not shaved, good men. They can supply many things we cannot normally get hold of, at a price that is good for us." Kwanza was told by the Angolans, when enquiring about the supply of the weapons. Normally this type of people will not divulge such information, but Mr Umbekie can open many mouths Kwanza thought to himself on being told this. What he didn't know was that Michael's 'cousin' was working for the same government as Michael.

The 'cousin' agreed to put Kwanza in contact with the Argentinians through Michael. "The Argentinians will only meet people by personal recommendation. I will recommend Michael, giving them Michael's contact details, they will meet him and through him they will meet you. That is how they insist they do business. They need to ensure that they are not trapped by the authorities. When they know Michael is my cousin, they will know to trust him, and he will ensure they trust you."

Kwanza was not entirely happy with Michael being involved, fearing that Mr Umbekie would overlook Kwanza in favour of Michael, but agreed as it was the only way he could be involved. On their journey back to Brazzaville he made sure that Michael knew his place, after all Kwanza had been trusted by Mr Umbekie for many years and could talk privately with Mr Umbekie. The promise to Michael of a good position by Kwanza's side ensured Michael's loyalty. What Kwanza didn't know was that his lust for power had been exactly on what the Michael's government had been banking on to get the Argentinians close enough to Umbekie.

On his return Kwanza went straight to Umbekie to tell him about the potential new business partners he was arranging a meeting with. Umbekie cautiously wanted more information before jumping head first into a potential trap, so he used his contacts to put feelers out to find out more about the Argentinians. The information that returned was very positive, the Angolan deal was confirmed, as were other deals in Africa. The information regarding the Sudan deal was what finally convinced him that the Argentinians were the men he wanted to talk business with. He gave Kwanza orders to arrange the meeting quickly, specifying when he would like it to take place.

Kwanza studied the two Argentinians during the meal, he was satisfied that the men the Angolans had described were the same two men sat in front of him.

What Kwanza didn't know was that the Angola deal was part of a wider operation, which was essentially an American operation. The destabilisation of the country would make it easier for the Americans to gain control of its vast oil resources, something the current Angolan administration were not too keen on happening. After all it was their oil and they should be the ones to get rich from it, not the Americans.

The government Michael worked for knew of this operation and arranged for the Argentinians to manage the weapon transfer to gain further credibility in Africa, ensuring that they could get closer to their target in the

Congo, Umbekie. In the end, everyone was happy, apart from the Angolan government who although still had control of the oil, were forced to buy more weapons to fight the rebels, get in more debt, so become more open to the western money being offered to them for their oil rights. Sooner or later they would have to relinquish control.

Kwanza was not smart enough to understand the wider political implications of such operations, he just understood that rebels needed weapons and that there were businessmen who were able to supply them. Now he was the main contact for such businessmen, he is keen for things to move quickly. He can smell the success.

"I can arrange for you to meet Mr Umbekie, tomorrow if you want to talk about some business with him."

Rob nods, whilst Andy looks at Rob and tells Kwanza that they would very much like that.

At that moment Kwanza excuses himself for a moment, gets up and goes to the side of the restaurant, where he makes a phone call. He talks for a while, nodding excitedly.

Michael turns to the men, speaking to them in a hushed tone. "He is very keen, I can tell by the look on his face, this can give him a lot of power within Umbekie's organisation and he wants it to work. He was watching you both very closely, he already has it in his mind that he trusts you, I can tell by his excitement." He whispers to them. "You look like the Argentinians described in Angola even to me."

Rob is proud of his meticulous preparation. "Well we have done this many times before, we could have won Oscars for some of our performances."

Andy makes a slight quip, now being totally at ease. "Though if we did, instead of enhancing our careers, winning an Oscar would probably ruin them!" A quip which passes totally over Michael's head.

Michael is watching Kwanza through the corner of his eye, speculating on what he is doing. "Kwanza is also trying to impress you with his power. I told you earlier that a meeting has already been arranged for tomorrow in the market. He is not arranging anything on that phone. He is most likely confirming to Mr Umbekie that you are the Argentinians that supplied the Angolan weapons, but wants you to think that he has the power to call a meeting with Mr Umbekie."

Kwanza puts the phone down and returns to the table, with a beaming smile. "Mr Umbekie will meet you tomorrow at noon in the Market, by the bottle store in the middle. He wants to ensure that you are all I say you are, before he can talk business with you properly in a more private location."

Rodrigo is very courteous. "That sounds very good to us, Señor Umbekie seems to be a very wise man."

Kwanza nods in agreement. "That he is." Kwanza is already thinking ahead of the increased status this will bring him.

Michael agrees. "Yes, Wise he is."

Rodrigo raises his glass again. "To tomorrow!"

They all follow suit. "To tomorrow."

All four finish their drinks then all get up to leave. Kwanza goes to the counter to pay, waving away the attempts by the other three to pay towards the meal. "This meal was compliments of Mr Umbekie, a goodwill gesture for our future business."

Rodrigo and Adriano express their thanks and inform Kwanza that Mr Umbekie is a generous man, whom they look forward to meeting.

Outside Kwanza, before he says his farewells, informs them of the plan for tomorrow. "Michael will drop you back to your hotel. I will see you tomorrow at the market just before noon. If you make arrangements with Michael, he can take you to the market tomorrow."

Rodrigo shakes Kwanza's hand, Adriano then takes it. "It has been a pleasure meeting you Kwanza, we look forward to seeing you tomorrow."

Kwanza walks off waving, while the rest get into Michael's car and drive away.

Rob turns to the other two after they have driven away. "It couldn't have gone any better."

Michael offers some insight. "Kwanza was very impressed and he wanted to be, he needs this. It's all to do with a power struggle within the group. With a set-up like this, he will firmly be the second in charge."

"We've heard that many times, it's the main way we get close to leaders to do our work." Andy recalls similar situations where they have easily got into a trusted inner circle via an over eager lieutenant keen to move up the power ladder. Setting up a supply network for much needed weapons is often the simplest way to move up the ladder, especially if it is offered to you on a plate.

Michael asks when they will be fulfilling their contract. He will be keen to distance himself from the action as he could be a prime target in a subsequent power struggle.

Rob clarifies. "Not tomorrow, we won't do it in a place as public as a market, we should be able to set up another meeting with Umbekie in a more private place. We'll ensure that you don't need to be there for that."

Andy is keen to reassure Michael, having an inside contact in Africa is very useful for future jobs, the easier a job can be, the increased likelihood they have of completing it safely. "Yep, you'll need a good alibi, so we will try and get a meeting with Umbekie where he comes to us. We can make a good getaway then."

However Michael has been on the inside for a while, studying Umbekie's habits in detail. "That may take a while, he rarely meets in places where he has not got a lot of firepower. He has many enemies both in the country and outside. He does not take many risks."

Andy wants the contract to be as easy as possible. "Well, we will have to find a way to get him with as few people as we can, we don't want to turn it into a bloodbath. That happened in Sierra Leone, where it got a bit hairy, ended up with the marines being brought into the country to keep the peace."

"You caused that?" Michael is concerned, as the Sierra Leone conflict was fairly recent and caused a lot of problems, especially when other countries got involved. Many gangs lost a lot in the conflict, including their lives.

Rob expands on Andy's fairly rash statement. He believed that it would have happened with or without their intervention. They just expedited the situation. "You could say we caused it indirectly. We kick started a lot of it off by removing the whole leadership of the most powerful rebel group instead of just the leader, which caused a huge power struggle amongst a lot of trigger happy minor players. The total anarchy amongst the remaining rebels in the group led a lot of other minor rebel groups to try and take power in the region, eventually leading to a minor civil war. The thing is, we were only supposed to take the one guy out, but he had surrounded himself with so many cronies, so many that we could never get rid of them, we just had to take the lot out."

Andy grins. "Still got paid though and a few mercenaries made a wad of cash out of it in the end!"

Rob attempts to reassure Michael further, emphasising their professionalism, rather than just being in it for the money. "At the end of the day we still got the job done, it just turned very messy, in a way no one could have predicted."

He has succeeded, Michael looks a little less nervous. "I suppose. Who can tell what consequences occur in Africa when the smallest of actions is taken. Whole countries have been wiped out before because of a dispute over rivers."

"Anyway, we will spend the next few days assessing the situation and trying to manipulate the best time to chop down the tree."

"Yes, tomorrow could be a busy day, but also could be a dull day, only time will tell."

They pull up on the corner they were picked up, as they are getting out, Michael clarifies the arrangements. "OK, I will see you here at 11:45 in the morning. I don't want to keep Mr Umbekie waiting."

"Sure, you've been a great help, see you tomorrow."

"Just doing my job, Good night."

"Good night."

They get out of the car and walk into the hotel, where they retire for the night.

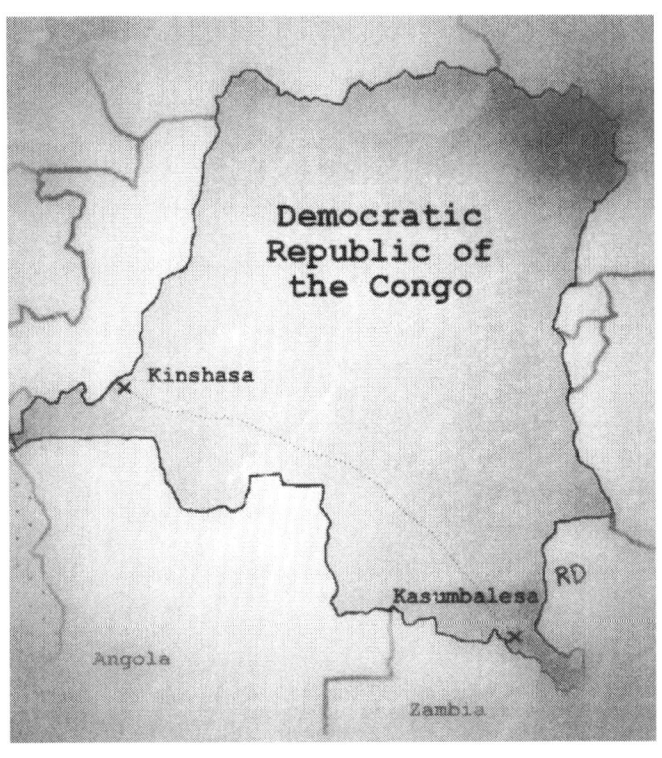

Capítulo Cinco

Both men get up early the next morning. Sleep wasn't a problem despite the uncertainty that lay ahead. Andy takes an early morning swim in the pool to relax, swimming lengths of the pool for 15 minutes. When he returns, the breakfast trolley has been left in the middle of the room. Rob is lying on the hotel bed with a concerned look on his face, with his empty plates left on the trolley.

Andy doesn't like his friend's expression. "What's up?"

Rob points towards the trolley.

"That breakfast left a lot to be desired."

Andy lifts the covers off the untouched plates on the trolley to reveal some cooked eggs, cold cuts of meat and some fruit, his expression openly displaying how unimpressed he is. "Well what do you expect in a 3 star African hotel?"

Rob shakes his head. "I'd like not to be throwing my food up two or so hours after I ate it, it didn't taste right."

Andy, with a sly grin, teases his friend. "It's probably nerves about today."

Rob just looks at Andy with disdain so Andy quickly changes the subject. "Shall we go loaded today?"

Rob has already planned their day as well as he can. "It's probably best if we do. One, we can check to see if the hiding place works, two, you cannot have arms dealers walking around situations like this unarmed."

This surprises Andy as his own thoughts on the day were different. "Thought it may be a good trust thing if we were unarmed, to show that we just mean to do business rather than be a potential threat."

Rob is leaving nothing to chance. "My trust boundaries don't extend that far, it only takes one situation where we can't take control and your kids are fatherless." He knows they have a better chance of fighting their way out of a bad situation if they have weapons.

Andy ponders this and is happy to go along with the plan. He knows his friend has thought of every eventuality in far greater detail than he has and will have a back-up plan for each one. "Fair enough, it will be interesting to see if they frisk us, to see whether they go anywhere near our gun placement. I suppose if we can't explain the guns satisfactorily, we shouldn't be in this business."

"Exactly! We have half an hour until Michael picks us up. Enough time to get sorted, also enough time for you to grab some other food than that breakfast, I don't want you passing out on me!"

They spend the half an hour preparing for the day, dressing in jeans and Argentina football shirts covered by jackets. Rob has the home kit and a black leather jacket, whilst Andy has selected the away kit and a brown suede jacket, specifically different so they don't look like they have a casual uniform. Andy pops out to grab a quick snack, returning just in time for them to conceal a pair of Glocks on each other's bodies before they leave to meet Michael as planned, who has pulled up outside the hotel in the same Toyota from last night.

Rob gets into the front seat and after greeting Michael wants to know if there is more information about the day. "Anything we should know before this meeting?"

Michael has been busy overnight, finding out exactly what the meeting entailed. "Not that I have not already told you. There should be about 6 people as well as me that are surrounding you. However, you should be aware that there will be a further twenty or thirty of Umbekie's men around the market, all keeping an eye on the meeting. There will be one on each entrance."

"Each entrance?"

"Yes." Michael clarifies. "Four main entrances, one on each side."

This concerns Rob. "This isn't an indoor market by any chance?"

"Yes, it is." Michael clarifies, failing to see the importance.

African indoor markets are notoriously bad places to get out of if things go wrong. There couldn't be a worse place to meet dangerous people. Rob knows this. He had had a similar meeting to this in an indoor market before and didn't like it. You have to think on your feet when you are walking into a meeting, work out several different aspects like escape routes, quickly devising the easiest way to get to them, knowing exactly who would shoot at you if it came to the crunch, what other type of person is in the market. All crucial aspects which could only be worked out on the spot when walking into such a meeting.

An indoor market is the worst place to do this, as there are less escape routes, they are more cramped than outdoor markets and there are more hiding places for the sort of person that may shoot at you. An indoor market was also noisier, which meant that it was harder to hear potential risks.

Rob is not happy, he had not been mentally prepared for an indoor market, although it was something he had planned for, it wasn't a plan that he wanted to invoke. There was a plus side though. Meeting in such a place increases the trust someone is willing to give you. Either you are very brave and stupid, or genuine. If all went well, they would have more of an open door for subsequent meetings.

Rob explains to Michael why he is not overly happy about an indoor market. "This makes it riskier for us, less escape routes and harder to identify all of the threats. We also won't be able to identify all of Umbekie's men easily as everyone in the market will be looking at the two Musungus with their normal African curiosity."

Michael sniggers at the use of the word Musungu, a word which Africans find amusing coming from the lips of Musungus.

Andy has other concerns about the meeting, despite it taking place in such a venue. "Michael, have you spoken to Umbekie today, any indication of his mood, does he seem genuinely keen to do business?"

"No I've only spoken to Kwanza, who will meet us outside the market. He hasn't stopped talking about how the business with you will make him rich, so is keen to be seen as the man who introduces you to Umbekie. He will take you into the market. I will follow behind, though I am not too keen to be associated that closely with you in front of the other men. Less they see of me, the less I will be linked with you and what you will do."

Andy grins. "We haven't done anything yet."

Michael pulls the car up outside a very shoddy looking building, resembling a warehouse. There is a large gaping entrance, clearly stating that it is a Market. "Here we are. There is Kwanza waiting for you. I cannot stop for long so will just let you out, I need to park across the road, so will follow as soon as I can. This is where I will pick you up here afterwards."

Kwanza is smiling broadly at the Argentinians as they approach him.

"Hello my Argentinian friends. Did you sleep well?"

Rodrigo smiles and offers his hand to Kwanza. "Very well thank you, is everything OK today?

Kwanza cannot contain his excitement and pride. "Everything is A-OK. Mr Umbekie will be at the meeting point waiting for you. He will have some bodyguards with him, but they are not to worry you, they are for protection against peoples in this country who would benefit from harming Mr Umbekie.

Adriano shakes Kwanza's hand also. "Fair enough, will they need to search us?"

Kwanza is a little surprised. "Yes, why? Are you armed?"

Rodrigo smiles at Kwanza, offering an explanation. "We have some small arms, it would not be prudent to be unarmed arms dealers in any situation."

Kwanza nods, rolling his eyes in self-mockery at being so stupid for even thinking that two arms dealers would not be armed in the middle of Africa. "I will tell them, being upfront allows for Mr Umbekie to trust you more. This will be very good."

Kwanza gestures to the Argentinians to walk into the market. They turn and walk into a shabby entrance, half blocked by old cardboard boxes. The dirt floating in the air invades every pore in the skin.

The three men walk through the entrance hall, Kwanza nods to a man waiting by the inner door, where they are joined by a further two men. All of the men accompanying them are small like Kwanza and casually dressed. The Argentinians are now fully alert and are taking in every aspect of their surroundings. They note every potential threat. They move their heads as little as possible, preferring to use peripheral vision and reflections as much as possible, darting their eyes around their surroundings to change a view. The man on the door was fairly uninteresting, however did have a handgun poorly concealed in the back of his trousers. The reflection in the door behind him gave it away.

Rob and Andy have developed a complex yet fast way of describing all of the features of a place to each other over the years. They engage their host in a simple conversation of pleasantries about the place they are in, asking what are the wonderful items they see around them. Using a clock face to identify direction, they always identify something at 90 degrees to a threat.

It has served them well in the past and as they are never pointing directly at a threat, it is hard for the uninitiated to spot. There would be too many people in here and they would be too hard to spot, so they had agreed outside not to do the normal routine. They would simply identify everything directly in Spanish to each other. This was a method they had used once before, which had worked well.

As the party enters the market, Rob and Andy see that, as expected for a market, it is filled with stalls selling fruit, vegetables, fish and meat products, most of poor quality, along with various colourful stalls selling household goods, all decorated heavily with the commonplace item on every African stall, the plastic bag, each stall containing many plastic bags of many varied colours.

The lines of sight in the market are far worse than expected in the first section they pass, combined with a lot of bustle of the busy market, to make the location of threats and escape routes more difficult than they would like.

The whole market is very noisy, with each sound being enhanced by the acoustics of the massive building. The dominating sound is the shouts of the stall holders, each trying to outdo each other to attract custom, combined with this are the sounds of produce being chopped, thrown around and occasionally dropped.

There is also the sound of metal being grinded, tiny transistor radios and sound systems, trollies being pushed around, the metal wheels grating on the concrete floor. It was all overbearing on the senses, but the Argentinians are totally focused and manage to block much of it out.

The Argentinians are aware that they are being looked at by everyone they pass, some offering their goods, others just taking an interest in the rare sight of Musungus in their market. This makes it near on impossible to tell who was working for Umbekie and who just had a curious interest.

They catch a glimpse now and again of people that could potentially be Umbekie's men, but there are so many it is impossible to know for sure where the threats actually were. They move through a small section containing a series of large stalls covered in plastic bags, being offered bags by every vendor.

The vivid colours of the bag stalls are almost as much an assault on the senses as the overwhelming noise of the market. Here the line of sight past the stalls is greatly reduced as each one has an awning that towers above head height which heightens the tension, a tension that the Argentinians hide well. Neither man speaks to each other, or the men accompanying them, who also remain silent during the long walk through the bustle.

Fortunately the next group of stalls are lower, just tables selling fruit and vegetables. Most of the produce is of poor quality, indicated by the dulled familiar colours they would normally see for similar produce in the west.

Andy catches the flash of a knife in his peripheral vision to his right as a stall holder brings it down sharply on an apple.

He turns his head, spotting a large man staring at them from the far end of the line of stalls. He is starting to feel very tense and could tell that his colleague was tensing slightly.

The market is full of movement in every direction, far too much for them to ascertain very quickly what is relevant and what is not. This market is the worst place they have been for a meeting for a long time.

The Argentinians' senses are overflowing trying to get a clear picture of their relevant surroundings. Kwanza guides the men around the various stalls, heading for the centre. He keeps pointing the way excitedly, assuring the men not to worry, as they have started bumping into people and apologising.

"This is a very busy place, the busiest in our city." Kwanza informs them with pride. They would be hard pressed to think of a less busy place they have ever been in.

The Argentinians are constantly aware of the activity and motion of people chopping meat and other produce all around them.

The market is almost a do-it-yourself butchers shop in one section they pass, which is not good for the nerves, the amount of knives being displayed and used on a variety of different meats, cutting and slicing the meat, causing blood to seep onto the floor making it slightly slippery, would put the calmest person on edge.

A sharp metallic clatter erupts as a stall holder drops a set of pans on the floor causes them to jump slightly, their hearts starting to beat faster.

Kwanza just smiles, pointing to the stall holder scrambling to pick up the pans, he shouts at the man. "Clumsy!"

After a few seconds, the Argentinians nerves fall back to their previously levels, albeit still heightened.

Rob and Andy managed to keep focused, their heads still, but constantly move their eyes around, before eventually they both spot a hexagonal dark green wooden hut in the centre of the building, it appears to be the only permanent construction in the whole market. Kwanza points directly at the building, indicating that this where they are heading, whilst also nodding at every stall holder he passes.

Kwanza is swelling with pride inside. He knows the stall holders will all have more respect for him after today. They will fight to serve him, giving him preferential rates, even free goods.

The group pass a few more stalls displaying sacks of seeds and pulses before turning into an aisle which leads them the final twenty metres to the green hut, which they can now see is decorated in the 7-up logo, it has stacks of soda cans piled up outside, cans of 7-up, Coca-Cola, Fanta, plus other local brands they are not familiar with. It is two storeys high with bars instead of windows, giving many vantage points all over the market.

Standing on one corner is a group of imposing men, all looking sternly in the direction of the approaching group. The men surround a large well-dressed man, who stands directly in front of them.

He is much larger than the rest of men around him, both taller and broader, with a very round intimidating face, which is smiling broadly. No one else is near the hut and none of the stall holders look directly at the men surrounding it.

Kwanza leads the Argentinians up to the hut and nods at all of the men around it in turn. Two of the larger men come forward and indicate that they want to frisk Rodrigo and Adriano. Kwanza says something in Congolese to the well-dressed man, who directs the bodyguards. They frisk the Argentinians and find the two unconcealed guns. They turn to the man showing him the guns, he nods at them. They return the guns to the Argentinians, who put them back where they were found.

The well-dressed man steps forward offering his hand, in a very deep booming voice which some would find very intimidating. "Buenos Diaz, gentlemen, I am Mr Umbekie. I trust you can speak English which is far better than my Argentinian, so forgive me if all of our business is conducted in English otherwise we would not get much done."

He smiles as Rodrigo and Adriano nod.

"Firstly, it shows good trust that you told Kwanza that you were armed, I am showing you trust by letting you have them back. Kwanza is very positive after your meeting last night and I have good faith in his judgement. I hope my men do not intimidate you, but this country is a troubled one, there can be many dangers to a man in a position such as mine."

Adriano offers his hand. "Pleased to meet you Señor Umbekie. English is fine with us. We could not do business internally without a good command of the English language. I am Adriano Cabrera. This is my colleague Rodrigo Diaz. I can understand you having such an entourage, in our line of business it is commonplace, so we are not intimidated. I trust Kwanza has told you favourable things about our meeting last night, we felt it went very well."

Umbekie nods at Rodrigo. The other men have not relaxed yet, still staring hard at the two potential assassins.

"Kwanza could only say good things about your meeting. I have also made many enquiries in other circles, our Angolan and Sudanese comrades have recommended you very highly." Umbekie is keen to impress on them how well connected he is.

Umbekie continues to try and impress the Argentinians. "You cannot be too careful in this business, a man makes many enemies. I only take on new business partners by personal recommendation, fortunately I have had many good recommendations about you. From what I have heard about you I hope we can set up a good working relationship. Firstly, I want to find out a little about you and what you can do before we set about having a private meeting and to arrange the finer details."

Rodrigo takes the lead. "You are a very cautious man, the sort of man we like to do business with. It is not good practise to deal with people who jump into partnerships without any background knowledge, as these people will be more likely be the type of person trying to stop our business. These are the people we cannot trust, as they will publicise their dealings with us to agencies that we would rather they did not know about us. We only do business with cautious people, and we also only do business with people from personal recommendations. How does the old saying go? Loose lips sink ships. We want to ensure that the ships bringing weapons to our partners are not sunk by people talking to the wrong people."

Umbekie is enjoying everything he hears. "Precisely. We can talk freely here; my men can hear anything I can hear. Everyone else will stay out of range so won't hear anything of use. What specifically are you able to do for us? Kwanza spoke about banned items, but was unclear about what precisely."

Rodrigo knows that Umbekie is keen to deal with them, but he needs to ensure that Umbekie hears enough to be 100% committed. "We have direct sources in the manufacturing plants of suppliers that can get us any item you require, which will be untraceable, but not including nuclear or chemical weapons, you can pick or choose anything you want. You will always deal direct with us, so there is no concern about who may be at the other end of a fax or who may pick up an email. It is us and whoever you name as the contact, a contact that we will get to know in person."

"This is exactly what we need. We used to get supplies from an American, but he has been put under pressure from his government to stop supplying groups in Africa. What sort of people do you supply?"

"We deal with many groups over the world, but not groups that conflict with each other. We prefer dealing with non-western groups. We have fought against western powers in our past. My first introduction to this was in the Malvinas when our bad leadership allowed us to lose to a force we could have beaten."

Umbekie smiles at the mention of the Malvinas. He had never actually heard anyone call the Falkland Islands that before. "I have been told that and I admire it. I like you two, I like everything I have heard about you. I think we can progress further. I would like to set up a proper meeting where we can discuss details. Would two days' time be suitable?"

Rodrigo is pleased with the speed things are progressing. "Yes it would, we are free to fit in with any schedule you have, although we have to leave in three days to conduct some business in the southern parts of Africa."

Umbekie looks puzzled, he would like them to be around for much longer. "You have flights booked?

Adriano clarifies. "No, it would have been silly of us to fly with these weapons on us. We drive from a base we have set up further south. On follow up visits when time is tight we will fly, but by then we will have a small base here."

Umbekie has now completely warmed to the Argentinians. He likes business partners who plan well. "Ah, I am very impressed, the airports are watched more closely than the border crossings, your presence will not have been noted by the security forces."

"That was the intention, in our business it is not good practice to have everyone knowing where you are."

"I will arrange a time and Kwanza will let you know where you will be picked up. In the mean time I want to get to know you more and in conjunction with your visit I have used my extensive contacts to arrange something special for tomorrow night which I would think you will be interested in."

Rodrigo is intrigued, he was expecting to be wined and dined before any business deal is agreed upon. "We would be delighted to spend some time building our business relationship with you, we would be honoured to attend whatever you have laid on for us."

Umbekie is still keen to impress how important he is upon them. "Once I had details of your visit, I arranged an event in one of my safe houses, where there will be many people attending from various organisations who will interested in meeting you, maybe obtaining some of the goods you have to offer. There will be people from other African nations and.." he swells with pride at this moment. "I have managed to attract some visitors from overseas, some very important people will be there. There will be many benefits to both our parties if I can put some of these people into contact with someone as useful as yourselves."

Rodrigo has heard such postulating before. He does not expect that there will be anyone apart from a few small rebel groups from minor nations. "We would be happy to come, this sounds like it could be very beneficial to us, do we need to bring anything?"

Umbekie smiles even wider than before. "Only yourselves, all refreshments are on me. I can send a car round for you at six tomorrow night. One rule though, all weapons would have to be left at the door, there are some people so important at this gathering that we cannot compromise their safety."

This changes the plan slightly, both men are very wary of attending anything without weapons, but Rodrigo already has a plan for such eventualities. Sometimes they have had to complete their missions in areas of high security, they already have a trusted way of circumventing weapon controls. "Yes, that would not be a problem, why need weapons when all we will do is talk business and socialise, we will look forward to it."

Umbekie is satisfied that their business for the day is complete. "I have many things to arrange for tomorrow night, so you must excuse me if our initial meeting has been brief, but we will spend much time speaking about details tomorrow. Please allow Kwanza to show you the delights of our fine city until tomorrow night, there is much to see. He can also get you anything you desire."

Adriano offers his hand. "It has been nice to meet you and I look forward to a fruitful relationship."

Umbekie grabs both their hands and shakes them very firmly, beaming with a large smile. "This could be the start of a great partnership."

Rodrigo finishes the pleasantries. "It has been our pleasure, until tomorrow."

Umbekie speaks to Kwanza in Congolese for a few minutes then he orders the five burly men away, who are still staring at the two Argentinians.

Kwanza turns to them with a large smile, overtly displaying his excitement. "He was very pleased. I have to make some arrangements for you for the next two days. We must go, we have attracted a lot of attention and people may start to talk." He indicates to some of the stall holders and some officials who have gathered to watch the meeting from a distance.

Kwanza leads them back through the market to the entrance where Michael is waiting for them in the car. He turns to them before they get in. "I must go and make arrangements. Can I meet you for dinner tonight? Shall I send Michael around for you at say, 7?"

Adriano accepts for both of them. "Yes, that would be good, you OK with that Rodrigo?"

Rodrigo nods.

Kwanza shakes their hands again as they get in the car, then he goes around the other side and says a few words in Congolese to Michael, before he drives off into the busy traffic.

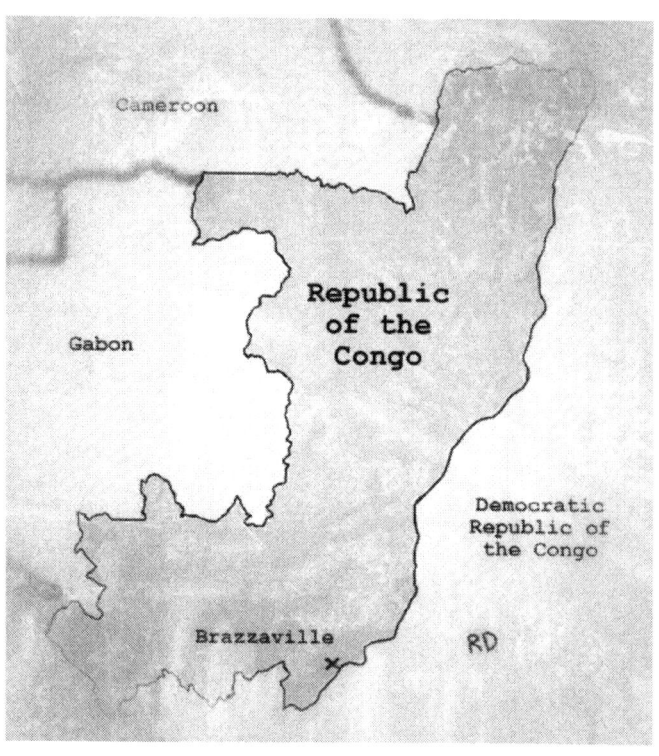

Capítulo Seis

Michael turns to the Argentinians when they have settled in the car. He knows it must have gone well by the reactions of Kwanza and the fact that they aren't dead, however he asks out of politeness. "How did it go?"

Rob explains. "Very well. He had done a bit of homework on us, which provided us with a lot of credibility, making things a lot easier. All credit to your government's planning of the Angolan operation. He is very keen to progress with business, so is setting up a meeting for a couple of days' time."

Andy is concerned about their earlier invitation. "One other thing, he has invited us to a party tomorrow night, which I don't know is a good sign or not."

Michael is puzzled however. "Party? I have not heard that he is having one, I'd be very wary, that could be a trap."

Andy is now even more concerned that this party is very secret. It doesn't seem right. "He did specify not to be armed, due to the people that will be there."

"I need to find out more about this, this is an unusual situation, Mr Umbekie does not have parties regularly, on the rare occasions he does there is a lot more notice. Something is very odd." Michael sharing Andy's concerns, shaking his head. "This is not normal behaviour for Mr Umbekie."

Rob is more relieved that they got out OK from what was the worst meeting venue he had been to, they were too vulnerable for his liking. He now focuses more on the party and the potential threat this could be. "See what you can find out, we will try and find out more from Kwanza when he is giving us a tour of his city."

Andy fills Michael in on some more detail. "Umbekie did say there will be lots of important people there who would want to do business with us, maybe it is so hush-hush that this is not like a normal party, it is just coincidence that we just happened to be here at the right time."

Michael knows he will need to try and find out what is going on from other sources. "I will see if any of our local agents knows of any unusual arrivals on any borders, and ask our Angolan contact what he knows, but it could take longer than a day to make safe contact with him as he has to maintain a very low profile."

Rob is confident that they can handle any situation, believing Umbekie is just trying to exaggerate his power and influence in order to impress them. "Just see what you can find out, we can go prepared for a hostile situation, I'm sure we can handle anything Umbekie and his cronies try and pull on us."

Michael has seen what Umbekie and his associates can do. "He can be very ruthless, caution is the best policy. I have seen his men butcher many people that have posed a threat to him, even a very minor threat, sometimes they have done this in crowded places to make a point. He has also got many of the police on his payroll, they have looked the other way when the most hideous of crimes have taken place lately."

Rob has a more logical view on the situation. "At the end of the day, if it is a trap for us, would they have created such an elaborate situation for it? All they would have to do is get Kwanza to poison our meal when we meet him."

Andy didn't consider this. "Oh great, didn't think of that, so all you are saying is, if we get through the meal tonight, we are not on his list of people to rub out."

Rob looks for confirmation "Essentially, yes, would he employ such a tactic Michael?"

"Possibly, he uses many methods to get rid of his enemies, you are right though, organising a trap for you is a bit elaborate for him, unless he plans to extract information from you. From what I have seen he prefers to be more direct than to concoct elaborate plans for removing people from the equation."

Rob reassures Andy. "Best not get too worried about it until we get more information, Kwanza should give something away by his mood tonight."

The car pulls up outside the hotel. Michael informs them that he will be round at 6:45 to pick them up. Rob and Andy bid farewell and leave for their room.

When the two are back in the hotel room alone, Rob talks in code while Andy undoes the light fitting and breaks the bug. He then scouts the room for signs of other bugs using a small electronic detector. The room is clear, indicating that they have not aroused any more suspicion than normal. Rob goes into the bathroom and turns the shower on.

When he returns to the room, Andy asks Rob what he thinks.

Rob offers his assessment of the situation. "In all honesty, I think that this is a genuine party, one that he wants us to attend to be introduced to some of his guests who are more important than him. If he wanted to get rid of us, or torture us, he would have done it by now."

"Yes, I'm starting to think that now. If he suspected anything, Kwanza would have been leading us to a back room instead of an open area and they would have taken action then. These people are too keen to get power and money, to impress those above them that they were willing to accept us before we turned up."

Rob is still thinking ahead. "Which is fine by me, but also leads to the question, when is the best time to do it? This party could be an opportune moment, if we get him outside on his own."

Andy displays some of his rare caution. "Could be too risky, I'd be surprised if he lets his guard down, anyway, we don't know who else will be there yet. It could be a situation where there are some very dangerous people." He pauses. "Best wait until Michael can find out a bit more. I'm still up for doing it in a private meeting, that way we will have a better opportunity to get away safely. The less people that are around as witnesses the better for us. If we did it at the party, the only guarantee of getting away safely would be to take everybody out, which if they are more experienced than Umbekie, isn't going to be easy."

Rob wants to keep all options open at the moment. It may be their only chance to complete the contract. "We'll have to plan for it though, just as an option, he may even cancel our meeting if he makes arrangements at this party. It would make sense for him to be showing off to people by making a big arms deal in front of a lot of people. These people like to be dramatic, if that happens, then there may be no need for another meeting."

"Good point, best plan for that situation, though I'd still prefer to push for another meeting where we can get close to him afterwards. Rather spend some more time here than cause a complete bloodbath. A massacre is the sort of thing that gets press coverage and too much interest from the authorities."

Rob picks up a pad and begins to make notes, while Andy moves towards the bathroom. After his shower they rest for a few hours until Michael picks them up.

Michael greets them with enthusiasm. They exchange niceties before Rob enquires if Michael has found anything else out about the party.

"A little. I have been asked to drive you tomorrow night. It is in a house in the suburbs that I know. Mr Umbekie uses it as a hiding place for men who the authorities are searching for. I don't think they will want to attract any undue attention by killing someone there."

"That's a relief. Any news on the guests?"

"None at all, no one seems to know who is coming. I have left a message with an agent, but he has not come back to me. I have spoken with Kwanza, but he seems to know very little about it also, it seems only Mr Umbekie is the one who knows all the details. Kwanza did say that this has happened at short notice and that Mr Umbekie has been taking many calls in private. I don't think it will be anyone as important as he is making out, probably a couple of small groups from neighbouring countries, nothing to worry about."

Andy was hoping Kwanza would know some more, so tries not to sound disappointed when he speaks. "So we don't hold out much hope for getting any more ideas tonight?"

Michael pulls the car up in a fairly non-descript street. "I would not think so. Ah here we are, this restaurant on the end."

Kwanza has been waiting for the men inside the restaurant. He is happy to see them, as always.

"Hello, hello, my friends how are you?"

His greeting is reciprocated with equal warmth. Michael just nods at Kwanza; He rarely speaks when Kwanza is present, an acknowledgement that Kwanza has a higher rank and a sign of respect.

Kwanza points to a corner of the restaurant. "We have a table over here."

A waiter leads them to a table at the side of the room. He places menus in each person's hands, which they all peruse. "Would you like to order any drinks sirs?"

Kwanza takes the lead. He is still eager to impress the Argentinians, he nods at Rodrigo in a gesture designating that he remembers exactly what he drinks. "A Bottle of wine and some water for my friend."

"Very good sir."

After the waiter leaves the table, Kwanza speaks very excitedly about the new developments, also giving feedback on how their initial meeting went. "I have spoken with Mr Umbekie and he is very pleased with the meeting today. He is looking forward to tomorrow night's event, where you will be important guests. He will be introducing you to many other important guests, hopefully you can do more business with some of them."

Adriano is inquisitive. "We look forward to it. What people will be there?"

They pause as the waiter returns with the drinks and pours them out. "Are you ready to order yet, sirs?"

Kwanza informs him that he is ready but his associates may not be as they have been engaged in business conversation. He is already trying to impress upon people he does not know that he is a man with power. When the Argentinians are ready, they order the fish and potatoes, giving Kwanza a further opportunity to emphasise his importance as he ushers the man away after stating that he will also have the same as his associates. Michael orders the same as the waiter is leaving, his order being the only thing he says during the meal, preferring to let Kwanza take the lead.

"Kwanza eats the same as the Musungus." He bursts with pride as he overhears the waiter telling his colleagues in awe. Kwanza had made sure the waiter knew his name before the others came in, although the waiter did not use it as he requested.

"Here is your table for you and your friends, Kwanza." is what he was instructed to say, to impress the importance of Kwanza on all present.

The waiter forgot, but Kwanza did not notice as he ushered the Argentinians to the table. He was too busy looking around to see who would be impressed with the man with the Musungus. He had his moment of pride as a couple looked up from their meals to look at him, nodding their respect in his direction. He was feeling prouder as each hour passed, knowing inside that he would be rewarded very well, very soon.

Kwanza continues where they left off before being interrupted by the menial servant. "Mr Umbekie has been very secretive about the guests, even I do not know. He has just assured me that they are very important, so important that you will be aware of their names. He says that you can do a lot of business with them. When you meet them, you will want to."

Rodrigo wants some more clarification. "I take it these people would not be enemies of people we deal with?"

"I assure you, Mr Umbekie would not invite people who would fight against each other here. All the people will have the same common cause, the cause you are against, the western imperialists."

Adriano suppresses his disdain as he voices his opinion. "That is a relief to hear, would not want the evening spoilt by arguments and vendettas."

Kwanza starts to get very excitable as he reveals his motives to the men. "I am very excited about all of this. It is a very good opportunity for us all. It will benefit Mr Umbekie, he will reward his friends, so we will all grow in stature, we will make much more profit."

The Argentinians know they have Kwanza in the palms of their hands. He has been blinded by his own greed. This will make it easier for them.

Rodrigo raises his glass in a gesture. "If you make more profit, we will make more profit and we will be able help even more in the fight against our sworn enemy."

Adriano follows suit. "Everyone wins."

Kwanza continues to impress on the Argentinians how much he is set to gain. "Mr Umbekie has said that I will be the main contact with you when we have a business plan in place. I will have a lot of power, I will be able to set up all the orders we need from you."

Adriano is keen to show Kwanza that the Argentinians are pleased for him, which will increase the trust he has in them. "That is very good for us, as we know you and can trust you. When will Mr Umbekie be finalising our business plan?"

Kwanza becomes business like again, remembering that he has to seal a deal before he will see any rewards. "I am not sure, he has not set a final date, though I will have the power to arrange all the details. Power that he is trusting me with, which is very good for me."

Rodrigo enquires further. "So he has not set a time for a meeting with us?"

Kwanza makes a guess, not really being sure, but not wanting to dissuade the men that a deal may not come. "He will do that at the party, I think."

This simple attempt at appeasement has made the Argentinians' decision easier. If a deal is sealed at the party, they may not meet with Umbekie for months with Kwanza being given authority to take over. Once Umbekie has delegated his power, he has no reason to meet with the dealers anymore. They know this and glance at each other. The Argentinians will have to go to the party armed and kill Umbekie there, providing they have sufficient opportunity. This could be the toughest thing they have done, especially if there are many dangerous guests.

Rodrigo acknowledges Kwanzas statement with a smile, just before the waiter returns with the food. They have a pleasant meal with not much more being discussed. Kwanza asks about their life in Argentina, which they respond to by reciting their well-rehearsed cover story to him, enthralling him with stories of the fight against the British in the Malvinas.

The group finish their meals, before taking their time to finish their drinks, by the time they are set to leave it is close to midnight, but Kwanza has one final surprise before they leave.

"Tomorrow, I will be your guide for the day. Mr Umbekie insists that I show you our city. Not many westerners get to see its delight and I will be pleased to show the best of it to you."

Rodrigo had wanted the day to prepare, to ensure that every eventuality was covered, but it would be frowned upon if they flatly refused. "The party doesn't start till seven, right?"

Kwanza nods, while Rodrigo continues. "We have to conduct some business by phone during the day, as you'll understand we have other deals we need to manage, but we can spare around three hours for you to show us some special places."

Kwanza happily accepts this compromise. They shake hands again before the Argentinians leave with Michael to go back to their hotel.

The two men wake early again next morning in their hotel room. Andy takes an early morning dip in the pool while Rob starts to put together the plan for the evening's activity. After his swim, Andy comes into the room and dries himself off in the middle of the room, which annoys Rob.

"Do you have to do that there? There is a bathroom you know." Andy just grins at him, he needs his moments of light relief to keep him focused.

Rob wants Andy to be fully aware of his plans before they go in. He has allowed some time for a small rehearsal in their hotel room, one plan which will be mostly based on the scenario that very few people will be armed at the party, with the other being a mass shootout.

"Anyway, I've put together a couple of plans for tonight. I want to go through them with you before Kwanza arrives at eleven. My main concern is that Umbekie will hand over the organisation of the details to Kwanza. He may not require another meeting with us, especially one with the privacy we prefer."

Andy is still keen to push for the private option. This could be a risk he does not want to take. "I only want to do this tonight as a last resort. I would rather keep pressing for a private meeting, as a goodwill gesture just to seal the partnership."

Rob explains why he thinks tonight may be their best option. "I think he is too cagey, He met us in the worst place possible for us, ensuring that he would be as safe as possible. He seems to be too smart to want to spend too much time with people he cannot be 100% certain of, but would be happy to seal a deal in front of his powerful friends. I'm looking at a 90% go for tonight and I want us to be ready."

"Who do you reckon his friends may be?"

Rob offers his opinion, although not too convinced himself of its accuracy. "Just a few local tribal leaders, maybe a few rebel leaders from neighbouring countries, no one of much importance outside this region. He is not a very big player in world politics."

Andy concurs. "That's my view. These people live a fairly sheltered life, trying to impress only the near neighbours. They don't seem to think big."

"It would suit us if they are only small time, as they will put up less resistance plus our actions won't attract much attention outside this area."

Andy cheers up as he realises the potential of doing it at the party. "If that is the case, it will be put down as a tribal argument, so we won't be given too much grief on the way out of the country."

Always planning ahead, Rob suggests they load the car with all the bags to make a quick getaway, although that is one area of planning where Andy is superior, getting away. "I am already on it, I packed all our unnecessary stuff in the car when I paid for the room, we just have a couple of bags left in the room, we can grab them quickly if needed."

Their conversation is halted by a loud knock at the door. They are not expecting anyone, so ensure their guns are near to hand, but hidden, before answering.

"Who is it?"

The familiar voice behind the door states that it is Michael. Rob opens the door slowly, to see Michael standing there on his own. He opens the door fully to let Michael in.

Rob looks at him sternly. "Why have you come around now, you are not supposed to be here until tonight?"

Michael is panting. "Great urgency, I have news about tonight, an agent has contacted me with urgent news."

"Go on."

"There has been a great deal of activity with a lot of well-known terrorist groups."

"What groups?"

"Some Arab ones the western agencies were able to monitor. There has been unusual activity, they think something is happening but they are not sure what. All agents have been asked to look out for the possibility of a gathering. It could be here tonight."

Rob shakes his head. "It could be coincidence too though. They do this sort of thing a lot to keep everyone else on their toes."

"But our men on the borders have reported seeing more Arabic looking people than normal crossing in remote places. This may be a small gathering of some major players, if it is we may ask you not to do anything to Umbekie, as he may be more important than we believe. We may need to abort this operation completely."

Andy is not pleased with the possibility of Arabs being in attendance. His view is that Arabs are generally armed and very trigger happy. "But how will you know? and more importantly when will you know? This may affect our attendance at the party tonight, as we don't want to end up promising things we can't deliver to the type of people that have the resources to hunt us down until the end of our days. We do have a career to maintain."

Michael assures them that he will know more before he picks them up in the evening, he has been told just to prepare them for this. His government is slightly concerned that a small job could turn into an international terrorist incident. That would bring an unwelcome spotlight down on some of their other activities.

Rob is keen to carry on regardless. This could be good for the Argentinians. "It was always going to be risky, we are prepared for that, the presence of some major players may enhance our reputation, enhancing our ability for future work. I say we go, put a hold on any shooting until we have assessed the situation, putting the emphasis on trying to get a meeting with Umbekie alone. I don't think the two of us would have the firepower to remove a lot of people safely. Well safely for us. We have a good plan, if it looks more likely that we won't carry it out at the party, we can just socialise with these people and earn their trust."

Andy is still a little sceptical. Local tribesmen he can handle. Arabs he is not too keen on. "If that is at all possible, all the Arabs I have met do not trust anyone until they have known them for a long time."

Michael states that he thought they should be aware of this information before they go in, so there were no surprises when they walk in the door.

Rob is confident that all will be OK. "Hopefully all this fuss will be for nothing. I can't imagine that major players in the terrorism world would risk their safety to come here. It's not the safest place in the world to reach undetected."

Michael is still not convinced that the reports he has received are unrelated. "We will see, I will meet you as arranged at six tonight, I will have the information then, we can talk on the way, it is a long drive."

Andy thanks Michael as he leaves, then turns to Rob. "Well what do you think?"

"I think they are getting over excited, I would be very surprised if anyone thought this a safe place to gather some of the most wanted people on the planet. We should just go with our plan, but be prepared to amend it slightly to account for the fact that the guests may be a bit wiser and more trigger happy than just a few jungle leaders."

Andy has decided that he just wants to get this job finished any way he can, rather than hanging around for too long, getting too deeply involved with any major players. "Totally agree, it may be a good idea to take a lot more of the chloroform. That could get us out of a tricky situation quickly and quietly, we can knock out everyone, and shoot Umbekie. It would be a better option than staying here longer than I am comfortable with and I am getting very uncomfortable right now."

Rob ponders this. "It's an option I will consider, but I am not happy with trying to drug lots of people, there is too much uncertainty on how it will work on large groups. We can take some in with us, but I think it is best to speak to Michael first, he will tell us more before we go through the door. I would rather stick with a more permanent solution to get away safely."

As he finishes speaking Rob looks at his watch. "We have thirty minutes until Kwanza comes to take us on his grand tour of this wonderful city, let's run through Plan A one more time." The sarcasm is not lost on Andy, who smiles to himself as he sits down to study the plans again.

Kwanza arrives on time as expected. As he walks into the hotel they are in reception to meet them. He is being driven in another black Toyota, by one of the men that escorted them through the market. As they approach him, he gets out greeting them with his customary wide smile.

"Hello my friends, it is a pleasure to see you again, are you ready to see my beautiful city?"

Both Argentinians smile as they greet him and get into the car. "What delights have you in store for us Kwanza?" Adriano has his tongue firmly stuck in his cheek.

Brazzaville has a lot of French influence, originally being part of a French colony. It was specifically built across the river from the Belgian Léopoldville to stem the Belgian influence. It had also been devastated by years of very bloody civil war, the infrastructure still bearing the scars of many years of fighting. The Argentinians were not expecting to be overwhelmed by a vast amount of architectural and cultural beauty. In this respect they were not disappointed as Kwanza showed them sights they would forget within a couple of days.

He took them to all the main sights the city had left for tourists, describing each one with enthusiastic detail en route, even detailing some of the limited history he knew about each one, providing so much detail that they knew they would be disappointed before they arrived at each venue.

They saw sights such as the Nabemba Tower, a tall office block in an elongated concave shape that looked more like a very long lampshade, to which they feigned wonder. They also saw the underwhelming Congressional palace, St Anne's Basilica, a modern angular construction with a bright green roof, the city Museum and the Brazzaville Zoo, which ironically housed fewer animals than can be found in the wild in the Congo, in a far worse condition than they would be in the wild. The tour was concluded by a drive through the area where Kwanza grew up, a ramshackle area of badly constructed and poorly maintained houses, which Kwanza seemed especially proud of.

The tour was finished within two hours, to which Kwanza was very apologetic for. "I would have liked to show you more, but time is limited, I have been asked to escort some people to the party tonight."

Adriano was grateful for the brevity. "Don't worry Kwanza, we have seen enough to make us want to see a bit more in the next few days, maybe tomorrow when we have some spare time you can show us more."

This pleased Kwanza, everything they said seemed to please Kwanza. He was very eager to reap the benefits his new friends would bring him, so did not want to upset them.

The driver dropped them off at the hotel around two, giving them a few hours to relax and make some final preparations for the evening.

Kwanza with his usual enthusiasm bids them farewell, assuring them that they would have a great time that evening, with many drinks together.

Capítulo Seite

It is dark by the time they have to leave the hotel, but their distinct attire of football shirts and jeans makes them easy to spot for their driver. They approach the black Toyota parked outside reception, but stop when they notice that it is not Michael's normal car, it is smaller and more decrepit. As they stop and look around for their lift, a man in the driver seat of the parked car gets out and beckons them over.

Rob waves the man away, thinking he is a taxi driver touting for business. "It is OK, we are waiting for a friend."

The driver approaches them. "I am here to pick you up. Michael had to pick many other guests up, his car bigger."

Andy is guarded, a change to the plan is the last thing they want. "Who are you supposed to pick up?"

"Two Argentinians, men who met Mr Umbekie at the market yesterday. You two, I was with Kwanza as we walked through the market."

Rob looks hard at the man, finally realising where he has seen him before, he was the very small man who was following behind them in the market yesterday. He was much smaller than the rest of the Africans. He didn't say a word during the whole time and looked the most nervous of all the escorts, something Rob correctly assumed was due to inexperience. He was memorable for his brightly coloured rastacap, which he is still wearing. Rob looks at Andy and nods cautiously.

"Ok, this is most unexpected though."

The driver tells them that it was a short notice change and that he'll explain along the way. They get into the car with Andy taking the passenger seat. Anything untoward and he will end this swiftly. As the car pulls off and heads along the road, introductions are made.

"I am Adriano, Señor, and this is Rodrigo."

"I am Mulaki. I was sent to pick you up as Mr Umbekie needed a larger car to pick up many guests. Many more guests arrived than he expected, very important people. I have small car so I drive you. I have not worked for Mr Umbekie for very long, I am honoured to have such an important task as this. I hope you are happy with me driving you."

Rodrigo is satisfied that everything is in order, especially if what Michael had told them earlier in the day was turning out to be true. "Yes thank you Señor, we did not expect anyone different than Michael to pick us up. It does not matter who takes us to this party."

He was getting very curious as to who would be in attendance tonight and wants to glean as much information as he can from Mulaki before they arrive, exploiting Mulaki's inexperience to see if he is keen to share everything he knows to try and impress them. "Who are these very important people?"

Mulaki shakes his head. "I do not know, men from overseas. I do not get told, I am not important enough. I only do errands for Mr Umbekie. He told me to assure you that everything is OK, he is sorry for changing the plan. He does not like changing plans. He will see you at the house and will make sure you are fully satisfied."

"How long will it take to get there?

"An hour only. It is in the suburbs, very big house, I have only been there one time."

"Will you be staying at the party too?" Every bit of information could be vital. They were expecting Michael to be waiting outside for them, allowing a safe and quick escape. This may not be the case now.

"Sadly no. Mulaki is not important enough for party. I will return later to take you back to hotel. I will be near telephone and you will have the number to call me when you are ready. I cannot stay outside the house as it attracts attention, so I will be at bus station, 10 minutes away."

"Ok, that is good planning from Mr Umbekie."

Mulaki nods in agreement. "He thinks of everything, he is most clever." He rarely gets to run such important errands for Mr Umbekie so is keen to offer praise which may be passed on in conversation to Mr Umbekie. Every good word that Mr Umbekie hears Mulaki to have said will improve his standing, in the long run this would help him to support his family better. The living to be made from running a bottle store is only a meagre one. He wanted some of the things he saw on satellite television from the west.

Every good word passed onto Umbekie will make him aware that Mulaki is loyal and useful to him.

Adriano joins in for the first time, despite not being happy with this change in arrangements. "So we see, we are most impressed with our dealings with him so far."

The car drives through various suburbs of differing quality, some very poor, some shanty towns, until they reach the richer areas. The further into the more affluent areas they go, the more wealth they see being flaunted until they reach an area full of walled houses, all protected by broken glass on the wall tops. Although these houses are basic by western standards, in a city such as this they are the height of luxury. A separate room for everyone who lives there with heavy security protecting them.

Mulaki pulls the car up outside a large one storey house, built in a North African Mediterranean style. Terracotta plastered walls adorned with arches and shuttered windows. A couple of men guarding the entrance gate wave Mulaki though, allowing him to drive the few yards to the entrance where he pulls the car to a halt.

Mulaki turns to the Argentinians with a smile. "Please phone me when you are ready to leave, enjoy the party. Give my regards to Mr Umbekie." He hands them each a piece of paper with his name and number written very neatly in capital letters.

Adriano shakes his hand. "Thank you for the lift señor, we will speak to you later."

The Argentinians get out of the car and head to the door, which opens for them as one of Umbekie's men standing guard knocks on it to announce their arrival, nodding at them as they enter a large lobby. Here they are stopped and are frisked by another guard. He finds nothing, but wasn't expected to do. Rodrigo and Adriano are experts in concealing weapons; it's the nature of their work, the most basic aspect.

A smile also goes a long way to ensuring that the frisking down is not as thorough as it should be. The only item they find is Adriano's asthma inhaler, which puzzles them until Adriano demonstrates how he sprays it into his mouth, then rolls his eyes and displays a euphoric face, to which the guards respond with expressions of acknowledgement and giggles.

Adriano didn't go so far as actually spraying anything in his mouth, the chloroform in it would have knocked him out. It's one of the small tools he likes to carry on every mission, serving very useful in the past.

As the Argentinians walk into the house, they hear some familiar music playing, but can't remember the song name, they just recognise it as bad western pop. They find themselves inside a large rectangular room with whitewashed walls, decorated with African rugs. It seems to be sparsely furnished, which they assume is due to the need to create some space for the party. Only some sofas have been left arranged in a semi-circular fashion around the room, which is full of people, most standing, with only a few guests making use of the sofas.

The room is a hive of activity, with a lot of greetings and introductions being made. Surveying the guests they notice that some are of Arabic appearance, some Indian, but most appear to be African. The Argentinians are the only white people present. Rodrigo conducts a rough count, estimating at around thirty people. There would be more people scattered around the house as they couldn't see some familiar faces such as Kwanza and Michael.

Adriano is concerned by the amount of people, it is far more than they anticipated, more than they have faced at once in the past. Their work would be cut out if they went for completion tonight, it would be nothing less than a bloodbath with the chances of them remaining unscathed very slim. Their best chance would be if most of the people present were slightly drunk, slowing down their reactions, making it easier. The problem here would be that they assumed most of the Arabs wouldn't be drinking. The Arabs were the group that would present the most danger, far more danger than the Africans.

Rob and Andy had completed a mission in a similar situation in the past, however that was over four years ago. That time they were using fully automatic weapons, lots of them. Their entrance to the venue consisted of a fast surprise assault, even then lightning fast reactions and swift movements to pick their targets were the key to success. Tackling such a problem with a few handguns and the lack of surprise they preferred would be the biggest challenge they had ever faced. For the first time in many years, Andy was feeling slight apprehension about completing a mission unharmed.

As the Argentinians stand by the entrance surveying the room, Mr Umbekie spots them and walks over to greet them with open arms and a large smile.

"Welcome my friends."

They exchange pleasantries, whilst Umbekie leads them into the centre of the room. He gesticulates around the room, emphasising to all how much he values the two Argentinians, whilst also impressing on them the importance of the guests.

"You have come to a gathering of a lot of important people. Many who you will have heard of, some you will not, but you will know who they work for. I apologise for the secrecy but as you are no doubt aware, there are many people who would benefit by knowing of this meeting. I will introduce you to many of them through the night. But first I ask you to take a drink and soak up the atmosphere, while you meet some new acquaintances, many of whom I have told about you and what you can do for them."

Umbekie leads the Argentinians over to a man serving drinks. They each take a drink. Rodrigo only takes an orange juice whilst Adriano takes a beer, before they move over the side of the room to watch Umbekie go to greet another guest entering the room. The Argentinians look around the room emotionlessly, taking in everyone who is there, mentally noting every detail they can. The guest list is like a Who's Who of the CIA's most wanted list, there seems to be representatives of every major terrorist group in Africa and the Middle East.

Rodrigo, whispers to Adriano very lowly. "Crikey, have you seen this lot, how the hell did they manage to get all of them here without alerting someone?"

"I don't know, but they managed it without raising too many alarm bells. Michael said that they suspected something was up, but I'm sure they suspected nothing like this, even his government were not sure what exactly was up and who was involved. So much for detailed intra-governmental intelligence, they've missed nearly everyone they must have been watching closely."

An Arabic looking man comes up to them and introduces himself. He is tall, dressed in a thawb, the traditional male Arab attire. He looks them up and down, spotting the football shirts under their jackets. "Ah, you must be the Argentinians Mr Umbekie has told me all about. My name is Hasan, I represent some people from southern Morocco. We have some needs that I have been told that you will be able to meet."

Rodrigo greets the man in English with the faint Spanish accent he has perfected for many years. "Hello Señor, We would give you our card, but we do not carry them around, you never know when the wrong person might pick them up and give you a call."

This causes all three to laugh knowingly.

Adriano takes Hasan's hand, indicating a show of trust and a willingness to do business. "I am sure we can make arrangements to set up a meeting to arrange for your needs to be met. This is something we are very good at."

"That would be most beneficial to us. Mr Umbekie has told us that you can be very accommodating and resourceful, we do have something in common, we want to defeat the same enemy."

"On that I am sure."

All three laugh again, while Hasan pats them on the back. Rodrigo has been watching all the people entering the room with great interest. He notices that the door has been locked, Umbekie is moving towards the centre of the room, where he claps his hands for silence before he addresses them in his booming voice.

"Gentlemen, I welcome you all here. You are all safe in here, my sources tell me that there is no unusual activity from the authorities, so assume your presence is unknown and you can relax. I wish you a happy night, a night where you may discuss business and personal items safe in the knowledge that the walls do not have ears. I will be making introductions to those who do not know each other, but as many of you do, my main introductions will be of my two new Argentinian business partners over on to the side, who I am sure many of you are aware of, they now supply me with the weapons I need the most and they will be happy to supply any of you with them too."

He gestures towards Rodrigo and Adriano, who nod their heads. The rest of the room nod their heads at them. Rodrigo and Adriano show no sign of nerves as they become the focus of attention for the sort of the people they make a living out of killing. Umbekie, meanwhile carries on.

"I have refreshments of every nature here, plentiful traditional Congolese food, drinks of all kinds, many imported. For those who prefer pleasures of the flesh I have a supply of beautiful clean women, feel free to use any room you wish. There is only one more guest to come and as he does not need any introduction, I will let him make his entrance quietly, where he can speak to those of you he wishes to.

Please ENJOY!"

The last word booms around the room. He raises his glass, as everyone else in the room raises a glass in salute to him. He then moves to one side to speak to some people. Most of the guests returning to their previous conversations while some immediately make their way out to the other rooms and the pleasures of the flesh that Umbekie spoke about. This leaves only around twenty people in the main room.

Rodrigo had counted exactly 28 people in the room during the speech, including the doormen, but not himself and his colleague. He is still unsure of the amount of people that were in the rest of the house at the time, but he is increasingly confident they can handle the situation and fulfil their mission tonight.

They each have two silenced Glocks with four additional magazines, concealed underneath false compartments attached to their backs. Compartments specially created out of latex moulded to their body to be totally undetectable. This gave them ninety shots each, more than enough for everyone present. The challenge lay in getting those shots off, this is what Rodrigo was now thinking through. He had several options in the plans he had made and was mentally modifying one of them, getting it straight in his head to ensure that there wouldn't be any failure.

After a pause, Hasan continues his conversation, indicating how he is keen to utilise their services.

"So, where were we? Ah yes, how do I go about setting up a meeting with you? I am very keen to sample some of the wares I have heard you can supply. I have friends in the Sudan, they told me that two foreigners from Argentina got them all the arms they needed, guns, rocket launchers and even missiles. That is the sort of business I would like to do."

Rodrigo continues surveying the room, thinking, smiling and nodding at anyone he makes eye contact with, while Adriano speaks to Hasan. "It seems our reputation has preceded us, we did do that business in Sudan, but we have improved our supply chains since then, so we should be able to meet all your needs quickly, as long as you have, how should I say it, ...the right funding." Hasan nods his full understanding, as Adriano continues.

"As for a meeting, we have an arrangement with Mr Umbekie. He will be our primary African contact in future as he already has excellent communication lines in place, as tonight demonstrates very well. He will set-up the initial meeting in a place of your choice, after that we can make our own contact arrangements. As you can guess we have to be very cautious. Mr Umbekie has a trusted deputy, Kwanza, who will act as the initial intermediary in all our African business. He can be very helpful and will sort out all the details, which ensures that we do not fall into an entrapment situation arranged by the very people who want to stop us, which may eventually stop you in your quest."

Kwanza would be delighted if he knew he was being described as a trusted deputy. Adriano suddenly realises that he still hasn't seen his beaming smile yet.

Hasan finishes his nodding, which had taken place at the end of each word. "I understand fully, I thank you, I am excited about building a strong business relationship, I will speak to Kwanza tonight as I have met him before. I look forward to our future transactions."

"As do we." Adriano shakes his hand, then Hasan re-joins a small group of similarly dressed Arabs who he seems to be familiar with, leaving the two Argentinians on their own.

Adriano turns his attention to Rodrigo, who has been working out all the possibilities. Addressing him in Spanish. "What are your thoughts about this so far?"

"It's a big possibility, I'm working on a small modification of the second plan we went over earlier, but as the odds of getting out unharmed look slimmer than I anticipated, it will be best to leave it to later, when the drink has been flowing. Best you stay on the orange from now on though."

Adriano knows the second plan well, it would work OK here and he agrees with the beverage option. They start to move around the room, acknowledging people as they go, keen to gain familiarity and trust with as many people as possible. As they move past the sofas, a large African man stands up and greets them.

"Hello my friends, I am Frédéric, from Burundi, I am a good friend of Thembezi Umbekie, we have traded for many years, we fought the same struggles in our countries. He speaks very highly of you and explained to me what you can do, what you have done for our friends in Angola and Sudan. I may need your services in the future, but not right now. It is nice to meet you and I hope we will meet again, soon."

He shakes their hands as he walks past to greet some other people. It appears that Umbekie has not been shy about impressing on his guests how the Argentinians could help them and what they are able to supply. All of this, without the Argentinians having actually provided any evidence that they could provide the things they say, it was all on reputation.

This suited them perfectly, as they had no intention of actually supplying any arms to any of the people here. The urgency of a few small players trying to impress their peers with the amount of power they have, has led everyone to freely accept the Argentinians at face value. Thankfully the finer details of actually obtaining weapons could wait until another day, as most guests were here to network and seek out future opportunities rather than finalise a deal.

The Argentinians continue to survey the whole building, whilst also mingling with the other guests, shaking many hands, repeating the details of the deal they have with Umbekie, explaining how to initiate business deals with them, to many of the other guests.

They eventually move out of the main room to survey the rest of the house, first walking through the only visible door which leads down a wide corridor with a row of doors each side, eight in total.

Heaving moans and groans are coming from most of the rooms, both male and female, enjoying the pleasures of the flesh as Umbekie so eloquently put it. The final two rooms are devoid of any noises, conspicuous by their silence.

They come to the end of the corridor, pass through another door into a large rectangular dining area, where a few men are sat around a table talking. They instantly recognize one of the men, who when he looks around and sees them, leaps up to great them with his usual beaming smile.

"Hello, hello, my friends."

"Hello Kwanza how are you?"

"Very, very good. I trust you enjoyed your trip here? Mulaki is a good man still with lots to learn, I am sorry we had to change drivers but Michael was needed for our special guest who has a larger entourage than you and Michael has the biggest car. I hope you are enjoying yourselves at our party, it has been a long time in planning, we especially arranged for your trip to be at the same time, it is a good opportunity for all of us to conduct more business."

Adriano makes Kwanza's night when he tells him that all the business opportunities they make here will be conducted through Mr Umbekie, using him as the main contact.

Kwanza's eyes light up with this revelation, he smiles wider than they had ever seen him or thought he possibly could smile before. He gets very over-excited. "I thank you, I thank you, this will be very good for Mr Umbekie and me, oh me and of course you."

Rodrigo tries to calm him down. "Don't get too excited, it is very early days, for us it makes perfect sense at this stage. We cannot give out business cards or phone numbers, so the best solution is to use the communication lines we have already established, so that my friend, means you, but don't get too carried away until some of these deals have been conducted, we have been let down by promises before."

Rodrigo's attempts have been futile as Kwanza starts to leap at them and hug them. "I agree, I agree. Oh thank you Señores, this will make sure everyone knows who Kwanza is. Thank you."

Kwanza turns to the men at the table and says something in Congolese to them. They all cheer and he holds his hands up, punching the air. He turns back to the Argentinians.

"Can I get you anything? A drink, a woman, a smoke, anything else? We are here to ensure that everyone has everything they need. If you need anything, come and see Kwanza."

Rodrigo smiles at Kwanza. He will be putty in their hands from now on, not that he wasn't before, but this will make gaining everyone's trust easier during the night as Kwanza talks about potential deals to the guests.

Adriano is keen to survey the rest of the building. "We are OK for now, we are just walking around soaking up the atmosphere."

"No problem. Just come and find Kwanza when you need something."

The Argentinians nod, before looking around for other doors to examine, only spotting two, one an exit to outside, with the other door opening as one of the guest emerges to the sound of a toilet flushing. Kwanza spots them looking at it and helpfully informs them the nature of the room. "The bathroom."

Rodrigo is sure there must be other rooms. "Kwanza, this house is very large, how many rooms does this it have?"

Kwanza proudly informs them that it has ten, plus a bathroom. The Argentinians expected more in a building that looked so big from the outside, but the rooms are large, using up all the available space. They are satisfied that they have seen all that there is to see, but are a little disappointed that there seems to be few places that offer good cover for them in an assault situation.

The Argentinians are just about to return to the main room when the back door opens, one of Umbekie's bodyguards enters, followed by three Arabs. They instantly recognise one of the Arabs. He is Malek Ali Bezir, the man whose face has appeared in countless newspapers and TV programmes since a terrorist outrage in the west. He is top of the FBI most wanted list and with a five million dollar price tag on his head, he is without doubt the most sought after criminal in the world. In the flesh though, he is far less imposing than they thought, very slender, appearing to barely reach five foot tall.

He walks past and nods at the two Argentinians, who nod back. Ali Bezir is flanked by two much larger Arabs, who are carrying large holdalls, all three wearing traditional Arab dress. They enter the first empty room in the corridor, in silence.

Kwanza nods after Ali Bezir. "The important guest."

Adriano just looks straight at Kwanza, trying not to be sarcastic. "So we guessed."

Kwanza is now keen to share what he knows about the night. "He has finance to give everyone. It cannot be done using banks anymore. Too many people watching. He uses such gatherings now, we are delighted that he chose ours to give money to people in this area. We will have the envy of all our enemies and they will fear us more now we have a powerful friend."

Rodrigo and Adriano look at each other, they know they need to get somewhere private to talk, this has changed everything. By killing Umbekie, someone they viewed as a big fish in an insignificant country, they would expect not have faced many repercussions. However as he is the friend of such an influential man in world terrorism, this could put them in danger for the rest of their lives.

They need to alter their plan, they need to take their action tonight, they need to leave no witnesses. Most importantly they definitely need to take advantage of the opportunity that has arisen. This could be their big opportunity, they know they can earn more money tonight than they would earn from their line of work for the rest of their lives. They would be able to retire comfortably and if all went well, safely in anonymity.

Adriano plays down the importance of the new arrival to Kwanza, not wanting to seem too keen to meet one of the most infamous people in the world. "I am sure we will meet your honoured guest during the night, although he probably does not have the need of our services as your other guests do, they may be able to afford to do a lot of business with this extra funding."

Kwanza smiles again, business for them now meant business for him. "I will be here if you need me."

The Argentinians go back along the corridor, enter the main room and stand to one side, away from the rest of the guests, where Adriano starts to speak in Spanish. "We cannot miss this opportunity, we can retire on this, which would make our families happier, well mine anyway. Besides if we remove all witnesses, we will be able to get away with this without having to worry about reprisals. No one would have known we were here, well amongst the terrorist fraternity anyway."

Rodrigo has already rethought his plans. "I agree, with MAB as a distraction, this may actually have made things easier for us. Let me elaborate."

The two Argentinians drink from their drinks using their glasses as a shield, looking over the rim at the others gathered in the room to ensure that no one is listening to them. Everyone else is talking away similarly, in small groups of two or three, so no attention is drawn to them as the room is starting to buzz with the knowledge of the new arrival and what it means for those present, the increase in wealth and a new powerful ally.

One of Rob's fortes is being able to think fast on his feet, to be able to deal with a situation in a way which ensured minimal risk. It had earned him a medal in the Falklands. They also had enough experience to draw on to be able adapt previous jobs.

"Well, remember the two jobs we did in Namibia, we can combine the methods to do this."

Andy nods. He remembered the jobs well, they were some of the first they had done freelance, whilst they were still in the Army. They had involved surprise and speed more than anything else and from the outset appeared to be impossible. The first involved taking out a small group of enemy scouts near a waterhole in the middle of the desert. They had done this by disguising themselves as nomads, they then lead some horses right up to the middle of waterhole to water them. When they were watering their horses, the scouts had lost interest and had gone back to sorting out their own water bottles. Rob and Andy then had drawn silenced pistols and shot all of the scouts in an arc.

The toughest part of the whole exercise was to walk to the centre of the waterhole, where they were surrounded. It had taken a lot of balls to do this and as such put the scouts off their guard as they didn't believe an enemy would be so foolish to do such a thing. The other had involved the kidnap of a rebel leader in a bar. This was easier, they sprayed him with chloroform, when he collapsed they supported him and took him outside for some fresh air. When they were outside they shot the man's bodyguards and jumped into a car. Likewise the hardest part of this was walking up to the man and shaking his hand, something that took a lot of bravado. If there was something that Andy excelled at, it was bravado and he had the confidence in himself to pull it off.

Rodrigo continues with the plan. "This is how I see it, firstly, we cause a diversion using your Asthma spray on MAB. When he is falling on the floor, we can take out his two cronies with headshots as they go to his aid. After this we each take one side of the room and arc very quickly in opposite directions taking everyone else out in this room, with Umbekie's guards being the first targets, as they are most likely to be armed.

That's about 12 people each, it will only take a few seconds, we won't need to reload but even then we cannot afford to miss one shot as it may give someone a chance to shoot back with any hidden weapons they may have. Then we take out the kitchen, leaving the corridor rooms to last. Speed and accuracy will be the important factors, the surprise will cause confusion and hopefully hesitation."

Adriano is pleased with the plan, when explained, it seemed so straight forward. He had no doubt that they would execute it perfectly, especially as they would be able to use methods that had been so effective before. "Suits me. We'll just wait until MAB is in here, the rest would have dulled their senses with alcohol and wealth, we approach him to friendly introduce ourselves, then I'll spray him. The rest will be history."

As they finish, Umbekie comes towards them, they greet him with smiles. "My Friends, come and meet some of my close neighbours. I spoke with Kwanza, he delighted me with what you told him. I want you to meet everyone! We can create a lot of business today, these people over here are from Cameroon and they are fighting to overthrow their government. They will have money after tonight but need supplies. You are the men for these supplies, you are going to get rich tonight, I will get rich tonight, everyone will be happy." The irony of this last statement meant they didn't have to feign their smiles.

He leads the Argentinians over to a group of Africans, making simple introductions. "Friends this is Mr Adriano and Mr Rodrigo, they can help you with any needs you have on the weapon front. Be nice to them."

The Argentinians shake all of their hands, smiling. No names are given by the Cameroonians. The largest of them aggressively asks what they can be supplied with.

Adriano tries to talk business. "What do you need?"

The man laughs loudly as if this is a joke. "Ha ha ha, everything! Did you not hear the news that our rebels were defeated?"

News such as this rarely travels further than the bordering countries. The rest of the world is rarely interested in small rebellions. "No, we have not heard of any news. We can supply you with everything. If you can match the price, we can give you the device. We supplied some tank busters to the Angolans last year, who were very happy with the merchandise. They used them to reverse a couple of defeats."

Another member of the group from Cameroon joins in. "I have heard of that, I have a cousin who was with the Angolans, he talked of the tank missiles. Sadly he was killed just after and ever since I have not been able to find a way to contact his comrades and find out how they got them. That was you?"

He is impressed and says something to the rest of the group.

When the Cameroonians finish talking, Adriano continues. "Yes, it was us, now you can get in contact with us through Mr Umbekie, who will be our primary point of contact in this area. If you tell him what you need, he will get Kwanza to contact us, we can have it with you in 48 hours. We have yet to work out the finer details, but we will speak with Kwanza tomorrow, to let him know a total list of our prices so he can deal with your needs."

The Cameroonians talk amongst themselves again, all smiling at the thought of what they could now achieve. Umbekie is watching them, smiling the broadest, sensing a lot of profit and power through his new association. He pats the Argentinians on the back.

"It is not what you know, but who you know eh? Ha ha ha. My brother spent years saving and studying and he has not got the wealth or power I have, even more of which I will have after today."

He laughs one of his booming laughs before taking a large swig from an imported liquor bottle. Umbekie is then beckoned by one of his men in the corridor. He goes over and returns smiling. He claps his hands loudly.

"Our most important guest will be coming in now to speak to several of you, to help you out with your fight against the forces of evil."

Malek Ali Bezir appears in the doorway flanked by his two men. He goes over to the Moroccan, Hasan, speaks a few words to him before shaking his hand and handing Hasan a bag. They speak for a few minutes. The rest of the room is relatively silent, with everyone still in small groups, all with one eye on Ali Bezir expectantly. Adriano grabs a glass of water from one of the guards serving drinks, while Rodrigo watches Ali Bezir's every move, who is now approaching Umbekie, to engage him in conversation.

Umbekie spots this and beckons the Argentinians over when Andy returns with his drink. Ali Bezir nods his head as they approach.

He introduces himself. "I am Malek Ali Bezir, as you may well know. I would like to thank you for helping the fight of all of these people against the Western oppressors and their puppets. I have spoken to Hasan and Umbekie, they both speak highly of you. I am here to supply these groups with finance to continue their fight. Finances, which will no doubt end up with you, so I cannot spare any reward for you. What I can offer is my eternal gratefulness for enabling us to do what we do."

Rodrigo knows that this is the time to initiate their plan, all the eyes in the room have turned back to their groups as they wait for Ali Bezir to make a move towards them. Rodrigo does the talking. "We thank you most gratefully, we were involved in a similar fight against the same forces decades ago, as we grew too old to offer our physical strength, we decided to offer the means to do it, please meet my colleague Adriano Cabrera."

He utters a little cough as he finishes, which Adriano knows is the signal, although they are not in the centre of the room as planned, they can still utilise their arc method.

Adriano offers his hand out to Ali Bezir. Ali Bezir takes it and bows down. As he bows, Adriano uses his asthma spray, which he has concealed in his other hand. It is unseen by anyone else, the chloroform acts instantly, knocking Ali Bezir to the floor still gripping Adriano's hand.

Ali Bezir's men see Ali Bezir falling and quickly jump to his aid, bending down to see what is wrong. Adriano has turned to the Africans behind him with a look of shock on his face to take their focus off him, fortunately they are all totally focusing on Ali Bezir, their main thoughts of the finances they have not yet received.

Rodrigo and Adriano reach behind their backs, pull out their hidden guns from their false back, one in each hand both silenced. The adrenaline is pumping really hard through their veins, but they are totally focused, devoid of any emotion or fear.

Rodrigo uses his Glocks very quickly on the backs of the heads of Ali Bezir's men, blood sprays from their front of their heads all over the carpet, just missing two men sitting on one of the sofas, who are so engaged in conversation they don't see what is going on.

Adriano turns his back to Rodrigo and concentrates on the people in his arc of the room, firstly placing two quick silent shots in the heads of the two Cameroonians, the blood from their exit wounds spraying over the white walls behind.

This happens so fast no one has been able to comprehend what is happening and react.

Adriano quickly turns his attention to the guards on the door who are starting to move, but are not quick enough to avoid the bullets that hit them in the centre of the forehead, causing them to slump to the floor in the lobby.

Rodrigo is as swift with the people in his arc, taking out Hasan and Umbekie side on, before turning his guns on the two men on the sofa still in deep conversation, still oblivious to the carnage that is evolving around them.

They die in mid-sentence remaining peacefully in the same position.

Adriano turns to the group of four on the right hand side, accurately putting a bullet into each of their heads before they are able to move.

The remaining six people left in the room have started to slowly react, although none has uttered a sound, they start to drop to the floor before they can do anything. Two are dead before they hit the floor behind the sofa, victims of Rodrigo's accuracy and speed.

Adriano has cleared his arc, so turns swiftly to help Rodrigo finish his, shooting the man that has managed to take one step towards the corridor, then before the body hits the floor, he despatches the man who was serving drinks, which causes the first loud noise of the offensive as the tray full of drinks crashes to the ground.

Rodrigo swiftly despatches two Arabs that had dropped to the floor, placing a bullet each through the side of their heads as they crawl on the floor trying to find cover. The last man left standing in the room is a drunken African who has not noticed what is going on, obliviously staggering towards where the drinks were.

Adriano walks over to him and swiftly and emotionlessly ends his life with another head shot.

The Argentinians ensure they keep a mental note of their actions, using unique hand signals to verify to each other what has been cleared and what is left to do. This ensures they do not miss anything in the house.

One room cleared, nine plus a bathroom left. 24 killed. One incapacitated.

The whole exercise has not made much noise and taken less than ten seconds to complete. The whitewashed walls covered in the crimson results of the ruthless assassins' deadly accuracy. The thumps and the noise of the drinks tray has aroused curiosity from the kitchen, from where two of the Umbekie's men have started to make their way down the corridor. They see a couple of bodies in the main room and let out a yelp.

Rodrigo appears at the other end of the corridor and shoots them both accurately. He then runs down the corridor into the kitchen where there are three people sat around the table. Kwanza looks up at him with his customary large smile, a smile he dies with, his head unmoved. The only tell-tale sign is a trickle of blood running down his nose from a small entry wound in his forehead. The others do not have time to move far before Rodrigo plants a bullet in each of their heads.

Two rooms cleared, eight plus a bathroom left. 29 killed. One incapacitated.

The bathroom is next. Rodrigo runs over to the bathroom and puts two shots into the door at waist height, a groan and a slump indicating they have hit their target. He opens the door and puts a hole in the head of the African sat lopsided on the toilet, leaving a red splash of blood on the white wall behind.

Two rooms plus the bathroom cleared, eight left. 30 killed. One incapacitated.

The noise has aroused concern in the rooms where Rodrigo believes there are a further eight men and an unknown number of women occupying some of the eight rooms. There is shouting coming from one of the rooms from an unknown male voice with a strong African accent.

"What is going on?"

"Umbekie?"

Adriano, who is covering the main room entrance of the corridor, shouts back. "There is nothing wrong, just someone who drank too much."

The Argentinians now set about clearing the remaining rooms of at least seven men and four women. There is an art to clearing rooms which Rob and Andy have perfected, always aiming for obvious hiding spaces inside the room through the wall from outside, never putting themselves in a position where anyone in the room has the chance to take a shot at them from cover.

The door nearest Adriano opens slightly and a head pokes through, which falls back through the room with a bullet in the forehead; in the split second it took, Adriano registers that it was a woman's head. There will still be at least one man in that room. He moves forward, knocks open the door without standing in the open doorway, he crouches down low and takes a look inside. He cannot see anyone inside so crawls back out of the room, stands up and puts two bullets into the wall that the door has just swung back on. A body slumps to the floor with a groan. He crouches again and rolls into the room, quickly checking for other occupants but it is empty. He pulls back the door and makes sure the man is dead with a headshot.

Three rooms plus the bathroom cleared, seven left. 32 killed. One incapacitated.

Adriano turns and puts four bullets into the door return wall of the first room at the other end; there is another slump on the floor. He kicks the door open, rolls in and scours the room. There is a man and a woman cowering on the floor. They are dispatched silently and without mercy before he makes sure of the man behind the door.

Four rooms plus the bathroom cleared, six left. 35 killed. One incapacitated.

There should be five men and at least three women in the remaining six rooms. Rodrigo checks the two rooms nearest the kitchen, they are both devoid of people, but seem to contain the luggage of some of the guests.

Six rooms plus the bathroom cleared, four left. 35 killed. One incapacitated.

Rodrigo kicks open the next door along the corridor, then lies on the floor, minimising the target he presents. In the room are 3 naked men, two cowering Arabs and an African who is tied to the bed face down. Rob sees they are unarmed and not a risk, so coolly stands up and walks into the room, shooting the two Arabs first, then the African. If he did feel any guilt about his actions, the killing of this man would be what he felt most guilty about, an unarmed restrained target who couldn't see his face, but he didn't feel guilt, the feelings of guilt left him years ago. It was a necessity, he wouldn't want this man to be able to tell his story or pose a vengeful threat in the future.

Seven rooms plus the bathroom cleared, three left. 38 killed. One incapacitated.

Rodrigo then checks the room opposite in the same way, but it is empty.

Eight rooms plus the bathroom cleared, two left. 38 killed. One incapacitated.

Rodrigo and Adriano have reached the last two rooms, nod an indication to each other of which one they will take first. They both put some bullets in the door return wall, but there is no sound. Suddenly a machine gun from inside the room fires a volley at the door. Rodrigo drops to the floor before he pushes the door open. The gun fires again but at waist height. The Arab firing the machine gun is not expecting to be shot from floor level, he drops the machine gun when two accurate headshots spray the contents of his head against the back wall. The woman he was with tries to grab the machine gun, but is stopped in her tracks by a pair of accurate bullets to the temple.

Nine rooms plus the bathroom cleared, one left. 40 killed. One incapacitated.

They have one final room to tackle. Adriano crouches on the floor and pushes his door in. He is not met with the same amount of force as Rodrigo was in the previous room. It is occupied by a couple who are still in the throes of passion on the bed. Their passion and vigorous movement stops with two short bursts from Adriano's gun.

Ten rooms plus the bathroom cleared, none left. 42 killed. One incapacitated.

House completely clear.

Rob turns to Andy. "You OK?"

"Oh Yes, that was much easier than I expected."

Rob looks at his watch, less than two minutes have passed since they started firing, but it seemed like several hours, such was the intensity of the moment.

They both know that next part of the job will be much trickier, they have to get out of the country safely and Rob wants to do it as quick as possible.

"Let's get the bags of cash, grab Ali Bezir and get the fuck out of here."

Andy realises something he had not thought of before. "How the hell are we going to get Ali Bezir out of here and, more importantly, to somewhere we can claim the reward?"

Rob is casual about this problem, he already has figured a way to get Ali Bezir out, smiling wryly. "I have already thought of something."

Suddenly, there is a rapid knocking at the door.

"Shit, the gate guards."

Rob has already gone for the back door, while Andy goes to the front door and rattles the lock. He hears a couple of thuds from outside before he unlocks it.

Andy opens the door to let Rob back in, dragging two bodies. "It is OK, I can't see anyone else here, only Michael who was still outside in his car. He is coming in."

"He's not going to like this, it could cause him some problems. He will be the only one of the attendees left, he could get asked some tricky questions, he is bound to be the main suspect in a power struggle."

Rob is totally unsympathetic, he knows that Michael would have had worse trouble if he had been found out to be a traitor by the gang. "Well he has to verify that we have taken our target out."

They hear Michael coming in the back door, so join him in the kitchen. He looks at the bodies slumped around the table, pausing for a moment to look at Kwanza's motionless, smiling head. He wanders into the main room, looking at the carnage in the corridor along the way, shaking his head. He is in stunned silence for a few minutes.

"Oh my god, oh dear, what have you done?"

Rob justifies their actions. "We had no option, this was an opportunity not to be missed."

Michael wanders around looking at the bodies again, shaking his head, muttering to himself.

He stands over one of the dead Africans. "Oh no, this man was a lynchpin for the peace in Burundi. The country could disintegrate if there is a power struggle."

Rob needs to stem Michael's concerns very quickly and get him back on track to help their quick exit. "He was being financed by Malek Ali Bezir. He couldn't have been that peaceful. In fact all of these men were here to take finances back to continue their wars against the West. We cut off a vital supply of funds to all of these people. The groups they represent will find it hard to get significant funding now."

Michael is puzzled. "Ali Bezir? How do you know?"

Andy is a little more sympathetic towards Michael. "He was here, in fact you drove him here."

Michael is even more puzzled. "I was unaware of who I drove. They all had their faces covered."

Andy walks over to the unconscious Ali Bezir and shows him to Michael. Michael gasps.

"This is more serious than I thought. All sorts of bad things could have happened if these men had a man like Malek Ali Bezir backing them."

"Not any more it won't. Well not for a while anyway. Our big problem now is to get the hell out of the country before anyone discovers this and we have a lot more people gunning for us than we can handle."

Rob has come out of one of the empty rooms, holding two large canvass bags. He opens them. One is full of money and an assortment of precious stones. The other contains various rifles. He empties the weapons out and throws them to one side. He places the bag next to Ali Bezir.

"Perfect."

Andy looks at him with a smile. "You're not thinking what I think you're thinking are you?"

Michael looks at them both, his puzzled look has returned.

It was fortunate that Ali Bezir was not a large man. Like many powerful leaders he had compensated for his lack of stature with a strong personality. Rob looks up satisfied that his plan will work.

"Probably. Unless you've got a better way of getting him out of here?"

Andy shakes his head. "Not really."

Michael still does not know what is going on. "Get who out of here?"

They point at Ali Bezir.

"Why do you want to get him out?"

Andy is now puzzled by Michael's ignorance. "Oh, for a five million dollar reward maybe."

"I thought he had to be alive for that reward."

They both look at Michael, condescendingly. He suddenly realises that Ali Bezir is not dead and looks even more worried.

Michael shakes his head. "This is worse than I thought. You are going to take him to the US Embassy, but there is not one in this country, has not been for five years since the revolution. The nearest Embassy is in Angola."

Andy is aware that there isn't an embassy in the country, Kwanza had pointed out the impressive but empty building on his grand tour of Brazzaville. "Sadly we know, that's why we need to put him in a bag and get out of here."

"Oh no, it will be very difficult to go to Angola, when word of this gets out many road blocks and searches will occur."

Rob has folded Ali Bezir's legs and is attempting to fit him into the bag. "That's why we need to get out of here quickly, so a little help would be welcome!"

Michael looks around again, shaking his head. He looks at Kwanza, who looks peaceful and happy in death, unaware that his new friends were his enemies. Although he knew Kwanza was involved in bad things,

Michael did like him, he was an affable man, just misguided. Michael had hoped he may have got out of this business and learnt a lesson when Umbekie was gone. It was too late now. Much too late.

Rob and Andy have managed to get Ali Bezir into the bag. After having tested the weight, it is heavy, but can be carried by either of them. Rob is still trying to impress the urgency to leave quickly upon Michael, every second they spend talking about the justification of their actions was a second closer to having to talk about it to the wrong end of a gun. "Right, let's go. Can you drive us?"

Michael reluctantly agrees. "I suppose, where shall I take you to?"

"Just outside the hotel. I will get our bags and the car and we will leave tonight. You can then breathe a little easier."

"I will not breathe easy for a long time."

Rob slings the bag containing Ali Bezir onto his back, while Andy picks up the bag with the money and the precious stones, they walk out the back door and get straight into Michael's car. They can hear the sound of sirens in the distance and hope they are not heading towards them.

Capítulo Ocho

Michael drives off and concentrates on driving steadily without drawing any attention to his car. Before they even get to the end of the road, Michael raises his concerns. "Those sirens are heading this way. Someone must have heard the gunshots and called the authorities. They will be setting roadblocks up right now."

Andy is sceptical. "I doubt if anyone heard the gunshots, you didn't and you were right outside. In stressful times like this, every siren you hear will put you on more on edge, making you think they are for you. We have had similar worries many times, they were always unfounded."

Two police cars speed past them in the opposite direction, heading directly for Umbekie's house.

Rob looks out of the back window, watching the police cars, starting to show signs of concern himself.

"Those sirens could be a result of us this time, maybe the house was being watched after all the attention generated by the guests arriving. I hope it wasn't as a result of the gunfire, we could run out of time quickly if it was. If they discover the contents of the house there will be roadblocks set up all over this area."

Michael starts to panic, sweat starting to drip from his forehead. "This is very bad, very bad, if I am arrested and linked to the murders, my life will be in grave danger, the rest of the group will hunt me down."

Andy offers some cynical but reassuring words. "You will be OK, You are probably the leader now we have taken everyone out above you, there probably aren't many left in the group to be called a group."

This hasn't helped Michael. "There will be a power struggle and they will suspect me if I am still alive. They knew I would be there. Oh No. It is very bad. I will have outlived my usefulness to the government I work for too, so they won't want me, I will be jobless and on the run for my life."

Andy hasn't given up, they need Michael to stay calm and focused. "Look on the positive side, you've helped many governments to remove some of the biggest international threats ever known, you'll get a nice pension and a new life somewhere much nicer than this place."

It was a futile effort. "No, I will be not much use to any government now, I was only useful for being Congolese and knowing some bad people. What use is that now that now they are gone, there may even be another war."

Andy tries to calm Michael with a humorous insight. "We have all their money to buy guns, so the chance of a war is slim!"

Rob is getting fed up with the panicking Michael, he needs him to focus on helping them escape, he needs to ensure that Michael will not do anything rash like turning himself in, so Rob becomes a lot more assertive.

"Michael, pull yourself together, you've been involved in situations such as this many times, we need you to focus on getting back to the hotel as quick as possible, we have enough money here to ensure you have a good retirement. You cannot let us down, especially after what we have just done."

This does the trick, Michael's focus returns, partly out of fear of the two men in his car. Rob's words have made him realise that the worst scenario for him at the moment, is if they get caught, he could be silenced before he has a chance to tell his side of the story to the police. Suddenly he becomes totally silent, concentrating on getting back to hotel as quickly as possible.

They travel the same way as they arrived, through the suburbs of varying quality, pulling up opposite the hotel an hour later. Michael turns the car around and parks by the side of the road in preparation for his quick escape. Andy quickly gets out of the car and runs across the road to the hotel. A minute later a light goes on in a room, the window opens, two bags are thrown out, followed by Andy, who climbs out of the window. He jumps to the floor, picks up the bags and goes around the back to get the car. Another minute later the 4x4 slowly drives out of the hotel, crosses the street and parks next to Michael's car. Rob gets out, he puts the bag containing Ali Bezir into the back of the 4x4 first, before returning for the other bag.

Andy gets out and walks to Michael's car window. He leans in and shakes his hand.

"Thanks for all your help, we are very sorry it did not turn out exactly as planned."

Michael is starting to feel relieved, he has fulfilled his part of the bargain, he now feels that he will finish this unscathed. "I am glad I have got you here safely, I must go now, I must find a way to sort this mess out and ensure I don't have to spend my life looking over my shoulder, plus I may need a new employer soon, I need to see if I have a future."

Rob finishes packing the car and walks around to join them. "Michael, thanks for everything and just to put your mind at rest, we were never going to harm you, I just needed to get you focused. We are retiring from this business now, our pension is in that car."

He indicates towards the 4x4. "To show our gratitude and to make amends for the trouble we have caused you, please take this."

He hands Michael a handful of cut diamonds and a small bag full of American Dollars, at a first glance it appeared to be in the tens of thousands of dollars.

Michael displays the happiest face they have seen him express in all of their time with him, breaking into the largest smile, slightly weeping tears of joy. "Thank you, thank you very much. This is more than I expected, much more, it will secure my future, I too can retire." He is very still very keen to get away quickly to ensure his safety, to sort out his future plans. "Have a safe journey." He firmly shakes them by the hand, before they walk away from the car and get into the 4x4.

Michael sits in his car looking at the diamonds in his hand for a few seconds, he smiles to himself before driving off in the opposite direction to the 4x4.

Andy drives, leaving the navigation and the planning of their next step to Rob. He hasn't had much time to think of this stage, but knows that Rob would have been assessing options in his head on the way to the hotel. "I hope you have started to think of our options, I'm not sure which way is the best way."

"We are heading for Angola, via the quickest route."

Andy is surprised, Angola was one of the places they wanted to avoid, he thought they would head north. "OK, but it wouldn't have been my choice and it's not going to be that easy, don't we have to go via the DRC again?"

Rob has planned part of their journey, but is still searching for options in the map. "The normal route would take us back to Kinshasa, there is no way we would get over that border with this cargo and I don't want to take that ferry again, it will cause too much delay, plus I'm not sure it will operate at night. I've spotted a route to cross which takes us via Kinkala, but I suspect there may be a few roadblocks en route, the more of them we encounter, the less likely we are to make it, so I'm looking at other options."

As they talk they spot a roadblock two hundred metres further ahead in the road, which causes Andy to stop the car at the side of the road and turn the lights off. This must be linked to what has happened at Umbekie's house, the chances of two things happening to cause such a fuss in the same area were slim. They didn't know how safe they would be though, the possibility that the police were looking for known local criminals was foremost in their minds, they doubted that two westerners would be top of the police list, but in countries such as this, everyone can be a suspect.

Andy starts the car and turns it around in the road. "Hang on I have had an idea, but we need to go back to the hotel."

This causes Rob to stop studying the map and look directly at his friend. "This isn't going to be one of your silly ideas is it?"

Andy has remembered a plan they have used before, which has potential in this situation. "No, I'm thinking of trying the same plan that we used in Uganda four years ago."

Rob is a little disappointed that he hadn't considered that option, despite it working perfectly. It had relied a lot on an opportunity that had luckily presented itself to them. "That was a silly idea, a very silly idea, but it worked so I like it. Only thing is, would they have that service here?"

"Yes, I saw one advertised in the hotel. If we are going to do this, we best go back to the hotel for the night. We have only been away for half an hour so they will not know we have left. This way we get are more likely to be get out of the country safely." Andy is pleased with himself, he rarely gets to initiate a plan that Rob hasn't considered.

Rob likes the plan, but not the extra time waiting. "More likely to get out safely, but also more likely to get caught before we get a chance to get out."

"We can do it."

Rob puts the map down and rummages through the bags in the back, pulling out a clean River Plate football shirt, which he changes for the blood covered shirt one he is still wearing from the party, feeling a little annoyed that he didn't change before. The sight of the blood would have resulted in an extended detention for questioning. Andy, who had changed quickly in the hotel, carries on driving to the hotel. They pull up, park in the car park, get out and calmly walk over to their room. It still has the light on and the window open. Andy walks over and puts two bags in through the window. There are a lot of insects flying around the room.

"Damn, if I knew we would be back I would have shut this window."

Rob drags the two large canvass holdalls to the window and is helped by Andy to put them into the room before climbing in himself.

"Jeez, there are more bugs in here than out there."

He climbs back out, gets in the car and moves it so the headlights can be seen from the room. He turns them on, while Andy turns the hotel light out. Slowly all the insects fly towards the car. Rob turns the light off and climbs back in the window, closing it behind him, before turning the hotel room light back on. They both stand in the room looking at the two canvass holdalls.

Rob walks into the bathroom and turns the shower on, while Andy opens the bag containing Ali Bezir. "I'll give another dose of spray to our guest. Don't want him waking up and making a fuss, or even worse, killing himself."

Rob agrees. "That would cost us."

Andy opens the bag and looks at their unconscious guest. He sprays chloroform on the inside of the bag. He also puts tape over Ali Bezir's mouth and tapes his hands to his legs to ensure that there would be no escape if he did wake up. Rob goes into the shower to clean off the grime of the evening's events. It is one of the longest showers he has had in a long time, as he uses the opportunity to relax and contemplate their situation. When he finally emerges, Andy hurriedly runs in to do the same.

They surprisingly have a very peaceful sleep as the night passes without further incident and wake later than normal the next day. They dress before they check the status of their guest. When Andy opens the holdall, he is greeted by a pair of wide open, blinking eyes. He grabs the chloroform spray, pulls back the tape covering Ali Bezir's mouth to administer a couple of squirts which slowly close the blinking eyes, before Ali Bezir can utter a sound.

After the necessities, it is time to try and initiate their escape plan, so they leave the room and head into reception. Andy goes up to the desk, while Rob carries on outside.

Andy smiles at the receptionist. "Hello, how are you today? Have you got a telephone I can use please?"

The receptionist responds well to his charms. "Certainly sir, there is a public payphone across the lobby." pointing at a payphone a few feet away.

Andy walks over and picks it up. He looks at the leaflet he has picked up, dials and speaks for a few minutes before nodding his head and hanging up. He walks back past the desk and says thank you, leaving by the main door, making his way to the car park.

As he gets into the car, Rob starts the engine. Andy is keen to relay his phone conversation. "All set. He is happy to take us. He knows the rainforest well so can land us in a good spot. Well that's what he thinks."

Andy liked planning escapes, his survival instinct made him better at escaping than mission planning. "I have planned the route we need to go. Along the Kouitou River following it right out into the sea. Then just along the coast to Angola. The only tough part will be getting permission to land there."

He is especially pleased with himself, until Rob reveals a slight change of plan.

"That's a good plan, but we won't be going to Angola, I wanted to avoid it, but as we were going to travelling overland, it was the best option. Now we have other transport, I've assessed our options and we're heading for somewhere else, somewhere much safer, where I know there will be some help and some friendly faces."

As they pull away, Andy turns on the English language radio station and listens to the news. There is no mention of last night's massacre at Umbekie's house. The main news on the radio broadcast is of a dramatic escape of a dangerous criminal from one of the city's jails. It caused a major police operation, with road blocks being set-up all over the city, one of which managed to apprehend the absconder.

An interview with one of the heroic policemen who made the capture was broadcast, but the English was so poor it was hard to understand. This news brings great relief and a big smile to both of their faces.

It doesn't change their escape plan, but will make it far easier, it gives them more confidence that it will work, but Rob is a still little frustrated.

"We could have been well out of the way by now, the house and its contents will be discovered soon, someone that wasn't there will start to get curious, combined with the small chance we will run into someone that knows we were there, that driver for example, I would be much happier if we weren't here, especially as we are now heading back towards the house."

Andy agrees, but prefers this plan, especially as they are not going to Angola now, he is more comfortable travelling in this direction, the map he is navigating with shows their destination as being well away from the house.

"I think our friend Mulaki may have discovered it by now, but whether he raises the alarm is another thing. He was so green he will be shit scared that he would be blamed, plus he was told to wait until we called, I wouldn't be surprised if he is still waiting at the bus station for our phone call, just thinking it was a wild night."

As they drive towards their destination, they pass a bus station, were they see Mulaki's car parked up. Mulaki does not see them, he is busy sat on a small table outside the terminal playing cards with three other men, with his back to the road. They instantly recognise the brightly coloured rastacap.

Andy watches Mulaki in the wing mirror as the car passes the bus station, noting that Mulaki is just joking around with the three other men, which he presumes to be the other drivers for the party. "Well at least he is dedicated. They may never find out about the contents of the house if he carries on waiting for our call. Those drivers must have been expecting an all-night party, with some very late calls to pick up their guests."

Half an hour later they pull into a small aerodrome, very basic by normal airport standards, one small main terminal and a couple of small hangers on one side of the dirt runway. They drive straight to the nearest hanger, where a man is sat waiting by a small twin engine propeller driven plane, which Rob recognises as a Piper Seminole, a very common and reliable plane. The bonus is that this one seems to be in very good condition, a sparkling white airframe with nothing dripping from the engines. They have flown in worse, much worse. The car stops next to the hanger and they get out and approach the man.

Andy offers his hand. "Are you Señor Kwacha?"

The man takes Andy's hand, shaking it firmly. "Yes and you must be the man that I spoke to on the telephone earlier. Call me Mbuji."

"Yes Señor, as I explained, my colleague and myself are from Buenos Aires University, we are conducting a study on your rainforest compared to the South American rainforest. We need you to fly us east to conduct a study on the interior forests of the DRC."

Mbuji pauses for a minute, he is not interested in where they are from, but he is happy that they only want to fly around some rainforest, Crossing an international border is not a problem, he knows many places to do it without resistance or radar cover. "I am delighted to be of assistance, I know the area very well, better than any other pilot in the area. As I told you my rates are one hundred and fifty US Dollars per hour flying time, regardless of the destination."

"We will need you for about eight hours, as we need to circle the forest taking photographs for a long time, as well as potentially landing in the forest if we can find a suitable spot."

Eight hours work is the longest he has had in a very long time, he cannot hide his excitement, especially as this will be a safe journey, no flying mercenaries across a border, dodging gunfire, the thought of just circling around a rainforest for the cause of science was his perfect day. "That will be excellent, I will enjoy today's trip as much as you. I will try to give a guided tour as I do know the area very well. We will not waste time, have you much luggage?"

"No, only four bags, mostly Camera equipment."

The day is going to be good for Mbuji. "Ok, while I file a rough flight plan with my authorities, you can load all of your bags into my plane. It is that one, the white one."

Mbuji points to the Piper Seminole , the only plane in sight, before wandering off to the main terminal. When he is out of sight, Rob and Andy grab the bags from the car and load them onto the plane, ensuring that their passenger is safely secured in the spare passenger seat at the back. When Mbuji returns he has a pair of fifteen gallon fuel containers on a small trolley.

He smiles and beckons Rob to help him load the fuel into the back of the plane, as they lift the fuel inside, Mbuji explains the obvious reason why he has got extra fuel. "Everything is OK, we can go now. This is spare fuel; if we are flying for eight hours we will need more than the plane has, so I can refill whenever we land, no need to land in an airport."

Andy has a smug sense of self satisfaction, happy in the knowledge that he has once again picked a pilot for an escape who is keen to help and will remove any unforeseen problem from the equation, such as running out of fuel before they reach their destination. He displays this openly to Rob with a deliberately smug smile and a blink of the eyes. Rob just chuckles, he now has full confidence this is their best way to get away.

Mbuji starts to wave his hands at them as if shooing animals into a pen. "Please get into the plane, we go now."

As they get in the passenger seats, Mbuji runs around to the pilot seat and quickly starts the plane up, ignoring all standard pre-flight checks before immediately taxiing down the runway when the propellers start rotating. The plane reaches the end of the runway, turns and accelerates towards a thankfully uneventful take off. It climbs to 11,000 feet over the next five minutes and heads east towards the DRC.

As he flies the plane, Mbuji displays his overly talkative nature and complete confidence in his piloting abilities. He gives them his full life history.

"I am the best pilot in the area to fly you around the rainforest, I know it very well. I used to be in the Air force, flew many missions over all of this area during the civil wars, I know every hill, every valley, every river and every way to avoid radar and rebel fire. This last skill, we will not need today, but if we did, I am the best and you will be safe.

I flew many missions, I shot down many enemies, in planes and on the ground, I was a hero, they gave me a medal and the President gave me his plane, which I fly today for tourists. Not many tourists want me though, mainly mercenaries and smugglers, as I am the best pilot to get them where they need to go."

Andy has got the seat next to him, so spends the time ensuring that his ego is sufficiently boosted. "That is why we called you. Everyone we spoke to told us you were the best."

This puts a large smile on Mbuji's face, who continues. "It will take ten minutes to pass the border, another ten minutes after that to the rainforest, then I can take you to the best trees."

Rob is studying the map and gives directions. "Señor Kwacha. Can you head east? We want go to the end of the Kasai River. We have started our reference grid from there."

"I know that route very well, it will take a few hours, I can describe everything below us in detail as we go to make your journey enjoyable."

Rob and Andy assume that this means they are going to get a guided tour of Mbuji's exploits and adventures when he was an air force pilot for the next three hours, so Rob hands Andy a small digital video camera from one of their bags in the back.

"It would be a good reference to take a few shots as we fly over the rainforest."

Andy agrees. Anything to take Mbuji's mind off himself is a good thing. "Good Idea."

Andy films some of the rainforest while they are flying. Mbuji is suitably impressed as he flies the plane over some stunning rainforest for half an hour, not interrupting once, more interested in trying to watch the film on the camera, which he manages whilst keeping the plane level and on course. He may have had a big ego, but it was justified with his pilot skills.

Mbuji points up ahead. "There is where the Kasai River branches off on its own, how far do you want me to follow it?"

Andy looks out of the window at the river. "Right to the very end, there is some virgin rainforest that we need to see." The mention of the word virgin makes Mbuji snigger like a child.

They follow the river for another hour, Mbuji talking all the way. He talks about all of the dog fights he has had, some impressing Andy a great deal, the civil wars in the area were very vicious, the countless missile attacks, most of which were unguided so were easy to dodge, but still requiring great skill. He also revealed some of the charter flights he had made, many of which would have led to a lifetime sentence if he had made any incursions into the west, but as this was Africa, the rules were different, there just weren't any.

Mbuji reaches the very end of the river and turns to find out where they want him to go now. As he turns, Andy sprays him with the chloroform, knocking him out instantly, causing the plane to suddenly dive towards the ground. Fortunately they have sufficient height for Andy grab the controls and level off the plane.

Rob grabs Mbuji from the back, pulls him up over the seat and puts him in the spare passenger seat in the back of the plane. He ensures that Mbuji is belted in tightly as annoying as he was, he doesn't want to cause him any harm. Andy climbs over to the pilot seat, giving Rob room to clamber over next to him. They know where they are now and can navigate themselves, heading directly south east for the next couple of hours.

Andy turns to Rob, showing some signs of excitement. "Malawi here we come. No chance of any roadblocks here and looking at the display, no radar coverage either, so we are not going to be noticed flying across all these borders. Mbuji will not be missed for eight hours, but by then we will be long gone and he will be waking up with a headache wondering where he is."

Both Rob and Andy had earned their private pilot licenses. In the line of work they were engaged in it was a necessity rather than a luxury, allowing them more options when they had to get in or out of a tricky situation.

Rob is aware that they will need to refuel to get to their destination, the plane only has a range of 1,000 miles, but it was 1,200 to their destination in Malawi.

"I'm going to start looking for a quick landing spot, we need to get this spare fuel loaded. Then I can relax and let you take us to safety."

Andy also starts scouring the land for a clearing, but nothing can be seen, the only areas not covered in forest were the roads, he didn't want to risk the chance of another hijacking. He looks at the fuel gauge, there is enough for another hour of flight, so they have some leeway, but not much, he will need to find a suitable spot soon.

He is navigating totally by compass, following the direct south east heading, if they carry on in this direction, they will pick up Lake Malawi, the third largest in Africa, snaking over 300 miles along the spine of the country. Once they have reached the lake, navigation is easy, they won't need a map or a compass to find their destination.

Ten minutes later Rob shouts Bingo. Andy looks at him. "You were playing without me?"

"No, you fool, look there, fields." He is pointing to the North West where there is a huge clearing about five miles away.

"Gotcha." he veers over to the clearing, descending rapidly, taking a note of where he is now so he can get back on track when they resume the route. As he approaches the edge of the clearing, Andy is relieved, it is flat and very wide. There is a slight problem, there seem to be people gathered around the southern edges. Lots of people. As the plane flies over, the plane is spotted and everyone on the ground looks up, a plane is a rare sight in these areas. At the northern end there are some buildings, but the area in the middle is completely empty, so Andy heads directly for the middle, which is over a mile from the edges. He performs a bumpy but almost text book landing in such conditions. Rob jumps out before the plane has stopped, he doesn't want to waste any time and give any of the people, whoever they are, a chance to reach them.

Andy stops the plane, but keeps the engine running and gets out to assist Rob. They pull the two fuel containers out, place them on either side of the plane, then put the nozzles into the filler caps for the two fuel tanks. The containers have a hand pump fitted to make the job easier, which they are grateful for as they are aware of activity at the edges of the clearing and vainly hope that the activity isn't a result of their presence.

Emptying the containers only takes a couple of minutes, they pump harder with each stroke to speed up the process as they have realised that the activity is a result of them. The people that were at the edges have started to move towards them, some quite fast, fortunately it will take the fastest runner over five minutes to reach them, but it's what those people may be carrying that hastens their urgency. If the people are armed, the time until they are in range will be much shorter.

Rob keeps looking at the approaching crowd and the amount of fuel left in the container. "How much have you got left?"

"About a third, it will take another minute, but we need every drop."

A minute will be cutting it close, for the first time in a few hours, fear rears its head in both men, their adrenaline glands pump harder than any time in the last few hours.

Finally both containers are empty, the approaching people are still three hundred metres away. The appearance of the approaching crowd can be seen much clearer now, they are all dressed in what appears to be a uniform and all are carrying something that is long and glinting in the sun, raising the urgency even more.

Rob and Andy unhook the fuel lines, throw the containers clear of the plane, before hurriedly getting in each side. Andy pulls on the throttle and turns the plane away from the approaching crowd, he accelerates quickly and the plane takes to the air, much to Rob and Andy's relief. As they climb, they fly over the buildings at the northern end, which are arranged like an army barracks, before circling round to pick up their previous flight path.

As they pass over the crowd of people below, all of whom have stopped and are gesturing up at the plane, Rob uses the camera to zoom in and get a look at them. He snorts a small laugh as he zooms in to see the crowd chained together, being approached by some people dressed in a darker but different uniform. These other people are armed, he can clearly see their rifles, but they don't point it at the plane, just at the crowd of people.

"Prison, it was a prison, we've just refuelled in the middle of a prison. They must have been a work party clearing the tree line and looked at us as a means of escape. It was Machetes they had in their hands." He emits a sigh of relief, especially as the plane was now climbing well away from the land, more importantly, in the right direction for their destination.

The news that it was a prison is little comfort to Andy. "They still would have chopped us to death if they had a chance, they just wouldn't have got near enough to have that chance."

As the plane levels out into a steady flight, Rob climbs into the luggage compartment in the back of the plane and starts rummaging around. The noise of his video camera is heard. "Well, I'm not going to sit back and enjoy the ride. I need to sort stuff out, this isn't over when we land, it could be just the beginning of something else, although it sure beats a two day car journey."

The sight of the forest below them is a comfort, the lack of infrastructure indicates a lack of technology and more important for them, the lack of radar cover. This allows them to pass undetected over the DRC border into northern Zambia, changing direction to due east to minimise the amount of Zambia they have to pass over. The area they pass over is the wetlands, which makes a welcome contrast from the hours of tree cover they have just flown over, although the wetlands has little infrastructure, they are aware that Zambia is more developed than the DRC and an unknown plane in their airspace may attract unwanted attention

After an hour over the wetlands, they see a large snake like body of water straight ahead. This is what they are looking for and on reaching it, Andy continues the plane into the dead centre of the lake, where they encounter what looks like pillars of smoke rising from the waters. The tops of these pillars now reach above the plane which has descended to only 1,500 feet. There are no obstructions they could hit but there is a chance of being picked up on long range radar at much higher levels. Andy takes great care to steer well clear of the pillars, which both men have seen many times on their visits to the country.

The pillars were not smoke, but billions of swarming lake flies, flies which live their whole lives in the swarms moving around on the lake, occasionally hitting land. When they do hit land, they engulf everything they come into contact with, unintentionally clogging anything mechanical. The locals looked forward to the times when the swarms hit land, using buckets to catch the flies before crushing them into cakes which they then fried. It was a useful source of protein, but not the most delicious of dishes. Andy had experienced the delights of fly pie, he had also seen the effects the swarms had on some of the basic machinery found by the lake shore.

It was an experience that made him too aware of the damage they could cause a plane, bringing it out of the sky with clogged engines and a covered fuselage. The flies would pass through every available gap and would fill the cockpit in seconds. He gave the pillars a very wide berth.

Rob and Andy could see their landing zone now, one of a small pair of islands in the middle of the lake. Andy steered towards the larger of the two islands and more importantly, towards the tiny dirt airstrip he knew it contained.

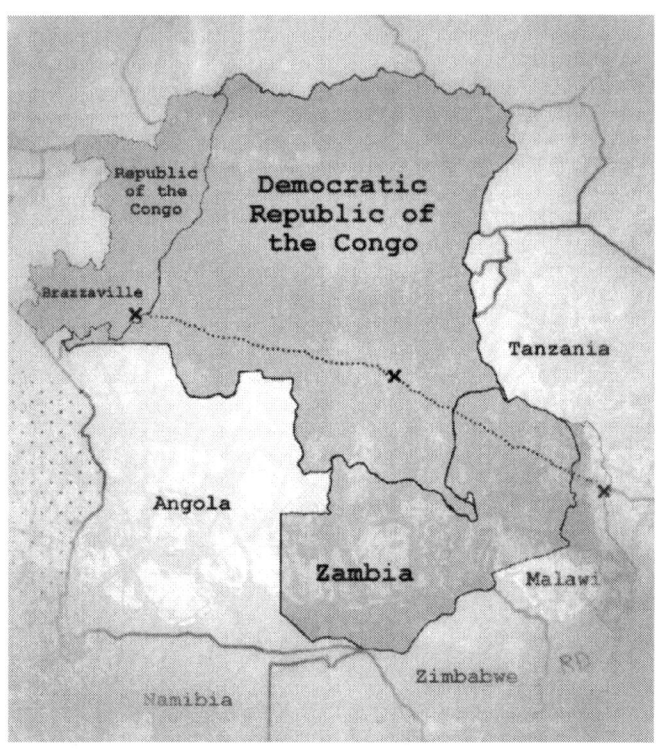

Capítulo Nueve

The plane lands on the dirt runway, finally stopping after taxiing to the end, where there are a group of people waiting. The plane comes to a halt next to them. The people approach the plane as the two occupants get out.

Rob is the first to get out and greet the waiting group with a large smile. "Hi."

The group is mainly Africans with two westerners at the centre, one of the westerners steps forward.

"Hi Rob, it's been a while, Oh and Hi too Coops."

He embraces the new arrivals with a strong grip. The second westerner waits until they are released to repeat the same actions.

The first westerner is tanned, with medium brown hair and a friendly face, casually dressed in cotton trousers and a plain t-shirt. "You should have called, we wouldn't have laid on such an imposing welcome. When Kwende saw a plane approaching, he quickly gathered this motley bunch in case it was trouble. We've had a few smugglers attempt to land in the last few years.

Being only a few kilometres from the Mozambique coast, this is an ideal drop-off location for people trying to get goods into the country illegally."

"Sorry Chris, we couldn't, we had to take a chance that you were around to meet us, you'll see why. Can we talk in private?"

Rob beckons him and the other westerner over to the plane.

Out of earshot of the accompanying Africans, he relays the story of the last few days. "You know what we do, well, we had a mission in the Congo that has turned out differently than expected. We needed to get as far away as possible, very quickly. We needed somewhere we could trust to be safe and I instantly thought of here, especially as it doesn't have good communications with the mainland, which helps stop leaks. When you see what we have, you'll understand why."

Chris grabs Rob before he reaches for the plane door. "Rob, please don't show us if it's something illegal, we can't help you if it is, Giles here had a bit of a run in with the authorities on the mainland a few months ago and they will use any excuse they can to deport him. The authorities don't like our operation here, its making them look inadequate, they'd like to get their hands on it at any costs. Although there aren't any phones to the mainland, they do have people watching in the main town who will send a message back to the mainland when the boat next arrives."

"Don't worry, it's not illegal, but it is very sensitive. When does the boat next come in?"

"It's not due for three more days."

"That's good, we'll be gone by then, hopefully in three days secrecy won't be as important as it is now."

Rob opens the door of the plane and discreetly opens the bag containing Ali Bezir, who is conscious and blinking his eyes at the sudden influx of light.

Chris is dumbstruck. "Is that who I think it is?"

"Yes."

Giles speaks for the first time. "Fuck me." He looks nervously over to the rest of the people that had met the plane. "That is something I didn't expect, I don't think any of the guys with us will know who he is, but I would wait for a while until we ensure it is safe to bring him out."

Chris agrees. "As there aren't any televisions or newspapers on the island, it is unlikely that any of the locals will know who this unexpected guest is, but I'm sure some of our lodge guests will, we will need to ensure they don't see him."

They weren't going to take the risk with the staff, they need to contain the knowledge of Ali Bezir's presence to a small amount of their most trusted staff. Ali Bezir's face had been widely displayed in the international media for the last ten years and they didn't want the staff gossiping to the guests about their mysterious visitor. Any simple description could lead the guests to guess the identity of Ali Bezir.

Chris walks back over to the waiting group of locals, he speaks with them for a while, before half of them leave in the direction of the nearby town. When they are out of sight, the plane is unloaded, the approaching dusk helping to conceal the precious contents, which are carried by towards a series of nearby buildings by the lake side.

Giles and Chris had spent several years building up the unique beachside lodge known as Kaya Mawa with the help of the local islanders who provided the labour. The lodge was built out of stone and timber, in a unique architectural style which melded in so perfectly with the natural landscape that it almost appeared to be a natural rock formation.

They dragged the cargo into the bar restaurant which was only used during the daytime and tonight would be devoid of guests, all of whom dined in the luxurious main restaurant in the evenings. Here they finally were able to remove their hostage from the bag. They place Ali Bezir on a chair and tie him firmly to it in the centre of the room.

Their other passenger, Mbuji, is moved further down the beach to a smaller backpackers lodge by some of the staff, where he is put into a bed in one of the chalets to sleep off the remaining effects of the chloroform. He would wake the next morning with a headache and several thousands of dollars for his trouble.

The four westerners stand around Ali Bezir staring at him, while he returns the stare, individually looking into the eyes of all present, focusing on his captors the longest. Giles breaks the prolonged silence. "What are you going to do with him?"

To Andy, the plan was simple. "Hand him over to the yanks and claim the bounty on his head."

Rob knew the logistical operation would not be as simple as Andy made out. "We will need help from you though, if you are willing."

"Of course we will be willing, we always help out old friends, I guess the main help you'll need is transport, that is the least we can do. I've got a car in Nkhata Bay on the mainland you can use, it would be perfect, 4x4 with blacked out windows. I can get you there in my boat in the morning."

In one foul swoop, Chris had swiftly solved Rob's logistical concerns.

This delights Rob. "Excellent, we can relax now, I guess our guest is hungry and thirsty, he's been in that bag for nearly 24 hours."

Andy walks over to Ali Bezir and tears the tape off his mouth, unleashing a torrent of abuse and threats.

"I will hunt you all down to the end of the earth and inflict a death so painful on you fuckers that you will regret the day you set eyes on me. You don't have the faintest idea how far my influence reaches, I have friends everywhere, they will release me and you will be in a world of shit."

Andy silences him with a swift punch to the side of the head, causing Ali Bezir to display a dazed expression for a few seconds, then opening his mouth again to carry on his tirade, before sensibly having second thoughts.

One of the staff brings out a supply of cold fresh mango juice for the guests, including one which is contained in a sports bottle that they use to provide Ali Bezir with some much needed refreshment. After quenching Ali Bezir's thirst, the gag is replaced again to ensure his silence.

"It could be a problem getting him to eat something." Andy suddenly realises. He is not sure how they are going to do this, but knows they need to feed him to keep him alive.

Giles has already thought of a solution, something that was used on him when he had his tonsils out. He was unable to chew for a few days and a pastry chef found a novel way to feed him using the tool normally reserved for icing cakes. "Nothing is a problem when you have a blender and a pastry bag!"

This puzzles the two guests, but brings a smile to Chris' face.

"Let me demonstrate."

Giles goes into the kitchen, brings out the pastry bag to show them how a blended selection of nutrients could just be squeezed into Ali Bezir's mouth. As soon as he shows them the bag, the penny drops and further demonstration isn't needed, so he continues talking.

"Before we feed him, we should eat ourselves, the sight and smell of us eating will make him far more hungry and far less resistant, maybe even grateful."

Andy isn't convinced. "That I doubt, if I was about to be handed over to a nation that hates me, I would be doing everything I can to make it difficult, I'd rather we got it out of the way before we eat, at least we can enjoy the food and drink more then."

Rob agrees. "Yep, I'm with Andy, I would like to get him fed and safely secured, especially if you guys start on the spirits during dinner, it may be too much for me to handle on my own afterwards."

Giles nods and goes back into the kitchen, from where the sound of a blender is heard for a few minutes. When he returns the pastry bag is full, he offers it to Andy, who takes it grudgingly. Rob grabs the back of Ali Bezir's head and holds it pointing skywards very firmly. Giles rips off the tape and Andy forces the nozzle into Ali Bezir's mouth, squeezing gently. Ali Bezir swallows the entire contents without any fuss. He doesn't get a chance to say anything as the tape is quickly replaced after the last drop is squeezed out.

Giles claps his hands. "Excellent, we can now undertake some fine dining."

"I'd like to secure him a bit more first." Rob points at Ali Bezir. "I want to be sure he cannot escape, but somewhere I can keep an eye on him. We then need to make some firm arrangements for tomorrow. I've had too many late nights with you two where we've missed our transport the next day. If everything goes OK tomorrow, we can get back here and have a bit of relaxation for a while."

"Sounds like a plan." Chris beckons Giles over to move some of the tables to one side, clearing a space to where they drag Ali Bezir against the wall and chain him firmly to it. "Now we eat."

They all sit round a large circular dining table to one side of the room whilst the chef starts serving them local fish cooked with spices and wrapped in a banana leaf surrounded by balls of Nsima. Nsima is the local staple food made from ground maize flour, considered as essential to most local dishes as the potato is in the west. The smell of the food, when it arrives, is enough to make

Rob and Andy salivate heavily, especially when they realise they haven't eaten a proper meal for well over a day.

Kaya Mawa's finest wine is also brought out for the guests, although Rob sticks to the mango juice. All four around the table tuck into the succulent food, as they start reliving past experiences.

Rob and Andy had first visited Likoma Island on exercise with the army. Likoma was perfect for exercises, there was no other air traffic to content with, so the army could practise land and sea manoeuvres and more essentially, evacuations. It was something the locals enjoyed when they occurred, albeit infrequently, as it was a welcome distraction from the mundane side of an island life with little infrastructure.

Rob and Andy had returned to the island several times to get away from the bustle of the west, spending a few weeks just relaxing on unspoilt beaches and swimming in crystal clear waters. The same beaches and waters that attracted Chris and Giles several years later, when on a backpacking trip, they took a chance stop off from the old steam boat that serves as the lifeline to the many communities that live along the coast of Lake Malawi.

Giles and Chris saw an opportunity, which they seized, resulting in them spending many years building Kaya Mawa and its smaller cousin further along the coast, Mango Drift, to give other Westerners the opportunity to experience the beauty of the relatively unknown island. It was always a puzzle to them why it was so unknown, as its uniqueness should have made it a top destination for world travellers.

The main town was full of stone huts significantly different in style from other traditional African huts, it was dominated by the third largest cathedral in Africa, one that would dwarf many cathedrals in the west, it was a testament to Victorian engineering as it was partially built in Britain and shipped across the world to be planted on this tiny island. The difficulty in reaching the island though was probably the contributing factor to the lack of tourism, with only a weekly visit from the MV Illala, the steamboat plying its trade up and down the lake, being the practical way to reach the island for many years.

There was also the added obstacle that before Giles and Chris built their island lodges, there was nowhere official for a tourist to stay on the island, definitely nowhere with the height of luxury that Kaya Mawa could now offer with its bespoke guest rooms, suites and specially designed honeymoon cottage almost isolated on a rock jutting out into the lake. All of the accommodation was furnished exquisitely with some of the rooms boasting their own private pools.

It was a labour of love for Giles and Chris, the end result was stunning. Rob and Andy had seen it in development and would become some of its most frequent visitors when it was finished, building up a strong and lasting friendship with its creators. A friendship that was reflected in the hospitality they were receiving now.

They ate and shared stories of many fun nights spent on the island and also on the mainland. Such as at the full moon parties of Nkhata bay, where the festivities were heralded by fleets of small man powered fishing boats each bringing a handful of guests, each boat displaying their traditional lanterns on the bow that were used a lure for the fish. As the boats landed, the music would start up, a combination of western dance tunes and the traditional African drummers who lined the beach. They were some of the most magical party nights all had had, far more memorable than a night in any nightclub.

It was on one of these nights that they had met Mad Mike, an Australian who had a penchant for living an almost hermit like life, trying to find the remotest place he could live for a while, but also be in reaching distance of amenities such as bars and women when he needed them.

All four were standing around the bar at the back of the beach when they heard a massive scream of "SCORPION" followed by the toilet door being bashed open and a tall skinny, very scruffy man hopping out holding his foot. They had quickly gone to his aid and held him as they debated who would be brave enough to suck the venom out, when they came to the consensus that it would be better to get the squashed Scorpion to determine whether it was life threatening enough to warrant one of them going anywhere near the man's feet.

A quick search of the toilet brought them relief as all they found were the embers of a cigarette that looked as if someone had stood on. It matched the wound on his foot and after soaking his foot in a bucket of water, he decided they were all going to share his bottle of whisky for helping him. He turned out to have a wondrous amount of travelling stories and he was going to make this part of Malawi his home for a while. He liked the vibe. Introductions were made amongst the group and even though he stated he was born Mike, he explained how he had earned the name Mad Mike, a name given to him by a group of British travellers who were amazed at his nonstop partying and unpredictable conversations. It was a name he liked so much, he now introduced himself to people using it.

They all remembered him and that night fondly, prompting Andy to ask rhetorically. "I wonder what happened to him, where on earth he ended up? I bet it's somewhere we haven't even considered going yet."

"That's an easy one." Chris knew exactly where Mad Mike was. "He has built himself a little hut in the trees on Chizumulu Island, over there." Chris pointed towards the smaller of the two islands on the lake, a few kilometres away.

"He loves it, hardly gets bothered, can do whatever he does to keep himself occupied, the good news for him is that there is a bar over there that supplies him with drinks for the occasional odd job. He rows over here every couple of months, to spend an evening entertaining the guests with his stories and sometimes his guitar playing, which I must say has got a lot better than when we first met him."

This news went down well with Andy and Rob, they liked Mad Mike and took great heart to know that he was OK and was still providing the same entertainment for others that he provided for them on their first meeting, where he'd initiated drinking games, danced with tourists and locals and ended the night diving off the highest part of the cliff into the darkened waters of the lake. The world needed people like Mad Mike, harmless but amazing fun trying to find his own path in life.

"Say Hi to him from us next time you see him, hopefully we'll meet him when we get back here."

Rob was looking at his watch, it had gone ten and they were looking at a 6am start for the two hour boat ride to Nkhata bay, then after sorting a few things out in the town, a five hour drive to the capital, Lilongwe, which they intended to get to before the US embassy shut for the day, to drop off their special delivery.

They finished the drinks they had, retiring to bed at about ten thirty, with Rob and Andy being given one of the unoccupied premium rooms, ensuring they had a very relaxing sleep, safe in the knowledge that Ali Bezir was chained firmly to a wall in the en-suite bathroom.

They awake at around five thirty in the morning, with the sun just starting it's rise into the cloudless sky, lighting up the lake with incredible hues of red and orange. A quick shower was followed by toast and juice, which set them up for the day, saying goodbye to Giles and the staff that had helped them, before they carried all of their bags to Chris' pride and joy, an impressive power boat, one of the only private sources of transport on the island. There were no cars, only a few could afford boats, so Chris was quite often in demand as an expensive taxi for those who could afford it.

The boat could easily manage thirty knots, making it the fastest available way to the mainland over water, something they were all grateful for, as Rob and Andy were keen to offload their hostage now and remove all reasons to be concerned for their own or their hostage's safety. Little was said during the journey, apart from Giles giving an update on the lodges in Nkhata and the changes of ownership that had occurred recently.

All were run by westerners looking for an idyllic life away from the urban environment, but sooner or later they would get yearnings for some of the basics that weren't available. The lodges would change hands every few years, some more frequently than others. Some things in the town had remained constant, but that was mainly amongst the African business owners, who had no other life to get homesick over.

The boat arrived at the dockside at around eight in the morning. Chris moored his boat as close to the town as possible. The authorities paid little attention to him, he was a frequent visitor and they viewed his business on Likoma as a benefit to the area. One man on the mainland did pay attention to the boat and was waiting by the dockside when it came in.

Moses had met Andy and Rob many times, having had spent many drunken evenings with them in Nkhata Bay's only bar which had a live sports feed, watching English football as the two Brits educated Moses about the rivalries between certain teams.

Rob is the first to greet him. "Hi Moses, it's been a while."

Moses embraces Rob looking over to Andy. "Hello Mr Robert, hello Mr Coops, it is good to see you. I had no idea you were coming, if I had I would have got a lot more Green in."

He then embraces Andy in the same affectionate way. Moses ran a local guest house and the largest bar in the town. A bar which came alive later at night after the sport had finished, causing the much smaller sports bar to empty. His bar stocked the two main Malawian beers, Carlsberg Brown, preferred by the Africans, and the more expensive Carlsberg Green, the lager resembling the version found in the west. Malawi had the only Carlsberg brewery in Africa, it was an important institution in Malawian life, with its beverages being found in every bar.

Moses finally lets go of Andy, who catches his breath. "We are only on a brief visit this morning, we need to get to the capital, but we hope to be back in the next few days, then I'll have lots of your Green, maybe we can even get my friend to have some."

He nudges Rob who finally considers that when they return, it will be a good time to have a celebratory drink. "If all goes well, I'll be definitely having some."

Meanwhile Chris has retrieved his 4x4 from a lockup at the dockside and pulls it up next to the boat, getting out and opening the boot to put the luggage in while the other two catch up with Moses.

"I've got one favour to ask, can I borrow your phone?" Rob knows that Moses has one of the few private phones in the town and he wants to keep this conversation as secret as possible. Moses is keen to help his friends and leads Rob down to his guest house a few hundred metres from the dock. Rob emerges a few minutes later, looking fairly happy, before bidding farewell to Moses.

Chris gets out of the car which Andy has pulled up next to the guest house. "Don't worry about the car being traced back here, I have anonymous plates on it. Have a safe trip buddy, hope to see you very soon." He shakes Rob's hand, who reciprocates the farewell. "Hopefully it will be very soon, if not something has gone wrong!"

He gets in the car and they set off through the small but busy town, lined with market stalls, selling household goods, clothing and an assortment of maize, tomatoes and fish, sadly all of a quality that wouldn't make it to the supermarket shelves of Britain.

They leave the town and climb the hill that takes them on the road to Mzuzu, through the coffee and tobacco plantations that cover the area, giving it a vibrant green appearance. They reach Mzuzu in an hour and don't stop as they pass through. Although it's the capital of the northern region, it's an unattractive city and after staying there once, they prefer to travel straight through it, knowing it has little to offer them.

The journey south takes another four hours, through some sparse forest before they hit the plains, which have the occasional hill in the distance. After a couple of hours, during which they passed unhindered through a couple of police roadblocks, they arrive at Kasungu, the small town at the centre of the tobacco industry, surrounded by endless fields of tobacco plants. Kasungu is used for a brief stop to refuel and check their bags, Ali Bezir is still awake, but showing a more concerned look on his face, everything else is on order. Rob is concerned by the look on Ali Bezir's face. "We'd better get him some liquid, we'll stop a few miles outside of town to give it to him." To which Andy gives an indifferent shrug of the shoulders.

They stop again twenty minutes later, this time by the roadside where there are no people or vehicles in sight. Rob gets out, goes around to the back, opens the boot, opens the bag containing Ali Bezir and removes the tape on his mouth. Ali Bezir starts pleading with him, offering up a completely different tone than the previous night.

"Please think about what you are doing, you are sending me to a certain death and probably a lot of torture, for what? Five million dollars? I can give you double that to let me go, I will ensure you are protected, something the infidels cannot guarantee, you will spend the rest of your days looking over your shoulder, worrying about your family, not enjoying your riches. Only I can guarantee that you will be safe."

Rob is unmoved. "It's not about the money, it's about justice for the pain and suffering you have caused, the money is a bonus. We won't be worrying about you, we've spent a lifetime making enemies and that's something neither of us will dwell upon."

He gives Ali Bezir the drink, which is gulped down in seconds. Ali Bezir grabs a breath before trying to speak again, only to have the tape returned before he can start pleading again. Rob closes the bag and re-joins Andy in the front of the car.

"Let's go, I want to get rid of him as our problem as soon as possible."

Andy nods in agreement before he pulls away to drive the final two hours through the grassland plains until they reach the outskirts of the capital, Lilongwe.

As they approach the suburbs of Lilongwe, they pass through villages of circular mud huts with grass reed roofs, giving an indication they are near the airport. As they reach the airport, Andy pulls the car into the unloading area. Rob gets out with one of the bags, the one containing all of the money, precious stones and a copy of some of the video he shot. He enters the airport, where he deposits it in a secure locker as their insurance policy in case anything goes wrong and stops them claiming the reward the Americans were offering. Five million dollars was a fortune large enough to bring out the greediness in anyone they may encounter before they can safely hand over their hostage and ensure the reward is safely banked.

They drive for a further fifteen minutes before reaching the more developed urban suburbs, full of the large red roofed houses of the county's elite, situated amongst the tree lined valleys, the glint of the occasional swimming pool flaunting the owner's wealth, an unexpected sight in a country so poor.

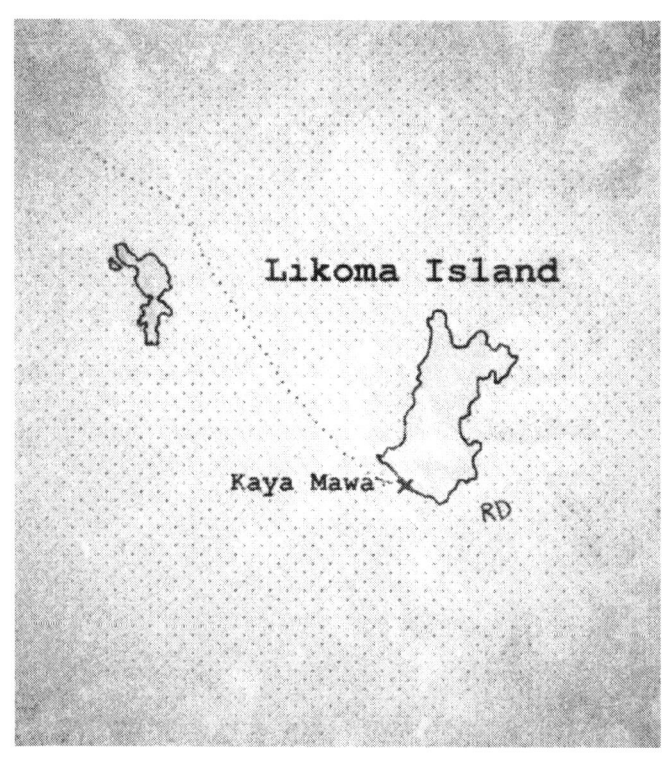

Likoma Island

Kaya Mawa ✕

RD

Capítulo Diez

Andy drives along some wide leafy avenues to reach the US embassy, a large compound hidden amongst the trees, where he pulls the car up outside of the gate to speak to the guard. He winds the window down and addresses the guard with a friendly smile and a hint of a European accent.

"Hello, we rang a few hours ago, we are expected."

The guard looks at them. "Names and Identification please?"

"Reinhart Drescher and Andreas Clausnitzer." They hand over their German passports, they were taking no chances, it was still best to conceal their true identities until they knew they were in the clear. They didn't want the possibility of any repercussions.

The guard takes their passports and makes a call on the phone. He hangs up after speaking for a few seconds and returns to address the two visitors. "Pull your car just inside the gate, someone is coming down to see you."

They pass through the gate into the embassy courtyard where they wait to be met. The guard uses a mirror to check under the car for anything suspicious and after a few passes is satisfied that there isn't an obvious threat. Over five minutes pass before three men emerge from the embassy, the central man is silver haired and very broad. He reminds them of an American actor, the name of which eludes them. He is accompanied by two leaner men in dark suits, all are displaying forbidding expressions, giving nothing away.

As the broad man approaches the car, the occupants get out and shake his offered hand. "Good Afternoon. I am Charles Sayer. I am an official with the US Embassy, I believe you have something of grave national significance for us, which was too confidential to discuss on the telephone." He doesn't introduce his companions.

Reinhart leads the conversation. "That is correct. When you see it you will understand why we couldn't discuss this over the phone."

"I will be disappointed if you are wasting my time, or this is some sort of prank, we will be forced to detain you for questioning, so I will give you this last chance to rethink, apologise if you were mistaken and swiftly leave."

"No, that is not necessary, we are quite sure you want to see what we have, you will most definitely want it."

Sayer studies Reinhart when he says this and is satisfied they are genuine and curious enough to want to see what they have, while the two other men stand motionless, arms folded with fixed stares directed at both of the visitors.

Reinhart leads Sayer to the car and opens the back, while Andreas stays with the other two. He unzips the holdall to reveal Malek Ali Bezir, who is awake and looking at them with blinking eyes.

Sayer is dumbstruck.

Sayer composes himself, returns from the back of the car and speaks to the two Americans.

"Right, this is something we are very interested in. It is of national importance to us and potentially the biggest story of the year. I cannot allow the Malawians to see this yet, we urgently need to keep it under wraps. We need to arrange to get the contents of this car into the embassy unseen. Can you arrange for all non US staff to gather in the rear courtyard while we unload the contents? A simple fire alarm should do it without causing too much concern."

The two Americans turn and walk back into the embassy, shortly afterwards the fire alarm sounds.

Sayer explains the need for secrecy while they wait for the staff to evacuate. "As you'll understand, the less people that are aware of this at the moment, the better. We want to interrogate our new friend without a lot of press interference. We will announce it when we are ready."

Sayer gets out his mobile phone and walks out of earshot. He spends a few minutes on the phone before he returns. "OK, can you move your car as close to the embassy door as possible, then we will load the bags directly into the embassy and take them to a safe room."

The Germans acknowledge him.

Sayer continues. "It is best not to talk until we get into the Embassy, where we can fully debrief you. We have some specialists on their way who have expertise in this area." The two visitors don't need a detailed explanation of which department the specialists work for, they have worked closely with many such specialists before.

Both Germans nod agreement before Andreas gets into the car and pulls it up next to the main door of the embassy. As they unload the bags, another car passes through the gate and approaches them, parking just to one side. It has US diplomatic plates on it. Several men get out of the car, all in dark suits, one of whom talks to Sayer out of earshot. He is seen nodding, then walks over to the waiting visitors.

He is fairly typical of agency staff they have worked with before, stern but plain looking enough not to stand out in a crowd or give a second glance, short cropped hair wearing a stereotypical dark suit and tie. He has an expression of someone who has just won the lottery on a rollover week.

"Hi. Jim Rogers is the name." He shakes the hands of both Germans, while Reinhart performs the introductions. "Reinhart and Andreas."

Rogers looks at them questionably for a second before continuing. "I'm here to help with this situation, Sayer has just briefed me fully on the contents of your car. I must say I'm impressed and I'd like to thank you guys for bringing this man to us. It has been a long search for him, a very long search where many lives have been lost. We will give you guys a proper debriefing inside the Embassy, but I'd like to find out a few details as soon as we get in the safe room, such as where and how did you get him and why did you come here?"

Andreas moves the car out of the way of the door as the rest all continue inside. The bags are carried inside by Rogers' colleagues, they pass through the main reception, into a side room and through a further door before descending some steps into a secured, soundproof area with several doors leading off a main corridor to adjoining rooms. The whole area is sparsely decorated in pristine white paint.

The bag containing Ali Bezir is taken into one room, while Rogers, Andreas, Reinhart and another man gather in the adjacent room. Both rooms are fairly large, with a one way mirror between the two, which is used to watch Ali Bezir being removed from the bag and untied. Ali Bezir offers little resistance, suffering fatigue from nearly two days containment. There is a table to one side containing food and drink, which is offered to him. He accepts the offer graciously, gulping down two litres of water before taking some fruit and slowly eating it, every action being watched silently from the room next door.

Rogers introduces the other man, a much older man, wearing a shirt and tie without a jacket. "This is my colleague, George Jones."

Jones shakes the hand of each man. "I'd just like to thank you two guys for bringing in what is essentially our number one target in the fight against terrorism. He has managed to evade us for many years."

Andreas smiles at him. "You are welcome."

Jones wants to ensure that the Germans will not withhold any information which could be vital. "I will be taking notes, but will only be noting information that is crucial to us. You and your dealings will not be noted and they need not sit on any official record."

When Rogers is satisfied that Ali Bezir will be occupied for a while and there will be nothing of interest he turns to the two guests. Rogers does all the talking, while Jones takes notes on a small notepad. "Well then, Reinhart and Andreas, which I doubt is your real names, but hey, I've been in the business long enough to know the relevant questions to ask and what to just ignore, so let's just get down to business, where the hell did you find him?"

Reinhart speaks for the two men. "Brazzaville."

Rogers is surprised. "The Republic of the Congo, not somewhere I would have expected to find him, but half an hour ago I wouldn't have expected the item of grave national significance for us that was being delivered in Malawi by two Europeans to be him either."

Rogers turns to Jones. "Find out if anyone else detected any unusual activity in the Republic of the Congo in the last few weeks and how He," indicating Ali Bezir. "has managed to slip past all of our surveillance and arrive in a major capital city, to be captured by two, what I assume are, at the moment tourists."

Jones goes to the door and starts speaking on a phone, returning as the debriefing continues.

Rogers turns back to Reinhart. "Anyway, please continue, I'm not sure I want to know what you were doing in the Congo, but I'd like to know how you came to bump into our friend here, especially as none of our agents in the country managed to do detect him, then how on earth were you then able to get him stuffed into a bag, then finally, how you managed to end up on our embassy doorstep over a thousand miles away."

Andreas looks at Reinhart, who shrugs and looks at Rogers. "We will tell you the information that will be valuable to yourselves, but you must understand that for reasons you must be very familiar with, we cannot reveal all of the details, most of which will be superfluous to your needs."

"OK, fair enough, but there may be follow up questions if I'm not fully satisfied." He knew that he would not be fully satisfied without all of the details, but is prepared to compromise with enough detail to be able to rectify his agency's failings, after all he is delighted to have the most desired prisoner in the nation, one that will enhance his career beyond his wildest dreams.

Reinhart continues. "Well, we were in the country doing research on rainforests."

Rogers raises a sceptical eye, but lets him continue, the reason they were there was far less important than why Ali Bezir was there and how they met and captured him.

"We had been there a while and made many local friends, the Congolese do not come into contact with many westerners, especially any that could be classed as friends. We were treated with the greatest hospitality wherever we went, it was like a massive status symbol to have a western friend. We used to eat at a few regular restaurants and one night we were invited to a party at the house of a man who we used to have a few drinks with now and again. He said he had some important friends from overseas coming and would like some westerners there, especially ones who would intrigue his guests with their knowledge of the local rainforests and their secrets."

Rogers is starting to look more cynical, uttering an elongated OK.

Reinhart tries to quell his cynicism before he wanted more details. "Well, we had been to a couple of local gatherings before, this man had been at many of them. He liked hearing how we would use a hot air balloon to travel around the canopy of the rainforest, gathering unknown fruits, seeds and epiphytes which could change the world, he liked hearing our views on what they could be used for. I think he was intrigued by the latent value these things could have to the west."

Rogers smiles, he wasn't buying the story, but it would do, for now.

"We went to this party, which was held in a non-descript house in one of the suburbs, there was nothing apparent to raise any alarms with us, there weren't any guards or an armed presence, but it had a few people we met before. Half an hour into the party some Arabs turned up, one of whom we recognised as Malek Ali Bezir, someone that anyone from the west would have instantly recognised. We feigned total ignorance, mainly for our safety, but he wasn't interested in us really."

Rogers is now puzzled. "So you get invited to a party out of the blue, with such important overseas visitors such as Ali Bezir, when we have had well trained undercover agents who had tried to infiltrate such events before, very unsuccessfully?"

"Call it more luck than persistence. Anyway, the party was just a standard affair, with lots of drinks and women available, as was customary at all the parties we had been invited to. We kept to ourselves, occasionally telling one of our rainforest adventures to some of the guests, didn't really see much of the Arabs, I had assumed they had left soon after they arrived, then after a couple of hours all hell breaks loose, the power went out, there was lots of shouting and lots of loud bangs and gunfire. I assumed it was a police raid, we just hid behind a sofa. I've never been in a situation like that before and I was scared for my life."

Andreas finally joins in. "like Reinhart says, it was a very scary moment, it was like being in an action movie.

I have never been so scared in my life. I don't know how we got out alive."

Reinhart continues. "But as you can see, we did. The noise and the shooting stopped after about ten minutes, but we stayed hidden for another thirty minutes until we knew it was safe. When we slowly poked our heads above the sofa, we saw nothing was moving. There was a smell of gunpowder in the room, the whole house was in total silence. We crawled out and started crawling around the room looking for the door, I found one, went through it and when we went into the room, we heard breathing, I crawled over and found Ali Bezir, still alive but unconscious, my first thought was to leave him, but then I thought of all the terrible things he had done, I knew we had to bring him to justice."

Rogers snorts a little. "Justice, very noble, nothing to do with a large reward then?"

"Of course we'd be lying if I said that hadn't crossed my mind, but getting a reward was a long way off, we needed to get him out of there and to a US embassy."

"A close embassy like one a thousand miles away?" Rogers wasn't buying their story but is persisting, thinking that there must be some truth in this somewhere, otherwise Ali Bezir wouldn't be here.

"I'll get to that later, first we had to get him out. I whispered to Andreas that we needed to quickly find a way to get him out of here, but we needed to check the coast was clear. It was a small house and we quickly searched all the rooms, no one was left alive, apart from Ali Bezir. His accomplices were dead, all the rest of the guests were African and some of them were armed heavily. We were the only ones left alive in the house though, I found a bag in one of the rooms, we stuffed Ali Bezir into it, then went outside and grabbed one of the guests' cars, they weren't going to need it that night. We drove instantly to the US embassy, but it was closed and unoccupied, so we needed to find another country to go quickly and there was a lot of police activity starting to happen."

Rogers leans over to Jones and whispers in his ear, which causes him to return to the phone, using it for a few seconds out of earshot.

Rob pauses for while the Americans speak, before continuing where he had left off. "We had very few options available to us, we didn't want to be stopped with such a wanted man in our possession, so we went to the only man we could trust, the pilot we had been using for our trips in the rainforest. We gave him a story about being chased by armed maniacs and needed to get as far away as quick as possible, he was eager to help, he said he was flying to Malawi the next day to deliver some goods, but could leave sooner.

An hour later we were in the air and on our way here. As soon as we landed, I have no idea what town it was, but it was in the north and had a small dirt airstrip, so we borrowed a car, phoned the embassy and drove straight here."

Rogers sits back, folds his arms and muses for a few minutes on the story he had just heard. He taps Jones on the shoulder and they go over to a corner of the room for a discussion, while Andreas looks at Reinhart and gives a nod of approval for the story.

After a few minutes' discussion, Rogers and Jones returns to their seats, Rogers places his thumbs in his chin in pensive thought, pausing for ten seconds before discussing his thoughts with the Germans.

"Right, that's a great story, it is plausible in places, but I'm not convinced, in fact I'm doubtful about most of it and I'm only prepared to accept a small part of it as potentially being the truth. The one piece I can verify is that the US embassy in the Congo is closed, we do not have a visible presence there for the moment, however there are US diplomats in the country you could have contacted had you the time. But I'm not going to dwell on that technicality."

He pages through the notebook that Jones has been using to write down as much as he can of Reinhart's story.

"Firstly, I find it very hard to believe that the world's most wanted terrorist would just happen to be at a domestic party in the Republic of Congo. The logistics of getting there, getting past all the border checks, avoiding all of our surveillance, just to have a few drinks with some Africans that are not even close to being on our radar, seem to stretch the limits of my imagination."

Reinhart opens his mouth to say something, but is stopped by Rogers' open handed gesture.

"Secondly, if Ali Bezir had managed to do all that and attended a party, I'm sure there would have been a lot of armed presence, security would have been extremely high, which brings me to my third point, with all that high security, I find it hard to believe that they would just happen to invite some unknown German ecologists. I've never seen a social event where ecologists and terrorists are mingling freely, but then again there are lots of things I haven't seen.

The next point is the shootout, I've seen such shootouts in films, but never in real life. They never ever end where the two innocent people and the most dangerous person in the room, just happen to be the last men standing. Then there is the trip from the party, even in war zones, that amount of gunfire would attract someone from authority, so it was impressive you managed to make it to an airport without passing any roadblocks or being stopped by police, finally, it's very coincidental that you happened to know someone who was willing to fly you a thousand miles at such short notice."

Rogers pauses for effect and to judge the reaction of the two men in front of him, but is disappointed by the total lack of reaction. "So I guess you can understand, if I'm a little cynical about your story, but I can offer my interpretation of your version of events, we can then negotiate a little to reach something we are both happy with."

Reinhart shrugs his shoulders. "OK, we will listen, but that is what happened and I can't see the point of negotiation over the story."

Rogers dismisses this, starting to offer his version of events. "OK, here's what I think happened. I'm happy with the setting being the Congo, I'm not sure why you would have made that up, although it would explain why we didn't detect Ali Bezir. If it was here or in one of the neighbouring countries, my team would have been on him like a pack of wolves before he had taken his second step. I'm not sure you are really ecologists, or even German, your accents are just not European enough.

He again looks for a reaction that doesn't materialise. "So, I believe you were in the Congo, it's the sort of place where guys that look like you can find highly paid security work. How long you were there, I'm not sure, but I can believe that you probably were mixing with some unsavoury people. Somehow or other, through these contacts, you came across Ali Bezir, used whatever skills you have to isolate and capture him, then stole a plane and headed as far away as you could to the safest country you could, which is why you are here. It's much simpler and much more believable, I'd just like to know the detail about the encounter with Ali Bezir, I'm not really bothered about how you actually got here, it is not something that will trouble our security services."

He sits back, looking very smug with himself, whilst Reinhart focuses on him intensely. "Can I speak with my colleague for a while, in private?" Rogers nods and leaves the room with Jones.

Andy turns to Rob. "I was almost convinced, but these guys are no mugs. I say we give them a little of the truth, they will be using all their resources to identify us anyway, just enough to satisfy his curiosity, hopefully he won't want to know much more."

They return to their chairs after knocking on the door, causing the two Americans to return.

Reinhart looks at the two Americans in the face. "OK, some of that may have been, shall we say embellished, but we will give you what you need. We were in the Congo doing some work for another government, the nature of which is unimportant. We had managed to infiltrate a local group there, who were having a little gathering of some players in the terrorist field, where the guest of honour turned out to be Ali Bezir. We were totally surprised, but didn't want to miss the opportunity, so we used chloroform on him and smuggled him out in a car. We then hired a plane and flew here, which was the nearest safe embassy."

Andreas needs to clarify, as being an agent could lead to even trickier questions. He also wants to show that there was not one dominant partner. It's a technique that they employ a lot, one that gives them a psychological edge in this type of situation. It is harder to break two men down than concentrate on one. "We are freelance, we were there to do a specific task. We just got very lucky to encounter Ali Bezir."

Reinhart continues. "There was a lot of secrecy involved, as you can imagine. No one mentioned he would be there. He was well hidden when he arrived. He was handing out money to some African groups."

Rogers is pleased he is now getting the truth he wanted. "Interesting, we will have to have an inquiry to find out how he slipped through our net. Freelance eh, I can guess the sort of work you are involved in, but as I said that is not important. What about the other guests? Were they aware he was there and more importantly would they be trying to find him?"

Reinhart feels no need to elaborate in his answers. "Yes, but I doubt it. We neutralised all the other guests. It was what we were required to do."

Rogers is intrigued, this could be better than he expected. "So no one actually knows about this, apart from us in this room, Sayer and my two colleagues who are looking after Ali Bezir?"

"No."

"Excellent, this will buy us a lot of time to extract some information from Ali Bezir. I trust as men in the line of work you are in, you can be trusted not to break the news."

"Without a doubt, we understand secrecy very well, we are really only interested in the reward."

Rogers smiles and pats Reinhart on the shoulder. This will be far less complicated than a diplomatic bargain for something from the US. "We will get along just great."

Rogers rubs his hands together. He is keen to get more detailed information, but wants to ensure the comfort of his guests. "Make yourselves comfortable. Do you want anything to eat or drink?"

Reinhart realises he hasn't had anything to drink for a while. "A coffee would be very welcome, black, no sugar."

Andreas is also thirsty. "Yes, I'd like a coffee too, fresh, not instant."

Rogers gets on an intercom and requests four coffees. "One of my colleagues will be in shortly with the coffee, we will wait until he has left before you continue with some further details."

The Germans nod. Thirty seconds later a man enters the room, carrying a tray of coffee. He places the tray on the table, puts a pot in the middle and puts a cup in front of each chair before leaving.

Andreas wants to get their motives out up front, lessening the chance of any political motivation. The last thing they needed was lengthy questioning about their politics, which is essentially sell out to the highest paying western government. "Well we did it for the money, but it was an important thing to do. As soon as we saw him, we knew we had to get him to the US authorities."

Rogers is satisfied with this version of events. "At the end of the day the end result is the same. We have our man. Now what we want to do is find out what we can learn from this."

Rogers explains what he needs to know in more detail. "Now, we want you to go slowly, ensuring you don't miss anything out. You are not on trial here, any illegal acts you may have committed will not go any further. We are primarily concerned with determining how our systems failed in picking this guy up, when yours worked. Now, when did you arrive in the Congo, why and who did you contact."

Andreas takes up the story. "Well we arrived in the Congo 3 days ago, as part of a job we had to do."

For the first time, Jones starts asking some of the questions, aware that he is the only silent person in the room, not wanting to seem like an insignificant note taker for Rogers. "What job was that?"

"We work for governments, eliminating undesirable people. They don't want any connection with the incidents, so they use us."

Jones understands. "I think we know the sort of work you mean, almost mercenaries but no need to go into full blown wars."

However Rogers wants to know more. Any government with interests in the region could have a conflict of interest with the US. "Which government were you working for?"

Reinhart knows the consequences of revealing this information. "It is classified."

Rogers pushes further. "It is something we need to know to be able to verify our source. Your dealings with them will not leave this room."

"It is still classified, we didn't even know ourselves. We only dealt with a middle man."

Rogers shakes his head. "These damn Europeans, they like to be seen as so squeaky clean, yet they have bloodier hands than the USA."

Jones doesn't want to get bogged down in trying to find out the country involved. They have a good idea about who would be interested in the Congo. "Carry on. We can get by without knowing the specific government. We can safely assume it's one of the Europeans."

Andreas continues with the story. "OK. Well, we made contact with a local man who was an agent for this government, he had infiltrated a local gang led by Thembezi Umbekie. Umbekie was our target. Our contact introduced us to a lieutenant of the gang, who was very keen to meet us. Our cover story was that we were Argentinian arms dealers who were keen to move into Africa. It did not take much to impress this lieutenant who was willing to believe anything we said, as he would gain a lot of credibility in the gang for bringing us in. All it took was a mention of missiles and large arms, with some profits to go to him."

Rogers was surprised. "This guy basically took you at face value?"

Reinhart clarifies. "We had prepared a good cover story, which we have used before. He actually got to hear of what we could do via a third party, who praised us so much, we could do no wrong in his eyes. This is what we are very good at, the preparation work. It helps us keep alive."

Rogers is disturbed by this revelation, which may have fooled his government. "I see. We may have to look into this, as we had been getting reports of some Argentinian arms dealers doing well, but could not trace them back to South America. Your cover story could have been too effective that we may have targeted you."

Andreas continues with the events of the past few days. "Anyway, this guy, Kwanza was his name, he took in everything we said and arranged for us to have a meeting with Umbekie, effectively being our credibility sponsor, as opposed to the agent working as our middleman. We met with Umbekie the next day, he was very forthcoming. Kwanza had obviously been praising us up to him and like Kwanza, Umbekie saw us as a potential way to impress his peers. He invited us to a gathering he had in one of his houses, which was last night.

We were fully trusted, which was odd since it was after such a short time. However it was easy to smuggle weapons into this gathering. We didn't have a plan to do the job last night, just to set up a one-to-one with Umbekie. We weren't happy about going into something like that unarmed, as it could have been a trap. Our contact had warned us that there was a lot of border activity, but there was no confirmation of who was involved. It wasn't a trap though, it turned out that there were a lot of high profile terrorist leaders there."

Reinhart interjects. "Guys we recognised from news coverage."

Jones confirms. "We did notice a lot of unusual border activity yesterday in the region. However there was a lot more activity on some of the north eastern state borders that took the attention away from the Congo. That is very clever of them. We'll have to look out for border traffic diversions in future."

Reinhart corrects him, which causes a stern look from Rogers. "Not any more you won't."

Rogers corrects Reinhart. "The fight against terrorism will never be over."

Andreas takes up from where he left off. "Then Ali Bezir came in. We knew this was going to be an opportunity not to be missed. Luckily, we had formulated a simple plan when our contact said about the border activity, which we were able to modify. There were about 30 or so people in the house, in about half a dozen rooms. We started when Ali Bezir was introduced to us, quickly neutralising him with chloroform spray. When the others went to help him, we struck. We were quick. They didn't expect an attack from the inside, so were taken completely unawares. It took less than a minute to eliminate everyone. We used silencers so were not heard. There was an instance when a few shots were fired at us from one of the other rooms, but they were muffled, very little would have been heard outside."

Jones is concerned. "You took everyone out? This could cause power struggles in some groups. Have you any idea who they were exactly? We need to know this so we can act quickly."

"Some Moroccan called Hasan was the only guy we really spoke to, but there were Africans from the DRC,

Burundi, Cameroon and some Arabs, but I can't really remember their names."

Jones turns to Rogers. "We need to get our guy in the Congo to find out some names of missing people, so we can put a plan into action."

Rogers confirms. "I'm on it."

Rogers walks over to a phone and starts speaking into it out of earshot. This confuses the Germans, as they were under the impression that Rogers was in charge. The Americans are playing the same game as them, ensuring that they didn't know who was the dominant partner, which served no particular purpose, in this case.

Jones continues with the questioning. "So there was little resistance and you managed to get away easily?"

Reinhart takes his turn. "None really considering. It was very easy, there were very few weapons in the house. We stuffed Ali Bezir into the holdall you have now, then just walked out to our waiting contact, who drove us to our hotel."

"Did he ask many questions?"

"No. We just told him the job had been done and to get us out of there quickly."

"And he knew about Ali Bezir?"

Reinhart decides its best that Michael is left out of this. "No, we weren't going to tell him, as he may have panicked. And anyway, the less people that knew about it, the easier we would find it to smuggle Ali Bezir out of the country. Five million dollars is enough for any person to want to try and get a share."

Jones is satisfied. He has dealt with the type of men who do similar work to Reinhart and Andreas. He has always been impressed by the way they conceal information from those they work with. Their contact did not need to know about Ali Bezir, so why would they tell him, he could turn on them and take the reward for himself. "Good. You are very thorough. So you got back to the hotel, how did you get out?"

"The hotel understood that we were research scientists studying the rainforest, so we were able to charter a plane through them, explaining that we needed to perform some night study. As far as they were concerned we were only flying up river for several hours and it was still early in the evening so they didn't ask any questions."

"I'm amazed at the ease with which you managed to pull this off. It should have taken a massive military operation to get this guy. But you have managed it, partly through luck and partly through good planning."

"Good planning keeps us alive. After all, what's the point of carrying out jobs like this if you aren't able to spend the earnings."

Andreas finishes off. "We went to the airport. Told the pilot where we wanted to go, then knocked him out when we were airborne. The flight plan meant that the authorities would not expect him back for over eight hours. All he had to do was fly back when he woke up here."

Jones nods in approval. "Having Ali Bezir in our hands is more important than a minor predicament of some pilot who has to fly back home for a day."

Reinhart smiles. "Hopefully."

Jones continues. "There are a couple of points I want to go over. Firstly did you know how Ali Bezir got into the country?"

Andreas shakes his head. "They didn't say. He didn't turn up until after we had all been there for a while, he was heavily concealed. As you can understand, there was a lack of information being shared about his attendance."

"Any idea what he was doing in a place with such minor players?"

Andreas shrugs his shoulders. "None at all. I think he was trying to spread his tentacles, maybe trying to get all these groups working together a little more. He met with a couple of them in private before we took him out."

Reinhart points out the obvious. "It was a pointless meeting now."

"Did anyone else know that he was there, does anyone else know you had him?"

"No. We took out everyone at the party, including his driver and escort. I'd be surprised if they introduced him to anyone else before getting there."

"So would I, but you have to check. Did anyone else know you were there?"

"No. We were driven there by our contact, everyone else who had met us with regards to this was dead."

"Well, all the loose ends seem to be tied up. I don't think there is much else I need to ask you."

Reinhart is keen to see an end to this though, he wants to get back home and start enjoying his life.

"Surely you need to know the bank account with which to put our reward in?"

Jones laughs. "Ha ha ha, I don't deal with the finance side of things. I deal with the field operations side, but my colleague will ensure that you are rewarded in full. Thank you gentlemen, I now need to speak to our guest, I trust you will not mention this episode to anyone until we have made a press release, which will give us more time to chat with him."

"Rest assured, we have been in this business long enough to know not to talk about anything with anyone. Not even with each other when others are listening."

"I thought so. Thank you very much. I will leave you in the hands of my esteemed colleague, Mr Rogers."

Jones gets up, shakes the hands of both Germans and walks out of the room. Rogers walks back over. He addresses the two men. "OK, I have booked you into a hotel in the city. It is a good hotel and the US government will pick the tab up."

Reinhart and Andreas thank him.

"We have booked you in for two nights. I take it you do not need to stay longer than that. I will need a way of wiring the reward money for Ali Bezir's capture to you, obviously we don't deal in cash for sums that large. We will give you some local money to tide you over. I will also need your passports. I can ensure all Malawian entry requirements are met."

"Two nights will be fine. We will want to get back to Germany now our work is over. We will give you the details when I have managed to unpack our bags."

The Germans shake hands with Jones and Rogers, who beckons them up and leads them out of the embassy. "Excellent, there is no immediate rush." He still doesn't believe they are German, but it doesn't matter.

They return to their car and follow Rogers in his car to a hotel only five minutes away.

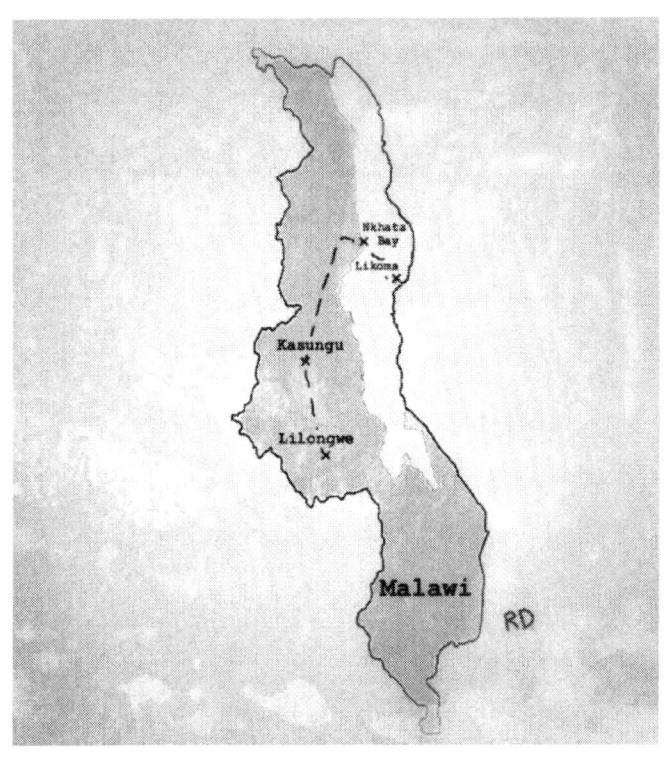

Capítulo Once

The Sunbird hotel is surrounded by a single storey whitewashed wall with a terracotta roof. It is a pleasant hotel, but not the most luxurious place they have stayed in the last week. They are not about to say this to the Americans.

Rogers handles all the formalities at reception before he gives them several hundred dollars in Malawi Kwacha and saying farewell. They are shown to a room which is clean but basic compared to western standards. When they are finally alone, Rob turns to Andy. "Well, what do you think?"

Andy is not about to say anything inappropriate until he is sure no one is listening. "Very nice room."

Andy starts removing light fittings and looking at other small hiding places that could conceal listening devices, finding several around the room. Andy shows some of them to Rob, who decides it would be better to leave them to avoid arousing any more suspicion, mouthing the letters C I A slowly, followed by "leave them where they are." Andy nods.

Rob grabs a notepad and starts writing. He hands it to Andy, who reads the note. "I'm not completely happy, I think they were completely shocked with what we brought them, but they weren't shocked enough and seemed too obsessed with us."

Andy writes on the pad then hands it to Rob. "I know, we need to be very careful, I don't trust them, they seemed very keen to keep this under wraps, there could be a lot to gain from taking all the credit for Ali Bezir's capture."

Rob writes a note which says. "I'm suspicious of these guys, something is not right, too many questions about who knew about it. They were far too happy that no one else did." Andy nods in agreement.

Rob stops writing and starts speaking for the people listening. "Well I'm tired, I am going to take a shower and get some sleep. It has been a busy couple of days."

Andy nods. "I need to rest too."

Rob walks into the shower. "After I have had a shower, I'm going to nip down the town."

Andy. "Good idea, I'll have a shower and come with you. It will be nice to have a bit of time to be a tourist,

I've not seen the delights that Lilongwe has to offer for a while."

After they have showered and rested, they leave the hotel and walk down to the local market, only a few streets away from the hotel, talking discreetly as they walk, very aware that they may well be being followed. Night has fallen, but the city is still bustling, with the population trying to make a living off the meagre amount of tourism.

Stopping at the first stall they reach, they sift through the trinkets it displays while Rob speaks, displaying some concern in his hushed tone. "I trust them as far as I can throw them, we should definitely be on our guard. There could be many reasons why they don't want it known they have MAB."

"I know. His capture was not as well received as I'd expected. They even seemed a bit pissed off about it. Our guard must be up all the time."

"Don't worry my guard is not coming down. I just want to get this over and retire in peace, I am starting to think that it may not have been worth bringing Ali Bezir to the Americans as the other bag we have has to be close to what the reward is worth. I took a quick count in the plane, it's well into seven figures. US dollars, plus all the value of all the stones."

Andy picks up a small drum from the stall, feigning an interest in buying it. "Have you noticed the guy following us?" The stall owner starts to haggle with them, to which Andy responds with a shake of the head as he replaces the drum.

Rob has spotted the man trailing their every move. "Yes, he is out of earshot though. As long as we don't do anything that causes him to take any action, he can follow us all day, just doing mundane touristy stuff should bore him until he loses interest and drops his guard."

Andy is not so sure. "Well, I'm all for doing some mundane things, but I'm not sure he will lose interest before I do. I take it you have been formulating some plans in case there is a situation where we have to get out quickly."

Andy knows Rob too well, who has been assessing their options continually. "Of course, but there are so many possibilities that for once I'm a bit stumped. Our best option is that the yanks just pay up and leave us alone, which I think still is the most likely option. I hope they are just being cautious following us. If things start to get out of hand and we are at risk, we have a few options, make it to the airport as quick as possible and hope the bag is worth enough for a comfortable retirement. Another option is to confront them, which is the last thing I want or we could just hang around here for a few days, when some friendly faces will be around. Whatever situation we face, I have prepared something which will force their hand with option one."

Andy is puzzled by the last two statements. "Friendly faces? And what have you prepared?"

"I'll tell you the first part shortly, but we need to find somewhere quieter for the second."

Andy knows how Rob thinks and trusts him to reveal what he needs to know at the opportune moment. The stall owner has continued haggling unilaterally, dropping his price to a few Kwacha, a price Andy finds hard to refuse and reluctantly buys the drum.

Rob indicates a nearby street which has several restaurants. "Let's grab a drink and something to eat, it's been nearly a day since we had a substantial meal, I don't want our energy levels to drop."

They walk up the street and select one of the many restaurants that line it, sitting at one of the tables by the side of the street, giving them a perfect view of the whole street. Their tail tries to walk past inconspicuously, selecting a table at a restaurant further up the road. He is satisfied he hasn't been spotted when his two targets pay no attention to him.

A waiter comes to serve them, they order fresh fruit juice and omelettes without looking at the menu. They sit in silence as they wait for the food, just observing the activity on the street, making certain they cannot be overhead.

Andy's curiosity cannot be contained any longer. "So what have you got prepared?"

"Insurance, I made sure we had video evidence of Ali Bezir, so I filmed him in the plane. I also took some good footage of him with the day's newspapers when you were busy drinking on the island, I even got him to speak a few words. There was also other footage of us handing him over to the Americans, I had the camera running in the car as we entered the embassy. The videos are safe, I've only got the footage to force the Americans' hand if needed. And don't worry, we don't feature in it, there are a couple of copies just to make sure, with one copy in the bag at the airport as a backup. I have some plans to get it released to the media if necessary. Hopefully it won't come to that, but I don't want us to be in a position where we have nothing to bargain with."

Andy is impressed, he knew Rob would have taken precautions, but hadn't realised he had been so thorough. "Is there anything I need to know about the video, just in case?"

"Nope, it's all taken care of. Now it's just a waiting game, I'm expecting the Americans to show their hand within the next day, so let's just finish the food and have a night on the town." Andy smiles at this, he knows that a night on the town here will be a tame affair.

As they finish eating, some music starts up at the bar across the road, an acoustic guitar being played at a frantic speed, accompanied by some very out of tune singing in an accent they cannot fail to recognise. The noise causes many in the street to move slightly away from the bar, but not Rob and Andy, they hurriedly finish their drinks, leave some bank notes on the table which will cover the bill plus a large tip and walk over to the bar, where they see the familiar scruffy sight of Mad Mike over-enthusiastically belting out his unique version of Rockin' in the free world.

The bar is one of the largest in the street, often popular with westerners. It has some external seating in front of a long rectangular room filled with tables, chairs and a bar running down the right hand side. It is also one of the few bars that has a large video screen on the back wall. It is plainly furnished, mainly in wood, but would not look out of place in any Mediterranean tourist resort.

Mad Mike spots them, waves, causing him to miss a few chords, then totally loses track of the tune, continuing out of sync with the lyrics for a minute before giving up. He slings the guitar over his shoulder and bounds over to his two friends.

His enthusiasm is limitless as he grabs them both in a strong bear hug, shouting at them in his strong Australian accent. "Fellas, fellas, how totally unexpected, wow, I never knew you were in the country and for you to be in the area when I was gigging, wow, awesome, I mean for you to be here and bump into me."

Rob has new possibilities that are racing through his mind, of all the people they didn't expect to bump into, Mad Mike was one of the most welcome and could be the most useful distraction.

Andy is the first to get a word in. "Mike, we never expected to see you, how are you doing? How come you are here, we thought you were on Chizumulu?"

These are too many questions in one go for Mike, but he attempts to answer them all at the same time. "I'm, I'm gigging earning money to rebuild my home, good thanks sort of, it was trashed in that storm, you know, the one that delayed the boat."

They didn't know, but let him continue regardless. "Lisa came and got me, brought me here to help sort things out, I've been good, but could be better, my house is trashed, but these gigs will help, but I ain't been paid yet." He looks over at the bar owner and shakes his fist, the bar owner does not know what Mike is gesticulating about and expresses this with a shrug of the shoulders as he carries on cleaning glasses.

"I need to get some wood, rebuilt my house, but it ain't free and they don't understand the value of a quality musician." He shakes his head, then spots Andy's earlier purchase. "Nice drum!"

Rob tries to calm Mike down, as his volume has increased to a level that could be heard across the street and he wants to ensure that the conversation cannot be heard by their spectator. "Maybe we can help, I understand the value of your entertainment, it's always good to help friends, especially old ones. We may need your help too." He pulls up a chair and sits down, prompting the other two to follow suit. He is also slightly puzzled as he has never known Mike to play for money.

"Right, firstly, who is Lisa? Where is she and where are you staying?"

Mike looks puzzled. "You know Lisa, English chick, a bit short, long dark hair, lovely, stays with me sometimes on the island."

They didn't.

"She has a flat here, where she stays when working in the city, you know, you've been there, I'm crashing on the floor, it's OK, but it's not like my home, too noisy."

He looks at them pensively, then a flash of inspiration appears on his face and he stands and starts waving frantically at the bar. "Bar tender, quick, six shots of tequila and some sugar." The bar tender shakes his head and starts pouring some drinks.

Rob tries to stop Mike. "It's OK, we really haven't got time to get wasted, plus I don't drink, remember?"

Mike doesn't remember. He is too animated to pay much attention, keen to enact his plan to show some hospitality. The bar tender brings over six shot glasses with some lemon and salt and places them on the table, before walking off muttering to himself. Mike clinks the glasses and downs one of the shots, ignoring the lemon and salt, not noticing that the others are not reciprocating, but continuing regardless. "Anyways, Lisa will be here soon, she'll be delighted to see you again, we'll have a wild night." He has completely forgotten his gig, much to the relief of the bar owner and the two customers who didn't leave when Mike started up.

Andy tries to humour him. "Yep, it'll be great to see Lisa again and catch up, but we do have some pressing business, so will need to leave soon I'm afraid." He has spotted that their pursuant has moved to another restaurant with a clearer view inside the bar they are dominating. He doesn't want Mike to become entwined in any of their potential problems, it could lead to trouble for all of their friends in the country. Mike was not hard to trace, he left a wake of chaos wherever he went and sooner or later that trail would lead back to the islands.

As they talk some tourists pass the bar and seeing westerners inside, they decide to patronise it with their custom. Soon the bar starts to fill up as the presence of westerners acts as a magnet for more to stop as they pass. If there is one thing a tourist likes, it's the comfort of their own when selecting a venue for a night out.

This is what Rob needs, as they start to become harder to observe from outside. "No, we can stay for much longer, I've got something I need to do though." He looks directly at Andy. "Can you stay with Mike catching up for a while, I need to pop out somewhere, I won't be longer than an hour."

Andy starts to ask where he is going, but stops, knowing that wherever it is, it will help them in the long run, he doesn't need to know the details right now. He grabs one of the shot glasses, passes another to Mike and gives him a wink. "Me and you are going to have a wild time for a bit, while Rob goes and sorts some of his shit out." Mike doesn't need another invite and downs the contents of the glass, nodding at Rob as he stands up and heads towards the bathroom, which fortunately, has a window which he uses to exit the bar unseen from the street at the front.

Andy and Mike finish off the rest of the shots quickly. Once they are done, Mike remembers his unfinished gig and starts to stand and pull his guitar round to the front, but before he finishes, Andy puts an arm out to stop him getting up, slowly guiding him back to the chair. "Mate, let's just catch up and have a few drinks, the rest of the customers can experience your talents at another time." He doesn't want the bar to empty and reveal the lack of Rob to the street.

He orders some beers from the bar, settling Mike's tab at the same time, ensuring that the flow of drinks doesn't stem for the next hour, an hour spent playing drinking games interspersed with occasionally conversation, most of which comes from Mike about some of the fun times they have had and the people they had them with. Most of which Mike had got mixed up, Andy having been elsewhere, but he wasn't going to let the truth get in the way of a good story as Mike was still very entertaining.

Forty five minute later, Mike slams down a bottle of beer half way through drinking it down in one as a forfeit, leaps to his feet and throws himself at a woman that has just walked in. Andy doesn't know whether to stop him, but relaxes when she smiles and hugs Mike back. Mike had started many fights by mistaking people for others he knew, embracing the wrong woman can evoke jealous anger in the most tolerant of men, especially as Mike's embraces were very passionate affairs.

He pulls the woman towards Andy. "Lisa, look its Hoops, how long has it been since you've seen him?" He pushes her towards Andy while he goes to the bar to get Lisa a drink.

She is used to Mike's confusion over the past. "erm, it must have been all of my life since I last saw you. Hi I'm Lisa." she shakes Andy's outstretched hand.

"Hi, I'm Andy, not Hoops, although some close friends do call me Coops! I can see you know Mike well, he's told me a little about you, but assumed we had met and I knew everything." Andy has already warmed to Lisa, who despite appearing a little rustic, has a bohemian style about her. Her long hair was well styled and neatly brushed, all of her clothes were clean and pleasant smelling. She has the look of a tourist that stays in five star hotels, but is trying to fit in a little with the more independent travellers.

She speaks with a well-groomed English accent. "He does that all the time, he can't remember anything correctly, but I'm used to it now, it took a while at first though. I came across him when I started to run the Wakwenda Retreat on Chizumulu, have been doing that for a couple of years now, so that must seem like a lifetime to Mike. His accommodation was damaged in a storm last week, so I brought him here with me for a week, while it is being repaired. He's probably told you something completely different, but that's Mike, he's a lot of fun but hard work."

"Nope that's exactly what he told us, although he did say he was here gigging to pay for his repairs, which confused us as he never seems to lack for money. I've heard good things about Wakwenda Retreat, never been there though, but it seems an unusual place to end up running on your own."

Lisa displays a laid back but professional attitude. "It's owned by a friend, I was getting bored of the city life, I just wanted to get away from it all for a while, which I certainly have. Whenever I want to get away from the lodge for a break, I head over to Mike's just to listen to some of his stories. He's probably mentioned you in a few, but he does get the details mixed up now and again, so forgive me if I associate you with something that you were not involved in!"

Andy shakes his head. "Don't worry, it wouldn't be the first time we have been accused of something we were not involved in."

Lisa smiles, not fully understanding what Andy was insinuating. "As for him gigging to pay for the repairs, I don't think he would ever make enough money to pay for his front door. He has it in his head that he must work to fund the repairs, but he has already paid for them."

Andy chuckles as Mike returns to the table with a large cocktail for Lisa, adorned with umbrellas straws and a sparkler. "How's the catching up going?"

They both look at him as they simultaneously speak. "Good thanks." This is followed by a small giggle from Mike.

Rob suddenly returns from his trip, completely confusing the man watching the restaurant from across the road. He hasn't been able to get a clear view of the events inside the bar, but thought that none of them had left. When he sees Rob approaching from the end of the road, he decides he has to get closer to ensure he doesn't miss anything else. He follows Rob across the road at a distance and takes a seat inside the bar, closer than normal protocol dictates.

Rob sits down, looks at Lisa and figures out who she is. "Hello, I'm Rob, you must be Lisa, Mike has mentioned you were meeting him here."

Lisa is taken aback a little by the new arrival, someone who had not been mentioned until now, which made her start to wonder if there was anyone else due. "Hello, yes, I wanted to be as late as possible so I didn't have to watch him crucify some of my favourite songs. Is it just the two of you or are we expecting a mass gathering which Mike has organised without telling me?"

Rob knew exactly what she meant, he had spent evenings where Mike had separately arranged to meet nearly everyone he knew, to initiate an evening of wild partying, gatherings which Mike called festivals. "As far as we know it's just the two of us, we bumped into Mike by chance, he didn't know we were coming, so it's not one of his festivals."

This causes Lisa a little relief, she liked Mike's festivals, but they often got out of hand and were best held in a remote place where damage can be limited and the police couldn't be called. "Thank the lord for that, I have some things I need to do over the next few days, including a spot on television talking about Chizumulu. I don't want to spend one of them with a bad head."

Rob wonders why. "Chizumulu? Are you some sort of expert on it?"

Lisa raises her eyes to the sky in despair at her failure to realise that Rob may not know what she did. "Sorry, I should have said, I run Wakwenda Retreat on Chizumulu Island, it's how I know Mike. I've been asked to do a small piece on tourism on the island on national TV tomorrow, this is why I am in Lilongwe. It seemed a good idea to bring Mike along while his hut is repaired from some storm damage."

Everything makes sense to Rob now. He smiles as he silently thanks fate for delivering a potentially golden opportunity for them.

Lisa is starting to piece together some of Mike's stories which involved two English guys he knows very well. "I take it you know Mike very well, he has probably mentioned you many times, I know you're not the guys who live on Likoma, are you the guys that borrowed a fishing boat with him and went to catch flies for the world's largest Fly Pie?"

Rob and Andy look a little sheepish, while Mike grins inanely. It was a story he was very fond of telling everyone he met, while they thought it was something that had been lost in the mists of time. They had indeed been involved in the incident and were not proud of it as it had caused them some problems, not least due to the fact that the borrowed fishing boat was more of a commandeered boat, as the owner had not really given permission for them to use it.

Andy decides to provide the details, speaking quietly so any occupants at nearby tables would not overhear. "We visit Malawi fairly often, we first met Mike at a full moon event in Nkhata bay, at the Africa Bay lodge. We had a wild night and woke up on the beach the next day. We decided we were going to relax there for a couple of days, while our friends went back to Likoma. Around noon, Mike came leaping up to us all excited, as a fly swarm was headed towards the shore, but it changed direction and was heading back out into the lake. Mike wanted to taste fly pie, he heard of it and for some reason was desperate to have some. We both had hangovers, but he had a bottle of rum, which seemed like a good hangover cure at the time. Now under the influence, we were easily convinced to take part in the ridiculous suggestion that we were presented."

Mike grimaces when he hears it described as ridiculous. "It was a genius scheme, would have made us rich and famous."

Andy continues. "Well that I doubt, I can't see anyone becoming famous for making a pie out of flies. Anyway, Mike convinced us that we could row out to the column of flies, which was about a mile away, catch as many flies as we could in a large tarpaulin he had found and break the world record for the largest ever Fly Pie. It seemed like a reasonable idea at the time, logical aspects such as how we would cook it, whether there actually was a world record and whether anyone would actually care went completely out of the window. We needed a boat, so convinced one of the local fishermen to lend us his boat, well when we say convinced, we really just told him we were borrowing it, despite his protestations. We all jumped into the boat and started rowing towards the swarm, against all odds we actually made it. Mike unravelled his tarpaulin and used it to gather a huge amount of flies. That successfully done, we rowed back to shore, as directly as we could, although we were later told that we were anything but straight heading in all directions.

We got back to shore to be met by a police officer and the angry fisherman, who Mike somehow managed to pacify with his frantic over-enthusiasm to show them his tarpaulin, shouting Fly Pie so loud and frequently that they eventually joined in. A group gathered to pile up some stones to create a stove large enough for such a haul. We obtained some sheets of corrugated iron to be the hot plate and Mike jumped up and down on the bulging tarpaulin to compact the flies. When the stove was lit and burning well, a large crowd had gathered to watch with fascination. Mike bundled the tarpaulin onto the corrugated iron, where it sizzled for a while, then exploded with an almighty ball of flame that shot up into the air, scattering the crowd. We had to endure some intense questioning in the local police station, which cost us nearly a hundred dollars each to bring to an end. It's not our proudest moment as we like to maintain a low profile when we are here."

Lisa was in fits of laughter on hearing the story unravel. "Mike is always delighted to tell that story, I've heard many versions of it."

Andy shakes his head. "Who would have thought that someone would have used that tarpaulin to mop up the barrel of fuel that Mike had accidentally knocked over the previous night."

Rob finishes the story off. "Yes, who would have thought that we would have been too drunk to actually notice the smell! That was the last time I actually touched alcohol."

Lisa still has a smile on her face. "Well it's finally nice to meet the two other men that were responsible for the 'The Big Bang of Africa Bay'.

Rob and Andy both put their heads in their hands on hearing it described as that, it made it sound like a historical event. Rob looks up first. "Anyway, there is more to us than that, I'm not going to elaborate on everything, but I think you can help us a great deal, the more people that know about what I am going to tell you, the better it will be for us."

He relates the same story that he used in the embassy, but this time instead of the cynicism of the Americans, it was met with wide-eyed wonder from Lisa, Mike only paid attention some of the time, missing most of the story. Rob finished with the tale of the handover to the Americans, pointing out the fact that they were being followed, which was a concern. This was the only thing that Mike paid any attention to, igniting his mistrust in authority, he starts to demonstrate why he had earned his 'Mad' moniker.

Lisa is keen to help. "What do you want from me?"

Rob hands her a package from his pocket and whispers into her ear.

Meanwhile Mike stands up, grabs Andy's drum and goes to the bar to place an order. He is going to turn this quiet evening in the bar into one of his festivals. The barman starts lining glasses up on the bar, filling all of them with assorted spirits, only stopping to beckon one of his waiters over to give him details of what additional supplies to obtain.

Mike stands on a table to address the patrons of bar in his loudest voice possible after he bangs on the drum violently to attract their attention.

"Ladies and Gentlemen travellers, can I have your attention please."

The customers in the bar, which is now full, stop their chatter and give Mike their full attention, with more coming in from outside to see what the commotion is about. The room is silently focused on the tall scruffy Australian that towers above them.

"My name is Mike. Some people think I am mad and they call me Mad Mike. I am happy with that as I was given the name for being a party animal. Tonight I am going to demonstrate to all of you why I have earned that name. I am going to give you all a night you will treasure until the end of your days."

This statement is met with a moment of silence from the crowd, which is mostly young western backpackers, until someone at the back starts a loud cheer that quickly erupts around the room. The bar owner smiles to himself, but sensibly gets the remainder of his staff to start moving the furniture out of the way. This has happened before, only once, a couple of years ago, but his takings were the largest he had ever had in one night, larger than an average month's takings. It was the main reason he had tolerated Mike's terrible live music show.

Mike starts punching the air shouting

"FESTIVAL, FESTIVAL, FESTIVAL"

getting louder with each word

"FESTIVAL, FESTIVAL, FESTIVAL, FESTIVA-AL"

to the familiar beat of Sousa's most famous marching band tune,

"FESTIVAL, FESTIVAL, FESTIVAL", "FESTIVAL, FESTIVAL, FESTIVAL, FEST-IVAL"

He carries this on for four more times, by the end of which all of the crowd are on their feet and jumping up and down in rhythm with the tune

Drinks are starting to be dispersed amongst the crowd and are being downed quickly, without any thought of who will pay for them. Rob, Andy, Lisa and the American following them all try to decline their drinks, but Mike has had his eye on the American and has a plan. He jumps off the table and gathers some of the crowd into an arm locked circle, where they start dancing around in a circular fashion. He plans this well, ensuring that the American is swept up in the circle, not getting a chance to avoid it. Mike produces a pitcher of mixed spirits and passes it around, making sure the American drinks enough to dull his senses when it is his turn, chanting "more" every time the American tries to stop and hand it to someone else.

Rob, Andy and Lisa also have problems declining the drinks now the crowd are being swept up in the moment, so they take them and pour them on their fronts instead of drinking them.

Mike leaves his circle to carry on jumping around whilst sharing the pitcher, then starts up similar circles with the rest of the people in the room, starting off a pitcher in each circle. By the time he has finished there are nearly a dozen circles of bouncing people rotating, drinking and chanting. The only three people that manage to avoid being swept up were purposely missed out by Mike so they could slip away quietly.

After ten minutes, Mike jumps up onto the bar and claps his hands to bring the events to a halt.

"That was the appetiser, now for the Festival. Bring on the games, food, music, singing and dancing."

He waits for the cheering to finish.

But first, we must repeat the rules. These rules are an ancient tradition and must be followed at all times. Anyone failing to follow them must perform a forfeit in front of everyone on the bar. It is your duty to spot any non-conformists, to which you must point and shout at the top of your voice."

He pauses for effect,

"POOPER."

A muttering of the word pooper ripples through the attentive crowd.

"Now the rules, which you must repeat after me."

"EVERYONE MUST DRINK."

The crowd shouts "EVERYONE MUST DRINK."

"EVERYONE MUST SING."

The crowd shouts "EVERYONE MUST SING."

"EVERYONE MUST DANCE."

The crowd shouts "EVERYONE MUST DANCE."

"And finally, but not leastly,"

"EVERYONE MUST PLAY."

The crowd shouts "EVERYONE MUST PLAY."

He is delighted with the unified response.

"Now all together…

EVERYONE MUST DRINK, EVERYONE MUST SING, EVERYONE MUST DANCE and EVERYONE MUST PLAY."

The crowd in unison chants

"EVERYONE MUST DRINK, EVERYONE MUST SING, EVERYONE MUST DANCE and EVERYONE MUST PLAY."

He raises his arms and waits for silence to fall again. "And the final thing, which you don't need to repeat.

"I WILL PAY."

This solicits the longest cheer of the night so far, it will be one statement where he will be absolutely true to his word. Money has never been a problem for Mike, who is the black sheep of a very rich family.

He organises the all too willing crowd into random teams, arranging each team into lines in preparation for the first game, which is a series of drinking races, followed by a mass dance competition to some music played on the sound system. Some more drinking games follow, before platters of food are distributed by the staff as a local band entertains the crowd with Malawian versions of popular western songs.

Mike keeps his eye on the American, who by now has forgotten why he was here and is participating enthusiastically in all the events.

The band is followed by some more drinking games, then a mass karaoke competition between the men and the women, some more drinking games, a mass session of truth or dare, Mike's favourite, then he climbs back onto the bar and calls for a solemn hush.

"Ladies and Gentlemen travellers, it is the time of the night when we need to commemorate…" he again pauses for effect and instead of shouting he beckons the crowd in closer and emphasises every word clearly.

"The Big Bang of Africa Bay."

A waiter brings out a very large wok like object and places it on the floor just outside the door, which he starts to fill with a mixture of spirits, while Mike walks slowly up to the end of the bar nearest it.

"Ladies and gentlemen travellers, here starts a tale of such bravado and daring, that you must never repeat it to another soul."

He waits for some acknowledgement from the crowd before continuing in the same tone, a loud whisper, a very loud whisper.

"Many moons ago, myself and two fellow travellers set out to make the world's largest ever fly pie, a delicacy that is only found on the lakeshores of this fair country. To gather the ingredients, myself and these travellers fashioned a small boat out of driftwood, we then set about rowing into the middle of the lake, to catch the elusive flies, rarely seen up close by man."

He looks around the room catching as many eyes as possible with his wide eyed stare to ensure they were hanging on his every word, while the waiter who has finished pouring the spirits, covers the large metal wok.

"We rowed through one of the largest storms seen on the continent to our destination, barely surviving countless capsizes, but we worked as a team, we finally reached the fly column, a column which stood so tall it rose many miles into the sky."

Mike emphasises every sentence with exaggerated body language and wild hand gestures, displaying the height of the fly column by standing on the tips of his toes and reaching up to the ceiling.

"I unravelled my fly catcher, a tarpaulin so large it took the three of us to hold it and we set about catching the flies, flies who fought back with a ferocity so fierce not a square inch of our bodies went unbitten."

"We filled the tarpaulin after several hours of battle, then set about returning to land, a journey fraught with the same danger as the outbound trip. When we eventually set foot back on Africa Bay, we had been gone for nearly a day, we were exhausted, but determined to make the world's largest Fly Pie."

"The whole town of Nkhata Bay had gathered to build a cooker large enough for the pie, they had even crafted a special pie dish for the event. We were being cheered like heroes, but we had also had upset some people who were determined to sabotage the event."

"I emptied the contents of the tarpaulin onto the dish, while some of the locals helped mix in some special liquid flavouring for this delicacy. We were ready to go and I was given the honour of lighting the fire to cook this monumental delicacy."

The waiter hands Mike a flaming torch made out of a broom handle and some fuel soaked rags, which Mike waves around over the heads of the crowd.

"As I lit the fire, the sabotage became evident as the whole Fly Pie exploded in a ball of flames so high it was seen from all shores of the lake."

He waves the torch over the opened wok, causing the spirit mixture to explode in an eruption of flame that bursts several feet into the sky.

The crowd started cheering and wildly applauding, which Mike milks for a few minutes while the waiter pours the heated spirits from the wok into shot glasses which are handed around.

Mike calls for calm.

"Hush my friends, we will soon toast this event, but I first must reveal to you the cause of the sabotage."

The crowd quickly silences.

"Our attempt to create this massive delicacy upset some people in the area who wanted to keep the secrets of Fly Pie from the masses, they thought that this would bring knowledge of Fly Pie to the wider world, so instead of spices and flavouring, they mixed in an explosive fuel mixture, destroying our plans.

Fear not though, these people were apprehended and although the pie was not created, the legend lives on and the knowledge of this delicacy is spreading, thanks to myself and my fellow travellers."

The crowd applaud, while Mike holds up a shot glass.

"I call upon you to toast THE BIG BANG OF AFRICA BAY."

The crowd repeats in unison "THE BIG BANG OF AFRICA BAY."

The bar erupts into applause and loud cheers.

After the cheering dies down, Mike initiates some more drinking games, a mass sing-a-long with the band and some more competitions before the sound system is switched on and the crowd dances the night away to familiar western party songs.

It is starting to get light outside as the first reveller leaves, thanking Mike on their way out. It is seven in the morning before Mike can finally sit down and reflect on the glory of the night which he managed to put together at such short notice. He thanks the bar owner as he leaves, pays the astronomical bill on his debit card. As he leaves, he steps over the only other person left in the bar, the unconscious American who is laying in the middle of the floor, clutching the drum that Mike had taken from Andy..

As he steps into the street with a massive smile, he raises his arms and shouts "I am the MAN."

He walks back to Lisa's room fondly remembering the events of the night, the highlight for him being the improvised Can-Can competition, where he had managed to get each team dancing the can-can on the bar wearing skirts improvised from some table cloths.

He amazed himself with this improvised invention and was determined to introduce it as a permanent fixture for all future festivals.

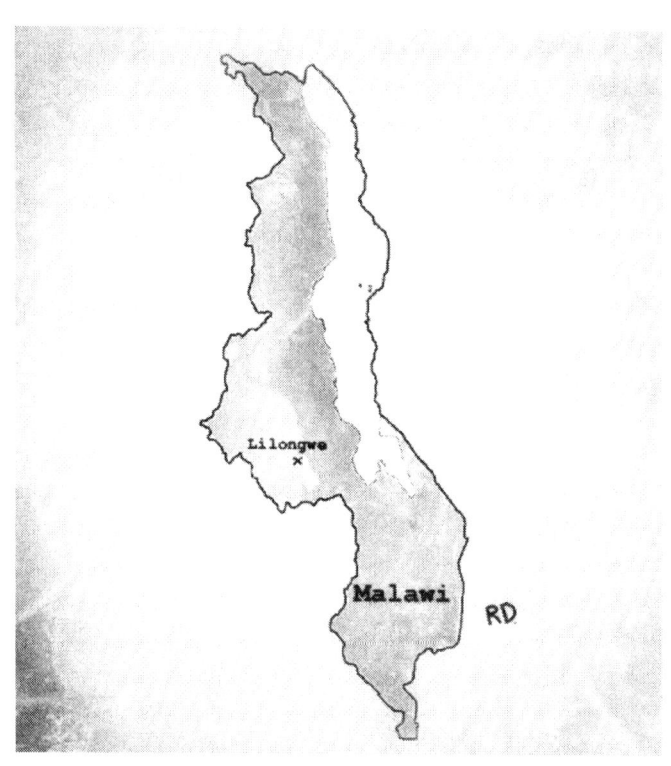

Capítulo Doce

After they slipped away from Mad Mike's Festival, Andy and Rob walked Lisa back to her hotel before they returned back to their own hotel room, heading straight for their beds. They sleep for a few hours, until they are woken by a loud knock at the door.

Andy drowsily looks at the clock, it is 7:30 and daylight outside. He shouts at the door. "Who is it?"

The voice that responds is definitely not African. "Room service, with some drinks. Compliments of the hotel."

Rob gets up and whispers to Andy. "Since when have they been employing westerners to deliver room service in African Hotels and why would they turn up so early in the morning?" Andy does not need to voice his concerns, he knows they need to take action quickly.

They flick the lights on and quickly fumble into some clothes, ensuring that they have their hand guns in the back of their trousers. They position themselves either side of the door. Andy turns the handle from the side. Four shots are fired through the door, which would have hit Andy in the middle of the chest if he had been standing directly behind it. The door bursts open and two burly men rush in. The intruders are stopped in their tracks by the sound of guns cocking at the back of their heads.

Andy is the first to speak. "This is a very odd sort of room service."

Both men are wearing dark jumpers and trousers, with no identifying marks. One of them states in a gruff threatening voice. "You don't know who you are dealing with."

Rob responds. "Sadly, I think we do."

Before they can answer, both of the assailants are immediately knocked out by swift blows to the back of their heads with the butts of the handguns.

Rob is now very concerned, they could be in more danger than they were at the party.

"We've got to get the fuck out of here quickly, I'll fill you in on some details of a plan I have outside."

Andy is keen to get what is due to them. "What are we going to do about the reward?"

"I am not sure they are too keen on giving it to us, but I may have to force their hand with what I explained yesterday. We just need to pack and get somewhere where they can't find us."

Andy hasn't lost his sense of humour in the tense situation. "How do we get to New York quickly from here?" Rob just raises a small smile as he sets about implementing his exit strategy.

They hurriedly pack their few remaining belongings into their bags, then calmly walk out of the room, down the corridor to a window at the end. They climb out of the window, hoping they are totally unseen with the lack of other people in the vicinity providing reassurance. Outside the window, they find themselves at the back of the hotel compound, with just a small wall to scale to get out. Scaling the wall is a routine two man effort, but is completed in a few seconds as they both drop over the other side into a small back street.

They make their way up the street, sticking to the sides where some cover is provided by the trees that line it. Eventually they end up on the main road, close to the main market area of Likoma, which is just starting to bustle with life, unfortunately not enough bustle to provide two Muzungus sufficient cover. They try and merge into the crowd, but stick out too much, as do the few other Muzungus that are in the area, one of whom spots them, alerting Andy and Rob to this by his overreaction as he beckons the other Muzungus to him whilst pointing at Andy and Rob.

They spot this easily and need to get away very quickly, anywhere will do. They slip into a side street and run to the end which leads into another busy street, presenting some more chances to merge into the crowd. Rob spots a matola across the street. Matolas are the standard form of public transport in the country, typically a privately operated minibus which darts passengers around quickly between unmarked stops, frequently stopping off anywhere to pick up as many passengers that they can fit in, with twenty to thirty occupants being common for a bus that is supposed to have only sixteen seats.

Rob nudges Andy in its direction. "Quick jump on that, we can work out what to do when we are away from here."

They cross the road and jump on the matola, clambering to a seat at the back where they are crushed against the other passengers. But it will do and they are able to see if they are being followed from the window.

The urgency of the situation has removed the need for covert conversations, so Andy openly speaks to Rob. "Any ideas as to where the fuck we go now?" The recognition of a familiar western swearword raises a few eyebrows amongst the other passengers.

Rob hasn't felt so threatened in a long time. "I'm working on it, I had made some arrangements in the time I was away yesterday, but not sure I want to use them now people are willing to shoot at us in the open. I don't want to endanger other people. We also have Lisa as our backup to force the news in the open later today, I hope it pays off before it's too late. Obviously we were spot on noticing their under-excitement about catching this guy, someone must have a lot to lose from his capture, I know it could reduce the total spend on defence in the US, but not immediately. I'm struggling to think why the agency would want to keep this quiet so much and would go as far as assassinating people in the street. We need to find a way to resolve this safely, but I don't know how yet."

Andy too is scared. "Well someone believes it is worth a lot more than we are worth alive, those two in the hotel room didn't seem to be your typical agency workers, they looked too much like hired thugs and I am struggling to think why there would be a need for people like that to be stationed in a country like Malawi."

This is something Rob hadn't paid too much attention to, but now he thought about it, Andy's statement made perfect sense. Malawi is a stable country, there would be a small agency presence, but very small, their agents would not be as large and noticeable as the two brutes that had burst into their room. The Americans would normally use agents that wouldn't garner a second glance in the street, people who could blend in to the uninitiated. "Shit, you are spot on, we may be thinking the wrong people are after us, I have been struggling to work out why the agency would want us out of the way, the capture of Malek Ali Bezir would be a great coup and would lead to intelligence they could use for years. It's got to be someone else and there is only one way we can find out."

Andy knows what he means, reluctantly. "We've got to capture one of them haven't we?"

Rob nods. "Sure do, it's the quickest way."

The mention of Lisa's involvement puzzled Andy. "Changing the subject, you mentioned Lisa, why would she be in danger?"

Rob reveals his insurance plan "I saw the perfect opportunity when Lisa mentioned she was appearing on TV, I gave her a spare copy of the video I shot of Ali Bezir, she will hand it over to the media unless I give her a call to tell her to stop. It's our failsafe plan, but I've also left another copy for some friends I was hoping to catch up with tomorrow."

Andy looks at Rob, questioning what he meant. "Friends?" then after some thought and a staring frown from Rob, the penny dropped.

The minibus slows for one of its stops, barely stopping to let passengers board before speeding off again. Rob looks out the window and notices a large car pull up behind them.

Rob makes a move to get out of his seat. "I think this is us, we can get a lift."

They clamber to the front and urge the bus driver to slow down. As the bus slows they jump out of the bus and slip round the front, watching the car closely. A man has got out of the following car and is looking inside the bus through a side window. Rob sneaks up behind him and knocks him out with his pistol. Andy makes his way to the car, pulling the driver out of it, before knocking him out and putting him in the back seat. He then searches for the man's ID, discovering a CIA badge. Rob jumps into the passenger seat as Andy climbs into the driving seat and quickly speeds away.

"Well, there sure are quite a few people out looking for us. We need to get to somewhere quiet where we can find out more from this guy." Andy indicates towards the American in the back.

Rob is rummaging through the glove compartment, but there is nothing of use in there. "A map would be handy, I've got a few ideas where to go, but I have no idea if we are going the right way."

Andy has an idea where to go. "I still know the place roughly, but it has changed a bit since I last spent any amount of time here." Despite visiting the country often, they only ever came to Lilongwe to use the airport, a visit that most times didn't involve a trip into the city. "They will be watching the bus station and probably the other Embassies in case we try for diplomatic assistance."

Rob shakes his head. "I doubt they have the manpower, they must have used all of their men out on the street looking for us, fortunately Mike would have made at least one inactive today."

Andy displays a rare bout of paranoia. "They probably have a dozen or so locals they can call on in times like this. Trained to spot a Muzungu and oddly enough there are not that many running around that fit our description that are being chased by large groups of people, which is why I'm heading for somewhere discreet to speak with our friend here." The man in the back is starting to regain consciousness and is making some small groans from the back seat.

Andy puts his foot down when Rob sees a sign pointing to a familiar location and indicates that they should head directly for it. A few minutes later they are in an industrial estate, where they pull up out of sight from the road, behind some unused units.

They both turn to the man in the back who is fully conscious and completely terrified. His youthful looks betraying his inexperience. Andy is in intimidation mode. "Right, what the hell is going on, why are we being followed, chased and shot at?" He glances at the ID badge, "Phil."

Phil is shaking. "We don't know, its normal protocol for us to track people who have an involvement in US national security, but you don't meet those criteria, even after what you delivered yesterday. After you had left the embassy yesterday, we started getting some unusual phone calls asking specific questions about you and what you had dropped off."

Rob stops him. "You were told about the delivery?"

Phil continues. "Yes, our whole team had a debriefing session, this is the biggest thing to happen to many of us, we needed to know the details to ensure that we had everything in place for the major unveiling tomorrow."

This is good news for Rob and Andy and an indication that the Americans weren't going to cover the capture of Ali Bezir up, but it doesn't explain why they were being shot at. "So, why were we being chased through the town earlier?"

Phil is still shaking. "We don't know, we are only a small unit, not much happens here that affects the US, well it didn't used to, but we had some information that there were some potential threats that had entered the country, which we assume were the people making the calls. We are still trying to find out who they are, we guessed that their number one target was Ali Bezir and that they intended to secure his release, but when they started going after you, Jones decided to put us all out on the street to try and find you, in the hope we could find out what they wanted with you first."

Andy shakes his head. "I would say that's pretty obvious now, they want us dead."

Phil is starting to regain his composure. "We know that, but don't know why and that could be something that affects how we handle the Ali Bezir situation. The good news is that we have a lot of extra people flying in to help, but they won't be here until tomorrow."

Rob's doesn't like being the target of unknown assassins, despite being one for much of the last ten years. "Tomorrow could be a little too late for us. We can't go back to the hotel, we know that has been compromised, your embassy will be being watched, so we can't go there, we need to find a safe place for the next twenty four hours. Thanks Phil, you've been a great help and we now know we can view your agency as friends, but we need to make our own plans for our safety until the cavalry arrives."

Rob and Andy get out of the car and walk away. Andy is keen to find out what Rob's intentions are. "What are your plans for our safety?"

Rob knows part of his plan, he is still working on it. "If we can get to the guest house run by our old friend, we can at least take some time to relax and work out how we are going to deal with this new threat, the longer we can stay concealed, the more chance we have of the Americans sorting it out for us."

Andy knows exactly which guest house Rob means. "Isn't it a bit far to walk safely?"

"Definitely not too far to walk in normal circumstances, but there is a chance we may be spotted, but that depends on how many people there are out there looking for us and which way they went when we disappeared."

Andy regrets that they didn't reduce the amount of people involved. "It's a shame that we didn't take out those two thugs permanently this morning, if I knew they weren't agency guys, I would not have thought twice about it and there would be two less people to be out looking for us now."

Rob doesn't have time to worry about something they have no control over, so focuses on what they have to do. "We can't do anything about that now, all we need to do is get to a safe place. Once we are out of this industrial estate, there are only a few streets to pass before we reach the golf course, which we can cut across easily. There should be less people around to see us there, I'm sure golf is not a mass participation sport here."

The two make their way out of the industrial estate and cross the road in front of them. They walk into a side street where they jump over a wall, landing on an unkempt golf course, which they start walking across.

Andy has been on the course before and knows exactly where they are. He had played a terrible round on this course and spent all eighteen holes walking all over every inch of grass after too many sliced shots. This had stayed in his memory for years, it was hard to forget such an embarrassing episode in his life.

Rob hasn't been on the course before, but has driven round it, so knows how big the course is. "I guess it will take about thirty minutes to cross the course, after which we have only a few blocks to pass on the other side, in total about forty five minutes away."

Andy has suddenly remembered something from his game on the course. "One thing, it may be a little early to be on this course, they don't open until nine and it's only just reached eight."

Rob was not a fan of golf, never having set foot on the course before. "We are not planning on playing, we only need to cross it, unless you want to disguise ourselves with golf bags."

Andy explains the relevance of what he meant. "There is not much choice now and I forgot about this until just now. The owners are very particular about who comes onto the course, especially when it is shut. If I remember correctly they have guard dogs to keep undesirables from sleeping on the grounds, quite nasty guard dogs, but I guess taking on the dogs is a better option than taking on whoever it is that is after us."

Rob weighs this option up for a while, before he concludes that the dogs would be easier to deal with as they were more predictable and far less devious. They continue walking across the field. After only ten minutes they stop and crouch when they hear something. They listen intensely and survey the whole area when Andy spots something he didn't want to see.

He whispers, pointing in the direction they have just come, at two figures around three hundred metres away. "There look, there are a couple of guys coming towards us, I'm hoping they are local security."

Rob has been listening intently. He has sharper hearing than his friend. "I can hear the panting of a dog."

They can make out the shape of some dogs running towards the outlines of the figures coming towards them. They know when the dogs have reached their targets as there is a loud scream and the sound of some dogs viciously attacking the men. They hear four quiet blows, which they recognise as silenced gun shots, gun shots which silences the sound of the dogs.

Rob spots a chance to find out why they are being chased. "Definitely not local security, unless they were too stupid to call off the guard dogs, I would also be very surprised if local security carried guns with silencers on them. Quick this way, we can get behind them if we use that banking as cover, but best to leave the bags in that bunker."

They leave the bags by the bank of a nearby bunker and move swiftly off to the left, using the natural banking of the fairway to get round to the back of the approaching men. The men are heading towards the bunker containing the bags, which from their direction are easily visible due to the contrast against the fine white sand behind.

The two approaching men become clearer, they are both dressed in the same attire as the morning's assailants, but they do not look as large, one has blond hair indicating they are a different pair, both are limping slightly, which Rob assumes to be a result of the dog attack, something that will be to his and Andy's advantage. When the men are only a few feet away from the bunker, they get down on their fronts and start crawling on the floor towards the bags, making them very easy targets for Rob and Andy, who silently sneak up behind and jump on top of them. The two assailants are disarmed efficiently and overpowered with a bit of a struggle, ceasing their resistance when guns are pointed in their faces.

Andy displays intense anger giving them short shrift. "Who the fuck are you and why are you following us?"

Neither man answers, they both just stare back.

Andy gets angrier, raising his voice slightly. "I'll only ask once more, Who the fuck are you and why are you following us?"

The blond haired man starts to speak, but they don't understand a word he is saying, all they recognise is a Slavic dialect, which could have been from anywhere in Eastern Europe.

Rob expresses his irritation. "Fuck. Eastern Europeans, this gets worse, we need to find one that speaks English now to find out what they want with us."

Andy agrees. "These two are useless, then, shall we inactivate them?"

Rob nods agreement. "Yep."

The blond man indicates that he has understood bits of what they were saying and starts to plead with them. "No, No, please no, we only hired to find you, to take you to big boss man."

Andy hasn't much patience left, he knows the story is unlikely to be true, the covert approach of the two potential assassins was not one of an attempted capture. "Who is this big boss man and what does he want with us?"

The blond man is shaking, but his English is improving. "I do not know, we have not met him, we were hired three days ago, I only met the others yesterday."

Rob realises that he may prove of some use. "How many others?"

"Ten, twelve of us in total, we flew here at short notice, we were told to find you two and capture you."

Rob knows this is bullshit, people are not normally captured by shooting through doors, his patience has finally run out. Rob and Andy knock out both men with their pistols, then tie them up with the assailants own belts.

Andy is satisfied that enough has been done for now. "They won't be going anywhere until the course security came across them and hand them over to the authorities."

Rob and Andy move back to their bags, pick them up and carry on crossing the golf course, using the bunkers and trees for cover as much as possible. It takes them another twenty minutes to cover the remaining ground, zigzagging much of the way, running when they can. When they are around three hundred metres from the far end of the golf course, they hear the sound of dogs attacking more people, followed by more gun shots.

They stop by a tree wall, to catch their breath for a couple of minutes and watch to see which direction their potential assassins are coming from. Andy tries to break the tension by stating the obvious. "Looks like backup has arrived." In the distance they see two more figures running towards them.

Rob has spotted that their assailants are on not on a direct course to intercept them, veering towards an exit in the corner of the golf course. "Looks like we may be OK, they are not heading for us, if we wait here until they go out and start searching the streets, in the time it takes them to realise we haven't left the course yet we should be able to get out via the nearest wall, avoid them and hopefully be somewhere safe before they realise."

Andy hasn't lost his sense of humour. "Hopefully? I'm not planning on spending the night in somewhere unsafe!"

Rob doesn't pay any attention, he is fixated on the two departing assassins, who have stopped and seem to be looking around. "Shit, don't move, they may not be leaving." Rob and Andy are sufficiently hidden by the tree to be difficult to spot from the distance, but Rob can see that binoculars are being used to scan the area. Too much time is spent focusing in their direction for his liking. The two figures start moving in their direction, walking slowly at first then breaking into a slow jog. The men are over three hundred metres away, so it will take nearly a minute for them to reach Rob and Andy, only half that time to get in firing range.

This is still enough time for Rob and Andy to make it to better cover. There is a thicker clump of trees less than fifty metres behind them, Rob nudges Andy in their direction while he picks his bag up, Andy doesn't need to be told twice, grabs his back and they run very fast to the trees, causing their pursuers to break into a near sprint.

Rob doesn't want to be caught with the odds against them. "When we get in the trees, just chuck the bags, you go left, I'll go right, when we are about fifteen metres apart just hit the deck, we should be able to hit them before they hit us."

Andy isn't as confident. "It does depend how good they are and what they are carrying, but I guess we will be favourites as long as it's just them two." Rob is not considering the option that there may be more assassins around the club, he prefers to focus on what he knows for sure. At the moment what he knows for sure is that there are two armed men chasing after them with a determination to kill him and Andy.

They arrive at the tress, which are dense enough to provide sufficient cover. Their pursuers are still two hundred metres away but gaining fast. The bags are dropped as they run to the back of the copse before splitting in different directions and dropping to the ground. Rob and Andy crawl forward so they can get clear views out of the trees without being seen themselves. This has slowed their pursuers, who have realised that they do not have the advantage any more. The men slow to a stop and speak for a while, before starting to move further into the golf course, following the tree line.

Rob has crawled up to Andy and whispers in his ear. "We need to track them so we don't lose the advantage." Andy doesn't need to be told the obvious and starts crawling through the trees in the same direction as the two assassins. They follow them for around a minute, when the two assassins suddenly change direction and speed to a sprint away from the centre of the course, closing in on the trees in a diagonal line. This confuses Rob for a second, but the sound of dogs barking supply him with an explanation.

The dogs quickly gain on the two assassins who are running and randomly firing shots behind their back.

Andy queries this tactic. "Why don't they stay their ground and take out the dogs in a controlled manner?" Before Rob can offer an opinion, six ferocious guard dogs come into view, heading at great speed, all bounding up and down presenting a very difficult target to hit.

As the dogs near the two assassins, two of them are hit by the gunfire, but the other four reach their targets, bringing them to the ground with the ferocity of a starved predator going for the kill. The dogs are all over the two men, biting and tearing at their limbs, one of the dogs is shot at close range, but the other three dogs are doing too much damage, ensuring their victims are incapacitated before any more shots can be fired, leaving the two men on the ground motionless but still alive, with the dogs maintaining strong grips on their limbs.

Rob and Andy don't need to watch anymore to know that this is their time to get away. The bags are retrieved before Rob and Andy creep through the trees keeping an eye on the dogs for any movement. Fortunately the dogs will not let their captors go to chase anything else.

Rob and Andy exit the trees to see they are only a hundred metres from the wall, which they sprint towards, arrive safely, climb over the wall and to their delight find they are on a totally empty street.

Andy is keen to get to the guest house as quick as possible. "This should make things a lot easier. We can use the main streets a bit more and get there quicker."

Rob prefers caution, the street is far too empty for his liking, he has been here before and normally there is a moderate flow of traffic. "I'd still prefer to stick to the side streets where there is less chance of standing out, it is only five minutes away and I'd like to ensure we get there in one piece."

Andy accepts Rob's logic. "Fair point."

They cross the road and walk up to a junction with a side road. Two dark cars are parked up the road, which start moving towards them when they are in sight. Both men jump over a small wall at the side of the road, reload their weapons and take positions in preparation for an exchange with the cars. The odds will be against them, but it depends on the amount of occupants and the weapons they have.

As the cars approach, they look too official to belong to the assassins chasing them. Both cars stop in the centre of the road adjacent to their hiding place. The cars are identical black Mercedes S class saloons with blacked out windows and diplomatic plates. The passenger door of the first car opens, a man gets out with his arms raised showing he is unarmed, as he turns they recognise that he is George Jones from the US embassy, causing them to release large sighs of relief.

Jones turns to the guys and beckons them over. "Quick get in the car, we've got to get you out of here, safely."

They don't need to be asked twice, jump over the wall, grab their bags and run to the car, still with their weapons drawn, just in case. The rear door of the Mercedes opens and they climb in the back seats. Jones returns to the passenger seat. The driver quickly pulls away before the doors are fully closed.

Jones turns to Rob and Andy to update them on the situation. "We got a call this morning from the hotel, informing us there were gunshots involving your room. By the time we got there, there was no one there. The people that attacked you had managed to get away, but we knew there was something bad going down."

Rob stares him in the eye. "We did think they may have been your agents."

Jones frowns. "We are Americans. We don't shoot people through doors, especially people who have just delivered the most valuable asset we could have imagined."

Rob tries to explain. "Well, you didn't seem over friendly when we dropped him off, in our line of business you sometimes don't know who to trust. We know different now, but who the hell are the people that are after us and more importantly, why?"

Jones composes himself. "Let me explain from the start. We got some intel to put us on alert, it seems there were some very unsavoury people heading into Malawi from Eastern Europe, some of whom were known to us as they were associated with one Matvei Kovalenko, a small time Russian arms dealer who we had been tracking for a few years. He's been trying to expand his empire and doesn't seem to care who he deals with to further his expansion.

Our agency has intercepted weapon caches he has shipped to nearly every major terrorist organisation in the world. Fortunately he hasn't got the infrastructure to enable him to develop a totally secure transport system yet, but that's only a matter of time with the increase in business he is trying to develop."

Neither man has heard of him, Andy wants to know the link with them. "We've never heard of this guy, we have always stayed well clear of the Eastern Europeans, far too unpredictable and dangerous, what have we done to warrant this all-out war?"

Jones shrugs. "That we don't know yet, but we will interrogate as many of his men we can. Malawian police have already arrested those on the golf course, but two of them will be in hospital for a while and may not be able to answer any questions as those dogs did a real number on them. Anyway, to continue where I was, we detected Kovalenko and his entourage heading this way, we managed to get some local help to track their plane to an airstrip up north, but they disappeared from our radar quickly. Then out of the blue we receive a cryptic phone call from you two promising us something, which at the time seemed too coincidental, so we were justified in treating you with caution, even after you had dropped your package off, it could have been a set-up, so we trailed you while we completed some background checks.

Surprisingly enough, we couldn't find out much about Reinhart Drescher and Andreas Clausnitzer, there didn't seem to be any travel or credit history, but we sort of suspected that would be the case, which is why we ran your pictures over to Langley, who were able to identify you, well sort of. Several different names came up against the facial matching software and we got about a dozen potential candidates returned to us, all of who looked a lot like both of you. Now I'm a cynical man, you have to be in my line of work and I found it odd the pictures of two men would have delivered so many different results from our computers, without them actually being the same men in each picture. We studied the identities, 6 different nationalities, so contacted the embassies of each nationality, guess which is the only one that came back with a positive ID?"

Andy tries to be coy. "German?"

Jones shakes his head. "Funnily no, it was British. We confirmed that you are Robert Dixon and Andrew Cooper, two highly decorated ex-servicemen. It made sense to me and fortunately for you gave more credibility to the reasons for your hostage delivery. Meanwhile, our agent trailing you ended up getting drunk thanks to some idiot Australian guy and we lost your trail for a while until you got back to the hotel. We left you there for the night thinking you would be safe, but didn't bank on the Russians turning up so quickly and somehow finding the hotel you were in. Luckily they didn't catch you unguarded and we were able to pick up your trail pretty swiftly, even though Phil was a bit shaken up, he was able to direct us out here."

Rob feels a lot of gratitude towards Phil now. They could have been in a world of pain if they had been intercepted by these Russians instead of the Americans. "We are very grateful for your help and we would like you to pass on our thanks to Phil, but what happens now? We have some dangerous people chasing us for a reason I cannot begin to work out and I don't think we can handle them all on our own."

"Good question. We thought that too, so we asked the Brits what we should do. You must have some friends in high places as they were very keen to get you well protected. So we are going to take you to the British embassy, where they will provide you with some safety for the night. We will see what we get out of the captives in Malawian custody before we come up with a plan for tomorrow. One advantage we will have tomorrow is that a large team of special forces will have arrived, primarily to escort Ali Bezir back to US soil, but they will now also be very useful in neutralising this other threat and if we get lucky, capturing Kovalenko, another man on our list."

Rob feels the Americans are owed an apology. "We are sorry for protecting our identities and causing you so much trouble, but I'm sure you understand our need for secrecy."

Jones smiles. "I do and we will be happy to maintain that secrecy, even when paying the reward and giving out the credit for the captures. For us, this could be the most important couple of days in the battle against terrorism in the last decade. It would be of great national pride if we were able to announce that it was a team of US special forces that captured Ali Bezir and Kovalenko. I'm sure you'll understand and won't be offended if we put out a completely false account of the capture."

For the first time in a couple of days, Andy and Rob feel that their retirement is close. Andy speaks for both of them. "Understand? We would be absolutely delighted for you to do that. We would be able to retire in absolute peace." Both men shake Jones' hand, while he offers some caution.

"You are not out of the woods yet, you can relax later on tomorrow when we have Kovalenko." His smirk indicates that he is not telling them everything, but they don't pursue it.

The cars drive on through the busy Lilongwe traffic towards the embassy district. Most of the cars around them are local cars, their age and poorly maintained state indicating the case, but other cars are mixed in with them. The driver of the rear Mercedes has noticed a brand new Nissan 4x4 conspicuous by its size, good condition and blacked out windows. It could be a diplomatic car which would use this route, but the driver is under instructions to report anything he is suspicious about and radios through to the front car. "White Nissan, three cars behind us, driver looks a little out of place."

Jones instructs his driver to take the next side road then head away from the embassy district, which he does. The Nissan follows. Jones surveys the situation out of the back window, humming to himself whilst looking at a map. "Take the next right, then head out west on Queens, we'll see how far this guy is going."

He explains his thinking to his passengers. "Queens leads directly out of the city, via some run down suburbs, unlikely that a car such as that would have much business taking that route." They get onto Queens and the Nissan is still behind, the only car behind now, but still maintaining some distance. Jones grabs the radio handset. "We will see if this guy really is a threat, we'll get up some speed and if see if we can lose him, follow our lead for the moment."

Jones' driver puts his foot down, accelerating to 90mph, above the safe limit for the road, with the second

Mercedes following suit. The Nissan also accelerates to keep them in sight. "He's shown his hand, we need to lose him. I don't want my guys to engage highly trained killers, many of them are fairly green and although there are five of us, we only have limited firepower and I'm not sure what those guys in that Nissan have in terms of either firepower or numbers."

Andy speaks up for the first time in a long time. "We can help, we have some experience in these sorts of situations, we can stop that car without getting any of your guys in danger."

Jones is unsure, but is willing to listen to any option, which when Andy finishes, he agrees to, his respect for his two passengers increasing. He tells his driver to go for it, the stretch of road is clear and straight, clear of urban areas with just sparse bush land to be seen for miles. Jones radios the plan through to the other car.

He looks at the map, another major intersection is just up ahead, which is perfect. Jones instructs the other car to speed up just after the junction, keeping to the right side of the road, which it does drawing parallel with the first car, both travelling at nearly 120Mph. They have now put over half a mile between them and the Nissan, which is struggling to keep up. Jones' driver screeches to a halt and makes a perfect handbrake turn while the other car continues ahead. Jones' car accelerates as fast as it can towards the Nissan, while Andy fastens the seatbelt around himself tightly. Rob climbs over him and opens the door, holding Andy while he hangs over the edge of the seat and pokes his head just enough under the door to see his target from under the door, using the bottom edge of the door for stability. Andy's head and hands are just a few inches from the speeding road.

Rob starts counting down as the Nissan approaches on the other side of the road. The Nissan driver has spotted the Mercedes heading towards them and starts to slow, winding down his window in order to take a shot, but the relative speed between the cars is increasing as the Mercedes is accelerating. The occupants of the Nissan haven't got enough time to prepare as well as the occupants of the Mercedes. Rob reaches zero as they are almost upon each other and Andy releases a volley of shots at the wheels of the Nissan, hitting both several times in the fraction of a second as they pass. The Nissan driver manages to get a single shot off which misses its target completely.

Andy pulls himself back into the car and Rob closes the door as Jones just looks dumbstruck. He has never seen such an effective way of immobilising a car at speed from another car and is impressed by the skills of his occupants. "Wow, you guys need to write that manoeuvre down for me, that's the sort of shit we should be teaching in Langley."

This pleases Andy, who had conceived the tactic and would be proud to have it taught to others. "I'd be delighted, you could call it the Cooper-Queens Manoeuvre!"

All the occupants of the car relax back in the seats laughing as they look back and see the Nissan immobilised by the side of the road. The driver takes the next left, heading back into the city, meeting up with the other Mercedes a few junctions later. It had turned back at the next junction it met on Queens, forking back to meet them as arranged. The rest of the journey was uneventful as they passed out of the bush land, back into the suburbs and straight into the embassy district, where they head directly for the British embassy.

As they pull up they are waved straight through the gate into the compound where they are met by a thin-greying man dressed in a beige suit. Jones turns to them before they get out. "This man doesn't look much, but he will ensure you are safe, I will speak to you tomorrow, it will be a big day." He thanks them again and shakes their hands as they get out of the car with their bags.

They walk up to the waiting man, who introduces himself. "Nigel Miller, I'm attached to the British embassy. I'll need to talk to you for a while get an idea of what has happened to date, but I'm grateful for what you have done for the Americans here. When I contacted the UK about you, I was told to show you every comfort we can provide and keep you well protected. You are held in very high regard by some important people."

His two compatriots shake his hand and he leads them into the embassy. Rob asks to use a phone when he gets inside and mouths Lisa to Andy, who understands perfectly. He doesn't want to jeopardise their retirement by the release of a story which will conflict with the American version.

Capítulo Trece

The rest of the day is spent in the embassy with Rob and Andy describing in detail their every move in the last few days, before they are shown to some basic but well protected rooms where they spend the night. It is one step up from being in prison, as there are sparse furnishings but they are free to order any food or drink any time. The security brings them some comfort and a chance to finally relax.

They wake early the next day, shower and get dressed before being shown into a briefing room around 9am. Jones, Rogers and two other men, who they assume to be US agents are already in the room as Nigel shows them in. The two men they already know rise and greet them warmly, with Rogers leading the talking. "Good Morning, I trust you have slept well after yesterday's activities, George filled me in on the details, I was especially impressed with the way you immobilised the chasing car, that technique will be in our manual soon."

The Cooper-Queens Manoeuvre." Andy informs him, which stalls him for a moment, before he continues.

"Well, we have a plan for today, we will ensure you get your reward, but that's not until this afternoon, there are a few things we need to do first, a few things we need you to do, but first may I introduce my two compatriots who have just arrived from the US." He gestures towards the other two men, who with their short hair, athletic physique and steely glazes remind Rob and Andy of countless servicemen they have worked with.

"John Smith and Joe Smith, they are with a special team of thirty who have flown over to escort Ali Bezir back to the states." The Smiths both nod acknowledgements, but stay silent.

"John, Joe and their team can bring a certain amount of shall we say, expertise, to the situation we currently have here. We will use them to neutralise any threat and if possible detain Matvei Kovalenko. They will also provide some welcome cover for you, as we will credit them as the assault team that captured Ali Bezir, I'm sure you will be happy with that."

Rob nods. "Very happy with that, I'm not one for publicity and I'm sure my colleague isn't either."

Rogers smiles as he continues the dialogue. "Anyway we will run through how they did it in a while, first we need to break down today's program of events. Our priority is to capture Kovalenko and to do that we will need to take out his men. For that we need your help."

Rob and Andy both could guess where this was going.

"We need to get you out in the open, to bring them out where our forces can get them. This may not be as easy as it seems as we know there are at least twelve of them. We have four of them, none of whom will tell us anything, so we don't know what weapons they have or what other resources they may have and we don't know what Kovalenko wants with you. As they are four short, they will be a lot more cautious so maybe a little harder to flush out. We may need you out in the open for longer than you feel safe for, in some very public places."

One of the Smiths speaks for the first time, they are not sure which one he is, but that is irrelevant. "We have selected a few things for you to do today, my team will be hidden around the areas in the plan. First we need you to go to the bus station and enquire about a bus to Blantyre. Then you will go to the open air market and spend some time browsing round there. We should be able to apprehend some of them there, then if there are more to get, we need you to eat at an open air restaurant on Mandala road. If there are still more of Kovalenko's men to apprehend, we would like you to browse the shops on the nearby street and maybe go into the little mall they have here. If we haven't been able to neutralise the threat totally after that, we'll send a taxi to take you towards the airport, which will hopefully flush the rest out. We are banking on Kovalenko being one of the ones that makes an appearance, but will review the situation if he doesn't. We will find a way to get him, a way where there will be minimum risk to yourselves. You will be in the line of sight of at least four of my men at any time, as Rogers said, there are thirty of us, so we have plenty of man power for this operation. Any questions?"

He had made it sound so simple and matter of fact.

Not matter of fact enough for Andy though. "Will we have our weapons and any bodily protection?"

"You can have your weapons, body armour may give the game away, but we will not let anyone take a shot at you."

This does little to reassure Andy, who just wants to get it over with as quickly as possible. "OK, when do we go?"

"Right now, we are ready, our men have been in place for thirty minutes now."

Rob looks at Andy, giving him a look of resignation, before turning to the rest of the occupants. "OK, let's go, we've faced more dangerous situations before." They have a strange feeling that they haven't been told the full story, but are willing to go with it for now.

They leave the room and go outside the embassy where there are two waiting cars in the court yard. Rogers turns to Rob and Andy. "We have a taxi waiting for you outside the gate. Turning up in one of our official cars may give the game away. We won't be too far behind you, there will always be someone close at hand in case help is needed."

Rob puts his bag over his shoulder and walks to the gate while Andy turns to Rogers. "Can we trust this taxi driver?"

Rogers snorts a little laugh. "You'll see when you get in it." This intrigues Andy who follows Rob out of the gate and into the waiting taxi, a typical battered Malawian car, painted dark green. As they get in the back, the driver turns to them. "Hi guys, Bob Smith, I'll be your driver today and I've got some firepower here in case we need it, but we should be OK until we get to the main centre of town." This brings Andy some comfort in the knowledge that the Americans seem to have everything covered.

Rob wants to know more though. "Hi Bob, have you guys got any leads on the Russians at all today?"

Bob shakes his head. "Very little activity since we've been here, although that's only been a few hours and we've been locked away planning for most of that. There are too few permanent agents here to provide any effective in depth surveillance, although there were reports of a break in at the Argentinian embassy last night. The reports are a bit sketchy, when we pass there in a minute, you'll see that there seems to be a car watching it."

This is interesting news for Rob, who has been racking his brain for a motive for the Russians. The Argentinian connection gives him some reassurance that they may not be looking for them under their real identities, which if it is the case, when this is over this is one thing they won't have to worry about. They pass the Argentinian embassy a couple of minutes later, hiding their faces as they pass a brand new Nissan 4x4 with blacked out windows parked across the street. As they drive out of sight, Rob taps Bob on the shoulder. "That was the same type of car which chased us yesterday, too much of a coincidence."

Bob knows exactly what Rob is implying. "Sadly, we cannot engage them until they pose a threat to you, we have to be sure, we need to flush Kovalenko out in the open, taking out his guys there would likely cause him to flee. It depends on how much he wants you two."

Andy still finds the time to joke about the situation. "Hopefully he doesn't really want us, this is all just a case of mistaken identity."

The line is totally ignored by the other two occupants of the taxi. Bob checks his watch. "Right, one minute and we are at the bus station, I will drop you at the top entrance. There is a wide open space you need to walk over to get to the terminal and make your enquiries, but I'll be here, watching every move, you'll be relieved to know that we have the area completely covered."

Rob and Andy are dropped off at the top of a hill. They look at over a hundred metres of a partially tarmacked rectangular area, the gaps in the tarmac covered in loose stone chippings. At the far end is their destination, the bus terminal in the corner, a one storey yellow building with only a couple of windows. Only the word 'Ticket Office' written in red across the middle gives away its function.

One of the only nearby parked buses provides adequate cover as they survey the area, which is far too open for their liking. With only a few buses parked at the top end, most of the walk will be without cover. They can see that the bottom end of the slope is lined with trees, a contrast to the line of shops at the top end. There was plenty of scope for a sniper to take a long shot. They would also be defenceless if a car came at high speed when they were in the middle of the rectangle, giving them little chance of getting to cover in time.

There were a few taxis near the ticket office, their drivers all sitting around on some plastic tables near the building. They could present a danger themselves, they could be concealing assassins, or in the case of a lot of gunfire breaking out, they could scatter, increasing the chance of being accidentally hit by one of them.

Andy turns to Rob. "What do you think?"

"I don't like it, I can understand why the yanks picked this place first, but we are too exposed. Our best chance is to go down the left hand side, to the treeline, then follow it along to the office, but that's not what we are expected to do to draw out the Russians. I guess we just go for it and hope the bus station isn't being watched right now.

Andy resigns himself to a tense few minutes. "OK, no point in waiting around, let's get this over with." They start walking briskly, with their heads down, right across the middle of the open space. They cover the first half in silence, with nothing untoward to bother them and start to relax a little, the chances of reaching cover if needed are increasing with every step.

The relaxed atmosphere doesn't last very long as the taxi drivers near the ticket office suddenly all get excited, simultaneously leaping up and heading for their taxis after some heated exchanges with each other. All of the taxis speed off up the hill, raising the adrenaline levels in Rob and Andy to extremes. It all looked too unnatural, as if something was about to happen. They start edging towards the tree line but still moving forward towards the ticket office, nervously looking around for any sight of danger. They spot what they are looking for at the top of the hill. Coming down towards them in a slight jog are two darkly dressed men both with blonde hair.

Andy does not need to be told what the plan is, he makes a run for the treeline, closely followed by Rob. Their pursuers speed up when they see this. Rob and Andy put their heads down and sprint as fast as they can towards the trees, with the intention of using them as cover to give them the advantage. They start taking fire a few metres before they reach the trees, fortunately for them the range is too far to be effective as they dive into the undergrowth at the tree base.

Before they have time to scramble round and return fire, silenced shots start ringing out from in front of them, their worst nightmare, sandwiched between assassins, their odds of escaping safely reducing significantly. It takes a few moments for them to realise that the shots coming from the trees are not aimed at them. The sound of the accent telling them to get down is most welcome. The Americans immobilise the two assassins very effectively, putting bullets in each of their limbs, enough to knock them to the floor and disarm them, but not enough to be fatal.

One of the Smith's heads appears in front of them from behind some foliage. "We need you to quickly go and drag those two guys over here. It's better if we are not seen yet, it could cause Kovalenko to decide the odds are against him and retreat."

Rob signs, but understands. He looks around and is surprised to see the Russians are so close, only twenty metres away. He grabs Andy by the shoulder, they both get to their feet, quickly run over to the men, kick the guns away and drag the first body into the foliage, returning to repeat the same with the second Russian, the whole process taking less than thirty seconds. They crouch in the foliage, panting as Smith pats them on the back. "Good job, take five to get your breath back, then we'll head off to the market."

Five minutes later, they walk through the trees, heading for the market which is only ten minutes' walk away, feeling a lot more confident about the protection they are getting. They reach the market, which is a sprawling array of wooden stalls, protected from the sun by canvass awnings, selling the typical African variety of goods found in markets, ranging from household goods and clothing to all types of food produce. They are happier in this type of environment where any attempt on them will have to be at close quarters, something they are adept at spotting and dealing with.

The market is busy, bustling with locals, many dealing with traders in a sea of sound and motion that Rob and Andy take a few minutes to focus out, enabling them to spot the patterns and sounds of unusual activity. They start to spot some of Smith's men mingling with the crowds, effectively passing as tourists to the uninitiated. Rob and Andy both hope that the Russians do not spot the Americans as easily as they have. They walk through the market, paying little attention to the stalls, despite every trader they pass making an extra effort to attract the two Muzungus and their money.

Rob and Andy spend twenty minutes weaving through the stalls, getting to the end of the first row and half way through the second row of stalls, when they first speak. "I have not seen anyone that fits the bill, we may have entered an area too busy for the Russians' liking."

Rob has spotted something that has alerted him. "I'm not so sure, we've been concentrating on looking for Mzungus, but have you noticed the four guys that seem to be trailing our every move, they seem to be locals, but fairly well dressed. Every time I've caught a glimpse of them they have not even bothered to take any interest in the stalls."

When they stop at a household goods stall, Andy uses one of the mirrors to take a look behind. "Yes, I saw those earlier, didn't pay them much attention, they looked too green to be a threat, but I can see what you mean, they have now stopped and keep looking in our direction. We can take them easily."

He keeps watching them, while Rob catches the eye of one of the Smiths, his nod back to the four Malawians, being returned. The Smith calls over a local policeman and talks closely in his ear, the policeman seeming to acknowledge every word, before looking over and quickly pointing in the direction of the four well-dressed men. The four locals do not see any of this, their focus being totally directed at Rob and Andy. The four start edging closer, which causes Andy to alert Rob. "They are moving." They both look round directly at all four, who freeze for a second before lurching forward as they draw out some knives, the blades immediately catching the beams of sunlight coming through the gaps in the stalls. The glint of the knives panics all the people around the four men, causing a mad dash out of the way accompanied by screams and shouts, leaving a clear path between the armed Africans and their two intended victims.

As the four men move closer through the throng trying to get out of the way, they pause for a second as they spot Rob and Andy are turning to face them with their hands behind their back, something they didn't expect. Before they can get their guns drawn fully, the potential attackers are stopped dead by very loud assertive shouts coming from a dozen local police who have guns directed straight at them from behind the closest stalls. They all raise their hands quickly and drop their knives, while Rob and Andy's guns are returned to their hiding places.

The four attackers drop to their knees and start pleading with the police, watched by a large crowd that has gathered around them in a circle. With the cover of the crowd, one of the Smiths approaches Rob and Andy with the Police commander, he taps them on the shoulder. "Don't turn around, my Malawian colleague here has the situation under control, he has translated what those four are saying, apparently they are pleading for mercy, saying they were asked to do this by a large Muzungu, they were only supposed to catch you, not kill you."

Rob keeps looking at the four pleading men. "What do we do now?"

"Walk right out of here, we don't know how many other locals have been paid off and we want to get you in a more open area to get the odds back in our favour, we can easily spot Westerners in somewhere like this, but Malawians present too much of a risk. Quickly get out to the end of this row where Bob will be waiting in the taxi. We have you covered, so just move as fast as you can."

Andy and Rob don't need to be told again, they turn and walk briskly out of the market, pushing forcefully past anyone in their way, causing some comments and hisses as they pass. Manners were not the highest item on their agenda at this time. As they pass the last stall they see the dirty green taxi they started the day in and get straight into the back. Bob greets them. "Tough day so far?"

Andy shakes his head. "We've had tougher, but I will be happy when this day is over. I don't like being the target."

Bob pulls the taxi away. "I'm just going to drive around for a bit, make sure we are not being trailed, then drop you off at the top end of the shopping area, it should be safer there, less bustle and less close contact. I've been in radio contact with the team all the way, they have taken out a few more locals who did not even get as close to you as this last lot. It appears Kovalenko has hired the men from one of the local crime lords. We still don't know why though."

Rob doesn't like this, the numbers against them are increasing all of the time. "The odds of us getting out of this unscathed seem to be decreasing by the minute."

Bob disagrees. "Nah, the local agencies have got enough intel on this crime lord to be able to neutralise him easily enough, he doesn't have as many men as we do. We have already taken 90% of them, those four in the market were his top men, so the rest will be a doddle."

Andy chuckles at that. "If they were his top men, I'm not worried, they froze like rabbits in headlights when they saw we were about to face them with firepower, but we still need to deal with six or seven nasty Russians, they are the ones that worry me."

Bob has been alert looking for the presence of cars that are constantly behind him and has identified two that have been with them since the market, so he takes the next left leading them away from the city, before taking some more turnings that will lead them back into the city. The cars he has singled out follow suit, a definite indication they are following him. He radios the details of the cars to the rest of the team before putting his foot down and heading into some leafy residential streets at speed. "We have some colleagues on the way, they will take out these cars, but we need to head out of town to minimise collateral damage.

"Fine by us." Both passengers have their guns drawn. At the moment they are the only defence the taxi has. Rob has been observing the two cars behind. "Both cars are driven by Africans, no sign of Westerners." He speaks too soon, as they pass a junction at speed, the white Nissan they saw earlier screeches out behind them and joins the chase. "Forget that, we have a car full of bogies behind now, a car which will outrun this car easily."

Bob smiles, shaking his head. "Don't be so sure, it may look like a typical beat up piece of Malawian shit from the outside, but we've got a lot of tech in this, including a beast of an engine. It's a special embassy car, all our embassies have them, they can prove very useful for blending in and performing when needed."

The Nissan is still stuck behind the two local cars, which are swerving over the whole of the road as the drivers struggle to keep up with the taxi, a good indication that the drivers are not used to driving at this speed and will be easy to lose. Bob executes a perfect sliding turn at speed at the next junction, which loses the first car, as the driver cannot execute the same turn of skill and smashes straight into a house situated on the corner. The car behind it spins on the corner screeching to a halt, most importantly blocking the road for the Nissan which collides with it, the force of which throws the passenger of the local car through his door. The cars end up entangled in the twisted metal of the local car, which took the full force of the impact. The Nissan only has cosmetic damage, allowing the driver to use the power of the Nissan to pull away, shearing off the front axle of the local car.

The Nissan regains the trail and starts to accelerate after Bob's taxi, which is in the far distance, but has slowed to allow the pursuers to catch up. Bob lets the Nissan get within fifty metres before accelerating to maintain the distance. He follows the straight road for few more minutes, monitoring the radio which is constantly updating the progress of his colleagues. "We should be OK after the next junction, the cavalry are waiting there."

As they pass the junction, he slows considerably as two black Mercedes pull out of the junction to intercept the Nissan, taking the driver completely by surprise, causing him to veer into the side of the road and collide with a wall. The Nissan is quickly surrounded by members of Bob's team, who pull the Russians out of the car and force them to lay face down on the floor. Bob flicks on the radio. "Great job guys, we are going to head back into town."

"Roger, go to agreed rendezvous, our friends could do with something to eat."

Bob turns to Rob and Andy. "Hungry?"

Andy shakes his head. "Food wasn't top of my list of things I needed at the moment, but I won't turn down a coffee."

Rob wants to know more. "What's at the rendezvous?"

"Nothing special, it's the restaurant we selected in the plan, we will have quite a few of the team there already, it has good vantage points so should be one of the safest parts of the day for you. If they take the bait it will be easy for us to take them out."

Barely ten minutes later the taxi arrives in the shopping district, which Bob drives through before pulling into the street full of restaurants that included Mad Mike's festival site. Bob pulls up and points to the restaurant they ate at two days before. "I've been told you are familiar with the food here, it's the optimum one in the street for us, I'll be round the corner listening to everything in case you need me." Bob explains everything with an excited enthusiasm, he is enjoying his role this mission.

Rob and Andy get out of the taxi and take seats at one of the tables outside. A waiter arrives to take their order. "Two coffees, black, one sugar each." The waiter nods but waits for them to order food, which Andy definitely does not want yet. "We'll order food when we have finished our coffees." The waiter openly displays his disappointment. "You order food now, we bring it after your coffees." He had seen many Muzungus order drinks, then leave before eating when they see the bar over the road filling up with other Mzungus. Rob decides to appease the waiter. "We'll have two tomato omelettes please." which causes a look of consternation from Andy.

After the waiter leaves Andy explains his dismay. "We could be here for a while, I don't want to be rushed into having our food now, then find we have to spend a few hours just waiting around, you know he'll bring those omelettes straight away."

"I know, I like your optimism, but I'm hungry and these Russians have been onto us like a shot everywhere we've appeared, I need to get some energy inside me before the next piece of action, even now I'm doubting that we will get a chance to tuck into those omelettes before we are under fire again."

"Sounds like a bet!" Andy has a glint in his eye.

Rob is never ceased to be amazed by Andy's ability to maintain some sense of humour in the most tense of situations.

The waiter returns with the two coffees, which bring some welcome stimulation. They are barely half way through them when Andy slams his down on the table. "Here we go." He has spotted two men that meet the same criteria as all the other Russians chasing them, large, stern looking and dressed totally in black. The

Russians walk past the end of the street, as they pass they look up the street directly at Rob and Andy, before they stop and stand outside a store on the corner, pretending to look at postcards. The Russians are obviously engaging each other in deep conversation, not even looking at each item they pick up. They maintain this façade for a couple of minutes, before slowly making their way up the street, pretending to look in every store that lines it.

Rob has been watching in the reflection of a square chrome box used to hold condiments that is on the table. A box that is different from the condiment holders on the rest of the tables, something he assumes to have been put there specifically for them by the Americans. Andy has not taken his eye off the Russians. He pulls his guns from behind his back in preparation, gripping them between his legs for a quick retrieval. Rob does not have this luxury as his back is facing the two assassins, but Andy has noticed this. "I know I won't say this very often, but if you reach between my legs, you will be able to grab something you like."

Rob is grateful for his partner's insight into the situation and slowly pulls one of the guns from between Andy's legs. The two Russians continue their pretence of being tourists, but their naivety of their opponents' support team is their downfall. As they stop in an open shop front only metres away from their targets, pretending to look at some souvenirs, they suddenly appear to jump into the shop, after which a few loud thuds are heard.

A minute later the waiter returns, but he has changed, instead of being the slim Malawian that has been serving them, he is a lot broader. He speaks to them in an American accent. "We've got those two, word on the street is that there is no one else in this vicinity, so why don't you guys head down to the little mall across the road, we should flush the last two out if you are more in the open, hopefully we can get to Kovalenko easier without his goons around."

Rob thinks about objecting, the omelette hasn't arrived yet, but knows that if they can get the last two as quick as the rest, they will be able to eat in a more relaxed atmosphere, maybe with some company. "Sure, do you want us inside or out?" He has been to the Nico centre before, calling it a mall is a little overstating it.

"Doesn't matter, we are all over the place." The American leaves the table, while Rob and Andy leave some money for the coffees, omelettes and a tip, getting up to leave the table for the walk down the street to the Nico centre, which is less than five minutes' away.

The two Brits arrive at the two storey bright orange building with a bright green contrasting roof. They go inside the arches that surround the ground floor level to peruse the shops, using the reflections in the many windows to observe everything directly behind them.

Around thirty uneventful minutes are spent wandering around the outside of the building. Rob and Andy start to get bored, but maintain their alertness, something they manage through their many years of experience. They go inside the mall, board the escalator and ride to the first floor. Rob looks up at the mirror at the top of the escalator. As they are half way up they spot two familiar but unwelcome figures pass through the front entrance, looking directly up towards them. They are accompanied by a burly grey haired man, who seems to giving the other two directions whilst pointing up at the escalator.

Rob nudges Andy, but he has already seen the threat. Rob and Andy start to run up the escalator, reaching the top as the three behind them reach the bottom. Rob turns to look down at the three, the two thugs that tried to kill them in the hotel the day before are accompanied by a man who dwarfs them both, his pockmarked angry face topped by a head of very short cropped silver hair. This is a face that he has seen before a long time ago, the exact location eluding him at this moment.

As they get off the escalator, they see their options are limited, with only a few shops arranged either side of a walkway, but they are banking on at least some of the Smiths being here. It is not as brightly lit as many Western shopping centres, but there is still sufficient light for them to be easily spotted. They need to find good cover or an exit, so run down the walkway glancing in each shop as they pass. Nothing obvious they could use stands out in the fractions of seconds they have to look in each shop. They do not see any obvious presence of support they are expecting either.

They approach the shop at the end, realising they are potentially trapped, but as they have no time for hesitation they need to take a quick decision. Andy makes that decision before Rob, grabbing a bin from the side of one of the shops then sliding onto the floor to take what limited cover he can behind the bin. Rob catches onto the plan immediately and follows suit, leaving them both prone on the floor, guns outstretched facing towards the escalator.

The three Russians reach the top of the escalator, quickly ducking to either side of the walkway as they fire a volley of shots down the corridor, none of which hits their very limited target.

A voice shouts out from one of the shops. "Kovalenko, you are surrounded and outnumbered considerably."

"Fuck You."

More gun shots rain down from the escalator end, smashing some of the shop windows in the corridor, raining glass down onto the walkway. Fire is returned by Rob and Andy, but they stop when they hear a familiar voice behind them. "Careful guys, we don't want any civilians hit, we have this floor cleared, but there still are some in the direction you are firing at, outside in the street."

Andy takes exception to this. "I'm not laying down here letting them fire at will at us, the more they fire, the more likely they are to hit something."

"It's OK, we have it covered." As Bob finishes speaking, two gas grenades are flung up from the bottom of the escalator, covering the far end in choking gas which causes the Russians to leave their cover, taking random pot shots down the corridor whilst covering their faces as best as they can.

More shots are heard as two of the Russians shoot out the window of the closest shop to them, then jump through the gaping hole, leaving one man out in the open, a man who is staggering down the corridor, his identity given away by his size. A single shot rings out, hitting Kovalenko in the shoulder, dropping him to the floor.

He is quickly surrounded by a dozen men in full assault kit who appear from shops half way down the corridor. They disarm and restrain Kovalenko whilst facing a volley of abuse in Russian and English. Some of the squad enter the shop after the two other Russians, but quickly return shaking their heads.

Bob, John and Joe Smith appear behind Rob and Andy, who have now got to their feet, receiving back slaps from everyone. "Awesome operation guys, we were told you were good, but didn't expect you be to be as good as us." John is impressed.

Andy puts his arm around John. "Years of practise my friend, which is now going to be put into retirement."

"That's a shame, we could use guys like you, a lot."

Rob isn't going to be convinced to carry on either. "It's nice to have the recognition and the offer, but that should be the last time we fire guns in anger, it's been a tough life leading it the way we have and now I want to enjoy the spoils of our work with some good company."

The group exits the shopping centre via one of the fire exits, where they are met by some embassy officials. Rob and Andy are escorted into one of the waiting Mercedes. A small crowd has gathered to look at the mall, the gunshots brought this part of town to a complete standstill. For a peaceful city like Lilongwe, gunfire was a sound that was rarely heard.

Rob and Andy are driven back to the US embassy, where they get out to be met by Jones and Rogers, who offer them more thanks. Kovalenko is carried into the embassy by four of the assault squad.

Jones addresses them. "I'm guessing you'd like to find out what Kovalenko wanted with you?" They both nod. "Well, if you have the time and I'm sure you do while we clear your reward payment for Ali Bezir, would you like to view our debriefing? I'm keen to find out what he wanted too, it will be a more civil situation for yourselves than last time you were in the viewing room."

Rob is delighted he will get to see the debriefing session, he wants to jog his memory and find out where he has seen Kovalenko before. "We would like to definitely take you up on that offer."

Jones smiles and escorts them into the embassy, down into the basement and into the viewing room where they have refreshments already waiting, including the two omelettes they ordered earlier. There are six other people in the room, but they are not introduced to any of them.

Kovalenko is in the other room, secured to a chair, having his wound treated. He is grimacing and still cursing. Once the medical treatment is finished, he is left alone for a few minutes, before Rogers enters the room with Jones who leads the interrogation.

"Mr Kovalenko, what a pleasure it is to have you with us."

"Fuck you, get me to my embassy, I have rights."

"I'm afraid not, your embassy does not want you, you have upset the Malawian authorities, broken several international laws and from our point of view, broken many American laws by indirectly causing the deaths of American citizens."

"FUCK YOU, get me my embassy, now."

Rogers nods to the one way window, one of the occupants of the viewing room gets up and leaves to be shown into the room next door. He sits down and starts to speak to Kovalenko in his native tongue, producing his identity badge after some aggressive backchat. As the man keeps speaking, Kovalenko looks increasingly agitated, his expression bordering on totally scared by the time the conversation has finished.

The man gets up and returns to the viewing room.

Jones continues his dialogue. "Now that you can clearly see that your country cannot and does not want to help you, I take it you will be as co-operative as you can be. We have some other high profile people in our custody here, the last thing you want to do is be tied in with them, as they will, how you say, be thrown to the wolves back in the US."

Kovalenko looks at them expressionless. "Malek Ali Bezir."

This surprises Rogers, Jones and all of occupants of the viewing room.

Jones wants clarification "Sorry? What do you mean?"

Kovalenko looks indignant. "Malek Ali Bezir, you have him here, those two Argentinian bastards brought him here. I tracked them." He looks smug as he says the last part.

Jones tries to feign ignorance, aware of the people who are next door. "I think you are mistaken, we have been trying to track Ali Bezir for years, we would know if he is here."

Kovalenko starts to show a little anger. "I know he is here, I tracked him. He was in the Republic of the Congo , those Argentinians kidnapped him and brought him here, they flew over the Democratic Republic of the Congo, over Zambia to the north of Malawi, then drove to your embassy. I tracked him all the way."

Jones and Rogers confer out of earshot for a few minutes, before returning to their interrogation.

"I'm impressed that you claim to have done something that every government in the Western world has been trying unsuccessfully for the last seven years. Pray tell me, how did you manage such a feat?" Jones' fails to hide his cynicism.

"Easy, I gave him a bag of weapons that had a tracking device attached and also a piece of jewellery with another tracking device. He was wearing the jewellery when they kidnapped him, they carried the bag with them all the way to here."

This raised the hairs on Rob's back, he realised that if the tracking device was on the bag he had stowed at the airport, it would be gone by now, which would reduce their pension considerably.

Jones knows that Kovalenko is probably telling the truth, but wants him to tell the whole story from the start. "OK then, can you run though everything you know? Right from the start, we can ask questions afterwards."

Kovalenko sits in silence pondering this for a while, then shrugs his shoulders, he has nothing to lose, what he says may make him more useful to the Americans. His whole story is relayed with an angry tone.

"I have been building my business up for many years, I have had some setbacks when various authorities impounded my legitimate imports and exports, authorities that want to keep the market for themselves and stop businessmen like me from making a living.

Combined with that, I had to compete with other similar businessmen, in a very tight market, a market where those Argentinians were my main competitors, I lost out on a big deal in the Sudan because of them, the more I tried to get into Africa, the more everyone asked me if I knew them. This pissed me off as they had all the business, everywhere I tried, everywhere they had been before.

So I had to find a new market and after many years of looking for a way in to the market which others were scared of supplying because the risks were too high, I eventually met with the man who would present the best business opportunities for me, Malek Ali Bezir. We did some small deals for his friends in the Middle East, but they did not pay well, the groups were small and they did not last long as the west destroyed them. Malek Ali Bezir wanted to expand into Africa, he said there was a big untapped following that could get him the power he wanted and I was the man that could help him.

I was becoming his main supplier and he promised me that I would be his main supplier for his African partners. I would not have to worry about Argentinians or Germans or Belgians again.

He had arranged an initial meeting in Africa, where he would start to set up the networks which would provide funding for people who would buy weapons from me. Once they had the power and control in their areas, they could finance themselves. It was to be my greatest deal, the one which would make me the Bill Gates of weapons.

I gave him samples to take and supplied him with some extra money for his fund to fuel the deals, several millions of dollars that I knew I would get back, I am a business man, sometimes you have to invest to get the rewards.

I supplied him the weapons in a bag that I had fitted with an electronic tracking device, as I wanted to see where my investment was going. He would not tell me, it was big secret. I would not become directly involved until infrastructure for deals was in place, after which he would not need to be directly involved. He said if I went for first meeting and it went wrong, everything would be lost. I agreed but was not happy, so gave him good luck pendant as leaving present, which also had tracking device. A smart businessman keeps eye on his investment.

I tracked him to Republic of Congo, so made some calls to contacts I have there to make sure I was given correct information about what was happening. Then everything went wrong because of Argentinians. Again they gate-crashed my deal and again they took my business partner away. I get phone call, saying something bad has happened, everyone is killed, money is gone, Malek Ali Bezir is gone. My contact thinks that the Argentinians were responsible, but they disappeared. He knew they were there as he drove them to the meeting with Malek Ali Bezir and many other of my new clients, but they did not phone him for lift home, later he saw their bodies were not in house.

I was angrier than I have ever been, they taken what was mine away again, but I had the advantage, I could see where they were, so I gathered some associates and tracked them here. I wanted them alive so I could get my money back and take over their business once I had extracted their contacts from them. They are the criminals, they stole from me and now you help them. You are criminals too. If I had sober men with me today who also were not cowards, we would have prevailed and you would have given over the Argentinians and my money and left me to do my business, a business which your government conducts every day with terrorists to my country.

So do not call me a criminal, I am the victim."

Rogers lets out a large gasp of air. "Phew, that was a great story. We will have to check its validity, but in our view, supplying the worlds most wanted terrorist with weapons does actually make you a criminal, one of the worst kind."

Kovalenko is still defiant. "We will see in court."

Jones is keen to wrap things up. "No doubt we will, but I suspect that may be some time yet, we will be shipping you to the US tomorrow to try and unravel all of your business deals. Myself and my colleague would like to thank you for your candidness today, it has resolved a few puzzles we had, especially as how a peaceful country like Malawi can turn into a bloodbath.

Jones and Rogers leave the room before Kovalenko is led to a cell for the night, returning to the viewing room which is still in a state of shock over the revelations they have just heard, something that Jones wants to clarify with a couple of the occupants. "Gentlemen, I hope that satisfies you with an explanation for today's events, even though many were totally unwarranted and we can draw a line under it. I would like to thank you all for attending. If I could have a quick word with Yuri and Chikosi, before you leave, I'd like to clear some things up before tomorrow, so there isn't any ambiguity over the situation between the United States, Russia and Malawi.

The occupants of the room leave the Russian and the Malawian to their briefing on the unveiling of Malek Ali Bezir tomorrow and the 'true' details of how he was captured, which were contrastingly different from the tale they had just been told.

As Rob and Andy were leaving, they wondered where they would stay that night, but it was soon clarified when they got into reception and Nigel was waiting for them with a friendly welcome.

"Hello again, I hope your day wasn't too stressful, I've had a full briefing and I'm proud that some of my compatriots have contributed so much to world peace today. The British ambassador would like to meet you tomorrow morning to privately present an award to you, before we bring you back here to finalise any financial regularities with the Americans. We have arranged a hotel room for you tonight, where I guarantee you will not be woken up by gunshots!"

Rob shakes his hand. "Thanks Nigel, I think we need definitely some sleep."

"And something to eat." Andy was still hungry. He now wished he had a chance to eat that omelette while it was hot. The cold version in the viewing room didn't appeal to him.

They are taken to the crossroads hotel complex, a large modern single storey complex, arranged around a swimming pool. The orange brick walls interspersed with a lot of glass, contrasting with the bright green roof.

The formalities are sorted out by an embassy official, while they are shown to their room, tastefully decorated in several shades of subtle brown and orange. A quick freshen up is required before they interpret the day's events. They are not concerned about listening devices in the room now. Andy does not perform his usual checks before speaking. "Well, what do you think?"

"I'm happy, Kovalenko doesn't really know who we are, I'm confident the authorities have everything under control, I'm just looking forward to getting the reward and having some rest and relaxation."

"Didn't you think that Kovalenko looked familiar? Although I'm not sure where I've seen him."

"Sudan, he was there when we delivered the shipment. Remember that argument that was going on in the background across the compound when we collected the payment, I think he was the one that was doing the most shouting."

Andy vaguely remembers, it wasn't important at the time, but there was an altercation over the other side of the compound, well away from where they were, it didn't seem relevant to them at the time. "We must have really pissed him off then, it's a shame that his contact in Brazzaville wasn't important enough to get invited to the party, we would have taken him out and Kovalenko would not have been chasing us, just Malek Ali Bezir."

"I think it was lucky for us, otherwise Kovalenko would still be out there with a grudge against us."

Andy considers this and is satisfied with the logic. "I still wish we'd put a bullet through Mulaki's stupid hat though."

Rob snorts a laugh as he checks his watch. "Turn the TV on, channel one, Lisa is due on to talk about tourism."

Andy turns the TV on, they sit on the bed to watch 'Malawi Tonight' which is a topical magazine show, similar to many in the west which combine news with more trivial entertainment and special features. The female presenter conducts the show in English, reading some mundane news stories, occasionally handing over to a reporter in a safari park, talking about the welfare of the animals. Half way through the show, she introduces Lisa, who is interviewed about tourism in Malawi, answering a series of questions on how the locals can improve their image, most of which receive routine responses. The interview is over in five minutes and fortunately would not set the world of journalism alight, like it would have done if Rob had forgotten to call Lisa and ensure she sat on the tapes he had given her.

Andy looks on the bright side. "I'm happy that it was as mundane as it was now, if we had been in the situation where Lisa had to broadcast the tape, I think we would have been in the firing line of the Smiths all day."

They smile, switching off the television before they go to grab some food, after which they retire for a good night's sleep.

Capítulo Catorce

The night's sleep is longer than normal. So long that they almost miss breakfast, but it was a sleep they needed, the first time in a long time that they didn't have anything to worry about that disturbed them during the night.

Breakfast is a slow affair as they help themselves to a buffet table laden with fresh fruits and pastries before tucking into a freshly cooked hot selection of eggs, sausages and potatoes. While they eat, Andy shares the only thing that was unresolved in his mind. "The Americans didn't mention the other two from the shopping centre yesterday."

Rob had realised this but wasn't worried. "I'm confident they were dealt with, there were so many people around that centre yesterday that they would have to be illusionists in order to disappear, Kovalenko called them drunks, if they did get away, they would make a slip up pretty quickly, drunks make too many mistakes in times like this."

As they finish breakfast they are joined by Nigel who is accompanied by some British embassy officials. "Good

Morning, I trust everything was to your satisfaction and you didn't have any unwanted interruptions."

Andy is still finishing his food, while Rob neatly places his cutlery on the plate before responding. "Morning, We had a fine night's sleep. Is there any news that we need to be aware of?"

Nigel shakes his head. "No, nothing has changed since yesterday, the Americans are busy briefing some other nations on the activities of the last few days, they want to ensure that there isn't any fall out before they make their big announcement, they are trying sort out the fine details to ensure no country will claim their borders were infringed illegally. It may take longer than expected as there is a lot of negotiation going on, but we are confident that it will be wrapped up today."

These details do not concern Rob or Andy, they just want to finish this episode of their lives and enjoy their retirement. They finish their breakfast and leave with the officials, with Nigel explaining the protocol for the day as they drive off.

"We will go back to the British embassy, where the ambassador will meet you for a few minutes to present you with an award from our Government for your charitable work in Malawi, we will then tie up some visa formalities. We will all then travel in an official cavalcade to the American embassy, where you will be presented to the American ambassador in an official reception where he will present you with an award, they will finalise any payments due to you, then you will be free to enjoy your retirement wherever you wish. The whole proceedings shouldn't take longer than an hour."

Neither Rob or Andy are keen for the official publicity, especially as it will be so close to the announcement of Ali Bezir's capture, it wouldn't take much for someone to link their awards with the capture. Even if it was a very tentative link, it would potentially put them at risk. Rob voices his concerns. "I'm not sure I'm completely comfortable with being in any official spotlight, I'd prefer everything was much more low key."

Nigel is very reassuring. "Don't worry, there will be no photos, no media coverage of either presentations, there will be just a tiny footnote in official records, with no mention of names. I wrote it myself, it simply states: 'Two aid workers are presented with the British Empire Medal'. An award that, although it is officially discontinued, is still given in exceptional circumstances where we want to recognise the achievements of certain people who do not want any attention drawn to themselves."

This satisfies part of their concerns, but Andy wants to clarify that the Americans will be as subtle,

"Are the Americans going to be as prudent?"

"Yes, they will be presenting you with the equivalent civilian award as the team who captured Ali Bezir, it will be completely behind closed doors, you will not even be a footnote in their history books, but they want you to understand how grateful they are for what you have done."

They arrive at the British embassy and are escorted into the official reception room, pleased by the small amount of people in attendance. Apart from themselves and Nigel, there is just the ambassador and an assistant. The British ambassador, Michael Hunt-Davies, was a slight man, younger than they expected, appearing to be only in his early forties. He greets the two men with a very warm smile. "It is a great pleasure to meet you. I am very impressed with the story of what you have done for our government and how you have helped our overseas friends, albeit in a very minor role, it is a role you must be proud of."

It is obvious to Rob and Andy that their full involvement has not passed up the chain of command from Nigel. Rob is not about to correct the ambassador, or give him any more information than he needs. "We were just glad to be in the right place at the right time to be able to help."

The ambassador shakes their hands. "It gives me great pleasure to present this commendation to two brave aid workers who have made a valuable contribution to our international partners." He presents them both with a silver medal attached to a purple ribbon, it is very reminiscent of many of the military medals they have received for various campaigns throughout their career, but it is one that they will treasure most valuably. The actions that led to the award rather than the merit of the award were what mattered the most.

The swift ceremony finishes in a few minutes, after some formalities of appreciation they are led out of the room and into a plain office, where Nigel hands them some paperwork, openly displaying how pleased he was with himself. "See, you had nothing to worry about there, I couldn't have planned it to be as understated as it was, I'm sure the ambassador has probably forgotten about it already. Now for some formalities, I have taken the precaution of replacing your passports to ensure your trail is totally covered and that all official entry requirements into the country have been formally met. I took the liberty of backdating your entry to three months ago, which I'm sure won't be a problem for you."

Both men shake their heads as they receive the passports, fully stamped with their arrival dates, Malawi being the only entry in the empty pages. They don't have the heart to tell Nigel that they never use their British passports, so there wasn't a trail to cover, letting him take pride in his efficiency, they thank him graciously.

Nigel hands them some more paperwork. "It is almost time to leave, but I've taken the liberty of booking you into your hotel for a further two days, it is entirely up to you if you use it, I won't be offended if you do not, but I would not be happy leaving you with nowhere to stay in the short term."

They thank him again as he escorts them outside to the solitary car waiting to take them to the US embassy, which did not meet their definition of a cavalcade. Nigel gets in the front and directs the driver to the US embassy, a journey only taking a few minutes. The US Embassy gate is opened for them as they arrive and they pull up in the courtyard next to the only other vehicle, a Mercedes with official Malawian insignia.

They are taken into the embassy where they are shown into a small plain room without any furnishings or decoration, just plain white walls. They wait there with Nigel until Charles Sayer enters with another man, who is as broad as Sayer, but not as tall and looks much younger.

Sayer shakes their hands. "Gentlemen, may I introduce David Morgan the United States ambassador to Malawi."

Morgan greets them and proceeds straight into formalities. "Gentlemen, forgive me if I am brief, but we have some pressing business here in Malawi today, I am sure you will understand later."

He receives a nod of acknowledgment before continuing. "It gives me great pleasure to present you with 'Secretary of Defense Exceptional Civilian Service Award' for your contribution to United States work in Malawi." He pins a gold coloured medallion hanging under a white ribbon on them and shakes their hands before leaving the room. It is far briefer than they expected, but it is far more than they hoped for.

Sayer stays in the room after the ambassador exits. "Forgive us for the briefness of the ceremony, but as you can understand today is exceptionally busy. If you would like to follow me, I have the authorisation for your payment, we just need to conduct the transaction before you leave.

Andy states what both men are thinking. "We are just grateful that it was that brief, we are not ones for ceremony or publicity, we would like to retire without looking over our shoulders each day. I get the impression that he didn't know the full story."

This raises a smile with Sayer. "He knows the full official story of how a team of brave American agents tracked down Malek Ali Bezir to a compound in an African backwater, where he was apprehended by a crack team of special forces, with very limited collateral damage, before being brought back to this embassy for debriefing while those forces rounded up the entourage that Ali Bezir had sent into the capital to start an insurgence. It's a great story you'll hear in full when we make the announcement and as you explicitly wanted no publicity, it's a story you'll be pleased to hear omits any involvement from yourselves."

"That suits us perfectly."

Sayer claps his hands. "OK, follow me where we can arrange your reward and sign some documentation." He leads them through to another room, where Rogers and Jones are waiting next to a computer.

Jones greets them with a smile. "Gentlemen, it is almost time for us to say goodbye, but we have some small business to conduct. As you are aware, there is a five million dollar reward for delivering Ali Bezir to us, you are also probably aware that we have prepared a detailed report of his capture, which credits US forces for the capture, something which is important for national pride and for us, to justify our budgets to congress. We would like to ensure that report is never challenged and that no conflicting stories surface in the years to come, although we are aware that conspiracy theorists will be spreading their own farfetched versions of events for their own satisfaction, we want to ensure that there isn't any hard evidence to back up any particular version."

The men start to feel a little anxious, this could go either of two ways, they didn't want it to go the way where they were physically wiped from any records, but this anxiety passes as Jones continues. "So, we would like to offer the full amount of the award to each of you, on condition that you sign this agreement, which will ensure that if for some reason your version of events ever surfaces, you will not provide any substantiation to it."

He waves a piece of paper in front of them which Rob takes and reads through. "I'm very happy to sign this, rest assured we will be at such risk from a great many people if for some bizarre reason we decide to go public, that I will never give you any reason to enforce your liability clauses."

They both sign the documents, while Rogers takes the details for the fund transfer. They watch the transfer go through, after which Rob is given a phone to clarify that payment has been made, the brief conversation satisfies him.

Jones is satisfied that his business with Rob and Andy is complete and is keen to get back to the arrangements for the rest of the day, something which for him will be a major milestone in his career. "I just like to finally thank you for all you have done, for the world, for America and for the staff in this little backwater, which will soon be in a spotlight we couldn't have dreamed of a few days ago."

He shakes their hands, followed by Rogers, who finishes the conversation. "Enjoy your retirement and your travels, if you ever need our help or have something that will help us, please contact myself or George, wherever we are and whatever posts we have, we will still owe our place in history to you." He hands them both a card with his details on, which they place safely in their passports, knowing that if they ever are in a situation where they have to use this card, it would be the most valuable thing they have at the time.

They bid farewell, Sayer leads them out of the embassy, to a waiting taxi, before saying his final farewell and offering some more thanks.

They get into the taxi, disappointed that Bob isn't driving it and ask for Glyn Jones Road. They spend the journey in silence, ever cautious over who might be listening into any of their conversation, so get out half way along outside a guest house. They don't go in, continuing along the road by foot.

After around fifteen minutes of walking they arrive at the large steel doors door of a small compound, set back from the road. Andy knocks at the door, the door opens and a man appears.

"Hi, we would like a room for the night."

The man is dressed in a pair of overalls, standing very guardedly in front of the door. "Sorry no rooms left, only camping in the garden is available."

Andy accepts, failing to realise that they do not have a tent. "That will do fine."

The man opens the gate and beckons them into the compound.

Inside there is a guest house in the middle, with space for camping all around and a large toilet block in the middle. There are also a couple of large trucks parked up, with a group of people cooking by the side of it. Both trucks display the very welcome and familiar Overland Wonders logo.

The man points at the house. "You register there please."

"Thank you."

Andy likes their choice of accommodation, he had been disappointed they hadn't made it a couple of days ago, it made him feel safe. "No one would ever think of looking for us in a place like this, too rustic, but I can see why you were keen to come here now." He indicates the two trucks.

Rob smiles. "You may notice that it's only the clients, the staff aren't with them."

Andy is not convinced. "They won't be far away though, soon enough you will be ignoring me for Julie."

Rob continues smiling, but wants to discuss the continuing niggle he has about the two unaccounted for Russians. "Hopefully if those last two are still interested in us, they will not think of contacting somewhere like this to see if two guys matching our description are staying. Luckily, our friend here will not give anything away."

They walk into the house, to a small reception, which doubles as a bar. There is a white woman behind the bar, slim, tall very attractive with long dark hair and a very friendly tanned face. Rob does not recognise her.

"Hello, we would like some camping for tonight, is Monsieur Dupré around? He is an old friend."

The woman answers in a French accent. "Bonjour. I am Marie, welcome to the Kiboko Guest house. Monsieur Dupré not work here often now, but is still around a lot, I have taken over the day to day running from my father." This news delights Rob and Andy.

The two men politely say hello in French, before Rob continues. "I remember his daughter from years ago, but last time I saw you, you weren't tall enough to reach over the counter! Is Anton around? We would like to say hello."

Marie shakes her head. "He is in town for the morning, but will be back later this afternoon. Forgive me if I don't remember you, Father knows a lot of people, so many have come and gone over the years that my memories as a girl have fogged." she studies Rob and Andy for a few moments. "You do remind me of the type of friend my father has from his past."

They both knew what she meant, they had worked with Anton for a few years before he retired. He was an excellent helicopter pilot who had dropped them in the middle of many dangerous situations, often putting himself at far more danger than he had to, but Anton was an ex- soldier himself, he knew just how much a few extra metres without being under fire could mean to the success of a mission.

Marie looks at them inquisitively and decides to give them the benefit of the doubt, her father would soon throw them out if they do not meet his criteria as old friends. "Officially, we only have space for camping left, all our accommodation is taken, but I have some special rooms which my father likes to reserve for his old friends, you can have two of them, there will be no charge. He will be back in less than an hour, I do hope he will be delighted to see you."

Andy reassures her. "He will, we go back a long way."

As they gather their bags and wait for Marie to show them the room, the phone rings, Marie picks it up. "Kiboko guest house, how may I help?"

The speaker on the other end cannot be heard, but Marie just listens to what is said, looking the two men up and down constantly, before ending the call politely. "If they arrive here I will tell you."

She puts the phone down and turns to the men. "That was odd, it was someone using very bad English pretending to be an American, he said there are two dangerous men loose they are trying to catch, if they try to book in, can we inform them. They matched your descriptions." She gives a wry smile.

Rob tries to offer an explanation. "Just coincidence."

Marie is unconvinced. "Maybe, but I am not a great believer in coincidence, my father has very few enemies, but some of his friends sometimes have many and I do not want their business affecting our business. So I am giving you the benefit of the doubt for the moment, I will not reveal your presence to anyone that you are here unless my father tells me anything different."

Andy comes clean, he feels that being honest with Marie will increase the chances of her allying with them. "We may have some people after us, we are not sure if they still have a motive, many of their comrades were captured by the Americans in the city yesterday, but we do not want to take any chances and we definitely do not want to affect your business."

This is enough for her, she is willing to help, as long as her father is happy. "I can help you, we have a way to stop the people getting in here, but we must wait until my father returns. I suggest you have a drink and wait in the back room in case anyone decides to pay a visit."

Anton arrives back within thirty minutes, entering reception to talk to Marie in French before he goes into the back bar intrigued over the identity of the unexpected guests. As he walks in he sees Rob and Andy and stops with his arms outstretched and a welcoming smile. Rob and Andy are delighted by the sight of their old friend, a man ten years their senior, but his thick black hair and suntanned face and athletic physique make him look the same age.

"My friends, my friends, it has been too long, far too long, what a most welcome surprise." He hugs both men, before turning to reception and shouting back something in French, which Marie responds to in English. "All your friends look the same as do your enemies, hello again Coops and Rob, apparently you are special friends, so I must remember you for the future!"

Anton is puzzled by their unannounced arrival. "What brings you here at short notice, why did you not call me to tell me you were coming to Lilongwe?"

Andy and Rob start to tell Anton selective bits of the story, carefully leaving out anything to do with Ali Bezir, their flight from the Congo was hastened by the Russian, who followed them here and was apprehended by the authorities. They do not leave out the fact that there still maybe two more after them supplying Anton with details of their appearance and the possibility that they may be drunk and definitely trigger happy.

As they talk away, the door of the reception opens and two Malawians walk in and order drinks.

Marie has never seen the men before and is suspicious, she calls into the back room in French, which causes Anton to leave his friends and speak to the two Malawians.

"Hello my friends, how can we help you?"

The Malawians remain silent for a moment, before one responds in relatively good English. "We just came for a drink, we are looking for some friends we met in the town yesterday, they told us they were staying here, they are from Argentina."

Anton knows that it is Rob and Andy they are looking for, the Malawians' weak back story has been concocted for them by the only people that are looking for Argentinians, the two remaining Russians.

He turns to Marie. "Give these men some special drinks on the house for their trouble." before focusing back on the Malawians. "We like to show the best hospitality to all of our guests, sadly the two men you are looking for are not guests here, we only have Europeans here at the moment."

Marie pours them both a drink, handing them to the two grateful men who drink them quickly.

Suddenly one starts to slur his words, before his legs buckle, causing his body to wobble around. "Thaaank shuuu vesshy, ve ...."

Both men slump to the ground. Anton turns to Marie, a bit taken aback. "How strong was that?"

Marie shrugs her shoulders. "I wanted to make sure."

Rob and Andy have heard what has gone on and come out of the back room now it is safe. They look at the men on the floor, before Anton explains. "They were asking for friends from Argentina, obviously working for the Russians looking for you. We take no chances here, Marie will get them picked up by the police for being drunk."

They chat in the bar for another hour before Rob realises he is late. "Sorry Anton, I didn't realise the time, we've got to meet some people in town, we must go."

Anton will not let them walk while their safety is at risk. "I will drive you down to the centre, I can spend the time contacting some of Malawian friends, explain the situation and make sure you have some extra protection."

They are not going to turn down a lift and are grateful for Anton's hospitality, they leave saying good bye to Marie, get in Anton's car, in which they are driven down to the city centre by one of Anton's trusted staff members with Anton riding shotgun.

The car stops outside Mad Mike's favourite bar in Mandala street, Rob and Andy take seats at the table already occupied by Mike and Lisa. Anton shouts a farewell, but will not be far away.

Mike is eager to recount the story of the gunfight the previous day, over-excitingly describing every embellished detail, making it sound like a full blown war that lasted hours, instead of the few short minutes it actually lasted. Lisa makes yawning faces as Mike relays the story, she has heard the story grow considerably each time Mike has retold it in the last day, but although he sees her yawning, he carries on regardless.

After he finishes explaining the helicopter assault on the Nico centre which brought the event to an end he turns to Rob and Andy. "Amazing eh? Who would have thought it in Malawi?"

They both smile, Rob shaking his head. "Not us, nothing like that ever happens in Malawi." He knows that the soon to be released information will make yesterday's events pale into insignificance.

Rob pulls Lisa to one side for a private chat. "You need to forget everything we told you two days ago, it's also important to get rid of the tapes, we'll give you a considerable sum for your trouble, but if you keep them you could be in danger. The Americans have a great back story explaining how they got the person we told you was on the tape and they wouldn't want anyone ruining it." Lisa nods, she is shocked to be given ten thousand dollars for her trouble, she brings the tape out of her bag and slips it into Rob's pocket. "I didn't want to keep this, it could have led to a world of shit, I was so happy that you phoned to stop the release, I only wanted to get involved if it kept you two and Mike safe."

"We are definitely safe now, well from that particular situation, I cannot vouch for anything else!"

As they talk, some familiar faces walk up to the table. Rob and Andy rise and greet all six with large hugs, while Mike and Lisa watch with bemused expressions.

Rob introduces the Overland wonders staff. "Chris, John, Mike, Steve, Julie and Kate meet Lisa and Mike, these guys work for one of the overland companies we met in Zambia, they are cool."

Greetings are exchanged, with Mike hugging each one of his new friends like he had known them for decades.

They chat amongst each other with Mike relaying the story of the mall assault again with some new embellishments, before they exchange travel stories, each finding out what they can about their new acquaintances, while Rob and Julie move to one side to catch up alone, embracing fondly before they talk.

"I was not expecting you to turn up here. When I got your note yesterday, I thought it was some sort of joke, but I'm so delighted."

"It's a long story, I wasn't expecting to be here either, but I'm glad that events have turned out like they have. We travelled for another day after we left you, before we ended up in a world of trouble. We accidentally drove into an area where terrorist activity was rife and I don't know how, but ended up being chased by a Russian mobster, we ditched the car and jumped on the first plane we could find, which ended up here, only to find that the Russian had followed us, he was determined to get us, so we hid in the British embassy while the authorities dealt with it, which they did yesterday. Apparently the guy was a huge arms dealer wanted all over the world, we had accidentally compromised his hiding position. He thought we were security forces and was determined to kill us. It was incredibly scary."

"Oh my god, we saw all the police activity yesterday and heard shooting, had no idea what it was, we assumed that it was a coup or something, which we found odd, after all Malawi is renowned for its friendliness and peace. Are you OK?"

"Yes, we were both unhurt, a little shaken but not a mark on us, we have been given some compensation, apparently this guy had a price on his head for any information leading to his capture, which was given to us, several million dollars!"

Julie is dumbfounded. "Several million dollars?"

Rob has a glint in his eye. "and there is nothing more I would like than to use that money to build a life with you and have some wonderful times together."

The smile on Julie's face could not be any bigger. "I'm not a materialistic person, we don't need that sort of money to build a life. I just want you."

Rob holds her hand, stroking it gently. "I just want you too, but the money is going to help though, I won't have to worry about a job and we can have a permanent holiday full of travelling experiences!"

This has sold it to Julie, who leans over and kisses him, which develops into a passionate embrace lasting for longer than the rest of the table are comfortable with. The embrace slowly stops when the couple notice that Andy is coughing very loudly to gain their attention. The couple look at the rest of the table sheepishly.

Food arrives and all enjoy a loud chatty meal, sharing portions of their food with each other before relaxing with some drinks until Mike has a great idea. "We can go and see the Nico centre, get some pictures of the war, I want to have my picture with my finger in a bullet hole!" The rest groan, but his new acquaintances already know that Mike will be persistent, so finish their drinks.

Chris speaks for the Overland Wonders staff. "We need to get back to Kiboko and prepare, we are leaving before nightfall to travel up to Kande to give our guests the full moon party experience on an unspoilt beach. We can do the preparation while Julie stays with you for another hour."

Rob is happy with that. "Sounds like a deal, we'll get Mike some gunshot photos, I'll get Julie back to you before you leave."

The group separates with the Overland crew walking back to Kiboko, the rest going in the other direction to the Nico centre. They have barely got half way there when Andy spots something which causes him to whisper very loudly. "Shit, it's the goons." Just across the road are the two remaining Russians, sitting outside a bar. They have spotted their targets and have already started to rise from their chairs.

Rob turns to Julie. "You wait with Mike and Lisa, we need to lose these two guys, we'll meet you back at Kiboko." She nods tearfully, shaking with fear.

Rob and Andy start running up the street, followed by the two Russians who are shouting after them in Russian, so whatever they are saying, their words are futile.

As Rob and Andy race up the small incline of the street, the gap widens with each step as they dodge other pedestrians along the way. Andy looks back to see that the Russians have slowed to a walking pace, bending over to catch their breaths. He prods Rob in the shoulder. "We can stop now, they are wasted, no point in tiring ourselves out."

Rob shakes his head. "No, I want to get a bit of distance between us, they could still start shooting."

They carry on running at a slow pace until they reach the top of the hill, before slowing and turning to look at their pursuers, who have completely stopped, with their arms on their hips, which hasn't relaxed Rob. "I don't think they will give up that easily, it could be a ploy."

Andy is more optimistic. "Or they could just be drunk!"

"If they are, they could be more dangerous."

Rob and Andy cross to the other side of the street, still keeping an eye on the two behind them, suddenly the urgency increases again as the Russians flag down a cab, a sight which causes Andy the most concern of the two. "Fuck, where is Anton when you need him."

Anton has been watching from further down the street with amusement, he knew the Russians wouldn't catch his friends, he had been watching them finish off half a bottle of vodka between them for the last half an hour, he couldn't envisage this being any trouble for his friends. If there was any chance they were in danger, his car was close enough to extract them quickly. He was far too busy laughing at the spectacle of the two drunken Russians' pathetic attempt at chasing down their prey to bring it to a sudden end.

The sight of them hailing a taxi was enough to stop his amusement and call his car over. He instructed his driver to pick up his friends quickly. The sight of Anton's car quickly coming up the road brought smiles to their faces.

As they got in the back panting, they were surprised by Anton's reaction to their dilemma, Andy was most distressed by the laughter. "It's not funny, they are dangerous psychopaths, we could have been taken out easily by them."

Anton carries on laughing, struggling to get his words out. "It was so funny, those goons couldn't even walk, let alone run after you, they were wasted, you weren't in danger, they were so drunk they left their guns on their table!"

Rob raises his head to the roof, shaking it slowly, while Andy starts to smirk. Anton's driver turns the car around at the next junction, they pass the two Russians further down the road in a motionless taxi gesticulating at the driver who has no idea what they are saying.

Anton still smiling has some new information for his friends. "I know why they are after you, I was close enough to listen to them as they sat and drank, my

Russian is a bit poor these days, but it was good enough to understand most of what they were saying."

He has the full attention of Rob and Andy all of a sudden. "Really, what did they say?"

"They were moaning and seemed to be feeling very sorry for themselves rather than being angry. They kept talking about a bag with jewels that they needed to get along with the fact that they were unemployed now and needed new work. They seemed to be ranting a lot about this bag and how they could get it, I did catch the phrase 'beat it out of them', but definitely nothing about killing you, it seemed they just wanted information, in their state I knew they wouldn't be able to beat anything of you."

This made total sense to Rob, he was already formulating a plan when he taps the driver on the shoulder indicating to pull over. They stop by their three friends and both men get out, they talk to the pedestrians for a while, giving Mike and Lisa big hugs, then they get back into the car with Julie.

"Right, let's go." Rob explains his plan to Anton as they travel back to Kiboko.

As Rob finishes, Anton has one more thing for them. "One thing I forgot, when they were in the bar, one of my men sprayed them with some invisible marker paint, they won't last long on the street."

This does not alter Rob's intentions. "I'm not taking any chances, we haven't come through everything in the last few days to let two drunken Russians ruin it all." They pull up at the green steel doors of the camp, which are opened for them after a few seconds.

There is a lot of activity in the courtyard of the camp as the Overland Wonders staff supervise the dismantling of their equipment, their clients packing it all into the trucks.

Rob and Andy collect their bags from the reception, bidding farewell to Marie, before loading them onto the truck. They both embrace Anton, offering their thanks, Rob's departing words giving him some comfort. "We will be back very soon when this has all died down, this place is shortly going to turn into a media circus, which we don't want to be around, you'll know what I mean soon."

This intrigues Anton as he watches the two trucks move slowly out of the compound, but he knows that Rob has been cryptic for a reason.

He will know what Rob meant sooner or later.

Capítulo Quince

As the trucks make their way through the Lilongwe traffic heading North, Rob and Andy are relieved to be leaving, looking forward to relaxing while this city becomes the focus of the entire world.

Across the city, the American embassy is starting to become very busy as all the news agencies based in the capital descend on it. The rarity of an important international announcement from one of the embassies is enough for them all to accept the invitation and send large teams to hear whatever will be announced.

The staff at the embassy had been working non-stop for the last twenty four hours, none of them have had a chance to go home as they have worked tirelessly to ensure the proceedings run without a hitch, driven on by the shock news they were given in the first briefing. Even the most minor staff member has been given their own script for any questions they may face from the media.

David Morgan has spent more time on the phone to Washington than he has before, being given unprecedented access to communication channels that are normally out of bounds to him. He has also had to appease the local authorities, who were dismayed at the incidents of the last few days.

He faced a lot of awkward questions from the Malawian foreign minister, who had reports of Americans shooting up a hotel, running amok on the streets, killing people in a shopping mall and most distressing for the foreign minister personally, causing the golf course to be closed for two days due to reports of the guard dogs being shot dead, all of which he assumes to be related to the Americans. The course was shut to allow the police to investigate, the owner was seeking compensation from the Americans. The minister's game that morning was cancelled personally by the owner to make a point.

Morgan had to utilise all of his diplomatic skills to their full and fought off his tiredness with gallons of fresh coffee as he spoke to the angry foreign minister, something he would rather have had Rogers or Jones do, as they were partially responsible, but the minster didn't want answers from minions. They had negotiated through the night, after a few calls to Washington, he was able to appease the minister with a substantial compensation package, substantial for Malawi, but a drop in the ocean for the Americans.

He finishes another cup of coffee as he makes the final preparations for the press conference. An assistant brings him a clean suit, which he puts on before he gathers his staff for the final briefing. They all have a nervous excitement.

Morgan clears his throat before giving his pep talk. "The next hour will be one of the most important hours of your careers, it is unlikely that you will have so much attention directed at you again, so enjoy it, every embassy worker in the world would love to be in your shoes right now. The shock and disbelief that you greeted the information we gave you yesterday will be magnified as every piece is analysed in intricate detail, each one of you will be asked the most minor details by the press, just stick to the official scripts we gave you, even a misplaced word can cause a line of questioning to change, these people are experts in obtaining information, but I am sure your professionalism and the coaching the press office has given you will be sufficient for you."

He starts addressing some of the staff individually to make sure that there are no last minute hitches.

"Ryan, have you checked the International feed is working OK?"

A scruffily dressed nerdy looking man in his early twenties responds. "Yes, we have arranged exclusivity with the local satellite operator, the feed is up and working perfectly."

"Hannah, have you got the press packs double checked and ready to be distributed at the end?" He doesn't want the journalists reading the press packs before the announcement. He wants the announcement to grip their attention the whole way through the show they will be given.

He is answered by a woman in her thirties, smartly dressed, her immaculately groomed appearance hiding the fact that she had been working endlessly for the last day and has not had any sleep. "Yes, I checked each one myself. I've taken the liberty of providing a list of everyone that is present for you, so you can address their questions with their names and the press agency they are with."

Morgan likes this extra touch of professionalism. "Doug is your team at their posts, ready to control the melee that may ensue afterwards?"

Of all the people in the room Doug was obviously in charge of security, his dark suit and tinted glasses accompanied by an expressionless face would have been enough to give him away, but the radio earpiece he wore made it obvious. "Everyone is in place, we have rehearsed for every possible scenario, there will be no stampede in or out, everything will be kept calm."

"Ruth, are all the refreshments laid out for the post conference meetings?" Morgan anticipated that there would be a lot of questions, so many questions that some of the press would want to address them in a more informal atmosphere, so he had asked for a buffet reception set up in the garden.

An African woman wearing a white uniform responds. "Yes, all the food is laid out on the tables, there is a wide selection and enough to feed fifty people for a whole day."

Morgan is satisfied. "Good, is there anything else?"

Ryan speaks up again. "The feed to the cell is working fine too, the switch to the shot of the captive with the team that got him will be smooth."

This delights Morgan, he had asked if they could do this for extra effect, but was told that they would need extra equipment that may be difficult to get at short notice. He was pleased that Ryan had been able to deliver this, it would be an image that would be shared worldwide for many years to come. He claps his hands. "Fantastic, I think we are ready, let's go and make history!"

He leads them into the reception room, where he takes the pedestal at the front, the rest of the staff line up against the walls of the room.

Jones and Rogers are already seated at the back. In front of them are around 30 reporters, sat on seats, arranged in lines facing the front, with a row of cameras behind taking live pictures. Everyone in the room is expectant of something, but not entirely sure what the news could be which the Americans had built up so much. They sit in silent anticipation, all knowing that there would be a worldwide audience.

Morgan taps the microphone, then addresses the audience.

"Ladies and gentlemen, welcome to the US embassy in Malawi. We have a major announcement to make, after which I will take questions. If you have more to ask than the allocated time allows, which I'm sure you will have, we have arranged a buffet reception in our garden for some more informal discussions."

He pauses for effect, knowing that this will be his big moment. He will appear on billions of TV screens in the next few days, so it's worthwhile making a show of it.

"First I would like to introduce the President of the United States of America." He turns to the large screen behind him, which shows the President standing behind his presidential pedestal, waiting for his cue from the live feed he has in front of him of the proceedings in Malawi.

He looks directly at the camera in front of him, before addressing the whole world,

"The United States Government is pleased to announce the successful capture of the terrorist leader Malek Ali Bezir. It was the result of many years of intense surveillance, involving the co-operation of many other nations, culminating in a successful assault mission by US forces in the African country of Malawi. The mission did not cause any civilian casualties."

He pauses for the news to sink in.

"Ali Bezir is now safely in custody in Malawi and is fully cooperating with our investigations. He is being very well treated and will be transferred to US soil in the coming days to face trial for his atrocities.

I am sure you will greet this news with delight as we have made a giant step towards world peace."

The President pauses again for the information to be absorbed, he doesn't face the press in person as he makes his address from the oval office, but knows that there would be a reaction of shock throughout the world.

"I am sure you have many questions and want more details, so I am pleased to hand over to the US Embassy in Lilongwe, Malawi, where our Ambassador, David Morgan will provide details of the mission which captured Malek Ali Bezir."

Morgan swells with pride at the mention of his name to such a global audience, he returns to his pedestal to face the world's press, his image now being relayed across the world.

"Thank you Mr President. It is a great honour to provide details of the successful capture by US forces."

He glances at the script detailing the mission, but he does not need to read it, he has memorised every detail.

"For many years we have been monitoring the activity of Malek Ali Bezir, who has been linked to many terrorist atrocities globally.

The intelligence we have gathered was very limited as Ali Bezir took great precautions in protecting his whereabouts at all times. He never used a mobile phone or a computer, relying on a network of personal contacts to disseminate his propaganda and terror. This made the surveillance very difficult. We relied on our allies throughout the world to share any information they may have.

Over the years, we learned that Ali Bezir would travel all over the world incognito, to meet with local groups he could support, funding them, supplying arms and training. We had many near misses in apprehending him, but managed to build up a map of his activities, allowing us to target the surveillance more effectively.

Several months ago, we detected some activity in west Africa which we believed to be linked to Ali Bezir. A man believed to be one of Ali Bezir's business partners, a Russian arms dealer known as Matvei Kovalenko, was conducting business with several insurgent groups. We tracked Kovalenko for many months, but there was no sign of Ali Bezir personally, just the money he was supplying for Kovalenko's arms.

Kovalenko gradually moved east, we were able to anticipate the countries he was likely to visit, increasing our surveillance in those countries with the full help of the nations involved. One of those countries was Malawi, a nation recognised as very stable and peaceful, with no history of insurgence. We anticipated that Kovalenko may pass through en-route to other nations, so we engaged the local authorities to monitor any activity that may have been of interest to us.

We received some interesting intelligence about some foreigners who were being very secretive in the northern city of Mzuzu, so we focused on there as Kovalenko was expected to pass through at some stage.

We watched the activity for many weeks, noting patterns that matched previous activity associated with Ali Bezir, for example, the coming and going of a messenger from a large walled house in the centre of the city, but we were not actually able to confirm the presence of Ali Bezir himself.

That is until earlier this week. We managed to install a listening device in the house, enabling us to listen to the conversations inside, leading to a positive identification of Ali Bezir. Once we had this confirmation, we notified the Pentagon, who gave the green light for a team of special forces troops to perform the extraction.

They immediately left the United States, arriving in Malawi within a day, where they were able to survey the residence at close quarters and efficiently plan Ali Bezir's capture. We were insistent that there must be no civilian casualties. The special forces were able to provide us with a plan that met those criteria in a very short space of time.

They installed themselves in Mzuzu where they were able to operate covertly for few days. Using the drainage system, they were able to get a line directly into the house, which was used to pump a derivative of the drug fentanyl into the house completely incapacitating the occupants harmlessly during the night.

When the unit was satisfied all occupants were incapacitated, they assaulted the compound, scaling the walls before efficiently neutralising the armed guards that were present outside of the house itself.

They entered the house with no resistance and after a quick search were able to identify Malek Ali Bezir and take him into custody, bringing him directly to the secure facilities we have in Malawi for debriefing and preparation for transport to the US.

After our troops left, local forces moved to secure the house, taking the remaining occupants into custody. The house involved is displayed behind me."

He turns to the screen which is displaying a two storey brick house surrounded by walls which hid the first storey completely, guarded by Malawian troops. There were gasps in the audience and several camera flashes as pictures were taken of the screen. All of the reporters present had their arms raised, but Morgan had not finished.

"After this successful operation, when Ali Bezir was safely in custody, we needed to neutralise Kovalenko, who had made his way to Lilongwe with a small force, giving us cause for concern that he would try and extract Ali Bezir, putting our staff and the Malawian people at risk.

Our special forces trailed Kovalenko, reducing his forces over a couple of days, before there was an armed confrontation in a shopping centre right in the centre of Lilongwe. Again our forces were able to successfully complete the mission without any civilian casualties and they were able to bring Kovalenko into custody.

Over the last few days we have made major gains in the fight against global terrorism, it gives me great pleasure to show you Malek Ali Bezir in the safe custody of the special forces that captured him."

He turns again to the screen, stepping to one side to give the full effect of the image displayed, which is a live feed from the secure unit below them. Ali Bezir is sitting restrained in a chair, with some of the Smiths behind him, their faces obscured by breathing apparatus with blacked out visors.

There are more gasps and more flashes, with the raised arms now being waved frantically.

Morgan steps back to his pedestal with Ali Bezir being displayed just to his left behind him on the screen, an image he would later have framed and display in every office he occupied.

"I will now take your questions."

The room bursts into a crescendo of shouting as every reporter tries to get their questions heard by Morgan. All of the reporters have sensed an opportunity of a lifetime, to get their question on screen in front of a global audience could make their careers. Morgan silently lets the noise die down, before pointing at a journalist he knows well.

The reporter stands up and fires in a question. "David Styles, USA today. Where is the secure location?"

Every possible question has been anticipated by teams of analysts in the Pentagon, each one has been drilled into Morgan. "It is at a location I cannot disclose for security reasons, but I can reveal that it is within Malawian territory, I cannot be more specific than that."

Styles has another question. "Was any reward paid by the US for the information leading to the capture?"

"We have compensated the Malawian government for their help and covered any expenses they have incurred."

"Mike Phillips, Reuters. Do you know why Ali Bezir was in Malawi and do you expect any repercussions from his capture?"

"Those are areas which are part of our on-going investigation, we believe he was here just to distribute funding to Kovalenko, rather than initiate any insurgency here, but I cannot reveal any further details at this moment in time. We will release further details when they become known over the coming months."

Morgan scans the room for further questions, with many for him to choose from, he points at a British journalist he has met before.

Laura Lee, BBC. "What will happen to Ali Bezir now?"

"He will be transferred to a secret location in the US, where he will be fully debriefed, providing effective intelligence in the continuing fight against terrorism, before he is put on trial for his crimes in the US."

Morgan handles every question asked of him perfectly over the next hour, many wanting further details of the mission and the men involved, Paris-Match were slightly disappointed that he wouldn't provide the name of the unit involved for obvious security reasons, but did ask it hopefully. Local news agencies wanted to know more about the house in Mzuzu, something Morgan is happy to provide, detailing the layout while the screen displayed detailed plans of each room. The Americans had covered every aspect in detail, leaving little room for anyone doubting the authenticity of the mission.

The ambassador wraps up the press conference with many reporters still having questions, but has let each one in the room get at least one question in while the proceedings are being screened live around the world.

"Ladies and gentlemen, we have run out of time, but we can address any further questions you have in our reception in the embassy gardens. I thank you all for your time."

The cameras providing the live feed are switched off, as news rooms around the world start to analyse all of what they have been shown, having been supplied enough detail to run with this story for the next few weeks.

Many of the reporters get up and leave urgently to write up the story to wire across the world, but a handful follow Morgan and his staff outside to chat more informally and enjoy the hospitality provided for them.

As Rogers gets up and leaves the press conference, he walks by the side of Morgan. "Well-handled David, it couldn't have gone any better, I can see a big promotion coming your way soon."

Morgan smiles. "Jim, I can see big promotions coming for all of us. This has been one hell of a few days, something I couldn't have dreamed of in a million years. Now we just have a few more hours of intense questioning before we can sit back and fully appreciate the implications of this whole episode."

The press conference had the largest global audience ever recorded. As news began to spread of the announcement people all over the world turned to their TV screens and the live feed from a country that many had never heard of before, a country that was now the focus of the whole world.

The broadcast was watched all over Malawi too, with people gathering in bars and other communal areas to share the news that would make them so proud of their country.

Outside one of these bars in a tiny roadside town, two large overland trucks are parked, both displaying the Overland Wonders logo. The news being received by the occupants with the same surprise as everyone else, not least Rob and Andy who were very pleased with what they had heard, but for very different reasons than everyone else.

The news they received with the most relief was that the final two of Kovalenko's men were apprehended by Malawian police, they were grateful to the reporter who asked Morgan if there was still any potential danger to the population of Lilongwe. Rob had made a mental note of his name and smiles as he imagines the reporter's reaction to the anonymous delivery of a new laptop he would receive in a few days.

The staff and crew talk excitedly over the news for the next hour over drinks, incredulous that it had happened when they were in Lilongwe. Only Julie displays a slightly different reaction to the rest as she embraces Rob fondly, kissing him before saying "You were so lucky and brave to have a minor part in the situation, I didn't know those men chasing you were so dangerous, I'm so glad that you weren't harmed." Rob vowed never to tell her how involved he actually was as they kissed passionately.

An hour after the press conference finished, Chris decides that they have spent enough time waiting around, they had already been delayed slightly by a slight detour to the airport where Rob had to pick a bag up. Chris was keen to get to Kande beach quickly where he could relax at a full moon party to end all parties.

They arrive at a Kande an hour later, pleasantly surprised to see that proceedings are in full swing, the news having brought out the need in every westerner in the area to let their hair down. The trucks park up and the occupants join in the festivities.

Above the noise of the party a very familiar voice can be heard, it's presence does not surprise Rob or Andy as they hear some familiar words.

"Many moons ago, myself and two fellow travellers set out to make the world's largest ever fly pie…"

Lisa stands at the edge of the crowd. When she hears Mike start his story again, she starts looking around for a distraction and eventually spots Rob and Andy standing a few metres away from the rest of the crowd. She runs up to greet them, giving them both a big hug and placing a bottle of Carlsberg green in each of their hands. "When you told Mike you were coming to Kande, he had to come, so made me drive him here. I guess you saw the news?"

Andy nods. "I think everyone saw it, we thought it was great, it was such a relief."

Lisa clinks her bottle against theirs.

"Time for a celebration!"

Andy agrees. "Oh yes, we have the money, we are officially retired and worry free."

Rob raises his bottle. "Here's to Good Times."

The other two raise their bottles. "Good times."

Rob gets one in before Andy can.

"And I don't mean the song!"

As they laugh to themselves, a massive explosion of flame bursts high into the sky, lighting up the whole beach as the crowd cheers and wildly applauds.

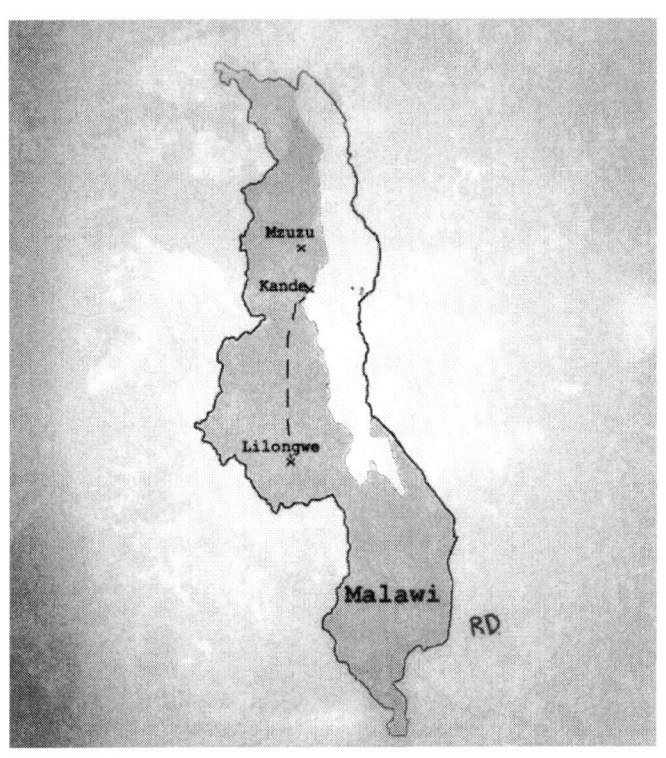

Epílogo

The news of Ali Bezir's capture dominates the global news for the next few weeks, before a natural disaster in Australia takes over as the dominant news story.

The house in Mzuzu is purchased by the Americans and given to the nation of Malawi, which maximises its moment in the spotlight. It proudly turns the house into a tourist attraction, which attracts thousands of visitors from all over the world. Once in the country, the tourists also start to discover the other delights that Malawi has to offer.

The upsurge in tourism brings many benefits, not least to Kaya Mawa which is the prime destination for the wealthier visitor, many of whom are flown in by Mbuji who liked the island so much he stayed, creating the first regular air service between the capital and the island.

The upsurge in tourism also benefitted Lisa, who became the head of the hotel company that she formed with Giles and Chris, its mission to create unique accommodation for the discerning and wealthy traveller.

One of her side projects was to create a chain of bars, 'Mad Mike's Festival Bar', a chain which spreads to some of the most lively tourist areas in the world, each one regularly receiving a visit from the scruffy Australian who entertains the bustling crowds with 'The Big Bang of Africa bay' and newer stories such as 'The Assault on Lilongwe Mall'.

He becomes a minor celebrity in all of the resorts.

All of the embassy staff published their own accounts of the events, some making a comfortable living out of appearing on shows debunking the conspiracy theories. Rogers and Jones rose through the ranks of the agency very swiftly before settling in very senior positions, Jones slightly aided by the introduction of the Cooper-Queens manoeuvre to the training syllabus.

David Morgan stayed in Malawi for another year before being offered the prestigious ambassadorship to the United Kingdom.

The authorities in the Republic of the Congo did not find out about the massacre at Umbekie's house. It was mysteriously destroyed in a fire the day after the massacre. Very few people saw the contents, the only locals that witnessed the inside of the house were the drivers that were waiting to pick up the guests, but they all disappeared before they could share their stories. The plot of land Umbekie's house occupied was purchased by the Americans a few weeks later, when they reopened their embassy in the country. The replacement house that was built there houses a Mr Smith.

All records of the missing people were accidentally deleted in a clerical error.

Michael unexpectedly received the offer of an excellent opportunity in Europe, which he took without any hesitation.

Kovalenko is put on trial very quickly. He receives a life sentence without parole in one of America's toughest prisons. All of his associates also receive life sentences. Ali Bezir is still waiting for his trial, with the process set to take many more years. Something the Americans are happy to wait for as they extract every piece of useful information from him in a secret location.

Andy brings his family out to see Petre, staying for several weeks helping out on the farm, which he eventually is forced to sell, albeit at a reasonable price, allowing him to retire in a peaceful sea front home in Cape Town. Andy eventually settles his family in New Zealand.

Rob and Julie spent the next few weeks on the island of Zanzibar, relaxing on its beaches covered in pure white sand, before returning to Malawi when the excitement had died down, staying with Anton in his newly opened more upmarket tourist lodge in the centre of Lilongwe. They spend the next few years travelling in luxury, before Rob pops the question and they settle down to raise a family.

Rob and Andy meet up twice in Kaya Mawa a year to reminisce.

Neither man handles a gun again.

Maps

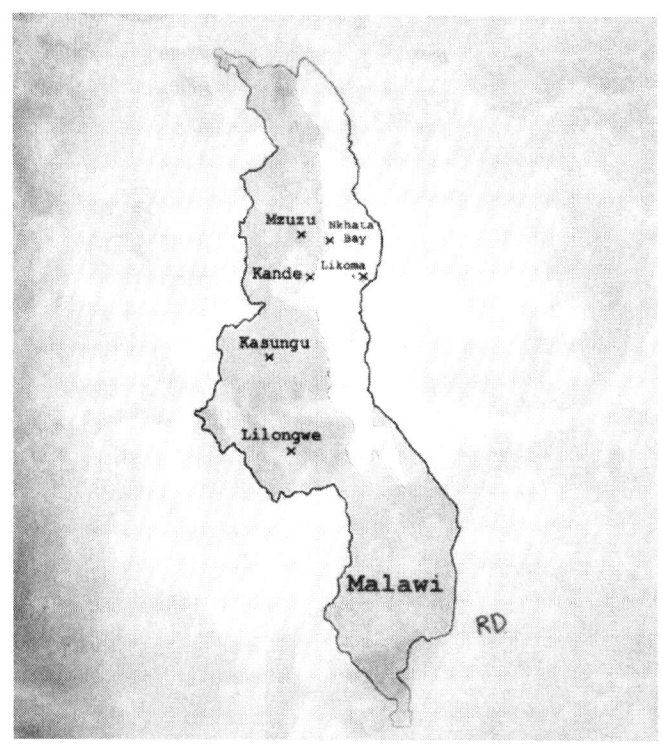

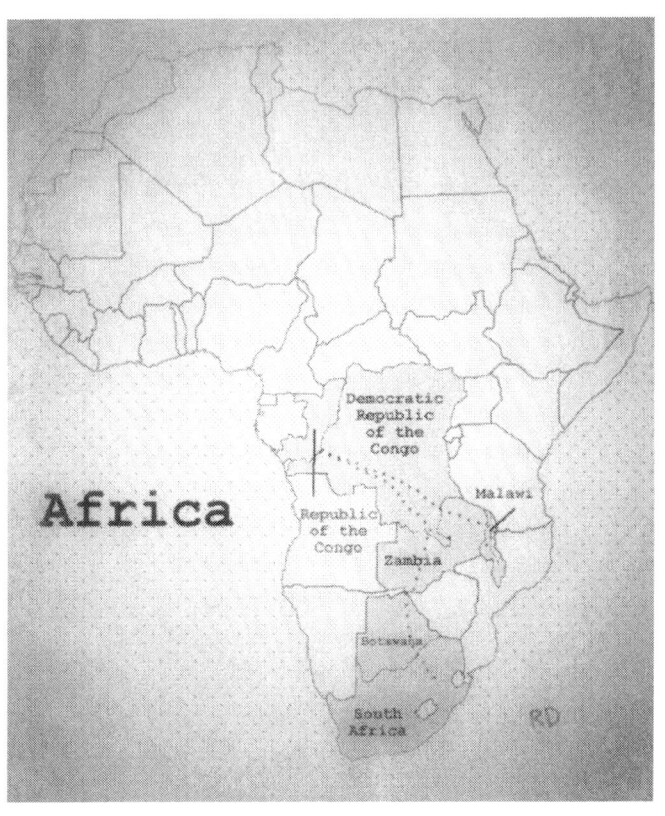

Africa

39470234R00272

Made in the USA
Charleston, SC
11 March 2015